Martina Murphy has been wr ~~ber.~~ She is the author of twenty previous novels under various versions of her name! Her books have been translated into many languages and include the YA award-winning *Dirt Tracks* and the Impac long-listed *Something Borrowed*. She also writes plays and is a qualified drama teacher. She lives in Kildare with her husband, two adult children and a dog.

Also by Martina Murphy

YA novels:

Livewire
Fast Car
Free Fall
Dirt Tracks

As Tina Reilly:

Flipside
The Onion Girl
Is This Love?
Something Borrowed
Wedded Blitz

As Martina Reilly:

The Summer of Secrets
Second Chances
Wish Upon a Star
All I Want is You
The Wish List
A Moment Like Forever
Even Better Than the Real Thing?
What If?
Things I Want You to Know
That Day in June
Proof

THE NIGHT CALLER

MARTINA MURPHY

CONSTABLE

CONSTABLE

First published in Great Britain in 2021 by Constable

A CIP catalogue record for this book
is available from the British Library.

ISBN: 978-0-34913-495-6

Typeset in Bembo MT Pro by Initial Typesetting Services, Edinburgh
Printed and bound in Great Britain by Clays Ltd, Elcograf S.p.A.

Papers used by Constable are from well-managed forests and
other responsible sources.

MIX
Paper from
responsible sources
FSC® C104740

Constable
An imprint of
Little, Brown Book Group
Carmelite House
50 Victoria Embankment
London EC4Y 0DZ

An Hachette UK Company
www.hachette.co.uk

www.littlebrown.co.uk

For my husband, Colm, who has been there for all
the thicks and an awful lot of thins.
Love always. X

Glossary

DG   Detective Guard

DS   Detective Sergeant

DI   Detective Inspector. 'Cigire' is the Irish word for 'inspector', shortened to 'Cig', pronounced 'Kig'.

IP   Injured Party

SIO   Senior Investigating Officer

SO   Suspected Offender

TE   Technical Examination

Tusla   Child and Family Agency – a child protection agency

TY   Transition Year: A sort of gap year between one set of exams in secondary school and a final set. Students explore what they may like to do career-wise.

The Captain

Eight months previously

But, Jesus, she'd been some feckin' weight, the size of her. And she'd been a screamer to boot. And he had struggled, feckin' struggled, to carry her from the bathroom, where she'd made a right mess, across the bog to the water tower. But it was done now, save for the auld fella in the house, mithering and moaning. He should finish him off too while he was at it.

But no. He'd proved himself and probably would again, so he'd leave him alone for the time being.

He wiped his hands down the legs of his jeans, bits of blood and spatter making a right mess of them. He'd have to do a great tidy-up on the place, so he would. Bleach the place.

Pearl, her name had been. But she was no pearl among women, that was for certain sure. An auld bitch, just like the other one, years ago. He'd given Pearl a chance, but her trying to work the old man against him was something he wasn't prepared to over-look. And the old man falling for it, all over again. That had cut deep, so it had. Pearl had died roaring. All in all, it was a sad state of affairs.

And now, after all the shouting and screaming, there was

silence. That pure, earthy envelope of quiet that you could only get way out here. All around him lay the bog, brown, with hints of purple in its spring coat. He could sense that the land was readying itself, getting set to bloom. In a few months the bog cotton would turn this place pure white. Marigolds and sundews would abound. But now the sky loomed grey and oppressive. He could hear the lap of the ocean past the road beyond, and meanwhile, the bog stretched away in every which direction, keeping its silence and its secrets.

The water tower where he'd put her was rust-coloured in the dipping of the evening sun. This bit of land would probably be his one day, he thought. One day soon. But he wouldn't take it: he'd sell up, put the money into his own place. Too many memories here, too many memories in his head. Too many memories on his body.

He put his hands into his pockets, took a final look at the water tower, a final look at the fields. It had not been meant to go like this.

The next one would be better.

Closer to home.

He knew which one.

He just had to bide his time.

Ready himself.

1

Day One

Present

The call comes at ten in the morning. I'm in the middle of sign-
ing off on an investigation that has ended well for me and my
partner, Dan. Without breaking a beat, I reach over and put the
phone on speaker while, one-handed, I continue to type the final
paragraph. 'Detective Sergeant Lucy Golden.'

'Lucy, it's William.'

I stop typing. The DI wouldn't call unless something was up.

'Hi, Cig, I'm listening.' Across the desk, Dan looks over, eyebrows raised.

'I want you and Dan to get on down to the bog at Doogort,
there's been a body found.'

'Doogort's bog, Achill Island?'

'Yes - you're local, they'll talk to you. We think it's that missing girl, Lisa Moran.'

I'd heard of Lisa Moran, not because she'd been a high-profile
missing person but because my mother had told me. I'd got in
from work three days ago and she'd met me at the door almost

3

bursting with the news. I'd barely got my coat off by the time I'd been given all the details. I hadn't taken much notice because Achill Island, my home place, was a nowhere land where nothing much ever happened. There had been a murder once, over twenty years ago, when I'd been stationed in Dublin, but apart from that, the island was a speck in the Atlantic Ocean, joined to the mainland by a bridge, whose sole purpose was to make it easier for tourists to come in the summer.

'Can you give us some background, Cig?' Dan asks, as we pull on our jackets.

'They'll fill you in at Achill Island garda station – they're clearing a space for you now – but what I can gather is that Lisa Moran, twenty-five, disappeared three days ago while walking home from her job in a primary school on the island. She had no drug issues that we can find, no depression or other mental-health issues. In short, according to the regular lads who investigated the case, there was no reason for Lisa Moran to want to disappear.'

'CCTV?' I ask.

'Some, but nothing from where she vanished. Get on down here. Joe Palmer and I are on the scene and I want you and Dan as part of the investigation. The super has appointed me SIO.'

'Okay, thanks.' I disconnect, and watch as Dan gulps the dregs of his coffee. He jokes that it's the detective in him, the habit of never leaving anything unfinished.

'So, Achill Island garda station, here we come,' Dan says, as we head out of our own station in Westport, which is fifty kilometres from Achill, to pick up our standard-issue Hyundai i40. Dan has got his jacket on upside down and is trying to wrestle his sleeve free.

'Yep.'

'A homecoming for you,' he jokes.

I make a face and he laughs, but in all seriousness, I seem to have spent my whole working life trying to escape the place and it keeps dragging me back.

Achill Island is approximately 150 kilometres square and is nearly 90 per cent peat bog. Scenic and wild, it has several small towns dotted around it. I was born forty-one years ago just outside Keem, near the far end of the island, proud boaster of one glorious beach and the highest cliffs in Europe, accessible only on foot. As a teenager, I couldn't wait to leave. I thought I'd drown in this all-seeing place where the views of the neighbours held such power. I had managed to escape the island to work in Dublin and I'd succeeded in becoming a detective garda, but thirteen years ago, I'd been sent back west, demoted to a regular uniform. I've spent the last decade clawing my way back up the ranks, proving myself over and over, and that was hard in a place where nothing really happens. I'd finally landed a promotion of sorts to Westport, but now it looked as if I was heading home once more. The only good thing to come out of the demotion from Dublin was that Luc, my son, benefited from being near my mother, and in that respect, I think sometimes it was worth it.

Half an hour later, I'm driving across the bridge from the mainland to the island. I drive through Achill Sound, taking the road that leads to the bog.

'Jesus Christ,' Dan mutters. 'Would you look at that fella!'

'That fella' is Eddie. Once a university professor, he'd had a breakdown and now he spends his days shambling along the roads of Achill, thumbing lifts, his trademark brown coat flapping out behind him.

'He must be freezing,' Dan says, as we zip by him. 'What happened to his shoes?'

'He thinks someone is poisoning him through the soles of his feet. My mother says he's going about telling everyone to watch themselves.'

'Is there no family?'

'A sister. She makes no pass on him.'

'Aw, Jesus,' Dan says.

The sister is old-school, under the impression that if she ignores his behaviour, if she brushes it under the carpet, no one will notice and it will go away. Far better to do that than admit to any sort of mental illness in the family. The west is full of such people.

'Give Achill garda station a ring. Ask them to contact Sylvia O'Shea – they'll know who you mean. Tell them Eddie is barefoot near Bunacurry.'

Dan nods and spends a few moments talking to one of the regular guys on the desk about Eddie as I drive the final few miles towards where the body was found.

As we near the site, I can see a crowd gathered. 'Damn,' I mutter.

'At least the media aren't here yet,' Dan says, just as we're overtaken by an RTÉ truck that pulls past and comes to a stop in front of us with a bit of a skid. Before I can react with a beep of my horn, Jayne Lowe, the western reporter for RTÉ, hops down from the vehicle.

How did she get here so quickly?

'They nearly took out the side of our car,' I snap.

I watch Jayne beckon the TV crew to follow her with a flick of a finger. There's no point in rolling down the window and giving her earache about her driving because she'd use the footage, probably to show how stressed we are or something.

'Let's see if we can find the Cig and see what Joe has for us,' I mutter to Dan.

'The joy of it all.'

We're both a little scared of Joe, the deputy state pathologist. His reputation goes before him, like the heat from a furnace. It burns if you don't take care.

I park our car right behind the RTÉ van so that they're blocked in and Dan chuckles. We climb out and start to make our way towards the entrance to the woods.

Jayne Lowe spots us.

'Detectives! Detectives,' she calls. I notice that she's cleared a little patch for herself and is now surrounded by awestruck onlookers. She looks like an exotic species compared to the locals, all flamboyant colours and bracelets. 'Can you tell us anything about the body found? Any idea who it is?'

Dan and I don't answer and she didn't expect us to but the camera gets a shot of us passing under the tape, suitably grim-faced. We hear Jayne saying to camera, 'As you can see the detectives have arrived.'

'If I gave her the two fingers do you think she'd say, "As you can see, the detective has just given me the two fingers"?' I copy her husky serious voice.

'She would,' Dan nods. Then, 'Who the hell is that fella?'

I stare in the direction he points. A shambling doughy man, with a large face and big features is panning the crowd with a mobile phone. He's about twenty-five, but looks older.

'That's Lugs,' I say. 'The local vlogger. And I mean "the".' Apparently, he has loads of followers. Luc gets a great laugh out of him. His vlog is called, wait for it, "My Boring as Shit Life".'

Dan chortles then says, 'I'll put in a request for one of the regulars to get that footage from him.'

We watch Lugs for a second more as he talks into his phone.

'I'd like to give him and that RTÉ wan a kick in the hole,' Dan says.

Me too. There they are, turning the scene of a murder into entertainment. Though no doubt they'd both claim that the public have a right to know the details. And, to be fair, it's probably the most exciting thing to happen here, ever.

'And there's that dorky kid from the *Island News*,' I groan. 'Here she comes. Hurry.'

A frizzy-haired, frazzled young journalist, holding her phone out in front of her and wearing a badge saying *ISLAND NEWS*, scurries towards me and Dan. 'Detectives? Who is this body? Has it been identified? What age—'

'Do not come any closer. It's a crime scene,' Dan snaps at her.

Her voice trails off. 'I wasn't going to. Can I just have a quote?'

We move away.

'Ah, come on!'

Once we leave the fuss and activity behind, the sounds of the road and the crowd recede and the peace of the place wraps itself around us. The bog stretches on and on for miles, roads running up and through it but not many people live here. Most of it is protected land now and the surrounding areas are isolated: the land is too barren, the ground too unstable to build on affordably. It's one of the attractions of the island, though – it even got its picture in a Bord Fáilte magazine. There's a huge biodiversity of life and rare plants and lots of types of trees and birds apparently.

Beyond the bog, further now than we can see, is the dip of the land into the ocean. Rain falls silently. The rich smell of damp earth rises as we walk and the sound of the ocean echoes thunderously in the gloom of the day.

It's easy to spot where Lisa was found because, up ahead, tape flutters in the brisk breeze, marking the area for about thirty feet in either direction, and regular lads are stationed at the scene.

'*Dia dhuit.*' One of the lads from Achill station greets me in Irish as he logs Dan's and my arrival in the book. Everyone entering or leaving a crime scene has to be logged in. I remember doing this job myself, back in my uniform days, and having to tell my then commissioner that no one was allowed on site. Even though he knew the rules, he was not a happy man.

We don special dust suits so we won't contaminate anything before making our way over to the Cig, Detective Inspector, William Williams. He's the only DI in the district so he's usually the one to take charge when something big comes up.

He has a habit of standing completely still, as if he's absorbing every detail of a scene, and today, in his brown jacket and trousers, hands tucked into pockets, he almost looks like part of the landscape.

'Lucy,' he says, his accent pure Limerick, 'I want everything on that missing girl by the conference this evening.' He says it without preamble, barely flicking a glance at me.

'Sure.'

'Jim D'arcy is the IRC.'

I'm glad about that. The incident-room coordinator has a big job: it involves opening a book on the investigation, coordinating all the reports and job sheets and ensuring that details don't get lost in the flood of material that comes into an investigation in the first few days. Jim has a solid head on him.

I turn to stare at the blue tent that has been erected over the body. The entrance flap flutters in the breeze. In the brief glimpses I get, I can see the forensic team at work, and Joe, examining the body, being careful not to disturb anything.

Finally, Joe emerges from the tent. He must be near sixty but looks older. The stuff he's seen over the years seems to have etched itself into the lines of his face. I hope I don't get like that. Even though, with the scar, my face is nothing to write home about as it is.

The Cig and I allow Joe time to get his breath back before crossing towards him, Dan behind us. Overhead, the jagged sounds of a helicopter can be heard. I try not to think that this whole scene, right at this moment, is on William and, by default, me and Dan. This is our case and we have to nail someone.

As we draw level with Joe, we get a better view of the body, which is lying on its stomach, face turned to the left, right cheek buried in the wet earth, spread-eagled, fingers wide, hair fanned out across the back. Barefoot.

'It's that missing girl,' Joe says, as he removes his gloves. 'The one you sent me the picture of, William.'

'Are you sure it's her?' William asks. 'She appears to be wearing a tracksuit.'

Joe shoots him a look of such disdain that even I wither. 'Unless two people with the same face have gone missing at the same time.'

'According to what I've been told by the regular lads, she was wearing a black mid-length skirt with a white blouse and black jacket and shoes when she went missing,' William says firmly.

'Maybe she didn't go missing on the day they thought,' Joe says.

'She failed to return home from work last Friday,' William insists, 'so it's a fair bet that—'

'Do you want to hear what I have to say or stand here arguing about fashion?'

'He wasn't—' Dan attempts to stick up for William.

'Go ahead,' William cuts him off.

Joe aims his comments at me, blanking the two men completely. 'You'll appreciate that I have to get her back to the mortuary first for a post-mortem. I'll let you know when so you can send someone over.' Then to William, 'Try to get a member who won't faint this time.'

Beside me, William stiffens. Apparently, the last murder he'd handled, a couple of years back, a new recruit had been sent to observe the post-mortem and ended up in hospital after cracking his head on the tiles on the mortuary floor.

Joe continues, 'You'll get a detailed report, but from what I can see here she's been dead since last night because of the level of rigor mortis. This is not the kill site. She died elsewhere, I'm pretty certain of that, as there is very little blood on site. From her injuries, there should be. She was badly beaten before death. Two of her fingers appear to be broken as is her left cheekbone and eye socket. She has a lot of ante-mortem facial bruising.' He shrugs. 'Because she's fully clothed, there isn't a lot else I can tell you right now. Forensics took some prints from the small areas of skin that are exposed. I'll give you a call sometime tomorrow with anything we get. I'll send through a preliminary report for the conference.' And with that he stalks off.

'Two people with the same face,' Dan mimics him. 'He's an awful arsehole, isn't he?'

'He's all right,' William says. 'Lucy, will you go in and have a look? I'd like your impressions. Dan, talk to the auld fella who found her. Find out what he knows. After that, yez can head out to talk to the mother – she's the one reported her missing. The liaison officer has been in contact with her already. It's Phil.'

'No bother. I know Phil. I have her number,' I say, approaching the tent and pushing back the flap. It covers a small patch of bog, brown and damp and cold, a place dying off but one that will bloom in spring. But Lisa, who has lain here for the last few hours, won't ever do anything ever again. The thing about a murder is that it's violent and cruel, yet the dead body and the space you find it in always have an emptiness about them, a stillness. I take a second before looking at Lisa more closely. She lies on her stomach, cheap grey tracksuit almost blending into the land. The smell of death is all around and the loneliness of her passing is something I can almost feel. What happened to you? I wonder, as I hunker down to look at her face. Outside, I can hear the bustle of Forensics and the low mumble of voices, but in here, it's like another world. Whoever put her here must have walked. He must have walked from somewhere because a jeep or a car on the bog would have been noticed. There'd be tyre tracks.

I take a final look at Lisa and I mentally promise her that we'll do our very best to get justice.

Emerging, I say to the Cig, 'Definitely not the kill site. I think we need to extend the cordon to the road at least. Whoever put her here walked with her.'

'Yes, I agree. No tyre tracks and the ground is soft. Anything else?'

'The way she was positioned, it looks deliberate. It's not as if she was hit from behind and fell over.'

'Good.' He nods. 'I thought the same. Talk to as many witnesses as you can today, build up a picture of her. I know when she went missing, the regulars did the usual door-to-door and handed out leaflets, but we'll have to redo. I'm just going to check with the garda Tech Bureau, tell them exactly what we want them to do and why. I'll see ye back at the station.'

I watch him walk off. William has been my senior investigating officer a number of times now, though we've never done a murder together. He's tough and thorough, just what you need leading an investigation. He doesn't have much of a personality, though, and the joke in the force is that he lost it in a robbery.

Not much of a joke but it's hard to joke about William.

'Where's Dan?' I ask a regular guard.

'Over there,' she replies, pointing to where Dan is introducing himself to an elderly man who is sitting on one of the stone walls that run like snakes through the bog. A black and white collie-type dog is dancing about his feet.

2

I know Milo McGrath, the man with the dog. He's friendly with my mother, though I can say that about everyone. She and Milo are in the same hot yoga class or something. Or maybe his wife and my mother are, I'm not quite sure.

Milo is an enthusiastic member of the Achill Island community: he's on the Tidy Towns Committee, the Street Painting Committee, and he manages the local St Patrick's Day parade. I know all this because he regularly appears in the *Island News*.

His eyes brighten a little as he recognises me.

He greets me in Irish. Achill is a Gaeltacht area, which means that Irish is the spoken language of the people. A tiny pocket of Ireland, holding fast to its ancient tongue, I love the place for it. We exchange a few words before switching back to English for Dan's benefit.

'It's great to have a friendly face to talk to. It's been a terrible shock, I don't mind telling you.'

'Take your time,' I say, hunkering down beside him, getting out my notebook. 'Just tell us what you remember.'

'It's marvellous to see you,' he goes on, determined to prolong the conversation. 'I knew you were working out of Westport and that you're back living here with your mother, but I've never seen you about?' The question hangs.

'Be bad luck if you did.' I smile and he laughs a bit.

'I do remember you from the telly, though,' he says then, 'that time on *Crimecall*, when you were telling the nation to lock their doors and such.'

Beside me, Dan suppresses a grin.

'That's right.' Most embarrassing moment of my life. It had been brutal. The lads in the station had pissed themselves laughing.

'And now, God bless us' – oh yeah, he's also on the church committee – 'you have this to deal with. That poor girl, just lying there, I got a terrible fright. I thought it was one of those shop dummies but sure . . .' he stops and shakes his head '. . . the smell. That told me it was real.'

'It must have been a shock.' Dan slides in to sit beside him. The dog nuzzles Dan. He pats its head and calls it a 'good girl'. Milo's face brightens at the gesture. Dog people like people to like their dogs. It always works on witnesses.

'I keep seeing her when I close my eyes,' Milo says, after a moment.

Dan gives him a second before asking gently, 'Can you talk us through everything that you remember?'

'I've already done it but sure I can do it again.' Milo makes himself a little more comfortable on the wall. He orders the dog, 'Lie down,' but she continues to jump about. Milo ignores her.

'I always take herself for a walk along here, every morning and evening. You could set your watches by us. Eight o'clock we set off from Bunacurry and then, sure, we turn up the bog road and then we just roam around the bog paths for a bit until half past

15

ten. It gives the wife time to herself in the morning. She likes that. Doesn't like me getting under her feet. Anyway, today it was the same as usual. It was quiet enough – I only saw one or two people, the usual people really. It can be busier but, sure, it's winter and getting fierce cold so not so many people are about now. Anyway, I let herself off the lead once we got to the bog, like I know it's illegal,' he darts a look at us and we say nothing, 'but, sure, everyone does it and she's a good dog, listens to me. Lie down!' The dog stares back, immobile, and Milo rolls his eyes.

'She mostly listens,' he clarifies. 'Anyway, Steph, that's her name, she was running along and next minute she veers off the path and she never does that because she knows it's dangerous but she started up a terrible yapping. Now she's never done that before either and I thought she was in trouble, had fallen into a bog hole or something, so I ran to her – well, I walked really because I didn't want to sink into anything myself, you know – and when I got to where Steph was, I saw that poor girl.' He blesses himself.

'So, you let your dog off yesterday?' I ask.

'It's not a big crime, is it?' He looks worried. 'She's a good dog and—'

'It's not a crime,' I say with a smile. 'But just to clarify, you let her off yesterday too?'

'I did. Just for a few minutes, like.'

'And when you came to this place yesterday?'

'She ran right past, no barking.' A pause. 'I do vary the route I take each day up here,' he continues, a little apologetically, 'but I would swear that girl was not there yesterday. Steph would have smelt it. If she'd been there yesterday, the dog would have known.'

'What time did you walk yesterday?' Dan asks.

'Same time. I got here about nine.'

'And on the walk back?'

'I would have passed here or near here about a quarter to ten or so.'

So, between nine forty-five yesterday and nine this morning that body was dumped. I jot it down. Talking to more witnesses will narrow that window. As will the estimated time of death.

'Who do you normally see on the walk?' I ask. 'Would you know their names?'

'The same people mostly. Some I know to nod a hello to and some I don't.'

'Who did you see yesterday?' Dan asks.

Milo screws up his eyes and squints into the winter sun. His dog does the same. 'Mrs Cassidy, she always walks through here in the morning. She's about ninety and as fit as a fiddle. Do you know Mrs Cassidy, Lucy? Your mother sings in the choir with her.'

'I do,' I say. Everyone on Achill knows Mrs Cassidy. 'Anyone else, Milo?'

'A couple of joggers, I'd know them to see. And a tall fellow – he's like Forrest Gump, always running up and down. He wears T-shirts with slogans on them. The one yesterday morning said, "Pain is . . ."' he scratches his chin, thinking. 'What was it now, it was ridiculous. Oh, yes, "Pain is your body's way of growing stronger." Did you ever hear such shite? Anyway, he's a nice enough chap, always nods a hello or whatever. Then there's another fellow that was out running yesterday. He was with a girl – both of them had headphones in and were going fast enough. And then there was another man with his dog. Now I didn't know him and, to be honest, he wasn't that friendly. Normally you'd pat someone else's dog and, sure, I patted his and he showed no interest at all in Steph.' Milo sounds wounded. 'I think that was about it for yesterday. And as for today, sure I was only out awhile when Steph found the girl so I didn't see anyone.'

It's most likely that Lisa's body was dumped last night because it'd have been dark. I make a note to request any CCTV from the Bunacurry road to the bog, if there is any. And our suspected offender might not have come that way: he could have come via Doogort or Keel. I look around. There are no houses to be seen from here. 'Can you talk us through what happened when you found the body?'

'I blessed myself and said a small prayer for the girl,' Milo says.

We wait. He looks expectantly at us.

Finally, Dan prompts, 'Nothing else? You didn't . . .' He lets it hang.

'I didn't touch it.' Milo shudders. 'And Steph just barked at it.'

'Thanks, Milo,' I say.

'Can I go now?' He stands up, and the dog, sensing a walk, bounces about.

'Yes, but if I sent a guard around to your house to take your boots and arrange a statement, would you have any objection?'

'Well, I'm fond of them and—'

'If the search throws up a number of footprints, we need to rule yours out.'

'I see. Well, I'm happy to help.' He reiterates his address.

'Don't talk to the media,' I say. 'We don't want to compromise our evidence or any trial that might happen.'

'Fair enough. Good luck.' He takes the dog's lead and starts to walk back. It's now near midday and I'd say his wife is wondering where he's got to.

'Let's put out a call for anyone who was here between nine forty-five yesterday morning and nine a.m. today,' I say to Dan, 'see who comes forward. And ask someone to get any sort of CCTV from the roads here and we'll trawl it for cars turning off up the bog road. Get car dash-cam footage and we'll organise a team for door-to-door.'

He looks at me. 'I can't see there being too much footage. Either our SO is a clever bastard or a lucky bastard.'

'Yep, but we have to try. I'll call Phil, see if Mrs Moran is able to talk to us.'

After a brief conversation, Phil assures me that Lisa's mother is willing to see us. She'll talk to anyone who can help her find out who murdered her girl.

3

Mrs Moran lives in a small cottage about twenty minutes' walk from Achill Sound. The drive takes about ten minutes from where Lisa's body was found. Whoever killed Lisa brought her home. I wonder if it's significant.

Or maybe she was killed by a local. There are plenty of odd-balls in this part of the world.

Dan and I give it thirty minutes or so before we head out because we're not the best with tears. And I'm fierce bad at remaining unemotional. They try to train you to do that, to be impersonal while at the same time having empathy. It's a load of shite, really. Like, how can you do both? How can you remain impersonal with some woman whose daughter's turned up dead and you have to call out and ask her more questions?

They tell you things to say as well. Things like 'I have a bit of bad news, I'm afraid.' That's utter crap too. It's such an insult to call it 'bad news', and yet you can't turn up at a person's door and say, 'I have news that will shatter your world' either, can you? Though most times, people just know. We don't have to say anything, they just collapse in front of us, like paper houses in the rain.

When we ring the bell, it's Phil who answers. She looks like she's upset, too, and from what I know of Phil, she's great at keeping her distance and being sympathetic. I suppose it's that Lisa was an only child, like my Luc. I can't comprehend the loss the woman must be feeling.

'She's inside.' Phil's voice is soft.

'How is she?' I ask.

Phil shrugs. What is there to say, really?

We walk through the hall and into the front room, which looks like it's falling apart. Margaret Moran sits, a blanket about her shoulders, staring at her hands. She lifts her gaze as we come in. I have seen grief before and now it stares me down again. 'I'm sorry,' I say, the words inadequate.

Dan and I watch as she crumples in on herself, her shoulders heaving. I feel helpless standing there, looking at her, unable right now to offer any comfort.

'D'you want tea?' Phil asks us. Her matter-of-factness, the asking of the ordinary, is reassuring.

'No, thanks,' I say, my voice as level as hers. 'We've just a few questions for Margaret if she's up to answering.'

'I'll answer a hundred thousand times if it helps get whoever hurt my child,' Margaret says quietly, but with a conviction that pains me to hear. 'Ask away.' She's Achill born and bred. She has the thick country vowels and the rhythm of a song in her speech. I used to sound like that too. I think she was a few years ahead of me in school. The captain of the camogie team, the girl who would be queen. She should not be here, weeping in a falling-down cottage.

I sit on a sofa opposite, Dan standing by the window, notebook in hand. He'll write while I question, he's saying. He'd prefer that. 'I know you've been through this only two days ago with some of our colleagues, Margaret, but let's go over it again, just in case you remember anything else.' Going over and over witness statements always reminds me of combing out lice from Luc's hair when he was a kid. Over and over until everything is extracted. 'Tell me about the last time you saw Lisa.'

She swallows hard, composing herself, and when she starts to speak, her voice comes out in spurts. 'It was that morning, she was running late. She was on the phone line, a helpline for children that she volunteered on. She tended to do all-night shifts every second Thursday. She normally went straight from the centre into work, but that day she came home. I think she changed her jacket.' A small smile, followed by such pain that I think I wince. 'Anyway, she rushed into the house, told me she loved me, ran upstairs to her room and came back down. And as she was leaving, I made a remark about it getting cold and that her skirt and top didn't look warm enough. I mean, it's December. I asked her if she was sure she'd be warm enough but she laughed me off. Then I handed her a tea in a take-out cup and off she went.' She says it like she still can't believe it.

'What did she have with her?'

'Just her laptop and her handbag.'

'Describe the laptop for me.'

'I think it was Lenovo, but I know it was pink and she'd put glittery stars on it. She liked that sort of thing.'

I nod. 'And the make of bag?'

'Michael Kors. Black leather. She brought it everywhere. Her dad bought it for her in Italy last year. It had a gold buckle.'

I wonder if she'd been assaulted for the bag. 'Did she have anything else with her?'

'No.'

'You're certain?'

'I told the others who came that she wouldn't have run off.'

'She was wearing a tracksuit when she was found.'

A moment of surprise. Then, 'No, she—' She stops.

'Does she own tracksuits?'

'Maybe it's not her.' She half rises out of the chair. 'Maybe you've got it wrong and—'

'You'll be able to formally identify her tomorrow,' I say gently, hating the way I extinguish the brief hope she has. 'Someone will be in touch about it, but we're pretty certain it's Lisa, and the sooner we get cracking, the sooner we'll have someone for this.'

Another moment before she slowly sits down. 'Yes, yes, of course. I . . .' A pause. Then she gathers herself – I can physically see it and it's painful to watch. 'I know she had tracksuits because she runs, but I'm certain she had none with her that day.' Another pause. 'Not unless she had her runners with her too. I can check. I could be wrong. I—' She stops.

'We can check in a minute,' I say. 'Just go on. You say she left with a laptop, her bag and a take-out tea. Then what?'

'A taxi dropped her to work. The Family First helpline provide a taxi for their overnight volunteers.'

'And where is the helpline located?'

'Newport. I'd generally drop her over, she'd do her shift, and the next day the taxi would bring her to work. That day, though, the taxi drove her here first, and she must have told him to wait for her while she got her jacket. On a normal day she'd walk to the school from here. It's not too far, just about twenty-five minutes, but when she was in the centre . . .' Her voice trails off as a tear rolls down her face. Phil pulls a tissue from a box on the table and gives it to her. She scrunches it in her nail-bitten hands, not even aware she's crying.

'So, she took the taxi and then?'

Margaret looks up at me and shakes her head. 'Nothing. She never came home.'

'What time would she generally be home?'

'Always by four thirty at the latest. She liked to correct copies or plan her classes in school, and then she'd come home, have a cup of tea and maybe go for a run around here or make some calls or do her voluntary work, whatever, really. On Fridays she went running with her friends.'

'Was there anything she had to do that day after work or some-place she had to go?'

'No. She would have mentioned it.'

'She ever mention being scared? Or wary of someone?'

A shake of her head. 'She did tend to protect me but I think she would have said if she was scared of someone.'

'Anyone you know who would want to hurt her?'

'No.'

'Work?'

'She got on great in work.'

I change tack. 'You say she went for a run on Fridays. Who did she go with?'

'There are about three of them that go out regularly. Sometimes others joined them. I know Liam went – he's an old friend of hers. There's a girl . . . I can't remember her name. Lisa wasn't mad about her. There's also another boy, Paul, I think – he called here for her once. I thought he was a boyfriend but she said no.'

'Why did you think he was a boyfriend?'

'I just thought at the time that there was someone . . . but whoever it was, it wasn't Paul.' A smile. 'She was horrified when I suggested it. And there was nothing wrong with the lad. He was grand and seemed very fond of Lisa but there was nothing there.'

'Why did you think there was someone?'

A shrug. 'I know my daughter. She seemed different. A bit secretive. Happy too. It was a while ago. If there was, it petered out because I didn't get any sort of a feeling since.'

'A while ago? Can you give me an idea?'

She thinks. 'Last March, April maybe.'

Nine months ago. 'Okay. She had no arguments? Fights with anyone recently?'

'No.'

Dan glances quickly at me. He's noticed her flinching too.

'You're sure?' I press.

A slight hesitation, then a nod.

That pause says it all: she's holding out on us.

'Margaret,' Dan leans forward, drawing her in, the way he's good at, 'if there is anything, anything at all, that you can think of that you didn't say before, it would be really helpful to us.'

'I can't think of anything,' she says. Defend. Defend.

'That's fine.' A moment before he says, 'But let me add that just because you think something about someone doesn't make it true. If you have a suspicion of anything, we'll investigate it without prejudice.'

And the pause that comes stretches out a bit longer than it should so you know she's thinking. Weighing things up. 'All right,' she says finally, sounding nervous. 'It's a silly thing. And Dom would never – I mean, he loved her so he would never but . . .' She stalls.

Neither Dan nor I speak. I want to shake her for only mentioning this now. She obviously didn't tell the other guards who interviewed her.

'It's a small thing,' she says, 'and it's only a suspicion but I think she had a fight with her dad. That's it. I have no proof but I think she did.'

'What makes you think that?' I ask.

'She refused to speak to him the last few times he rang. I ignored it – they do spark off each other and their spats don't last long. Dom loves her, I know he does. He'd never—' She stops.

'What would they generally argue about?'

'Everything. Politics, religion, where to eat on a night out. I think they liked it. But this time . . .' We don't fill in the gap. '. . . this time I think it was a bit more personal. That's all.'

I want to ask why she hasn't said this before. But she's grieving and—

'Why didn't you tell us this before?' Dan asks.

I flinch. He's right, of course.

Margaret is slowly ripping the tissue to shreds. 'Because I know that Dom would never kidnap his own daughter – I mean, never! It's ridiculous, but it's just now . . . things . . . I just feel . . . Well, I have to tell you all the small stuff. I'm sorry. I just didn't think it was that important.'

'It probably isn't,' Dan says, 'but we need everything you have. Anything else?'

'No.'

'You're sure?'

'Of course I'm sure.' She's indignant now.

We let a silence develop. You'd be surprised how many people talk into a silence. Only Margaret doesn't.

'What makes you think it was more personal, this argument?' I ask.

'She was angrier than normal, seemed to hold out on forgiving

26

him, but she could be like that at times. It could just as easily have been something and nothing.'

'Is there any chance we can take a look at her room?' I ask eventually. 'I know—'

'Of course.' She cuts me short and stands up. 'Come on.'

Dan and I follow her up the staircase. It's narrow and dark but looks as if an attempt has recently been made to paint it. It's a bit patchy, but it does brighten the place up.

'Who did the painting?' I ask.

'Me. I know it's not great but it's better than what was on before.'

We're on the landing now and Margaret turns to us before pushing open a door with a sign saying 'School's Out' and a picture of a sexy teacher.

'Her friends got her that when she qualified,' Margaret says. 'I didn't like it but she thought it was very funny. Go on in. I'll be here if you need me.'

She hasn't gone in yet. Some parents can't for a long time. Others take comfort in surrounding themselves with the smell and feel of their missing children.

I hand Dan a pair of gloves and we walk in.

There's a stillness about the room. The windows are closed, the air is stale. The bedcover is tossed, like she would have left it that last Friday. Tatty posters and collages of photographs cover the walls. The posters are of female athletes, running or on starting blocks. The photos look more recent, scattered about in frames all over the room or just randomly pasted onto a board.

'Who are the people in these pictures?' I ask Margaret.

She braces herself before looking into the room. After a painful moment, she says, 'Those ones there,' she points to some pictures tacked onto the board, 'they're the people she volunteers with. That picture in the middle was their Christmas party. Lisa's on the left.'

Lisa is smiling, a red paper hat on her head. Her last Christmas.

'Do you have names?'

'No, but it's the Family First helpline. They'll tell you who everyone is.'

'Can I take that picture?'

She nods and I pop it into a plastic evidence bag.

'All she wanted to do was give something back,' Margaret says. 'She didn't even get paid for her work on the helpline.'

'Give something back? How so?'

'She, well, I think . . . After her father and I broke up when she was young, she went a little mad. You know what it's like around here,' she eyeballs me, 'everybody knowing your business and talking. Lisa felt exposed, I think. Anyway, I got her help, she straightened out and this was her way of paying it forward.' Her eyes fill and she swallows hard. 'That was Lisa.'

'How long was she with them?' They seem a wholesome bunch. Sort of hipster and cool. And they all look young.

'Almost three years. As far as I know that's the maximum length you can volunteer for – she was due to finish up about now.' A holding of breath as it hits her how many things her daughter will never finish. 'And those,' she continues after a moment, with forced calm, pointing to another grouping, in Christmas hats, 'they're her college friends from Maynooth. Again, I don't know them. I've met one or two over the years. That fellow there,' she ventures into the room, points to a stocky, red-blond lad with a crooked grin, 'that's Liam. He likes her but she wasn't interested. They still hang out together, though, go running and that.'

Dan is peering hard at the picture. In it, Liam is looking at Lisa and she is oblivious, her head back, laughing.

'And over near the window, those pictures, they're her running group. Liam rang me when she never showed for her run that Friday. That was when I . . . Well, I knew something was wrong.'

I give her a moment to compose herself before I say, 'Tell me about Liam.'

'They've been in the same running club for years. It's on the mainland but on Fridays they meet in Achill Strand and run a few miles from there with a couple of others. Lisa and Liam have been friends since they were tots.'

'What is Liam like?'

She flinches. 'You couldn't think Liam . . .'

'We think no one as yet,' I say gently, 'but it's generally someone the person knows.'

She looks unsure, confused, but then shakes her head. 'He's a lovely boy. Like a member of the family. They grew up together. Though I remember thinking recently that they weren't as pally as before.'

'They fell out?'

'Oh, nothing like that, I'm sure. I supposed they were just growing apart. He wasn't up as much as normal and Lisa seemed not to be hanging around with him as often, that's all. Liam wouldn't be a boy who has rows. He's lovely.'

Dan catches my eye. 'You said she'd never take a tracksuit unless she had runners with her. Do you know how many pairs of runners she had and are they all here?'

'She had three.' She sounds certain of that. 'One for wearing, a second in case that pair got wet, and a spare.'

'So, if there are three pairs in the house, we know she didn't go running, which means she didn't wear a tracksuit. Would that be fair to say?'

Margaret nods.

I turn to the pink wardrobe, which has been decorated with sunflowers all down the sides. It looks like the furniture of a five-year-old. The door opens with a squeak and there, on the floor, are two pairs of Nike runners.

'Two pairs,' I say.

'There's a pair in the kitchen, too,' Margaret adds. 'So, there are no runners missing.'

The tracksuit was not hers, which is curious. I close the wardrobe. 'Thanks, Margaret. There'll be a search of the room to see if we can find anything of significance later. We'll be in touch and do call us if anything else strikes you.'

'I will.'

'Again,' I say, as I pass her in the doorway, 'we're both very sorry.'

She thanks us.

'Can we have Liam and your husband's address?' I ask.

She rattles them off, then watches us leave from the top of the stairs.

The gloomy day has given way to a dark afternoon. Rain spatters on the car windows as we slide inside. From somewhere a dog howls, the eerie sound echoing across the flat landscape. We sit for a second in silence, listening, before I say, 'Sorry, Dan, I know I should have asked that question about her husband.'

'She should have fucking told us before,' Dan snaps.

'Yes,' I agree. 'She should. But would it have made a difference?'

30

He shrugs. 'Do you want to go and see Dominic Moran now or,' he consults his notebook, 'this Liam fella?'

'I think we'd better do Dominic first. Then we'll head back to the station for the conference, see what sort of a team we can get together.'

'They'll be chomping at the bit,' Dan says.

A flip in my stomach. This is on you, Lucy, I think. William has given you a chance. Don't fuck it up again.

4

Dominic Moran lives off the island, about ten miles out, slap-bang between Achill and Castlebar, near the coast. His is the only set of apartments for miles, built when it seemed that everyone in the country was moving out of Dublin and going to commute to the capital, or when people thought it was cool to invest in property that, realistically, they had no chance of letting. The apartments might have been nice if the whole world hadn't lost interest in them. Three blocks, five storeys each with a balcony in the penthouse. The exterior is concrete and wood, now turning black and mouldy in the damp air. The grounds, facing the sea, have a few hardy plants trying their best to cope with the salt from the ocean. The grass is scrubby, as grass is in this part of the world, and the centrepiece water feature is turned off.

Dominic moved there after he and his wife split up more than ten years ago. He owns a penthouse and the view out of his window is stunning even on a day like today, with the leaden grey skies and the drizzle.

'Hi,' I say, as we enter. 'We've a few questions, Dominic, if you don't mind.'

He indicates for us to sit down. He looks battered by emotion. Stunned. He sits opposite, head dipped.

Dan had had Dominic's initial statement emailed to us as we drove and he'd read it out. The guard who had interviewed him had said he seemed a decent enough fella. And you can't be a guard and not have good instincts. It's in the eyes and the gestures and the voice. They all have to match. Dominic Moran's look like they match as he invites us into his apartment.

But the best of them can play people like a world-class violin.

I'm wary of my own instincts after everything that happened with my ex, Rob.

Dominic's place, like Margaret's, is a mess. Every surface is jammed with unwashed bowls and cups; jumpers and sweatshirts are thrown across chairs and the smell of Pot Noodle crawls in the air.

'I was about to go to Margaret's when ye rang,' Dominic says, as he rubs his unshaven chin and tries out a smile, which fails. He has the scattered air of a man in crisis.

'We won't be long,' I say. 'How are you doing?'

A glance about the room. 'Not great now. I just . . . well, I tried to tidy up, so I did, but . . . well . . . I can't seem to get a handle on doing anything.' His eyes are reddened and watery.

'We just want to ask you a few questions. Go over your statement.'

'Grand. Yes. Whatever.' His gaze is hopeless. It's like he wonders, What's the point? His daughter is gone and no amount of questions will bring her back. I'd say he was handsome enough at one time, but bad food and bad living have made him paunchy. 'Off you go,' he says.

'Can you go over the last time you saw your daughter?' I say.

He talks about meeting her in a local café six weeks previously. We let him talk. Then I go for it, like I should have done with Margaret. 'How often did you normally see your daughter?'

'Every two weeks, usually.'

'Why the six-week gap?'

And bam. He flinches. Eyes us warily. 'She, well, she got a bit stroppy with me, to be honest. Wouldn't meet me.'

'Stroppy?'

'Yeah, the way kids do.'

'Why didn't you mention this before?'

He flushes. Takes his time answering. Finally, after a few seconds, he says, on a sigh, 'Because I didn't do anything to her. There would have been no point in dragging it up. It would only have muddied the waters.'

'Dragging what up?'

'The row we had, if that's what it was.'

'Can you tell us about it?'

It hurts him to remember, I can see. His body sags and he squeezes his eyes closed, massaging them with his fingertips. I think for a second that he's not going to say any more, but then he says, 'It kills me, you know, that she wasn't speaking to me. I can't ever . . .' His voice breaks but he hauls it back. 'She wanted me to give her money. She said it was for Margaret and I told her I didn't owe Margaret a thing any more. How much longer, I asked her, can I pay for my mistake? It's over ten years now.'

'Your mistake?'

'The breakdown of my marriage.' Then, when he sees more is expected of him, he adds, 'It's the usual story, older stupid man and young woman.' His laugh is bitter, full of regret. 'It's a mistake I've paid through the nose for. Lisa hated me for a long time. She went a bit mad for a while, but she was only a teenager and I suppose it should have been expected. It was Margaret, not me, who helped steady her. So she's a lot closer to her mother.' His eyes fill. 'I've spent the last ten years making it up to her. But I wasn't giving her money for Margaret. I wish I had now.' He bows his head, gulps out, 'Have ye any idea what happened?'

'Not yet,' Dan says. 'Can we get back to the questions?'

'There is nothing more to be said,' he answers. 'I did have a bit of a row with her, but that was just us. She was the one took offence. I just said I was finished with supporting her mother.'

'Have you supported Margaret a lot then?'

'Margaret does not work. I have paid for that house, and the deal was I was to do it until Lisa turned twenty-one and then the place would be sold. As you can see, I haven't sold it because Lisa persuaded me not to, but I'm not paying any more for Margaret. Lisa was annoyed when I said it but she would have come around.'

There doesn't seem to be much there.

'Were you on speaking terms with Lisa in the past six weeks?' I ask.

'No.' The word encompasses a huge loss.

'How did it make you feel?'

A moment. 'How did my daughter not speaking to me make me feel? So bad I wanted to kill her? Is that what you mean?'

I don't reply.

'For Christ's sake!' Then, firm, 'I didn't feel anything. I knew it was nothing.'

'All right,' I say calmly. 'Let's go over once more the last time you saw your daughter.'

'I've already told you lot that.' People get belligerent when

35

they're asked the same questions over and over again. They think we're not doing anything, that we're not listening, but the thing is, it's harder to remember a lie. So, we go back and forth and sideways over the same stories to see where the differences are.

'This time, include the argument.'

'Fine,' he says. 'It was, I don't know, six weeks ago? As I said, usually I saw her every couple of weeks. There was no arrangement, really. She'd just call me or I'd call her, but it was usually once every two weeks. I'd give her money sometimes to treat herself. It was the least I could do, that's what I feel.' A pause. 'Felt,' he amends, wincing. 'Anyway,' he continues, with an effort, 'this day we went to Dixon's, in Mallaranny. It was her favourite place. Nice coffee. She liked her coffee. She was in great form until I refused to give her money for Margaret.'

'What did you talk about?'

'The usual. Her job, the children in her classroom.'

'Try to remember exactly.'

He goes through the bits of conversation he can remember. Word for word again. The same as before. No mention of trouble anywhere in Lisa's life. 'She loved her job and her life,' he finishes.

'Then what happened?'

He winces, rubs his hand over his face. It's an age before he speaks. 'We were talking, just chatting about things, but looking back now, I do think she seemed a little preoccupied.'

'How?' Witnesses who look back can convince themselves of anything.

'I don't know.' He shakes his head. 'She wasn't as sparky as usual. Maybe she was trying to build herself up to ask me for the money or something.'

'How did she put it?'

'Like anyone would. She said something like "Mammy needs money, she's finding it hard," and could I chip in, and I said no. I said it wasn't my problem any more, only I put it nicer than that. She tried to talk me around but I was firm about it. I'm normally not. Then she said she wouldn't talk to me until I changed my mind and,' his gaze travels upwards as he blinks rapidly, 'she didn't.'

I give him a second, then ask, 'How do you and Margaret get on?'

'Good.'

'Really?' I feign scepticism.

'Yes, really. I mean, we don't talk that much . . . but you know . . . it's okay.'

'How did you feel about her getting your daughter to ask for money from you?'

'Annoyed, but I said nothing. I just want a quiet life and Margaret knows that no means no.'

'And have you paid much extra money to Margaret over the years?'

'How is all this going to find my daughter?'

'Please, Mr Moran, just answer the question,' Dan says. 'Have you paid extra money to her?'

'Not much, a bit maybe, over the years, but the house is mortgage-free now and Lisa was earning so I knew they'd be fine.' He stops suddenly as a thought strikes him. 'Was it Margaret?'

'Was it Margaret, what?' I say.

'She told you I'd fallen out with Lisa, didn't she?'

We say nothing. It's best to keep it like that when someone looks as if they might dive off the deep end. They can say anything then.

'She knows I would never harm our daughter and yet . . . Christ. I mean,' he jams a finger at his chest, sounding bewildered and annoyed all at once, 'I was the one forking out for books and clothes and things, even though the money I gave Margaret was meant to pay for all that stuff.' Then it's as if something pulls him back and I watch as the reality of his life hits him again and all the anger and hurt seem to drain away through his feet and suck him along until he's just a shell of himself. He looks suddenly lost, staring down at his hands. 'Sorry. She was a good mother. Ignore that . . . Is it really Lisa? Are ye sure? It's not a mis—'

'It's really Lisa,' I say softly, changing tack. 'Of course, she'll need to be IDed but we're sure, which is why, as you can see, we're leaving no stone unturned, however unpleasant it is to you or your family.'

Dominic nods. 'I just . . . I never thought it would end like this. You don't, do you?'

But you do, I think. When a person is missing with no leads, no credit-card activity, no trace, you just do. Mostly, though, you suspect suicide.

'Is there anyone you can think of who might want to harm her?' I ask.

'No. She was a great kid.'

When someone dies, that's the bit that's hard to crack. No one wants to speak ill of the dead. But among everything, among all the platitudes and the eulogising, there had to be something. There usually was. 'All right.' I stand up, and Dan follows my lead. 'Thanks, Dominic, for your time.'

'It's all right. I should have told you about the row but I didn't because it has nothing to do with it.'

Neither Dan nor I say anything. Maybe it has, maybe it hasn't. We will find out.

We don't speak until we're out of the building and running back to the car through the rain, which has grown heavier. I think of Lisa, left in harsh bog land on a cold December night, and the anger at the injustice of a life taken hits me hard. I fling myself into the driver's seat, Dan into the passenger seat, half a second behind me. We stay for a second, me holding the steering wheel, him looking out of the windscreen.

'What did Margaret want money for?' Dan says.

'Indeed,' I say.

And even though investigating that might lead us down a rabbit hole and away from where we should be, I put through a call and ask that a warrant be prepared to request access to Margaret's bank accounts.

5

Although we should probably head back to the station to set up our new work spaces and talk to the DI, Dan and I decide to swing by Liam's place first. It's only a small diversion and it's best to go into the Cig with a couple of theories. The best friend or the jilted lover often proves to be the main suspect and it's good to get to them early while they may still be a bit shaky with a story.

Liam lives with his mother, in a house not far from Margaret Moran's. This house is bigger, more traditional. A square of farmyard out front where hens and ducks can roam, though today they're all in their coops. Beyond the two-storey grey farmhouse lie undulating bog fields, shrouded now in sheets of rain. Liam's mother answers the door, a harried-looking maternal type in a flowery apron. Even my own mother wouldn't be seen dead in an apron.

'Hello, detectives,' she says, all business, as she ushers us inside. 'We've been expecting you to call. This is a terrible business. We can't believe it. Poor Liam couldn't even go back to work this afternoon. He's in bits. Liam,' she calls up the stairs, 'the guards are here for you.' Then she leads us into the kitchen, her voice

dipped: 'Lisa meant a lot to him, though I have to say I wasn't—'
The sound of movement in the hall causes her to change tack
and say loudly and over-brightly, 'I made scones. Come and have
some.'

I could do with something to eat, I realise suddenly.

'I normally work,' she goes on, as we take seats at the kitchen
table and she scoots about putting on the kettle, getting plates
and butter and knives, 'but sure, I just can't. I keep breaking into
tears. I went on up to Margaret yesterday and, sure, I didn't know
what to say. It's just terrible.'

She plants an enormous pile of scones centre table. 'Almond
and pear,' she says.

'They look great,' Dan says, and she beams.

Liam enters, sliding into a seat opposite us. 'How are ye?' he
says.

He's red-haired and red-eyed, and underneath the mess of
freckles, his face is pale as if he's living in half a daze. Dressed in a
shirt and a pair of trousers, he still looks like someone who's just
tumbled out of bed.

'Hi, Liam,' Dan says. 'We hear you were a good friend of Lisa.'

His mother tsks. Then, at a look from Liam, she shrugs. 'He
was a good friend to her all right.'

'Mammy,' Liam says, sounding a little exasperated, 'do you
mind? I think they want to talk to me.' His voice is deep, thick
country, like his mother's, making the English language sound
more like Irish. He rubs a hand across his mouth and pulls his
chair forward, towards us.

'Sorry. Ignore me.' She takes a seat beside him, ruffles his hair,
and he pulls away under her touch. She looks a little hurt before
her smile reasserts itself.

'Maybe we could talk to Liam on his own,' Dan says. 'We just have a few questions and you look like you're busy.'

'He's very upset,' she says. 'He might—'

'Mammy!'

She shakes her head, and laughs as if he's a belligerent child. Palms flat on the table, she hauls herself to standing. 'Fine, fine, I'm going.' She flaps a hand in the direction of the scones. 'Please, eat them. They're best when they're fresh.'

We say nothing until she's closed the door behind her and the sound of the Hoover floats in to us.

'I am upset,' Liam says. 'She's right about that.'

'I can understand,' Dan says. 'We're here to see that whoever did this is caught, so any help you can give us, anything you think is relevant, will be your way of helping Lisa.'

Liam swallows hard. 'Aye.'

'Tell us about Lisa, Liam.'

And he does. How he'd known her from for ever, how they'd gone to school together, raced together, gone on holidays together. How she loved animals, how she got her job. And he talks of her with such affection, painting her with words, that I can almost see his grief hovering somewhere above him. He loved her, I think. He wears it like a badge. 'And now she's gone,' he finishes off, his voice breaking.

'It sounds like you two were close,' Dan says quietly.

'I'd like to think so.'

'She ever mention a boyfriend?'

He jerks like he's been shot, the question breaking the spell of the tale he's woven for us. 'She had a boyfriend? I don't . . . No, she never . . . She definitely had a boyfriend?'

'It's something we're investigating. But if you were as close

42

to her as you say, then in all probability she didn't.' Dan lets the comment hang. Waiting.

Liam hesitates. Seems to be on the verge, then in a rush, 'You'll hear it from the others anyway, there's no point in pretending but, well, I fell out with her, sort of, I think I did, about two months ago. She . . .' he swallows hard, looks up in the air to stop tears falling '. . . I know I told you, just now, how close we were, and we were, but actually, in recent times, she, well, she wasn't too happy with me, so she could have had a boyfriend and I wouldn't know.'

Dan flips through his notebook, 'How were you getting on with her last March?'

'That was fine.'

'This falling-out? What happened?'

Liam looks caught. 'I don't think it's relevant.'

'Let us judge that.'

We wait. You can sense sometimes when a thing is about to matter.

He rubs his face. 'I'm not sure we even fell out. Like, if I'd've asked her, she would have denied it but, like . . . it was different. And they all noticed.' He gathers himself, taking a steadying breath, before he goes on. 'Like she ignored my jokes or blanked me, but not all the time. And it was my fault too, like. I should have stepped up. Should have helped her.' His leg starts jogging up and down. He takes a scone and starts to tear it apart. 'I wasn't a friend like I should have been.' Regret and grief chase their way across his face. 'She, like, she asked my advice on something and it backfired and she was . . .' a sigh that seems to come from his bones '. . . she was pretty pissed off with me, I think.'

The clock on the wall ticks.

The crumbs of the scone pile up in front of him. 'I swore I wouldn't say and . . .' he swallows hard '. . . I can't.'

We wait. Finally, Dan says, 'She's dead, Liam. Breaking a confidence doesn't matter now.'

His head dips, a tear falls, plop, onto the table. After an age, he says haltingly, 'It was that helpline. She, well, she used to talk about the phone-line thing she did. I know she shouldn't have and mostly she kept it private but sometimes . . . sometimes a call would make her upset and she'd tell me, so she would. No names or anything like that, just stories and they were bad, and I'd tell her she was doing great and I'd swear not to tell anyone and then . . .' His gaze goes off into the distance as he remembers. 'There was one time, about, I don't know, two, three months ago . . . We were on a run and I gave her a lift home and she wasn't herself and I asked her why and she got really upset and she said . . . Oh, God.' He rubs a hand over his face.

'Take your time,' Dan says, catching my eye.

'She wanted my help and I, like I said, it backfired.' Liam closes his eyes and swallows. 'She hated me for it.' A tear slips out.

'I'm sure she didn't hate you,' Dan says. 'I'll bet the advice you gave her was the best you could come up with.'

'It was.' Liam is pathetically eager to embrace Dan's logic. 'She would have been mad to get involved with that child.'

And there it is, all shining in the sunlight. A piece of something new that makes my blood rush a little faster.

'What child?' Dan asks, and I can hear the note of hope in his voice.

'She never told me his name, it was all confidential,' Liam answers, 'but this boy, his mother wasn't treating him right, doing things to him, and Lisa kept telling him to call the guards or talk to someone but he was too scared and that upset Lisa - she was so kind, you see. She couldn't bear to think that that boy was so alone and so . . . Anyway, Lisa told me she wanted to try to find the boy or something but I said no. I told her it wasn't her job.'

'Did Lisa listen to you?' Dan asks.

I'm hoping he'll say no. I'm hoping this will be the crack we need to break this thing open. Maybe she went off to rescue some kid - it wouldn't be the first time. Maybe she crossed an unstable parent. I lean forward, pen poised.

'Yes.' Liam mops his eyes with his sleeve, shattering my hopes. 'She did because the following week, about six, seven weeks ago, she came up to me after our run and she said . . .' He has to take a second. Then he squeezes his hands tight together and half whispers, 'She said I helped kill this boy. That he had rung her again and she'd heard him being attacked down the phone. He was dead, she said. And I asked how she knew he was dead, which was insensitive, but how did she know? Anyway, she just looked at me like I was dirt and walked off.'

'Are you saying that's when things changed between you two?' Dan asks.

'I suppose she thought I'd given her bad advice. But like you said,' he gestures at Dan, 'it was the best I had to give.'

Dan nods, and Liam gives him a watery, grateful smile. I wonder if his hurt hides something more sinister.

'It was not a nice way to treat you,' Dan says. 'I'd have been furious, being blamed like that.'

'Nah, I was just . . . I wish I'd been man enough to help her, but I wasn't and I think she saw me as weak and went all cold on me and I didn't blame her. After that, she tended to hang back more with Paul on runs.'

'Is there anyone else she was particularly close to besides you?' Dan asks, after a moment. 'Anyone else she might have told about this boy or any boyfriend if she had one?'

'Selina is her best friend, she teaches in the same school as Lisa, and maybe Paul as well. She got very tight with him.' A hint of bitterness. 'He joined the club a while back. He's eager but he's not the greatest athlete. Lisa sort of took him under her wing. Or maybe she liked him, I don't know.'

'Do you know how he felt about her?'

Liam shakes his head. 'No.'

'How did that make you feel? Lisa taking Paul under her wing?'

'That was just Lisa, and honestly? If she was happy with Paul, I would have been happy for her. I know I sound like an awful eejit, but I, well, I was mad about her, always have been. I knew she didn't feel the same way but I could have lived with it.'

The poor bastard.

'Can you tell me about last Friday, Liam? In particular where you were between three and five.'

'I was in work until three. I left early that day, I – eh – got a promotion.' He says it like he feels guilty about it. 'I drove home. Got back about four. I work in a bank in Westport.'

That'd put him in the frame. I jot this down. We can check it on CCTV.

'I had some porridge then, for the slow-release carbs, you know, for the run. And I just spent the time after that in the room, gaming. And about six thirty, I drove to Achill Strand. We meet by the tourist office, and I got there about ten minutes after Paul and Sarah. And we waited for Lisa.' He winces. 'But she never showed up so I rang her mother and she started to get all hysterical. Said Lisa hadn't come in from work and that she was worried, so I went on over there. Sarah and Paul went for a run. To be honest, none of us thought it was serious.'

'Is there anyone who can confirm that you were home between four and six thirty?'

'Am I a suspect? I would never—'

'It's just part of the investigation. Dotting the *i*'s, you know.'

A nod. 'There was only my mother here. I made her tea. She wasn't feeling too good.'

'Okay, thanks, Liam. We'll be in touch if we need you again.'

'Right you are.'

He doesn't get up as we leave, just takes another scone and starts to crumble that too.

Liam's mother, who must have been keeping an ear out, joins us at the door.

'I hope you get whoever did this,' she says. 'She was a nice girl overall.' Then, in a whisper, darting looks towards the kitchen, 'I know what happened to her was terrible, but my Liam, he'll never be able to outrun the guilt she left him with. Never. She was a nice girl, but she made a doormat of him.'

I'd say mother and son had had plenty of rows over Lisa.

'Where were you last Friday between four and seven?' Dan asks.

'Here.'

'Were you in when Liam arrived back?'

'I was. He was in great form.' A pause. 'He got promoted in work.'

Dan jots it down, but the mother's alibi is as old as the hills, and I have thoughts that this one would go to any length to protect her son, especially if she perceives that Lisa provoked him.

Liam, for all his protestations of love, is definitely a person of interest.

6

There are only two garda stations on the island, and this one is nearer the mainland so it's been chosen as our headquarters. It's normally manned by three regular guards, Matt, Kev, and Jordy, who's been there since for ever. When a case breaks in a smaller station, which it rarely does, more guards and detectives are pulled in from other divisions. I know this station, having worked in it for a few years, and stepping through the door is like being plunged back into the dark ages.

For one thing, it's a listed building, which means that it's permanently freezing and not very well maintained, because to do so would probably use up the entire budget for the whole garda force for the next three years. On an evening like this, when the rain is hammering down and the wind sighing in every crack, it's a cold place to be, despite the heater going full blast and a state-of-the-art coffee machine cranking out hot drinks on the Formica worktop in the kitchen. The machine was bought last year by the three guards after a local died and left each of them a small sum in reward 'for all their hard work in making Achill such a safe place'. The purchase made the headlines in the local paper.

Matt Daly, who mans the front desk, tells us we'll be sharing office space with two other detectives from Ballina – Larry Lynch and Ben Lively, both of whom we know.

'Upstairs and into the right,' Matt tells us, before turning to talk to Malachy, a local doom-and-gloom merchant, who always wanders in when he's feeling a bit lonely and pissed off.

Dan and I grab a coffee each, then make our way past the two interview rooms and up a creaking staircase to our new office on the second floor. As a general rule, detectives work upstairs and the regulars, your run-of-the-mill wooden tops, are downstairs, dealing mostly with the public and petty crime. I think our upstairs office used to be some sort of sitting room because it has a massive tiled fireplace, also a protected thing, which we'll both grow to hate due to its ability to let the wind whistle through it. The room itself, with its big sash windows and wooden shutters, has been a dumping ground for files and boxes. Two desks sit in the middle of the mess, facing each other. Larry and Ben are sitting at desks by the window.

'Here they are, the drug squad,' Larry chortles turning to look at us.

'Are you not tired of that tired joke yet?' Dan asks.

'It's not even a joke,' I say, peeling off my coat. They call us that because Dan is Dan Brown, like the writer, and I'm Lucy Golden so together we're Golden Brown, like the song. You have to be a certain age to get the joke. The younger fellas just go blank when he cracks it.

'We were told to come down,' Larry says. 'I heard they found a body.'

''Fraid so,' Dan says. 'She was beaten, it looks like. We've to wait for Joe to confirm, though.'

'Any leads?'

'It's a girl, Lisa Moran, who went missing three days ago. Nothing else yet. Has the Cig been in?'

As if in answer, William's head appears around the door. 'Lucy and Dan, what took yez? I need to be briefed before the conference. Come on.'

Dan and I take our coffees with us as we follow him to his sometime office, which is only a little bigger than ours but seems larger because someone has obviously cleared it out for him and dumped the files in our space.

William's bonsai tree sits on his desk. He brings it with him from case to case but no one has so far been able to find out why. That he has guarded his privacy so well is some feat when you're dealing with detectives. The only thing we know about him is that he was from Limerick's Moyross. The area has changed a lot now, but at one time, it was as bad as it gets.

Jim D'arcy is in the office too. Jim is one of those unflappable people who never seem to get stressed. He's fifty and gives the impression of having seen it all, though having worked down here most of his life he certainly hasn't.

William indicates for us to begin.

Dan and I fill him in on the case to date, then on our morning, our preliminary thoughts and where we think we should go now.

'Okay,' he says, when we finish. 'Jim, I see DGs Larry Lynch and Ben Lively are here already. Larry is trained on the CCTV so get him on that. Mick and Susan, those two youngsters from Ballina, apparently are trained on door-to-door. Keep an eye on them, make sure they don't fuck up again. I'll leave—'

'Mick and Susan are good, solid guards,' I say, interrupting him.

'I'll leave the rest up to you, Jim,' he goes on, as if I haven't spoken, though his tone is icier. 'It's all hands on deck. Let me know what we need, and I'll see what we can do. Yez can go.'

Out in the corridor, Dan nudges me. 'Have you a suicide wish,' he chortles, 'telling him that Mick and Susan are good? He feck-ing hates them since they made headlines when they messed up the burglary case in court that time.'

'They fucked up once, just once,' I glare at Dan, 'and it's all anyone seems to remember.'

'Yeah, but what a fuck-up.' Dan laughs.

'It's not funny,' I say, with bite. 'Mess up once in this job and you have to drag it behind you till your dying day.'

'Aw, now, Lucy—'

'Aw-now nothing. Mick and Susan are good guards. Solid.'

And then something clicks with him. The laughter goes from his eyes and he opens his mouth to say something.

'This is not about me,' I snap, before he can get any words out.

We walk the rest of the corridor in silence.

'I'll go and type up the reports from today, will I?' Dan asks, when we reach the office door.

I appreciate the gesture for the small act of solidarity that it is. 'You sure?'

'You can't be called Dan Brown and not do a bit of writing,' he says, and I'm reminded once again why everyone likes him.

'Then thanks,' I say.

'No bother.'

7

The incident room is buzzing by the time Dan and I arrive for the first conference. That's always the way, and as the case winds down, it sheds staff as they move on to other things. For the next few days, though, this place will be a hive of activity as statements pile in from every direction. And each piece of paperwork creates yet more interviews and statements, and on and on and out and out, until the whole thing narrows down again, like a flock of birds suddenly landing.

It can be beautiful.

I spot the Cig sitting at the top of the table and he gestures for me and Dan to sit alongside him. As we take our places, the room quietens a little. William says nothing, just eyeballs everyone in turn until the place is as silent as a tomb.

'Be nice if we could stop the chat and get down to business,' he says pleasantly, and the younger regular lads flush, shuffling their feet uncomfortably. 'Right,' he begins, 'for those who don't know me, my name is William Williams.'

It's a mark as to the severity of the crime we're dealing with that not even a titter goes around the room.

'I'm the senior investigating officer on this case. Jim D'arcy is

52

the incident-room coordinator and I hardly need to tell ye that everything you get goes through me and Jim. Detective Sergeant Lucy Golden and Detective Garda Dan Brown will also need to be kept abreast of all you learn. Everything will be shared around. I don't want any senior member keeping information to themselves. No top-table syndrome will be tolerated here. Now, as you all know, yesterday morning, the body of a young woman, Lisa Moran, aged twenty-five, was found on Doogort East Bog, about three miles off the road.' He presses a button, shows us a picture of Lisa as she was. Pretty, young, her whole life waiting in the wings for her. She'd just graduated from college, it seems. Seeing her like that, it's a way for us to root for her, to want to try our best for her, not because it's our job but because we see her, see what she had the potential to be.

The picture changes to one taken yesterday of her lying, star-like, on the bog, a glimpse of face visible. 'The post-mortem is taking place tomorrow after the formal ID. Forensics have been in, and a fingertip search of the area is due to begin first light. In the meantime, we know that Lisa Moran was badly beaten before she died. Dan, did Joe send on that interim report?'

'Yes.' Dan stands up and reads, '"On Monday December the first last, at ten thirty hours, I examined, in situ, the body of a young woman, age approximately twenty-four, found in Doogort East Bog, to the north of Achill Island. She was found lying on her stomach, spread-eagle position, with her head turned to the left. The victim was attired in a grey tracksuit and was barefoot. She had a number of deep abrasions to her scalp, large contusions to the face, accompanied by swelling, particularly to the jaw. The index and middle fingers on the right hand also appeared to be broken. Due to the nature of the bruising, I believe that the beating was inflicted prior to death. The state of decomposition of the body indicates that death had occurred at least twenty-four hours previously. A post-mortem to establish the cause of death will be carried out after the body has been removed to the mortuary and been formally IDed.'"

'Thanks,' William says, as Dan sits down. Then he asks, 'Who's on ID?'

A young guard bounces up. 'I'm meeting Lisa's parents at the hospital tomorrow,' she says.

William nods. 'Good. I'll be attending the post-mortem afterwards.'

I smile. Fair play, I think. Joe is infamous for doing his utmost to make whoever is witnessing his post-mortems heave. The first time I attended, as a new guard, I'd watched as he poked and prodded until maggots had started to crawl out of the victim's mouth. He'd done it deliberately and his eyes glittered as he waited for my reaction. I'd been shocked at his total lack of respect for the victim and said so. He didn't fuck around with me after that.

William's gaze sweeps the room and Dan looks at me. It's time for the Speech. The Cig is famous for it. He gives it at all the bigger cases and it's always preceded by his eyeballing everyone in the place. 'For those of you new to this type of investigation,' he says, his words echoing a little in the high-ceilinged room, 'and there are a few of you because this is a quiet place normally, I'm setting down a couple of rules. You've probably learned them in your handbooks and whatever, but this is the real world and I need to say it straight. First off, do not assume anything. Ever. Do not think that it was her father or mother or her boyfriend. Do not think it was the rabid dog from next door.' A few chuckles. 'There has been many an investigation derailed by that sort of thinking. Good solid police work, laying layer upon layer, going one step forward at a time is the only hope we have of nailing the right person. Do not assume. Do not talk to journalists unless you've been told to. Do show initiative. Do follow up leads. Do keep the team informed. Do log everything.'

I tune out. I've heard it before and, though I agree with it, I also know that good solid police work hadn't found the suspect in my first big case.

Two children, taken from the street at noon on separate occasions, never seen again. A third, a six-year-old boy who was grabbed a few weeks later but claimed he bit his way to freedom. He was so traumatised that he couldn't remember a thing about his abductor. All he could say was that it was a girl.

We had taken baby steps all through that investigation, treading carefully, building up our case, and at the end we had a whole pile of nothing. Yes, there were suspects. Yes, we'd invited people in for questioning. A man on the sex-offenders register lived around the corner from one of the children, but he'd had a solid alibi. A man who'd lived on the road of another of the children had moved out overnight. Another dead end. We'd chased dead ends until we were banging our heads off walls. My thoughts are interrupted by the Cig saying my name, and I suddenly become aware that the whole room is looking up at me.

'Are we keeping you from anything?' he asks, with a smile that most definitely does not reach his eyes.

'Sorry, I was . . . Sorry.' I stand up hastily, my knee banging the edge of the table, making it jump and causing some files to slide sideways. I make a grab for them to the sound of sniggering.

Trying not to appear bothered, I take my time straightening the files and then I wait, perfectly still, my hands resting lightly on the table in front of me, for the laughter to die down. I know how important it is to take my time with this speech and to be in control of this bloody room. I need their trust and their belief. They all need to row in behind me and Dan.

'Thank you,' I begin, when the noise has died away. I inject just the right amount of sarcasm into the words. 'Though we haven't had a formal ID from her parents, this is undoubtedly Lisa Moran who disappeared three days ago. According to her mother, she never arrived home from work on Friday afternoon. This was initially treated as a missing-person case, which was the correct procedure. Progress was a little slow because she disappeared at the weekend, so it took a while to get CCTV footage from her place of work, where we know she was until four o'clock that evening. If you see here . . .' I nod at Dan and the CCTV appears on the whiteboard. It's always eerie to see footage of the last moments of a murder victim. It's something you never get used to. The picture is grainy, but Lisa can be seen leaving the school building in her black skirt and thick black jacket, her blonde hair swishing about in a ponytail. Her back is to the camera and she carries a laptop bag, with another bag slung over her shoulder, exactly as her mother described. The camera catches her crossing the schoolyard to the gate. It is deserted, all the children having left. At the last moment, Lisa turns and waves before moving out of shot. 'The caretaker in the school says he called out to her to enjoy her weekend,' I explain, 'and she turned to wave back at him. Next one, Dan.' As the footage rolls, I say, 'This was taken from the Bank of Ireland ATM just before she went into the main street. You can see her walk past and disappear out of shot. Dan?'

More footage appears onscreen, pictures of Lisa traversing the main street. She's alone, but her walk is purposeful. Dan puts up the final bit of CCTV.

'This is taken from the Credit Union, right on the corner, just before she took the road to Luck Lane. As you can see from the other footage, Lisa did not take her usual walking route along the R319, which would have led her by this police station, but headed up on a perpendicular road towards the Lane. For those of you not familiar with the Lane, it's a one-kilometre stretch of mainly farm and bog land, which is not covered by CCTV. There are a few houses along it, mainly one-off builds. It comes back out on the R319, further up the road, and is sometimes used as a shortcut when traffic is bad, which is almost never. Lisa never exited as far as we know. We have no sightings of her after that.'

On the screen, we see Lisa turn up the road. After a moment she disappears from view and in the incident room there is absolute silence as we watch her go out of sight. I allow it to settle before saying, 'This footage also shows cars taking that road around that time, coming in one end and going out the other. Once we get the regs from CCTV, we'll be assigning someone to ID those cars.'

'That'll be you, Jordy,' Jim says.

Jordy, the oldest guard, nods.

'In the interviews we've conducted so far,' I continue, 'her mother and father mentioned nothing out of the ordinary. She might have had a boyfriend, and she'd had a row with her father over money she wanted him to pay to her mother. Her father says he refused. I asked earlier for a warrant to have both bank accounts pulled.'

'I'm on it.' A tall lanky guard stands up. 'Ger Deegan,' he introduces himself.

'Thanks, Ger.'

'The only real lead we have right now is that she might have been trying to help a child in trouble,' I continue, 'so Dan and I will call out to Family First in the morning to see if we can get access to any records she might have kept of her calls on that line. All in all, there are about seventy-five witnesses to be contacted as of now. Jim?'

Jim stands up. 'I've the job sheets here. Now, as ye know, it's important that the book is kept in meticulous order. Every job, no matter how small, is logged, followed up, reported on. Any outsider must find it easy to understand how this investigation was run, d'ye get me?' Without waiting for an answer, he begins by tasking Susan and Mick with coordinating the door-to-door. He gives Larry the CCTV and dash-cam footage.

I watch as he pairs off guards he thinks will work well together.

'Dan and Lucy, you're on interviews. After you go to Family First, I'd like ye to call into the victim's workplace, see if any of them remembers anything of interest, and also get talking to her running buddies.'

I nod.

Pat O'Neill is put on Lisa's phone records. 'Requisition them for the last three months,' Jim says. Then, 'No, see if you can go back as far as Easter. Lucy says she might have had a boyfriend.'

Two guards are assigned to the roadway where she was last seen and two to canvass walkers on the bog. 'Talk to everyone who passes,' Jim says. 'Take the numbers from cars that go by. You know the drill.'

Finally, he assigns Kev Deasy, a young lad who has just joined the force, to the phone-line. He looks thrilled to have a role. That won't last long, I think in amusement, because the amount of

absolute shite that can come in during a single day from members
of the public dying to be part of an investigation would be funny if
it wasn't so tragic. 'Be courteous but do your best to get the time-
wasters off the line. You'll know yourself what's important and
what isn't. Anything, no matter how small, bring it back to us. For
the next few days, we'll meet each morning and see how progress
is. Don't hesitate to make it sooner if you feel we need to know.'

Everyone nods in agreement.

'Just remember,' Jim continues, 'every case has lots of lines of
enquiry. We have to keep it in control. Communication, people.'

A moment of silence, like mass or something, as he lets
that sink in. The Cig breaks it by clapping his hands together.
'Tomorrow we begin,' he says. 'There will be no holidays and no
leave until this guy is caught. Anyone who has booked anything
let me know. Let's go out and nail this bastard.'

The station is pretty empty when Dan and I finally take our leave
of it. There is only one officer covering the night shift.

'See you,' he calls after us.

I raise a hand by way of reply and push the door open into the
car park. The rain is still pounding down, and I'm glad at least
that Lisa Moran was found and not left out in weather like this. I
think of her mother and father and vow to get someone for this.

'Hey, Detectives, can you give us an idea of what happened to
Lisa Moran?'

It's that journalist again, all bundled up in a purple fleece,
digital recorder in hand. She is soaking right through and has
obviously spent the evening staking out the exits. What a truly
shit job. I'd say she believes that all her birthdays have come at
once with such a juicy story on her patch. There is nothing that

captures the public imagination more than a murder involving a young attractive female with a seemingly blemish-free life.

At least RTÉ have moved on, though they know better: they'll have contacts somewhere, feeding them titbits of information. This kid has no one, and nothing but her determination to stake out the station, which won't work.

I try to remember the journo's name. Stacy something-or-other. 'Please, Detectives,' she calls, getting closer. 'Can you just confirm that a young woman was murdered and her body dumped on Doogort East Bog?'

'Talk to the press office,' I call, as Dan and I walk quickly across the car park, but Stacy, being younger than us, is surprisingly quick too, even in her battered Uggs. By the time we reach the car, she's only a couple of feet behind me.

I'm not sure if it's stuck or if it's the force of the wind holding it back but the car door protests as I haul it open. Dan jumps in on the passenger side as I hop into the driver's seat, fire the engine and pull out of the station, passing Stacy on the way. She gives us the two fingers in the rear-view. Part of me feels sorry for her but she knows we rarely comment on cases without clearance. She was just chancing her arm.

I have to drive us back to Westport to pick up our own cars. We're tired so conversation is sparse. We throw around a few ideas about the case but then silence descends as the road whips by.

We leave Achill and drive onto the mainland. Twinkly Christmas trees in festive windows flash past as we eat up the road.

'Are you going to Fran's again for Christmas this year, Dan?' I ask.

He stiffens a little, a tightening of the jaw, then, 'No.'

'You're not going to Fran's family?'

''S what I said.'

I bristle. 'Sorry for asking.'

He doesn't rush to apologise, like he normally would if he's been unreasonable. Instead, he folds his arms and closes his eyes again.

We're both tired, so I let it go.

A while later, I pull into my drive. The journey has taken longer because it's one of those blacker than black nights. My mother is still up because there's a light on in the front room. She rarely goes to bed until I get in – she worries, though she'd never admit it. She moved in with me to mind Luc when I was demoted back here. It was just handier, she said, and though Luc is now eighteen and in Leaving Certificate year, she won't be moving out. She still has her own cottage in Achill Sound but she rents it to tourists and artists now.

I suppose I could have told her to leave but part of me likes the company when I get in. It's not fair to expect Luc to be around: he's eighteen and spends a lot of his time online talking to his mates, though lately there's been something up with him. He thinks he's being subtle, but I work in the body-language business. His behaviour is odd.

I try to think when it started and it was around his eighteenth birthday. Six months ago.

The only thing that reassures me is that he's still eating me out of house and home.

I let myself in and shout, 'Hello.'

'Hello, Luce,' my mother calls. 'I've just made some tea. Come in here and I'll pour you one.'

She's in the front room. I join her, flopping onto the battered old sofa with a sigh. 'You look tired,' she says, as she hands me a cuppa.

'It's been a busy day.'

The fire is blazing happily and the room manages to look cosy. My mother has a knack with stuff like that.

'I suppose you're busy with that poor girl who was found murdered,' she says, her hands wrapped around her mug. 'I heard all about it on the news and, of course, Milo was the man found her. He says his wife is not the better of it, even though she wasn't even there.'

'He wasn't supposed to talk about finding her,' I say drily. I pull my feet up onto the seat and throw off my boots.

'He only told me. Sure, I met him in Bunacurry earlier. He knew you'd tell me anyway.'

'I wouldn't. That's garda business.'

'Well . . . thanks very much. If you can't trust your own mother . . .' A sniff.

'Certain things are confidential, Mam. You know that.'

'Hmm.' A moment, as she sits down opposite me, closer to the fire. We spend a few seconds in silence, just listening to the crackle of the logs. 'They got a very good shot of you on the six-one news with Dan.'

'Really?'

'There's the detectives going into the gruesome murder scene,' my mother imitates Jayne Lowe. Then she adds, 'And I saw Lugs in the picture. Hasn't he put on some amount of weight all the same?'

'I didn't notice.'

'Will I tell you what else I noticed?'

'You're going to anyway.'

'Your roots could do with a bit of a going-over.'

My tea splutters out of my mouth and down my nose. 'My roots? Feck's sake, Mam. A girl died.'

'I'm well aware of that and it's tragic, but really, Lucy, big grey roots in your hair. It was like a landing strip.'

'I'm sorry if me and my roots offended you.'

'A bit of dye, would it be so hard? Or a hat.'

'I don't have the time to get my hair done. I have a busy job. A girl died.'

A beat. 'I'm sorry. I just thought I'd mention it.' Give her credit, she looks a little ashamed. 'It's terrible about poor Lisa, of course it is. And her so good at the teaching. And her father the brother of one of the best football players in the county.'

I just nod. My mother knows the whole seed, breed and generation of most people on the island.

'Margaret and Dom must be devastated.'

'They are.'

Neither of us speaks for a bit. I'll be paranoid about my roots now.

'It's always someone they know,' she says then, wagging her finger. 'I was watching *CSI* and, honestly, the twists and turns those lads go to to find their man, it's amazing. And these villains, always very clever. Geniuses most of them. But in a twisted way.'

'I'll bear that in mind,' I say, with only a touch of sarcasm. She thinks my working life is like *CSI* and no amount of telling her that most of the time it's boring and depressing will dissuade her. I change the subject: 'Is Luc in?'

'Down in his room on that computer. He says he's studying but he's probably not.'

I get up, leaving my mug on the coffee-table. 'I'll pop down to him.'

Luc's room is at the end of the corridor. It's the biggest in the house because I thought, as he got older, his life would get bigger and mine would get smaller. Rap music pumps out from behind the door. Some studying. I knock but he can't hear me, the music is so loud.

'Luc!' I call.

Nothing.

I push open the door and there he is, back to me, his fingers flying over the keyboard. The room is always a mess, clothes and sports shoes thrown over the floor. His schoolbooks are piled up against the wardrobe. Posters of bands are tacked to the wall, some peeling away they've been there so long. The room smells of boy. I watch him, my heart expanding with love for him. I drink in the way he's hunched over the laptop, his dark hair shaved, his pale face staring intently at the screen. I love the long limbs of him, his fine fingers, the careless way he dresses in trackies and sweats.

'Hey.' I cross over and put my hands on his shoulders.

He jumps like he's just been Tasered. He shuts his computer screen down but I see he's been on Snapchat.

I'd warned him not to go on social media but I should have known that was unrealistic.

'You shouldn't sneak up on me like that.' He pulls away from me.

'I didn't. I called and knocked but that music is so loud.' I make to turn it down.

'Leave it!'

His tone startles me. 'Don't talk to me like that.' I have to shout because of the noise.

'It's *my* music.'

'Luc, what the hell is wrong with you?'

'Nothing.' His eyes slide away. 'I'm grand.'

'What did I do? Did I do something? Can you just talk to me?'

He looks at me, brown eyes asking me a question I don't understand. I think he wants me to say something and then I think . . . No. No. My mind runs from the unbidden thought that this has anything to do with Rob. My ex and Luc's dad.

But Rob is out now and . . . No. To voice such a thought would only draw attention to it.

'What?' I ask again.

He holds the moment, then, 'Nothing,' he says, turning his back on me.

I spend a second wondering what I can say, then realise I've been dismissed.

I leave in silence.

I'll ring a couple of the boys in Dublin tomorrow, I decide, just to be sure.

8

Day Two

The Family First offices are situated on the mainland, in Newport, about a thirty-minute drive but well within our division. Dan, last night's terseness seemingly forgotten, fills me in on the helpline as I drive. 'Family First was established in the late nineteen nineties for children who were experiencing abuse or neglect or any sort of a problem that they felt they couldn't discuss with a parent. Their motto is "Don't worry, we've heard it all before."' He makes a face. 'Not exactly snappy.' Then he continues, as he flicks through the website, 'It's quite cool, seems to be aimed at younger kids mostly.' I take a quick glance and see a screen filled with block primary colours. 'They do a lot of fundraising and run courses every six months to recruit new volunteers to the helpline. Here's a bit on the guy who set it up.' As we pass over the bridge from the island, he reads, '"Aidan O'Flaherty set up Family First after his son's suicide in 1990. Aidan believes that if his son had talked to someone about how he was feeling his life might have been saved. 'Sometimes it's harder to confide in those we love,' Aidan says, 'because we don't want them to see us differently. This helpline is for any child or teenager out there who feels alone and forgotten. Don't hesitate to call, we've heard it all before.'"

'Can we get any more on Aidan?' I ask. The road ahead seems to be pretty clear and I'm cruising past fields and hedgerows that lie sodden in the winter drizzle.

Dan waves a sheet of paper in the air. 'Ahead of you. He's sixty years old, never been in trouble, three penalty points two years ago for speeding. Separated with two grown-up children, both working in Family First as full-time staff. Just your average law-abiding good-doer citizen. There are a few pictures of him chairing various events and being awarded humanitarian prizes but, by all accounts, he's still pretty hands-on with the helpline, though he's out of the country at the minute so we won't see him today.'

We lapse into silence, Dan staring out of the window, me concentrating on the road ahead. We speed past bog and swamped fields to the right and the ocean to our left. The land dips and rises and falls again. We enter Newport. In summer, it's an attractive little place, but today it seems to have taken on the gloom of approaching midwinter. Dominated by the disused railway viaduct, which spans the river, the town looks oppressive and moody.

Family First is housed in a dingy side-street, a way out, off the main drag. Its headquarters are in a tiny two-up, two-down house that was donated to the charity a few years back. We're obviously expected because, before we even ring, the door is opened by a young woman. 'Detectives?'

We introduce ourselves and she lets us into a tiny hallway. In front, there is what might have been a kitchen area in years gone by, while to the left, a small room seems to house, from what I can see in the narrow gap between door and wall, some desks and phones. Two people are taking calls. The whole place appears to be painted white.

'I'm Dee,' the woman says, with an attempt at a smile. 'Aidan is my dad. He's in France at the moment. Amanda, the head of the recruitment team, is waiting for you upstairs. Just go on up and it's the door facing you.'

We thank her. Amanda calls for us to enter just as we arrive on the landing. Dan pushes open the door and, like the room downstairs, it's white and small, with just a desk, some chairs, a phone, a computer and a filing cabinet.

'Sit down, please, Detectives,' Amanda says, standing up and giving us a firm handshake. Her accent is hybrid, hard to place. She's in her sixties, dressed casually, jeans and a green jumper, her long, silver-grey hair pinned back with old-fashioned gold slides. A swallow. 'It's terrible about Lisa. No one here can believe it.'

Dan and I nod in sympathy. No one can ever believe it.

After a breath to compose herself, she goes on, 'She was a wonderful girl. Never missed a day in the time she was with us.'

'How long was she with you?' Dan is the one doing the questioning today while I write.

'Almost the three years. She would have been coming to the end of her time here and we would really have missed her.'

'Why?'

'Because she was brilliant,' Amanda says simply. 'She had a way of talking to children. Maybe being a school teacher helped. And she always did the nights. It's hard to get volunteers for the nights.' A pause. 'It's unsociable, you see, and a lot of the most disturbing calls come in then, but Lisa was young and I thought she was well able for it. Sometimes she even did two night shifts a month, standing in for anyone who was sick.'

Dan could go in now and say he heard that some calls did bother her, that she wasn't as able for it as everyone thought, but instead he opts for softly-softly. Reel them in, get them relaxed.

'Tell me about working the helpline. What's involved?' He sounds interested rather than interrogative.

'The line is manned twenty-four hours, seven days a week,' Amanda says, 'which as you can imagine is a lot of work.' Dan nods along. 'The idea behind that was obviously to be there for anyone who might call. We recruit for volunteers every six months and they stay with us for three years. We don't want to burn anyone out.'

A bit like policing, I think.

'Every volunteer signs up to do ten hours a month. It usually means two four-hour shifts and one two-hour shift. The night shift is ten hours straight. That's what Lisa did. So, during the day on the lines, from seven in the morning to four in the afternoon, we have two full-timers, who get paid. Then from four to ten, a team of six volunteers rotates. They either do four hours or two. Then from ten until seven the next morning, the night volunteer comes in.'

'On their own?'

'There's no need for more than one volunteer at night. We use a taxi to bring them in and get them out of here. Aidan and I are always available to talk if necessary. We have shower facilities so they can freshen up before work and there's food in the kitchen for breakfast. It's also safe here, not much crime, and the guards are aware of us too. We get our volunteers to text into the station every hour. We take good care of them.' She sounds suddenly quite defensive.

Spending the night in this old house, in this area, curled up on an uncomfortable bed and being woken in the dead of night with a phone call from a distressed kid. Hearing that voice coming down the line into your head. It can't be easy. My admiration for Lisa goes up a notch.

'And then what?' Dan asks, ignoring her tone for now. All we want from this interview is to see what Amanda has to say about the child who called. If they were aware of him. Of his effect on Lisa. If they knew what she wanted to do.

'The calls are recorded, with no identifying information, by the counsellor in a journal. Every two weeks we have a debriefing session where we go through the most upsetting or difficult calls and speak about how we dealt with them. Everyone learns from everyone else.'

'And what calls did Lisa talk about?'

She hesitates. 'This is a confidential line.'

'I appreciate that, but this is a murder inquiry.' Dan splays his hands wide in a what-can-you-do? gesture.

We wait.

'Just the ones that upset her or that she found hard to deal with.'

'But you said earlier you thought she was well able for the calls.'

'She was well able to take the calls, help the caller in the moment and then move on. At least, most of the time. All the calls are upsetting, though, Detective.'

'I'm sure. When you say most of the time . . . ?'

'Most of the time she was good at dealing with calls and moving on.'

'And the times she wasn't?'

'She got upset. It happens. I suggested to her, on a couple of occasions, that maybe she should give the night shifts a break, but she was quite firm that there was no way she was leaving her callers. There was nothing I could do.' Again, that self-justifying note.

'How upset did she get?'

'How is this relevant? She didn't die by suicide, did she?'

The way she throws out that question is slightly shocking. 'No,' Dan says evenly. 'She was beaten and murdered. That must be a relief to you.'

Amanda flinches, closes her eyes briefly. 'I'm sorry,' she says then. 'I'm so sorry. I didn't mean it like that. I . . .' She gathers herself, says, a little tearfully, 'I've just been worried about Lisa ever since she went missing. She was so kind, so uncomplaining. I thought . . . you know . . . that it was my fault, that I'd pushed her too hard, let her do too much, because sometimes, Guard, when people volunteer, you just let them do it because it gets you out of a hole and, well, I knew Lisa was suffering a little, and I should have insisted she give up the nights but I didn't and . . .' She stops. 'But she was mostly steady as a rock.'

'But you're saying in recent times she wasn't,' Dan says. 'Can you tell us what in particular upset her?'

'There was just one call, far as I remember. She said she felt powerless, that this child was in danger and no one was doing anything and, well, I told her she had to let it go. And she did for a while and then there was one night . . . she said the child, the same child, had been attacked and that she'd heard it. It was upsetting, for us all, to hear that. I took her aside, told her to take a break, come back when she was able but, no, she wouldn't. She wanted to be there in case he rang back but, as far as I know, he never did. So, you can understand when she went missing I just thought she was distraught over this child, that she felt she'd failed him . . .' Her voice trails off. After a second, she says, 'I was convinced she'd killed herself.'

'No,' Dan says. Then, 'How long ago was this call when the child was attacked?'

'Maybe couple of months back. Maybe less.'

'We'd need access to her journal,' Dan says.

'You have to realise that this line is totally confidential. The children who ring here, we don't tape them, don't find out any details about them – they don't even have to give us a name. They need to feel safe.'

'And so do the public, Amanda,' Dan says. 'I totally understand where you're coming from but, as I already made clear, this is a murder investigation.'

'The journal is Lisa's so you're obliged to cooperate and hand it over to the investigation,' I weigh in, 'and I'm sure you want to help Lisa?'

'Of course I do,' Amanda says, 'but I don't see how . . .' She shrugs. 'But, yes, you're right.' She stands and pulls open a drawer of the filing cabinet.

'We'll also need access to all of the journals of your volunteers, I'm afraid.'

'All right. I'll get them sent to you or you can pick them up.' Resigned, Amanda pushes a bright pink diary across the table to us. It's akin to something a five-year-old would keep as the front cover is decorated with crazy flowers and butterflies. 'Here's Lisa's.'

I flick through the pages and see that the top of each page is decorated with stick-on stars. Lisa's writing is neat and precise, thanks be to Jesus. Once or twice, I've had a case hinge on a note and the writing has been illegible.

'She liked to say that the happy look of the diary helped ease the sadness in the pages,' Amanda explains.

'Right,' is all I can manage. The words 'beatings', 'drunk', 'drugs', 'scream' and 'help' dance across my eyes as I flick through it. No amount of stars could block the horror of some of these stories.

'Where's the call that upset her in particular?' I couldn't imagine a young girl not getting upset at most of this stuff.

Amanda holds out her hand. 'May I?'

I hand her the diary and she finds the relevant page. 'This story.'

'Can you summarise?' Dan asks.

We'll get someone to go through the whole journal back at the station, see if there are any links.

'Yes. It was a boy calling himself Sam.' Amanda scans the page. 'He was sobbing and hiccuping and he said he wanted to run away. Lisa asked him if his mammy was being bold again, so obviously Sam had rung her before. He said that his mammy was always bold, that she did bold things just to him. He wanted Lisa to come and get him and she said she couldn't, which was true. No helpline encourages active involvement with clients. She told him to contact the guards and he said he was too scared and then she said there was a scream, some sort of a noise, and he was gone.'

That ties in with what Liam said.

'Jesus,' Dan says. Then, 'Is there any record of Sam ringing her after that?'

Amanda flicks through the few remaining pages. 'No,' she says. 'Not that I can see.'

We sit in silence for a second.

'Did Sam contact any of the other counsellors?'

'I don't know,' Amanda says. 'I'll ask.'

'Thanks.' Dan nods. 'Did she contact the police after that phone call?'

'No. We move on to the next call. That's what we do. We can't get involved.'

Dan flicks me a look and I wonder if he's thinking the same as me.

'All right,' he says. 'Can we use this office for a few interviews of the volunteers downstairs?'

Amanda stands again. 'Be my guest. Take your time.'

As Dan writes out an evidence receipt for the journal, Amanda gathers together some bits and pieces before she leaves.

As the door closes after her, I say, 'Thoughts?'

'My first was that Lisa didn't seem the type not to get involved. We know she was thinking of it until Liam put her off.'

'Let's check to see if she did call it into the guards that night. I'll also get Jim to assign someone to checking death or hospital records for a young boy called Sam. Maybe that was why he didn't call after that.'

'That's a theory. So, we'll ask people here if they ever get personally involved.'

'Ask about Sam too, see if any of them heard from him.'

'That's a plan.' Dan grins at me. 'Let's go.'

An hour later, we've finished questioning the three volunteers from downstairs. All of them seemed certain that Lisa would never have become involved with a client. Only one remembered her ever getting upset in a debriefing but couldn't remember why.

None seemed familiar with Sam.

'But we only work during the day,' Dee says. 'Some callers just ring at night.'

'Can we get a list of people who work nights?' Dan asks.

'Sure.' Dee scoots him off the chair, presses a few buttons on the computer and, two seconds later, hands him a printout of the night volunteers. 'Lisa did it most. The others were floaters.'

'Is there a list of people who did it . . .' Dan turns to me and asks, 'When was that call from Sam?'

I consult the diary. 'Mid-October.'

'Who did the nights then?' Dan asks.

More button pressing as Dee searches for the volunteers in October. 'There you go,' she says, as it's printing. 'You'll find the night volunteers are listed at the end. I can get you their numbers if you like.'

'Phone numbers would be great.' Dan raises his eyebrows at me. It's rare you get such cooperation. 'Can we also have the name of your taxi firm?'

'Sure. We tend to use the same few drivers too.' She hands Dan a card and a list of phone numbers.

'Thanks.'

Then we're out of there.

In the car, a thought strikes me: 'If the night shift is from ten in the evening to seven in the morning, why didn't Lisa breakfast there, have a shower and go straight to work? Why did she go home first?'

Dan frowns. He picks up his notebook and scans the interview with Margaret Moran. 'She changed her coat,' he says.

'Let's swing by the taxi rank, talk to the driver who dropped her home, see if he knows why she did that.'

9

The taxi company Family First uses has its headquarters just around the corner. The driver on the night Lisa was last on duty is out on a job but will meet us in twenty minutes outside the taxi office. Dan takes the opportunity to grab us both a take-out coffee and a bun. My digestion always goes to shit when I'm working a case: it's bad food eaten too fast. As we wait, I flick through Lisa's journal, starting way back when she first began her phone counselling. Initially, she was on days. She didn't have too many calls, though she documented them meticulously. As she became more confident, she wrote less, though the context is still clear. I flick through and finally I find what I'm looking for. 'Here.' I jab the page. 'This is the first Sam call. Almost eight months ago.'

I hold the diary towards him so we can both read.

Sam. Seven. Very upset. His mother is being 'bold'. No elaboration. I told him to ring emergency services.

'That seems straightforward enough,' Dan remarks. 'Was it at night time?'

'Yep.' I flick through more pages, taking notes, writing down observations. Dan removes the top from his coffee, scooping up the froth with a finger. 'Ugh,' I say, as I always do.

He makes a production of sucking it off.

The phone rings and it's the taxi crowd telling us that Poitr has arrived in work.

I push the journal into my bag and we hop out of the car.

Poitr is eastern European, originally from Poland but living in Ireland close on ten years. A lot of his speech is peppered with Irishisms. He's a small man, skinny, and wears his blue trousers hitched up with a huge black belt. He also wears a black jumper that's a lot too big. He's jittery. Hopping from foot to foot. He remembers Lisa well.

'I drive her most times,' he says. 'She was very nice person.'

'Describe how she was that Friday morning,' I ask.

'She is smiling. She say she was busy with lot of calls and she look tired. She tell me to drive her home and I think she not going to work that day, but she is. Usually I drive her straight to work. That day I do it only after I drive her home first. So, I drive her to her house, then school, and we are a bit late, so she hop out and run off and wave at me.'

'How was her mood?'

He thinks. 'Like I say, she seem happy. Smiling, a lot.'

'Was she ever not smiling after a shift?'

'Yes. Hard work what they do in there.'

'Can you remember any occasion when she was upset?'

A shrug. 'No. Not that I know.'

'Did she say why she had to go home?'

'No. Not my business.'

'What did she have with her?'

Poitr thinks. 'A bag and a computer.'

'What sort of a bag?'

He laughs a bit. 'I don't know one bag from the other.'

'What size was it?'

'Just regular handbag.'

No tracksuit-carrying bag, then.

Dan thanks Poitr and hands him his card. 'If anything else strikes you, no matter how small, call me, right?'

We stroll back to the car. The wind has eased and the day is a little less bitter. It's nice to get out and walk, even if it's only for a few minutes. My phone rings.

'Hello, Detective, it's Amanda from Family First. I emailed all our volunteers and they're happy to be interviewed. I also asked if any of them had been contacted by a little boy called Sam, and one of our volunteers says he was but it was just the once about eight months back.'

'Thank you.' I'm surprised. 'That was quick work.'

'Lisa was very dear to us,' she says. 'I'll send you on all the details if you'd like to interview anyone.'

'Thanks.'

She hangs up.

I relay the news to Dan.

'Soon as we have the details,' he says, 'we'll get someone to talk to that other volunteer and see what he has to say.'

'Funny how Sam just talked to Lisa after that, isn't it?'

'She might have told him when she was working so he only ever rang her.'

'And if she did,' I say, 'it means she was involved.'

Dan agrees. But we can't assume. Not yet.

10

The school where Lisa worked is a typical country school set in
the centre of Achill Sound. I went there myself many years ago,
when it was just a three-room building with three teachers and a
principal. Built probably in the 1920s, it had served the community well until the 1980s when bits and pieces were added to it to
cope with the expanding population. The place smells of toilets
and bodies and that sandwich-gone-warm smell that I remember
so well from my own schooldays.

The secretary, a resolutely cheerful woman called Marge, opens
the hatch and peers out. 'Hello, Detectives,' she says, before we
even show our badges, 'we're expecting you.' Her voice wobbles
and she pulls a large hankie from her sleeve and dabs her eyes.
'Sorry, sorry. I'm so sorry. Poor Lisa.'

Dan has turned away and is examining the pictures on the
walls. Bright happy suns with blue skies.

'Is there a couple of rooms where we can conduct interviews?'
I ask.

'They're set out,' Marge says. 'Now, we've counsellors in
the school too, so it's all a bit chaotic. But one room is Delia

Dempsey's office. She's the principal. The other room is that one just there.' She points to a room two doors down.

Delia had been one of my teachers when I was in the school. Thirty-five years later, she's now the principal. I don't know if that's good or completely depressing. She had been one of those scary unpredictable teachers, red-faced, ready to slap with a ruler one minute and smiling the next. You'd always be on shaky ground with her. I'd got a fair few wallops of the ruler in my time. I wonder if she ever thinks of that now. Does it make her feel guilty?

I'd talked to her on the phone over the weekend and she'd sidestepped any reminiscences, instead cutting to the chase and professing herself very fond of Lisa, calling her a dedicated teacher who was loved by her pupils. It sounded like a cliché but maybe it was true.

I watch as Marge dials a number and murmurs into the phone. 'Delia's waiting,' she says to us, and launches into the directions.

'I'll head down to her. You take this.' I hand Dan the shorter list of interviews. 'When you're done, go and talk to any parents floating around. I'll nab the caretaker.'

He nods, asks Marge to get him Mr Connolly while I make my way to the principal's office.

Delia Dempsey calls for me to come on in. 'Sit down, Detective.' She gestures to a tatty chair. The use of 'Detective' tells me that there will be no walks down Memory Lane today. This place has not been done up in years, I think, as I take a seat. The walls could do with painting, and the flooring is old lino made to look like wood, only it doesn't. The only bright and humor-ous thing is the wall calendar, which shows a picture of a cat with a soother in its mouth. The rest of the room has an air of neglect.

Delia doesn't look to have changed much, except she's neater than she used to be. Buttoned up primly in a herringbone jacket and skirt.

'Mrs Dempsey,' I flip open my notebook.

'Delia, please.' Her voice is clipped.

'Delia,' I amend, 'I know you talked to my colleague last Friday on the phone.'

'Yes. Lisa was just missing then.'

'That's right. Anyway, I've a few questions for you, if you don't mind.'

'Anything to help.'

'Tell me about Lisa, how she came here. Just a bit of background.'

'This was her first job. She qualified two years ago with her best friend Selina Carroll, also a member of staff. Lisa had done some teacher-training here and we were very impressed with her. She was creative and good with the children.'

'And she was in work on the Friday she disappeared. Is that right?'

'Yes. Until just after four. Myles, the caretaker, saw her leave.'

'When did you last see her that day?'

She thinks for a second, running over a day that would have been forgotten in a short space of time, would have been logged unremarkable, except that Lisa Moran left work and never came back. 'I think it was at big break in the staffroom. I walked in and she was chatting and laughing with some of the others. I didn't speak to her. From what Selina says—'

'I'll talk to Selina. Just give me your impressions.'

'I have no impressions. She was the same as usual.'

'Define "same as usual".'

'Good form.' She doesn't elaborate.

'Anything that would have caused you concern regarding Lisa?'

The lightest of pauses, a tiny flicker of an eye. 'She was a fantastic teacher.'

That's not an answer, I think, so I press a little harder. 'How was her relationship with other staff members?'

'She never fell out with the staff.'

'Did she fall out with someone else?'

The silence that follows tells its own story.

'Delia, unless this is a tight secret, I will hear it from someone else. You might as well tell me what you know.'

'As I said, she was a great teacher and it was . . . It's difficult . . .' She looks warily at me, her primness and composure melting away, like ice in fire.

'I need to know, Delia. If you care about Lisa Moran, like you said, you will tell me.'

I can see conflict chase its way across her face. Then, closing her eyes briefly, she says, 'One of the parents complained that Lisa was too hands-on with her children.'

'Hands-on?'

'You've got to understand that parents can be very sensitive on behalf of their children. They blow things up.'

I wait.

She steeples her fingers and lowers her voice, leaning towards me across the desk. 'It was a month or so ago and it was . . .' she hesitates '. . . resolved. It has nothing to do with this. I—'

'Let me be the judge of that.'

My sharp tone makes her flinch. She's not used to being challenged. 'Things have changed in schools,' she snaps, and I get the impression she's not exactly on board with these changes. 'Parents entrust their children to us and yet we can't, it seems, be trusted. It's a minefield, a nonsense. Sometimes I'm this close,' she makes a small space with her fingers, 'to telling parents to keep their children at home and in ignorance, if they're going to question every motive of one of my teachers.' Another pause, before she says, 'This child, Kara, with a K,' another roll of her eyes, 'she fell in the yard. She's only a junior infant, a baby. Anyway, this fall was nothing serious, just a scrape on the knee, but apparently Kara was quite upset. Lisa was on yard duty that day and she lifted the little girl up from the tarmac, gave her a cuddle and brought her to the first aid.'

'And?'

'The parents complained that Lisa had no right to touch their child. You can't do that any more, Detective. If a child is crying and in distress, you have to comfort them verbally. Miss Moran knew that but she couldn't help herself. She said the tears got to her. Anyway, Kara's mother complained.'

'Can I have the name of the child's mother, please?'

'It really has—' She stops, knowing she'll have to hand it over. 'All right. I'll write it down for you.' She pulls over a pen and paper, presses a few buttons on her laptop, scribbles a name and address and passes it to me. 'Good luck.' She says it as if I'll need it.

I glance at the address. St Jude's Park. A rough enough area, just outside Achill Sound, on the Bunacurry Road. Compared to areas of Dublin, the social problems are mild enough, but it's still a place that doesn't make it onto the tourist trail. An estate of about fifty homes, designed for social housing, it was meant to have had some infrastructure included, but the crash came and that was the excuse the powers that be needed to abandon the place and its residents.

It makes me angry to think about it. Angry for the town and angry for the people who are forced, literally, to live on the margins.

'What happened then?' I ask.

'They complained, her more than him, really. He didn't seem to have an appetite for it. I've seen women like her before, Detective, looking for compensation. I told Lisa to write an apology and she did. But then, a week or so later, back Mrs Ryan comes again, complaining that Lisa was asking the child if she had a lunch and poking her nose into their affairs.' Another pause. 'I was obliged to pass the complaint to the board and I did. Lisa was very upset over it. She said she had done nothing wrong and I assured her that I believed her. So did the board. I made sure of it. Those people,' she shudders, 'they just wanted someone to sue.'

I wait for more. I know she has more.

'I have only a year or two left in this place and I will not see good teachers being hunted out by money-hungry parents. I support my staff, Detective.'

'I see.'

'Lisa's career could have been ruined.'

'And you saved it?'

She fiddles with the top button on her blouse. 'Would someone be murdered over something like that?' She looks up at me, like a kid needing reassurance. 'I'd hate to think that what I did annoyed them and he . . .'

'The only person at fault here is the murderer,' I tell her. I say that to everyone, yet I'm not sure it's true. There was a time I believed it absolutely. But now, having seen all I've seen, I know there are steps on the way to any crime, whether it's poverty or neglect or abuse, and it's only afterwards you can see those steps leading inevitably to wrongdoing of some sort or another.

'But if he—'

'We have no evidence to say that this man,' I glance down at the name and address she'd handed me, 'Mr Pete Ryan, has done anything wrong. Now, would you mind getting someone to cover for Selina Carroll, please? I just need a quick word.'

'I'll cover and send her in to you. Wait there.'

After she leaves, I take the opportunity to have a better look around the room. I sit behind her desk, in the chair she has vacated. Despite the tattiness, everything is in its place. Pens, pencils, box of tissues. Beside the laptop, there is a picture in a silver frame. A little girl, curly-haired with two front teeth, is smiling into the camera. Delia is holding her and laughing. It must be a grandchild. They look like they're on holidays, because there is a pool behind them and a bright blue sky above.

The door opens and a woman who must be Selina pops her head around it. She looks a little startled to see me sitting where her boss normally is.

'Come in, sit. Thanks for coming,' I say.

Selina smiles nervously at me before perching on the edge of the chair, her hands balled into fists. She'd be pretty except she looks like she might cry at any second.

'I wasn't going to come in today,' she says, talking before I can get a word in. Her voice is jittery, the words tumbling out, like a sudden rush of water. 'But you can't let the children see anything is wrong, can you?' I detect a trace of Cork. 'Like they sense these things, you know?'

I give a sympathetic smile and pass across the box of tissues.

She takes one, dabs her eyes and blows her nose, then wipes it vigorously. 'I teach sixth,' she goes on, between sniffs, 'they're much more aware of everything. They watch the news and they know all about Lisa. Some of them are very distressed and I have to pretend to be strong.'

'That must be hard.' I lean a little forward. 'Selina, I need you to tell me everything about the last conversations you had with Lisa.'

'Yes. Yes. Of course. What do you need to know?'

'Everything you can remember. Good and bad. Nothing you say can hurt Lisa now.'

A small 'Oh' escapes her. There is something about plain speaking that is rather shocking. She rubs a hand across her face, blows her nose again. 'There is no bad,' she says. A moment to gather herself. 'Lisa was just so lovely. Like really, really lovely, not fake or put on. Just caring and funny, and the children loved her.'

'You knew her from college, is that right?'

'We did our teacher training together. And then when we both got a job in the same school, it was a dream come true. I just can't believe this has happened. I'm—'

'Tell me about last Friday,' I interrupt, before she can get off the point. 'Begin when you first saw her.'

She hardly has to think about it. It'll be seared on her memory for ever now. 'She was running late, barely made it in. As I was walking my children to the classroom, I saw her out of the window. She was crossing the yard – I think she was on the phone but I can't be sure.' A small smile. 'And I laughed and knocked on the window and, you know, pointed to my watch and tut-tutted at her. She stuck her tongue out. She was gas. She cut it fairly fine most mornings but Delia would never say a word to her. She'd take the rest of us out of it, but she loved Lisa. That morning she was late 'cause she'd done a stint on the helpline. It's for children who've been abused and that.'

'Did she ever talk to you about the helpline?'

'It was confidential and I didn't ask.'

'Back to last Friday, how did she seem?'

'Grand. I suppose, if I was to think about it, maybe a little preoccupied. But that could be just me, remembering wrong, but I did have to repeat some things to her that I'd already told her, but mostly she was on the ball.'

'What did you talk about?'

'Anything and everything.' A moment of pain before she says, 'She advised me how to handle a boy, Owen, who she taught last year. His parents are headed for separation and he really is acting out. She was good with all that stuff.' A pause. 'Then she had a bit of a moan about her dad. She wasn't talking to him but I think she was only making him suffer because he wouldn't give her money.' There's a hint of bitterness in the sweet. 'Then I asked if she was going to a film on Saturday and she said maybe, that she might be doing other stuff and that she'd call me and . . .' a biting of lip '. . . and she never called. I was a bit cross over that but I never thought . . . And that's it.' She dabs her eyes with a tissue.

'Thanks, Selina. You say she gave out about her dad. Was that something she often did?'

'They fought all the time. She hated when she didn't get her own way over things. But she wasn't mad at him, she was just being . . . a bit mean, maybe.' A flush. 'Don't get me wrong, I love Lisa, but, like, most times she never knew how well off she was. Her parents were mad about her.'

'The only-child syndrome.' I smile. I'd always tried not to spoil Luc.

She shrugs. 'Maybe, all right.'

'Did she say what it was she might be doing on Saturday night?'

'No, just stuff. She said everything was up in the air and that she'd tell me on Monday and . . .' Her voice trails away, like smoke. 'I don't know,' she repeats, striving to get her voice under control. 'I don't know . . .' A tear plops onto her hand and she brushes it off with the tissue. 'I just can't believe she's gone. Who would want—'

'Can you think of anyone who would want to?'

A shake of her head.

'Did she recently have a boyfriend, say around last Easter?'

'That only went on for about two months.'

Her words fall into the room, like a gift. I lean forward. 'Any idea who it was?'

'She wouldn't say. She wanted to see how it would work out first but it didn't.'

'Why not?'

'She just said he was a prick, which I guessed to mean that he'd done something wrong.'

'No details?'

'No.' Selina frowns, 'I suppose that was a bit odd, like.'

'What can you remember?'

'That's it, really. It didn't go on too long and I think he broke up with her because she was really cross over it. It was like "How dare he?" or something. She was upset, but mad-upset, if you know what I mean. She liked being the one calling the shots. And she wouldn't talk about him so I didn't ask. I thought she might after a while – I mean, I was dying with curiosity.'

'Did she ever describe him, say where he lived? Anything?'

'No, he was just gorgeous, that was it.'

'Would she normally tell you who she was seeing?'

'Yes . . . yes, she would,' she says, as if it's only now dawning on her how out of character this was. 'That is odd, isn't it?'

I change tack. 'Did she say what she was doing on Friday night?'

'She normally went for a run on Fridays but I don't know if she was going to or not.'

'Did she ever talk about her running pals?'

'Not really. I suppose she thought I wouldn't be interested.'

'Would you know who, say . . .' I flip the pages in my notebook '. . . Liam is?'

She rolls her eyes. 'We all know who Liam is. They've known one another for ever.'

'How would you describe him?'

'He's a bit of a doormat but harmless enough.'

I've met dangerous doormats in my time.

'What about Paul? Did she ever talk about him?'

'She could have, I don't remember. I only know Liam because he socialised with us.'

'How was Lisa in work?'

She looks at me, wondering, I'd guess, what I know.

'I need you to be honest here,' I say.

'I suppose Delia told you about the Ryans?' she answers defensively. 'Did she tell you it was rubbish? Like, I know Lisa broke the rules but Lisa was like that. She just . . . well, she . . . and Kara, well, Kara is dealing with a lot for a little girl. I mean, her father was this high-flyer until he wasn't. Then there was some court trouble with him. They only moved into the area about

89

three years ago. The two of them are weird.'

'How so?'

'The mother was the one kicking up a fuss. He didn't seem to be too bad, but, what with his court case and that, we were all a bit wary of him. They made Lisa's life a misery for the last little while, though she never let on it bothered her.' A swallow. 'That was Lisa.'

'Was Kara in Lisa's class?'

'No, she's in Les Mooney's.'

'Can you get Les for me?'

'Sure.' She hops up, taking a couple of tissues with her, and just before she leaves, as she's halfway through the door, she turns to me. 'Please find whoever did this.' Then she is gone.

Les Mooney arrives a few minutes later, a middle-aged skinny man with greasy hair.

He plonks down into the chair in front of the desk and, in contrast to Selina, he doesn't appear shaken or maybe he's just hiding it better. His face is pale with over-large brown eyes behind black-rimmed glasses. He runs his tongue over his lips and leans forward, elbows on his knees. He's dishevelled.

'Is Kara Ryan in your class?'

'She is,' a jerky nod, 'quiet as a mouse. Why?' And then understanding hits. 'Between you and me,' he leans in further and his voice dips, 'that was handled very badly. I don't know what anyone else is saying, but those parents were perfectly right. Lisa should have been more professional.'

'I was told,' I pretend to consult my notes, 'that Lisa was just comforting the little girl.'

'You can't do that any more.' He snorts. 'What Lisa didn't understand, what she refused to understand, was that those rules are there to protect us as much as the kids. I said it to Lisa myself but she just brushed me off.' In a lower voice, 'She could be a right diva so she could.'

'Your principal disagrees.'

'You women,' he leans back and folds his arms, 'you all stick together.'

'Really?'

An unapologetic wave. 'If I did that, I'd be out with no future. The Ryans should have got a decent hearing from the board but, by all accounts, they didn't. If they had, I doubt they'd be as bad as they are now.'

'What do you mean "bad"?'

'The wife, she's constantly sending me notes, checking up. That's Lisa's fault, no one else's. I said it to her once and she laughed, but underneath she must have worried.'

She didn't worry enough to tell her parents about it, I think. Neither of them seemed to know. She never told Liam. Maybe she didn't want them knowing.

'Did you like Lisa?'

A shrug. 'I liked her well enough until she started making her own rules. That was odd, it was.'

'She normally obeyed the rules?'

'Far as I know.'

'Where were you on Friday between three and five, Les?'

'I was in school until three fifteen. Then I hopped in the car and drove to my mother's to bring her shopping.'

'Where?'

'SuperValu. I was with her all evening.'

I take a note of it, then ask him to get another of his colleagues. It's a small school, about eight teachers. It takes until one thirty to finish. It's then I ask Delia Dempsey to do me a small favour.

She agrees warily.

Dan has finished too, and his notes pretty much tally with mine.

'No love lost between Lisa and Les Mooney,' I say. 'He was the only teacher openly critical of her and of the principal. He's given me an alibi for Friday so I'll get someone to see if it checks out.'

'We have to talk to the Ryans,' he says. 'The teachers I talked to think Mrs Ryan was more to blame than the husband.'

'Still, he went along with it. Who knows what else he'd go along with?'

'Fair point. And maybe he was the one pulling the strings.'

'One of the teachers mentioned he'd been in trouble with the guards,' I say. 'Will you call the station and get that checked out? Then talk to the parents in the yard, if you can. I'll hunt down the caretaker. I'll join you for two o'clock. Oh, by the way, there was a boyfriend.'

He arches his eyebrows.

'And Margaret was right. It seemed to end as soon as it had begun.'

'Good work, boss.' He tips me a mock salute and trots off, already dialling, and I find the caretaker in a shed at the back of the school. He's tossing boxes into the back of a skip. *Lost and Found* is printed on one of them. *Old Boots* on another.

'Having a clear-out?' I say.

'Aye.' Then he pauses, looks me up and down. 'Guards, is it?'

'That's right. I just want to take you through your last sighting of Lisa Moran again.'

He pulls off his cap, scratches his head, puts his cap back on and comes to join me. 'Let's sit there,' he says, indicating the wall between the schoolyard and the shed. He plonks himself alongside me. 'Go ahead.'

'Thanks. Can you tell me what you remember about Friday?'

'That girl always left at four,' he says, looking down at his large work-worn hands and sighing. 'Regular as clockwork. I'd usually be around and we'd say our goodbyes. That was it. That Friday was no different.' He looks at me. 'No different,' he repeats.

'Did you notice anything unusual? Maybe a car around or someone hanging about the yard?'

He frowns. 'Would you not have that on CCTV? I'm not the best at remembering, particularly when I didn't know I'd have to remember.'

'I know it can be difficult.' I point to the left. 'The only area covered in the CCTV footage is there. What about to the right?'

He thinks, screwing up his face. 'There usually are a couple of cars parked there all right,' he says eventually. 'Cheap people do it to avoid paying the parking fee.' Then, with some surprise, 'Actually, there was a white car there Friday because I was going to go over and tell it to move and, yes, before I got to it, it did move on.'

My heart skips just a little. Instinct. 'What time was this?'

'Just a few minutes after Lisa left.'

'Can you remember the make of car?'

'No, the eyesight isn't what it was. All I know for sure is that it was white.'

'How many people in it?'

'It was too far off. I just wanted it to move because I hate the cheapness of some people.'

'What direction did it go in?'

'Towards the town.'

'Great. If you think of anything else, just call me.' I fish out a card and he takes it with a 'Thanks.'

That car might be nothing but, then again, it was out of CCTV coverage, just like everything to do with this case.

Dan is in the yard, talking to a group of parents. It's almost two o'clock and the younger classes have finished for the day. I see mothers and fathers arriving, like flocks of roosting birds. I'll bet the main subject of conversation is Lisa Moran, and Dan moves from group to group with ease, showing his badge and asking questions. After a moment or two, he spots me and trots over. 'Anything?'

I fill him in.

'We'll check out CCTV for a white car around that time,' Dan says.

'Yeah. What did you find out on Ryan?'

'It turns out,' Dan says, sounding like the cat that got the cream, 'he was up for assault two years ago, put a fellow in hospital.'

'Isn't that interesting?' I say.

Dan nods. 'Let's get the pair of them interviewed today if we can. I've asked for the incident report to be emailed over.'

'Great stuff.'

'What are we doing hanging about here?' Dan asks.

'Kara is due to come out of school now. I got the principal to point her out to me. Let's see for ourselves how she reacts with her mother.' My eyes are fixed on the door, waiting on the children to emerge. I spot Les Mooney as he comes into the yard, flanked by his tiny students. Some are running, others chatting hard, getting the last words in before they have to go their separate ways for the day. Like a flashback movie, I see Luc, aged six, tousle-haired, running straight at me, wrapping his little arms about my legs, saying, 'I missed you, Mammy.' I'd tell him I'd missed him too, then dump him on someone to be minded for the afternoon. Guilt is a physical pain, I've discovered. I focus on banishing the memory to try to spot Kara. She's there, in the middle of a little gang. And yet, despite being surrounded by five of her classmates, she's most definitely not a part of them.

'That's her, the dark-haired girl with the ponytail and the yellow bow.'

'I see her,' Dan confirms.

Her uniform is a little big and her navy coat a little small. Her bag, high up on her back, looks enormous.

One by one, her comrades peel off, running to their parents. Kara stands motionless, her eyes darting about and finally settling on a tall woman to the left of Dan and me. We watch as she raises a hand and Kara trudges towards her.

I'm glad to see the woman smile as Kara approaches. I watch as she crouches down and takes the bag from her. Then, holding hands, mother and daughter climb into an old white BMW and set off.

As I drive out to the place where we think Lisa was taken, Dan endures a very hostile phone conversation with Kara's father, who initially refuses to be interviewed but eventually calms down when Dan explains that we plan to interview anyone who had dealings with Lisa Moran.

'Eight o'clock this evening,' Dan says glumly. 'I tried to get him to go for an earlier time but he wouldn't budge.'

'Eight it is so.'

We lapse into silence.

After a few minutes in traffic, we come to the turn-off Lisa would have taken. It's a narrow road, with a grass verge for walking on. Altogether, it's about eight hundred metres long, going upwards, with laybys for cars to pass each other. There are a few houses along the route and it's not terribly isolated but there is a gap of maybe three hundred metres where there are no houses to be seen in either direction.

It's just begun to drizzle as I park the car in a layby about fifty metres from where we reckon she was last seen. The day is closing in, sun dipping over the edge of the mountains that dominate the landscape no matter where you are on the island. I pull up the hood on my old rain jacket and Dan zips up his state-of-the-art Superdry that Fran bought him last Christmas. As we get out, icy wind whips at our faces: after the mildest of autumns, winter has arrived. The trees that line the road are bare. Rotting leaves squelch under our feet as we make our way towards the two guards in high-vis vests whose job it is to stop and question the drivers of any passing cars. We'll run the registrations through the system later on. It's true that perpetrators of a crime sometimes return to the scene. The real killers, the ones that will do it again, I would say always come back, and I get the feeling this guy will do it again. Because of that, we'll also be examining all the footage taken yesterday. Lugs has probably been asked to contribute the results of his filming by now.

Dan and I nod a greeting to the two guards.

'Anything interesting?' I ask.

'No,' the taller of the two says. He's in his twenties with a country accent as thick as fudge. 'It's hard to know whether deh road is quiet because of what happened or it's just generally quiet anyway. All deh people in the cars this morning were locals, just going about their business, so they were.'

'We'll have a better picture later on. Someone is bound to have seen her last Friday and hasn't come forward yet,' the other guard chimes in.

Dan and I move on, walking the road she would have walked, trying to figure out where the abduction might have happened. Or if it was an abduction. 'She definitely came up this way,' I say, thinking aloud.

'Yes, and the woman who lives in the house back there,' he jerks his head in the direction we've come from, 'Myra Matthews, saw her. After that, no one else did.'

'That was four twenty. Could she have passed the other houses further on and just not been seen? It would have been getting on for dark.'

'Yes, but we don't have her on CCTV after she came up here, and if I was going to take a girl, I'd do it in this stretch.'

We turn and look back. We've reached the end of the three hundred metres. Another few feet and we'd be visible from another house. 'It would make sense if she was taken here,' I muse. 'Did Myra Matthews say she spotted any cars after Lisa passed her or just before?'

'There were cars, but she can't recall them.'

'And every car that went in was traced at some point as having come out? No one parked up here waiting?'

'That's right.'

'And no cars exited the route without first entering? No one parked up here the day before and then exited?'

'No.'

We're thinking aloud, going over what we already know. It's funny sometimes how that can shake things loose.

'And no cars took longer than usual to travel the eight hundred metres?'

'Not significantly. They're double-checking.'

'So, what we're left with is that a car came up here, the driver saw Lisa, jumped out, overpowered her and dragged her into it.'

'Or that she knew him and got in of her own free will.'

'Either way, it had to have been a car that came up here around four twenty or just before.'

'Yep. Or she could have gone into one of the houses.'

'We'll wait and see what Susan and Mick get on the door-to-door.'

It had been raining on Friday too. Maybe she'd been offered a lift. Maybe she'd hopped into the car of someone she knew. That thought, though chilling, is better than some random man just pulling her off the street. Those crimes are hard to crack.

We begin walking back to the car. I try to see the area as Lisa must have seen it that last Friday afternoon: the sun dipping, the sky turning purple with rain, the green of the fields bright against it. The endless stretch of bog further on, brown against the sky.

Dan's phone rings and he pulls it out. 'It's the station,' he says, and answers.

Was she hurrying somewhere or just waiting? Was she—

'You won't believe this.' Dan turns off his phone. 'Kev got a call from a Mr Clive Porter.'

'You're joking? Ex-Detective Inspector Clive Porter?'

'Yep, now *Private Investigator* Clive Porter,' Dan says. 'And after complaining bitterly that he couldn't get through to the super he told Kev Deasy that Lisa had asked him to do some PI work for her.'

Clive was a detective who'd retired three years ago. From Mayo originally, he'd worked all his policing life in Dublin. He'd been well known throughout the force because he'd been involved in some heavy cases over the years. At one time, about ten years back, he'd been a household name for testifying against some of the country's most notorious gangsters. He'd been shot at and, as a result, he now walked with the aid of a cane. I'd met him a couple of times since retirement, when he'd come to live on Achill, and had been in awe of him. It's not many people I'm in awe of.

'Let's go.'

11

Clive's offices are in Keel, the island's biggest town. Up a tiny side-street, you wouldn't know they were there at all unless you deliberately went looking. A bright blue door announces that he will 'INVESTIGATE ANYTHING!!!'

'Is there a reason for all the exclamation marks?' Dan asks, with a smirk.

'Yeah. He investigates *anythiiiiing!*'

Dan pushes open the door and the smell of expensive carpet, recently laid, envelops us. Clive's secretary, a pretty young woman spilling out of her tight top, tells us that Mr Porter will see us now.

'He's in that room there.' She points to the only room off the main office.

Clive sits behind an enormous desk, polished to a high shine. A nameplate announces who he is and his profession.

'Is that in case you forget?' Dan jokes, pointing to it.

I'm a little appalled at Dan talking to him like that.

'It's to remind me that I'm a lucky bastard not to be grubbing about in the mud any more,' Clive responds, then surprises me by coming out from behind his desk and man-hugging Dan while simultaneously walloping him on the back.

'This is Lucy Golden,' Dan introduces me. 'I work with her now.'

'Great to meet you, Lucy.' Clive shakes my hand vigorously. 'I think I've seen you before?'

'I grew up on the island,' I say. I don't add that most of the force and a lot of the country knew me at one time partly because of my notorious ex. Anyway, Clive is probably only pretending not to know me: a man like him doesn't forget a face.

'This fellow,' Clive thumbs in Dan's direction, 'was the brightest fucking light in Dublin South Central when I was there but then he transfers down west to the backwaters of nowhere. I'll never understand that.'

'You came down yourself,' Dan counters, with a grin.

'When I retired,' Clive says. Then adds, 'Plus office rents are cheaper and I get most of my clients online. You don't have to be in Dublin to do Dublin business.'

Dan shrugs agreement.

'How's life? Any girlfriend whipping your arse?'

'Nope. Now, come on, what have you got for us?'

Clive chuckles. 'You were always a secretive bastard. Right, come on so. I'll show you what I have.' He presses a few buttons on his laptop and we take a seat.

I flip open my notebook.

'Right. Lisa Moran came to me on October the fifteenth last, so about six weeks ago, asking me to trace a young boy, aged seven, that she knew as Sam. She said she had reason to believe that the boy might be in hospital or dead and that I was to check everything. She gave me a window date of the second of October to the fifteenth of October to search. If I found anything in deaths, I was to check out how these children died.'

'And?' I lean forward, unable to help the eagerness in my voice. This will save us some legwork.

'*Nada*. I mean, there were children but she rejected them all. There was something she was looking for and nothing I turned up satisfied it. She got a bit stroppy and accused me of not doing it right.'

'Bet that didn't go down well,' Dan remarks.

'The girl was desperate, I made allowances.'

'Going soft in your old age, what?'

'Probably,' Clive agrees pleasantly. 'Anyway, she refused to give me any details about why she was searching, which might have made it easier. On,' he consults his computer, 'the eighteenth of November, I told her I'd done all I could but she kept pushing me, try this hospital, try that one, see if you can access GP files. And then a curious thing happened about ten days ago.' He pauses. 'She told me to stop looking.'

What would make her do that? Was Sam back in contact? I take out the diary and flick through it again, seeing if I missed anything.

'I have to admit, I was curious,' Clive goes on. 'She seemed desperate for information and then she just shut the whole thing down.'

'Maybe she ran out of money,' Dan says.

'Nope.' Clive is pretty firm about that. 'Cash in hand, every week. She would have paid anything. I've seen her sort before. Something changed, and my guess is that she found the boy herself.'

'I'm just checking that,' I murmur, as the two men continue to talk.

'How did she seem on that phone call?'

'I got the impression she was happy. Relieved, even.'

'Did you ask her why she was calling it off?'

'Normally I wouldn't because, honestly, it's not my business. But it's rare people call searches off – they find the money somehow.'

'What did she say?'

'That she was grand now. That was the word she used.'

'Maybe she went for a better PI,' Dan says, half joking.

'You and me know there's no one better,' Clive says seriously. 'But that wasn't it. This girl was happy.'

I look up from the journal. 'After that call in October from Sam when he screamed and the line went dead, there's no mention of him in the journal.' I tap the book. 'In no place does it say she had contact with him after that date.'

'She was on her own in the Family First office,' Dan speculates. 'She might not have recorded it, especially if she was going to get involved with saving him.'

'Do you have a record of the date she called the search off?' I ask Clive.

'November the twenty-second.'

Dan takes out his phone and scrolls his calendar. 'Friday,' he says. 'She called the search off on a Friday.' He turns to me. 'Was she in Family First the night before?'

'Yes.' I scan the page. 'This is what's written, "Rose" – no age. "Her mother died two weeks ago and she is living with her father. His new children are mean to her. Her stepmother never takes Rose's side . . ."' I turn the pages, look up. 'Nothing about Sam.'

'Anything else you have?' Dan asks Clive.

'That's it.'

'Can we have a list of what Lisa paid you?' I ask.

'Sure.' Clive presses his intercom. 'Cherrie, print out the Lisa Moran invoices, will you?'

'No problem, Mr Porter. By the way, your six o'clock is here.'

'I have to get this,' Clive stands up and shows us to the door. 'You can collect the invoices from Cherrie on the way out. Good luck. Nice to meet you, Lucy. See you, Dan.'

As I fire up the car, I say, 'How did Lisa pay for Clive? There's no way her wages would stretch that far. It's a small fortune, what he charged her.'

'I was thinking about that,' Dan says, 'and I wonder, is that why she asked her da for money. To make up the shortfall. Is it a coincidence that she asked him for it six weeks ago?'

I think back. Lisa asking for money for her mother seems odd. Maybe Dan is right and it was for herself. I dial Margaret, who answers on the first ring. 'Hi, Margaret,' I say. 'How are you holding up?'

She answers in the sort of shocked, robotic way a lot of people do after they realise that this is their new reality. That what they had has been ripped from them and can never be replaced. I apologise for calling her again but she says it doesn't matter, call as often as I want. I give her a little summary of our day, then ask, 'Margaret, I have a question for you and it might seem odd but just be honest.'

'Okay.'

'Did you at any stage ask Lisa to ask your ex-husband for money?'

'No,' she says. 'Dom accused me of doing it yesterday – as if I would.' She sounds defensive. 'What is this about?'

'I'm not sure yet. Thanks, Margaret.' I hang up.

'If Margaret is telling the truth,' I say to Dan, 'which I think she is, Lisa asked for that money for herself.'

'And her father refused to give it to her, so where did she get it?'

And has it any bearing on our case?

The Captain

Lisa Moran is all over the news, her face beaming out like the Virgin Mary's into people's houses. Everyone saying how lovely she was, how kind she was, crap like that. Was she, though? As far as he was concerned, people were people. They shat all over you in the end. Best thing to do with people was use them.

Anyways, there was the gardaí putting out an appeal. Begging the public for information. But that would yield nothing. No one in this godforsaken edge-of-the-world place ever sees anything. The sighted blind, he called them in his head.

Maybe, after he took her, the car had been spotted. No way to avoid it but he'd been clever, bought himself a bit of time, so he had. And sure, then, when they did trace the car, they'd only find an address and the old man would keep his mouth shut. Of that much he was certain.

He smiles as he drives on through the drizzling rain, wipers swishing to and fro, like a boat.

The dark had come in early. Winter was here, he thought. His headlamps made tunnels of light on the road. A rabbit, which should have been sleeping at this time of year, froze in the lamps and he ran it over.

The slight bump was satisfying.

He makes it to his night class with a minute to spare, and from the top of the room, she smiles at him, all zen.

If she only knew.

'And breathe,' she says, from the top of the room. 'And breathe.'

12

At seven, just as Dan and I pull into my driveway to get a bite to eat before heading to the Ryan interview, my phone rings. It's Joe. In his usual style, he gets straight down to business. 'William told me to send you the post-mortem results,' he says. 'I can mail them to you but I thought you might want to hear them now.'

'Sure. Go. I'll put you on speaker so Dan can hear.'

'Right. Things that emerged during the PM. The victim had a small butterfly-shaped tattoo on her left shoulder with the word "begin" in script underneath. I'll send you on an image of that. At the time of death, she was wearing a Primark grey tracksuit. Size ten. Underneath she wore a black cotton top, size ten, a black bra and panties. In the bra, we found a piece of black material, most likely leather, folded up.'

'What?'

'Just reporting the facts. Now,' he goes on, 'no socks or shoes have been recovered. Her clothing and the black leather patch were handed over to William. The IP's face was badly beaten, and from the nature of the bruising, it's likely she was pummelled with some sort of padded glove. There was substantial swelling of the jaw on the left side, a broken left eye-socket, and three of her teeth, the top two incisors and the bottom left incisor, were knocked out. All the fingers on her left hand were broken. However, this isn't what killed her. We found haemorrhaging to the inside of the eyelids, which would indicate death caused by lack of oxygen. There were repeated blows to the larynx, I found a footprint on her throat. Scene of Crime have photographs of that. There was substantial damage to the larynx and hyoid bone in the neck. She died by asphyxiation. We also extracted dirt and some kind of organic matter from under her fingernails. On examination of her stomach contents, we determined that she had eaten a bowl of porridge about three hours before the assault. Blood was taken and sent to the lab. We should have results on that by next year, you know yourself. There were also traces of dust not just under her fingernails but all over the body generally.'

'You think she did it deliberately? Covered herself with evidence?'

'I'm not paid for an opinion. Her feet, which were bare, were covered with this dirt. She died sometime on Saturday afternoon,' he goes on, 'probably before lunch as her stomach contents were still partially undigested. Rigor mortis had set in and was well advanced.' He pauses. 'And there was no trace of sexual assault.'

Which means no DNA from semen. But it might bring Margaret some cold comfort.

'So, the attack wasn't sexually motivated?' Dan asks.

'For the third time, I'm just giving you the facts,' Joe snaps, as Dan gives him the two fingers.

'Anything else?' I ask.

'Not until the results come in. That should be any time from tomorrow to eternity,' Joe says. Then, half grudgingly, 'I'll press for them.'

'The bit of black fabric in her bra,' I ask tentatively, half afraid of annoying him. 'Did it seem as if it was there deliberately?'

He hates committing himself. 'It didn't get there on its own,' is all he says before he hangs up.

I disconnect him, and Dan and I sit for a few moments in silence.

'Why would she do that?' I ask.

'A clue?' Dan suggests. 'Maybe it's from where she was taken.'

That would make sense. I pick up my phone and dial Margaret again.

'Hi, Margaret,' I say, 'it's me again. I'm sorry. I have another question for you, just a small thing, probably nothing, but did Lisa like reading crime novels?'

'No, she wasn't a reader, really.'

My heart sinks. That's that then. She—

'She loves crime shows, though. She watches all those investigative ones, the true ones on Netflix. I used to hate them.' A sort of sad laugh. 'They always get their man in those.'

'Thanks, Margaret,' I say, and hang up.

'Good girl, Lisa,' Dan says softly.

It makes me feel incredibly sad.

13

My mother bustles about making Dan and me a cuppa and scrambled eggs. The normality of the kitchen, my mother, the food, helps keep me grounded and sane. I ask after Luc. He went out with some friends, she tells me, but came back an hour ago and went to his room. His friends looked respectable, she says. They had normal hair and wore jeans. She says it sort of defensively and I glance at her. She looks away.

'How was his form?' I ask.

'He's a teenager, his form is always weird.' She dismisses my concerns with a wave of her hand before placing an enormous bowl of scrambled egg in the centre of the table. 'You enjoy that now, Daniel.' My mother slides into the seat beside him. 'Any progress on the . . .' she hesitates, then lowers her voice reverently '. . . murder?'

'Just interviews so far,' Dan answers, filling his plate. 'This is great, thanks so much, Mags.'

'John, my husband, loved scrambled eggs,' she says, 'didn't he, Luce?'

'He did.'

We share a smile. My dad died when I was eight, so I barely

remember what food he liked, but whenever my mother comes out with something like that, I just agree. It makes her happy that I seem to remember him.

'Lucy says he died when she was young,' Dan says and, at her nod, he adds, 'Fair play. You bringing her up on your own and all.'

'She was a good girl,' my mother says loyally. 'But being a single mother is tough, and then, sure, it broke my heart when I saw poor Lucy having to do the same.'

No, Mam. Do not talk about Rob. 'I managed fine,' I interrupt, 'and you helped and it's all good.'

'It is,' she agrees. Then, mercifully, she does stop, pours herself some tea and there is a comfortable silence for a bit until she says, 'Milo says that Mrs Cassidy was interviewed yesterday by two guards. She was very offended that anyone would think she was a murderer.'

Dan's food splurts out of his mouth and my mother draws back hastily. I don't know what's funnier, Dan coughing and choking or what my mother said.

'No one thinks a ninety-year-old murdered anyone.' I laugh out loud. 'She was just interviewed to see if she noticed anything. She was on bog lands that day.'

'She noticed that she was being interviewed for a murder. Milo had to apologise for dragging her name into it.'

Oh, Christ. 'It's routine,' I say. 'It's what investigating a murder involves.'

'Well,' she says huffily, eyeballing me the way she would when I was a kid, 'excuse us in Achill for not being used to all that sort of thing. Poor Mrs Cassidy, she says she'll never get over the shock of it. It'll probably be me next.'

'To be murdered?' I say. 'Yes. Most probably. By me.'

'Very funny.' My mother's mouth twitches a little. Then she says, sort of off-hand, 'You will be careful though, won't ye? The two of ye?'

'I'll mind her.' Dan winks at me.

'I can mind myself, thanks. Now, partner, when you've finished horsing into every bit of food in the place, we'll go. Thanks, Mam.'

'No bother at all. Anytime.'

While Dan is finishing, I scoot down the hall to Luc's room. I never leave for work without saying goodbye to him. It's an old garda habit. You just never know what the day or night will bring. 'Bye, Luc, see you later,' I call.

He always used to open his door, poke his head out and say, 'Goodbye'. Or, failing that, he'd call. Now he ignores me.

'Love you,' I say then.

Nothing.

I should walk away. My logical brain is screaming at me to go, but I'm a guard and answers are what drives me. And if I don't find out what's wrong with him, and I know something is, I think I might go mad.

I realise too that I never rang the boys in Dublin to check on Rob's status.

'It's getting late.' My mother breaks into my thoughts as she calls to me from up the hall. 'You'd better get going.'

I turn to her and she quirks her eyebrows at me and we stay in silent combat for a few seconds. 'Dan is waiting,' she says then.

And slowly I turn away from Luc's door. As I pass her, she touches me briefly on the arm. 'He's fine,' she says. 'He's a good boy.'

It's a small gesture of support that half breaks my heart.

14

Achill Island is an incredibly beautiful place, wild and savage and blue and yellow and brown, the sound of the sea the backdrop to all our lives. When you leave, you take it with you, and when you come for the first time, you wonder how you never knew a place such as this existed.

That was the dream they sold the people in St Jude's estate. Dubliners made homeless during the recession were promised a better life if they relocated. Instead, they found themselves living in a badly built social-housing estate, miles from the nearest town. The estate comprises fifty grey houses, huddled together like survivors after a shipwreck. Ten years on, they are in varying states of disrepair, some with peeling paint, others with broken walls, gardens with scrubby grass and busted pillars.

Attempts have been made by Tidy Town volunteers to clean it up but you need more than a few shovels and plastic bags to make a place feel loved.

It's a shameful blot on our landscape and one that maddens me every time I visit it.

'How the fuck do walls break?' Dan asks, as we avoid a large block that has somehow found its way into the centre of the road.

Four or five youths stare at us as we drive past, like hungry dogs waiting for a feed.

The Ryans' house is the best of a bad lot on their street. An attempt has been made to cut the grass, though there are no flowers in the garden. The driveway is small, just enough space for one car that I notice isn't there. The door, once red but now a mix of peeling paint and rotting wood, has a bright polished knocker and bell. It's enough to make Dan laugh.

I ring, and the bell chimes inside. Nothing happens. I ring again and, after a bit, a shape appears in the wavy glass of the door and grows larger as it approaches. The door is opened a crack and the smell of garlic and chips floats out to us.

'Hello, Mrs Ryan? I'm Detective Lucy—'

'In,' Mrs Ryan orders, the door squealing as she opens it wider.

Dan and I step into a narrow hallway, painted blue. It's cold.

'I saw the two of ye in the yard today, looking at my child,' Mrs Ryan says, shutting the door after us.

'We only want a few minutes of your time,' I say, changing the subject. It would be unwise to admit to staring at anyone's child. I introduce us and say, 'We want to talk to you and Mr Ryan if you don't mind.'

Dan takes out his notebook and flips it to a clean page.

'He's not here,' Mrs Ryan says then, folding her arms across her chest. 'He had to go out.' There's a challenge in her eyes.

'He said he'd be here at eight,' Dan says.

'He was meant to but, like, he has a living to earn. If a job calls he has to take it. He can't be waiting around for the likes of yous to show up.'

'When will he be back?'

'Whenever his job is done. He drives a taxi for someone.'

Dan and I wait. She continues to stare at us.

'Right,' I say, after a bit. 'We'll talk to you first, then. Is there a place we can do this?'

'Mammy?' Kara's head appears over the banisters. 'Can I get a drink of milk?' She's talking to her mother but looking at us. 'Who are you?'

'They're just some friends of mine,' Mrs Ryan says, before we can answer. Her voice softens and she smiles up at her daughter. 'They just came to say hello.'

'What are your names?' Kara smiles now too and starts to descend the stairs. Her feet are bare, with toenails painted a shocking pink. She's in well-worn, pink fluffy pyjamas with a cartoon character on the front.

'I'm Lucy and this is Dan,' I say.

'My sister painted my toes.' Kara holds out a foot for us to admire. 'I wanted blue but she didn't have blue and then—'

'If you two go in there, I'll be right in after yez once I get this one her milk.' Mrs Ryan interrupts her daughter and indicates a room off the hall. 'Come on,' she says to Kara, placing her hands on the little girl's shoulders and pushing her along in front of her to the kitchen.

As Kara protests that she hasn't finished talking to 'those people', Dan and I head on into the front room. It's always a bonus when you get a glimpse of people's living spaces: it's a good way to tell how functional they are. Of course, if someone knows you're coming, they could clean up and shove things out of the way. Something tells me Mrs Ryan would not have made such an effort for us. She doesn't seem to care about making the right impression. In fact, it's as if she and her husband are going out of their way to make the wrong one.

The first thing we notice in this front room is the enormous TV hanging on the wall above a modest tiled fireplace.

Dan whistles, impressed. 'Imagine catching the soccer on that,' he says.

I think it looks a little ridiculous. The rest of the room is a lesson in how to do bland. It's as if these people have no investment in their house, as if they're ready to pack up and leave at a moment's notice. An off-brown worn-out sofa and two matching chairs are arranged around a brown rug. The floor is wooden but scuffed and the beige curtains hang crookedly at the window. In the alcoves on either side of the chimney, there are two brown IKEA shelves. One is crammed with books ranging from business manuals to romantic fiction. The other holds an assortment of pictures and ornaments. In the dim light it's hard to see them clearly but they seem mostly to be holiday snaps. The four of them all smiles and happy faces in shorts and T-shirts. A picture of Kara sitting on an older girl's knee, gap-toothed and tiny. There is a large one of Mr and Mrs Ryan on what must have been their wedding day. Mr Ryan does not look like someone who would give a mouthful of abuse to a guard but you never can tell. In this job, if a respectable-looking person does a criminal act, it's usually a lot worse than your average junked-up in-and-outer. Mr Ryan is a good-looking man, the sort they cast in films. He's the classic tall, dark and moderately handsome. Mrs Ryan married way out of her league: she's all mousy brown hair and pale freckled face. The white wedding dress does her no favours. But the way her groom is gazing at her, with such raw tenderness, captures me for a moment and tugs at something inside.

Once upon a time, I'd looked at Rob like that, dazzled by his wit and charm. He had blinded me so that I couldn't see anything or anyone else. He love-bombed me, made me feel special, and I had been in thrall. And it had all been a lie. When he was put away, I was alone, in a barren, friendless landscape. Only for my mother, I might have sunk into the quicksand.

'I'd say they had money once,' Dan interrupts my thoughts. He nods to a picture of Mr Ryan in a T-shirt. 'See the watch he's wearing? Nice.'

'We sold it,' Mrs Ryan says from behind, startling us a little. 'When ye're finished nosing around the room, can we get this over with? I don't need my daughter asking any more questions, so I don't.'

'Why did you sell it?' Dan remains looking at the picture as I take a seat in one of the chairs. I immediately wish I hadn't as the springs are gone and I feel like I'm being swallowed whole.

'Is this part of the interview?' Mrs Ryan takes the chair opposite me. Her voice is casual, but the rapid blinking of her eyes gives away her nervousness.

'It is now,' Dan says, with a smile.

'We sold it to buy clothes and uniforms for the girls,' she snaps. 'Now, can we just hurry up?' She directs this to me, ignoring Dan. I feel a little chuffed because normally it's me they dislike. Though, in fairness, she doesn't seem over-fond of me either.

'All right,' I say. 'Thanks for seeing us. We're here because we were told that you and your husband had a bit of a run-in with our victim Lisa Moran. Can you tell us about that?'

'Doesn't make us murderers, so it doesn't.'

'Of course not, we just need background.' I smile as she remains tight-lipped. 'Can you tell us what the run-in was about?'

'It was more than a run-in.' Her right foot taps nervously up and down.

This questioning is making her uneasy, which is kind of interesting. Slowly, so she can see, I pull out my notebook and flick a few pages, pretending I can't remember. 'I have here that you complained that Lisa Moran had been overly familiar with your child. Do you want to start there?'

'She wouldn't leave Kara alone,' Mrs Ryan says. 'Pete was on at me to leave it but I couldn't. He's gone spineless since . . .' She stops. 'That teacher was off her head. I don't know what she was on but she was a mad, interfering cow. She had no right.'

'No right to what?'

She glares at me. 'You know. You were at the school. They probably spun you their line.'

'I'm here to hear your line, Mrs Ryan. What happened with Lisa Moran?'

She eyes me warily. 'All right. I don't know how long it was going on but one day Kara fell in the yard. She barely hurt herself. That Miss Moran just swooped in and scooped her up and ran off with her. She had no right to touch her.'

'And you saw this?'

'No,' she says, like I'm stupid. 'Kara said that that was what happened and so did Natasha – that's my other girl. I believe my children, Guard.'

'Of course you do. Where did Lisa Moran run off to with your daughter?' I inject a note of alarm into my voice.

There is a small beat before she says, 'You can't do that with children, scoop them up like that and scare them. I know what's allowed. Kara isn't her child. She can't be going fussing over her.'

'Fussing how?'

'Kara said the teacher kept cuddling her while the nurse bandaged up her knee.'

'Kara was upset about it?'

'It was inappropriate. My sister even said so when I rang her.'

'And, as a result, you made a complaint?'

'Yes. We were concerned.'

'We? You and your sister?'

'Me and my husband,' she says, eyeballing me. I watch as she pulls a cigarette out of a packet and lights up. She has an elegant way of smoking, the cigarette poised, balancing delicately between her fingers. She blows a stream of smoke into the centre of the room, towards us. 'I realise it all sounds like nothing, but that girl was clever. In the meeting we had with the board, she denied everything. Twisted everything.'

'There was more?'

'It wasn't just the cuddling, she was quizzing Kara about us. About her home life. And then, at that meeting, she denied it. Said I made it up.'

'I see.'

'She made me look like a crackpot. I'm not a crackpot. I know what my daughter told me, Guard.'

'Anyone else see this?'

'Kara's word was good enough for me.' Her voice rises and she jabs her cigarette in our direction. 'My child is five – five. She is not going to invent this.'

'Of course not,' I say, though I think she might if she was getting attention for it at home. And I also wonder what possible reason Lisa Moran would have had for carrying on like that. 'How did you feel about Miss Moran at this stage?'

'I was pissed off because there's a fine line, a boundary.'

'There is, no doubt about that.'

'Was she not just trying to comfort your daughter?' Dan pipes up.

120

'By asking her personal questions?' She looks like she wants to punch him.

'Ah, now, Dan, there's comfort and there's comfort,' I say.

'This was more than just comfort.' Mrs Ryan takes a deep drag on her cigarette to calm herself down. 'You don't go hugging other people's children, these days, or poking your nose into their business.'

'Don't mind him,' I say. 'He hasn't a child to be worrying about.'

'We did our best to be reasonable,' she says, looking hard at me. 'Pete went and had a word with her and he said she apologised, but the next week she was back at it again. But that's Pete, he probably was too nice to her. So then I went in, and I'm telling you, I hauled her over the coals. She just smirked, said Kara hugged her. That was a lie. Kara isn't a huggy child. That was when I wrote to the board.'

Dan catches my eye. I know what he's thinking. This woman is halfway to crazy with this.

'And those – those bastards, they whitewashed the whole thing. We got nowhere. If Miss Moran hadn't died, we'd be bringing it further.'

'Miss Moran was murdered, Mrs Ryan,' I remind her gently.

It's like I've pulled a horse up short. Her mouth clamps shut and she stares at us. Finally, she mutters, 'Yes, and that's terrible and all, but she was not a saint. We might not even let it go.' She leans over and stabs her cigarette out on the fireplace. 'The way we were treated. It's not right for a teacher to be all over a child like that.'

'And this was when?'

'I just found out in October but who knows how long it'd

been going on? Oh, she stopped once the board got involved but I know that was only temporary. She was not fit to be there.'

'If you were so worried about Kara, why did you not remove her from the school?' I ask.

'And put her where?' The woman's voice rises again. 'The next school is five miles away. We'd have to pay for a bus for her, a new uniform, new books. We're not exactly coming down with money, you know. And if we'd taken her out and not sent her somewhere else, we'd be breaking the law and you lot would be banging on my door anyhow.'

'She has a point,' I say to Dan, and I smile at Mrs Ryan, but she doesn't smile back. 'I was wondering, Mrs Ryan, if you'd be able to clear up where you were between three and five last Friday?'

Her eyes meet mine. 'You think I killed her?'

'It's a routine question. It's how we do our job.'

Without breaking eye contact, she says, very deliberately, 'Me and Kara went to the school at three to pick up my older girl, Natasha. We walked from here, which is a long way, as Pete had the car. Then we came home and they both did their homework and I made the dinner.'

'You didn't go out anywhere?'

'Do I look like I can afford to go out?' She snorts, adds, 'I didn't go out and I didn't murder anyone. Are you finished?'

'We'll need to get a specialist interviewer in so your daughter can confirm these details,' I say.

'You don't believe me?'

'It's the way things are done, so if we need to we'll—'

'Nash!' She walks to the door and calls up the stairs. 'Come down here a minute, will you?'

'Mrs Ryan,' I begin, 'we really can't—'

122

'Nash!' she calls over me. 'Down, now!'

I glance at Dan, who shrugs. This isn't the way it's done, he's saying, but, hey, she's the one doing it. Our hands are clean.

'Nash' arrives in. Compared to Kara's neat little frame, Natasha is a broad girl, who certainly looks older than her twelve years. 'Are you all right, Mum?' she asks, panting from her run down the stairs. 'Mum' sounds such a strange word in this battered dining room that I look at her with more interest. There is none of her mother's bitterness or hardness about her. She's just a scared kid, sensitive to what's going on in the way her younger sister isn't.

'Sit.' Mrs Ryan pats the arm of her chair and Natasha snuggles in beside her, wrapping an arm about her mother's shoulders and looking at us a little warily. 'Now, Nash, the guards want to know what we all did last Friday. After school. Can you tell them?'

'Why?' Natasha sounds scared.

'Really, Mrs Ryan—'

'So, they can write it in their notebooks.' Mrs Ryan ignores me. 'Just tell them, Nash, and they'll go away.'

'I got out at three and you and Kara collected me and we walked home and it took ages because Daddy had the car. We saw Mrs Matthews and she waved and you didn't and—'

'Just tell the guard where we went and that,' her mother says quickly.

'We came back here and I did my homework and helped you cut the grass and the boys over the way threw their cans in and you threw them back and—'

'Then what?' the mother says again, interrupting her.

'We made the dinner, ate it and watched TV.'

'Did we go out anywhere?'

'We never go anywhere.'

Mrs Ryan looks at us. There now, she seems to say.

'Thank you, Natasha.' I nod to her. 'You've been very helpful.'

Rather than reassure the child, my words make her flinch. She pulls herself out of her mother's grasp and looks from me to Dan and back to her mother. 'You can't take my daddy away. He's good and—'

'They're not going to take Daddy,' Mrs Ryan says, flushing. 'Don't be silly. Why would they take Daddy?' She hops up, wraps her arms about her daughter and pulls her back in close. Over her head, she glares at us. 'They're just asking questions,' she says. 'It's because that teacher in your school . . . well . . .'

'Miss Moran? The bitch?'

Mrs Ryan flinches and has the grace to look a little embarrassed. 'That's what I call her. I'm sorry.' Back to her daughter, 'Yes, Nash, they're talking to everyone to see what happened to her. Now, come on, I'll bring you upstairs.'

After they leave, Dan raises his eyebrows in a question.

'You take it,' I say. 'I want to keep her onside for now.'

He nods.

We say no more until Mrs Ryan comes back in. 'You've gone and upset her now,' she snaps at us.

We let the silence develop for a bit, and then Dan asks quietly, 'So, can you tell us about the assault charge against your husband?'

Her gaze flits from me to Dan and back.

Dan edges forward on his seat, just a tiny fraction, his pen poised over his notebook.

'Do I have a choice?' Bitterness tinges the edge of her words, like salt on a margarita glass.

'You can refuse but I wouldn't advise it.'

'Just tell us, in your own words, about it,' I say.

'You know what happened. Your lot arrested him. Jaysus,' her lip curls, 'ye wouldn't arrest the proper people.'

'I believed he assaulted a young man?' I bring her back before she goes off on one.

'Two years ago.' Each word shoots from her mouth like a bullet. 'I hate this place. I hate the neighbours, the children on the road. Everything.' A harsh breath. 'We used to live in Dublin, in a nice area, then it all went wrong. We lost our business, money ran out and finally, after living in hotels and hostels, we were offered a chance to relocate to this place.' She tosses out a laugh. 'Pete was all for it and I thought, The country, sure that'd be nice. Turns out there are worse places than hotel bedrooms to bring up your children.'

'How so?' Dan asks.

'Don't give me that!' she says, like a slap. 'Have you seen this bloody place? It's a tip and there's nothing to do and the locals don't want us. They protested against the houses, for God's sake. It's so clannish on this island. And in this estate, most of them are all right but the ones that aren't . . . Jaysus.' A jab at the window. 'There's a family dealing drugs right outside our door, these days, young boys being recruited left, right and centre for these dealers and no one is doing anything.'

'If you give us a name, we can look into it,' Dan says respectfully.

She stares at him as if he's just crawled out of a gutter.

'Tell me about the assault charge on your husband.' I change the conversation back.

She looks like she wants to argue some more, but I guess she realises there's no point. She lights another cigarette and pulls hard on it before she says, 'Pete flipped, that's what happened. He was in Dublin about three years back and he saw this man who had owed us money and hadn't paid it, sitting in a coffee shop, like he hadn't a care in the world. Smug fucking bastard broke us, broke our company, landed us in hostels. Landed us here. Pete saw him and says the next thing he remembers is standing over him having broken his jaw.' A pause, then, with a note of defiance, 'It was just the stress of everything going wrong for us but he put that man in hospital.' Her voice catches. 'He got charged with assault. Eight months in prison. He's regretted it every day since. He's soft. But wouldn't you know it?' Mrs Ryan goes on, the bitterness in her voice inching its way across her face. 'That charge has followed him about like a bad smell. Somehow people find out. No one wants to have much to do with us. Have you any idea what it's like to be the talk of the town?'

I have, as it happens.

At that moment, a car pulls up in the driveway. She glances towards the window. The blind, a dirty white, is pulled right down, past the sill, so it's impossible to see out. Or in. A car door slams.

'It's Pete,' she says. 'Don't say I told you about the arrest. He's ashamed of it.'

'We'll have to mention it,' Dan says. 'Don't worry, we knew about it anyway.'

'He's a good man.' She leans forward, towards us. 'He works so hard and—'

The front door opens, slams shut. 'Are they still here?' Cultured, resonant voice. No accent that I can place.

'We're in the front room,' Mrs Ryan says.

In he comes. 'You all right?' he asks her, without acknowledging us.

'Yes, they just have a few questions.'

He sits on the arm of the chair, where his daughter sat, and takes his wife's hand. They certainly present an image of a united couple. Or a couple who need each other. 'Hurry up, then,' he says to us.

'Pete,' she warns, 'don't be like that.'

He visibly flinches, then recovers. His voice, when it comes, is softer: 'What do you want to know?'

Dan asks Mrs Ryan to leave, then says, 'We believe you had a run-in with our victim, Lisa Moran. Can you tell us about it?'

'Has my wife not told you?'

'Yes.'

'Well, then.' He shrugs.

'I'll rephrase,' Dan says. 'Were you concerned about the way Lisa Moran was with your daughter?'

'Yes.' He doesn't elaborate.

'And?'

'I talked to the woman and she said sorry but she wasn't.'

'How did that make you feel?'

A moment. Then, 'Annoyed.'

'I'll bet you were,' Dan says. 'Then what?'

'Nothing. I mean we wrote, had a meeting with the board and nothing. They didn't seem to take us that seriously.'

Silence. Dan moves in. 'Can you tell us when you initially came into contact with Lisa Moran?'

'Sure.' There's a studied casualness in his voice. 'She used to teach Nash, our older girl. We met her when we went to parent-teacher meetings.'

'And how did you find her at those meetings?'

'Grand.'

'No overstepping her boundaries with Nash?'

Mr Ryan shrugs. 'She might have.'

'But you've no proof?'

'Nash likes to keep the peace,' he says. 'She hates rows, all that sort of stuff. She might not have told us.'

'But she told you when it happened to Kara?'

'Kara told us. Nash backed her up.' His answers are short. Clipped.

'When Kara fell in the yard, was that the first hint you had that Lisa Moran was overstepping the mark?'

'Yes, and the second was when Kara told us that Miss Moran always asked her about her home and her lunches and that. My wife was concerned.'

'Just your wife?'

'And me, of course,' he tacks on. A moment. 'It doesn't mean we did anything to her.'

'Even though, some time ago, you assaulted a man in a café?' Dan says.

He swallows hard. 'I did my time for that.' A tinge of anger, which he manages to check. 'That man is the reason we're here. In this kip. I regret it, but in a lot of ways, he deserved it.'

We let that hang. 'And Lisa Moran?' I say. 'Did she deserve what she got?'

'What she deserved was to lose her job for unprofessional conduct.'

'I see.' Dan writes it down. 'Where were you last Friday, Mr Ryan?'

'Working.'

'Doing?'

128

'Driving a taxi. That's what I do now.' He doesn't sound particularly happy about it. 'I share driving with the owner of the taxi, and he pays me a wage.'

'So, the car outside is not the car you would have been driving on Friday?'

'From twelve until about three thirty I drove the taxi, a black Renault Mégane.' He gives the registration number without being asked. 'Then, when I was done, I drove to my boss's house and collected my own car.'

'Where were you between, say, three and five that day? Can you remember?' Dan asks.

He screws up his face. 'Just before two thirty I had a guy in the car who spoke no English. He was going to Knock airport. I remember because I got stuck in school traffic and he was annoyed. Then on the way back, I was told to swing by, pick up a woman and bring her to Mallaranny. I was finished by three fifteen. I collected my car and drove home.'

'Where did this woman live?'

'Up beside the bridge.'

'Fine.' Dan writes it down. 'And who is the man you share the taxi with?'

He gives us the name and address of his boss.

'You collected your car just after three fifteen and drove home from your boss's house? That's not a long journey, so you would have been back by five?'

'Yes.'

'Your wife never mentioned that you were here at five,' I say. 'And neither did your daughter.'

'What has my daughter got to do with this?' Pete's voice rises. 'You've no right to question her.'

'Actually, Mr Ryan, your wife insisted on it,' I say. 'And your daughter verified that she and your wife were here last Friday, but she never mentioned you coming in.'

'I was here,' he says.

'Maybe we'll just ask your wife to confirm,' I say. 'Dan, would you mind getting Mrs Ryan, please?'

A few seconds later he appears with Mrs Ryan.

Mr Ryan's foot has started to jerk up and down.

'What?' Mrs Ryan says crossly. 'Are yez not done yet?'

'What time did your husband arrive in from work last Friday, Mrs Ryan?' I ask.

Her gaze flicks to her husband and back to us. 'Last Friday? The Friday I just told yez about?'

'Yes,' I say. 'Can you look at me, please?'

'He got in at his usual time,' she says.

'Which is?'

The silence stretches like elastic at breaking point.

Finally, I think, she takes a plunge: 'Five or thereabouts.'

The room expands again. I flick a look at Dan, who raises his eyebrows a fraction. Nope, he doesn't believe her either.

'Thanks for that,' I say.

Dan gives me an almost imperceptible sideways glance, and I stand up. 'Thank you for your time. You've been helpful.'

Pete stands up too. 'When you solve this murder, maybe you might dedicate a few resources to ridding this estate of the wankers in it.'

We say nothing until the front door closes behind us.

'What a charming couple.' Dan lets out a breath.

'Maybe they were at one time.' I gesture to the car, a white nine-year-old Beemer, obviously a relic from their high-roller days. 'White. Interesting. The caretaker said a white car was parked up at the school last Friday.'

'I'll see if Larry has any CCTV of that car on Friday in Achill Sound.'

'Hey, are ye the guards?' a young teenager calls to us from across the road. He's wearing a beanie hat, oversized jeans, a large black sweatshirt with a logo and, on his feet, a pair of runners that go for about six hundred on eBay. He looks lean and hungry and mean. We'll probably be hauling him in some day in the not so distant future.

'Yes,' Dan says.

'Then take this.' He gives us the two fingers and cackles with laughter. Then with a salute he saunters off.

'I love this job,' Dan says, with relish, and I have to laugh.

15

Day Three

Dan is in early the following morning, which is surprising because I normally get in before him. He's at his desk, a little dishevelled, drinking a large mug of coffee.

'You're keen,' I say, as I take off my coat. 'Anything come in?'

'Ger Deegan left a note to say he managed to get hold of Dom and Margaret's bank accounts and that he pulled Lisa's too.'

'That was quick.' I'm impressed.

'He says, on first glance, there's nothing out of the ordinary on either Margaret's or Dom's. More interestingly, Lisa's full wages go into hers, the payments each month are the same. There are a number of large cash withdrawals, which must have been for Clive, but not enough to cover his fee. She got extra cash elsewhere to pay Clive.'

'Who'd give her that kind of money?' I tap my biro on my teeth, thinking.

'The gouger,' Dan suggests. 'To win her trust. Maybe she confided in him and he offered to help.'

That would make sense. 'It was cash so how do we trace it? I think we need to talk to the other friends today. Ask them about

Liam, see if he's being straight with us. Who have we left? Those running buddies, Paul and Sarah. Will you contact them? I've another call to make.'

Dan finds their details and starts to dial.

I ring Peter Casey, the arresting detective in Rob's case. We've kept in touch over the years. He works out of Dublin and keeps me abreast of what's happening there. He'd called me six months before Rob's release to say he was getting out.

'Hey,' I say, as he answers, 'it's Lucy. Then I add, 'Golden.'

'How are you doing?' His tone is easy, light.

'Grand.'

'And that boy of yours? Is he doing exams this year?'

'He is but you wouldn't know it,' I half laugh. 'He wants to do music so I hope it keeps fine for him.'

'They all get there in the end,' he says. 'I see you're busy with that murder case down there.'

'Yeah.'

'Poor kid,' he remarks.

'And you?' I ask.

'Young boy shot two nights ago. Looks like a feud starting.'

'Fuck's sake.'

'Turf war, we think. So, what can I do for you?'

'Do you know where Rob's gone?' I blurt out, and across the desk, I see Dan raise his eyebrows at me.

'Why?'

'I think he's contacted Luc. I have no proof but I know something's up.'

'What makes you think that?'

'I don't know. Intuition. Luc's gone very secretive.'

'He's . . . what? Eighteen now? They're all like that. They're keeping tabs on Rob in HQ, but you know yourself, you can only do so much.'

'Please?'

He promises me he'll do his best, wishes me luck with the case and hangs up.

I avoid Dan's gaze as I pick up our files and reports. 'Let's get down to the incident room,' I say.

He nods. 'Sure thing.'

I know he'll ask eventually but I'm not ready to go there. Not yet.

Everyone is on time, which is gratifying. It's good to see the commitment. I suppose, too, it's a chance for this district to prove itself against the big boys. No one ever admits that there's competition, but there always is.

Jim D'arcy starts by filling everyone in on the progress of our interviews. Then he gives the floor to me.

'As far as Dan and I are concerned,' I say, 'we have two possible lines of enquiry. One is that Pete Ryan, Kara's dad, followed Lisa that Friday and abducted her. He's a taxi driver and, by his own admission, he finished work in his taxi by a quarter past three, then took his own car home. His family said that he was there shortly after but only when asked to confirm it. The caretaker also says he saw a white car in the vicinity of the school around the time Lisa left that day. Pete Ryan has a white car. We need to see if he was at the school that day and not on his way home as stated.'

'I might have something here for you,' Larry says cockily. He coughs a bit and rubs a hand through his hair, which badly needs a wash. 'Yeah, everyone, Lucy rang me late last night, asked me to check out Pete Ryan's car's movements that Friday. I stayed late, roped in a couple of lads, and we picked up footage of him leaving his employer's place and later on, through footage obtained from shops in the area, we got him driving on the main road back to Achill. However, there was a CCTV camera at McLoughlin's Bar, which is the route his car should have taken that evening, and I know it certainly didn't pass that point by five. We do have a white car passing at five thirty but we can't be sure it's Ryan's.'

'Is there any other route he could have taken home? A byroad or something?' one of the regular lads asks.

'No,' Larry says, 'but I have him picked up on the camera from the Bank of Ireland ATM after four, which means he was at the school around the time Lisa came out, and then I picked him up on a camera at the Credit Union about ten minutes after Lisa walked up Luck Lane. I got a good look at the number-plate and it's a match.'

'Does he go up—'

'I'm not finished,' Larry says, to a bit of laughter.

The room comes alive, the air crackling with the hint of progress. Somehow, though, I'm thinking that it can't be this easy a solve. The murder was too well planned, in my opinion.

'There are eight cars that pass up the road Lisa walked between three thirty and five that evening. The first three arrived too early to have spotted Lisa. The fourth car, a Mini Cooper, called the station yesterday and said they saw a young woman walking that road around ten past four. The owner described our victim. After that, a blue Fiesta, shown here, went up.' We see footage of a car turning into the road. 'The number-plate is manky so I can't ID it, though it looks like a zero nine KE reg. The car that follows that, about ten minutes later, is white, looks like a BMW, but I'm having that confirmed later today. That goes up about four twenty-five, takes slightly longer to exit than the other cars, which would make me think the driver was travelling slowly, looking for something. Again, I don't have a clear look at that number-plate but I'll trawl more footage today because, most interestingly, the car that follows those two was identified as belonging to a Sean Reilly, whom we interviewed yesterday, and he has no recollection of seeing any young woman on that road. Neither do any drivers of the remaining cars.'

'So you're saying, based on what you have there and if your witnesses are correct, that Lisa could possibly have been taken by either the blue Fiesta or the white car.'

'Yep.'

The Cig nods. 'Okay. Go on PULSE. Find out how many blue zero nine Fiestas there are in the county. We'll widen that if we need to. Go through them all, find out who owns them and if any were in the vicinity on the day in question. Or, indeed, find out if there are any blue Fiestas on the island. Then, identify the make of the white car, see if you can get a proper ID on the number-plate along the road it travelled once it exited Luck Lane. Good work.'

Larry nods, pleased.

'If you manage to ID Ryan's car, we might be able to shake the tree and bring him in for questioning. At the very least he lied to us.'

'Will do.'

The Cig turns back to me. 'You had another possible scenario, Lucy?'

'I'll let Dan fill you all in.'

Dan tells them about Lisa's work with Family First and of how she seemed to have become obsessed with finding Sam. 'We also think there is a possibility that she may have arranged to meet this child, or take him away, and somehow got found out. She had also obtained money from someone to pay a PI Clive Porter to find the kid.'

'You think she arranged to meet him on an isolated road?' William sounds sceptical.

'Maybe. Or maybe she arranged to meet our suspect for more money to help the kid,' Dan says. 'We've some other friends to interview today but, so far, it seems the only person she confided in about this child was her friend Liam and, according to him, he told her not to get involved. She later blamed him for causing the boy's death. He could be lying. He might have helped her and it went wrong. He has an alibi for the time, though, says he was at home, which his mother confirms, though she isn't Lisa's greatest fan.'

I smile. That's accurate.

'And it's the mother,' William says. 'Always the alibi of the guilty.' He nods, thinking over what we've put before him. 'That could play. Any knowledge on who this boy is?'

'No. Even Porter, whom we interviewed yesterday, couldn't find out.'

'Let's get cracking on reading every journal from Family First. You never know, some counsellor might have forgotten that this boy rang them. He could have told them something Lisa didn't know. Also, contact the counsellor Sam rang around the same time as Lisa.' He points to two regular guards who have been roped in and asks them to get straight on it.

'Anything else on CCTV?' Williams turns back to Larry.

'Yesterday I went through the footage from around the bog

area, called in dash cam, which was precious little. There was nothing. It's not, in the main, covered, and anything we have got is unusable – it's too dark and the wrong angles. He could have parked his car anywhere on that road and brought the body across the bog. It's unlikely he would have been seen – ye know how isolated that place is.'

'I got a preliminary report on the fingertip search this morning,' Ben says. 'Any footprints we got are being analysed but we have no proof they came from our suspect. People do like to walk across the trails. Off trail, they did find one boot print, which was near to where the body was found, and we're currently comparing that with the marks on Lisa's neck.' He holds up an image for us to see. 'We're trying to trace the track mark on the boots to determine the size and make.'

'Good. Susan and Mick, anything on the door-to-door?'

Mick stands up. He and Susan are always put together as a team. Susan is the prim girl-next-door, wears her long thin hair in two plaits, has a smattering of freckles across her face and big glasses. She doesn't look like a guard, which I think sometimes works to her advantage. Old people love her. Mick, on the other hand, is tall and skinny, from Kerry. He has a long, pale, pleasantly humorous face, which goes bright red whenever he has to speak to a room. He coughs nervously. 'I have to say, we called to all the houses up the road from where she vanished and there was nothing new at all. Of the ten houses there, we got answers at eight. We'll call back on the other two today. According to the regular lads on door-to-door in nearby areas, there was nothing of significance to report either. Eh . . . one hundred and five properties canvassed and answers at seventy. No one saw anyone they didn't recognise. And—'

'No one saw anyone they didn't recognise?' Williams says. 'Sorry?'

Mick swallows, not understanding. 'That's what I said, yes.'

'Did you ask them who the fuck they actually saw?'

He darts a glance at Susan.

'It's in the questionnaire,' she pipes up. 'Question six, who did you see?'

Williams nods. 'Bloody better be. Never ask people what they didn't see, for Christ's sake. Anything else, Mick?'

Mick looks like he might combust with embarrassment. 'We also called on the people who came forward to say they were on the bogs that day. All of the people mentioned in Milo McGrath's statement have been identified, except for the chap with the slogan on his T-shirts. He hasn't come forward yet.' He pauses, reddens harder. 'One of the women, very elderly, I have to say, got very upset with us so if she complains, you know, we never meant it.'

'She did complain,' someone pipes up. 'Said in all her years she'd never murdered anyone.'

Mick rolls his eyes. 'Anyway, after a lot of legwork, we didn't find anything. People either saw her or didn't, and there was no in-between. We'll go out and do the other side of the island today and call to any houses we missed.'

'Grand. Phones?'

Kev Deasy stands up and makes a bit of a face. 'A few callers claiming they owned the cars that went up that way. They've mostly been interviewed, as you heard. Witnesses to say they saw her on the street. Clive Porter, who gave me an earful because he couldn't get through to the super. Still, he was useful. But the stand-out call was when someone claimed she was abducted by aliens, experimented on and her body dumped when they were done with her.'

There is laughter, which the Cig soon shuts down. 'This is a murder investigation,' he says, in the voice that sends chills up spines hardier than mine. 'Be good to remember it.'

'Sorry, Cig, we got very little, though.'

'Keep at it. Something might filter through.'

Kev nods miserably. ready to submit himself to another day of lunacy on the lines.

'All right,' the Cig says. 'Jim has the job sheets.'

Jim divvies out more job sheets, more interviews. 'Lucy and Dan,' he says at the end, 'be ready to bring Pete Ryan in if we get a proper ID on his car. I also want someone on background, so we have it all when he comes in. Ger, that's you, if you're finished with the bank accounts. Pat, while you're waiting for the phone records to come in, get checking the alibis of everyone so far, will you?'

After that he dismisses us.

16

Sarah's Place is the name of a cute little coffee shop tucked away in a side-street of Achill Sound. Inside it's all industrial lights and pipes, wooden floors and grey walls. Pictures of cool-looking people shot in bright primary colours hang along one side of the room. The smell of coffee drifts on the air.

Sarah, squat, square-jawed with short red spiky hair, greets us as we enter. Her clothes are odd: a pair of patterned loose trousers that look like curtains and a tent-style top with wide sleeves. She appears to be drowning in fabric. 'I'm taking my break now, Ruby,' she says to the young girl behind the counter, who is chopping some ugly vegetable. Her voice has the lilt of the island. To us, she says, 'Ruby's after making up some sandwiches. Would ye like one, would you?' She pronounces it 'sangwich'.

It's akin to offering manna to the Israelites after their trek through the desert. Dan and I hop on the offer like we've never had a sandwich before.

Sarah tells us to sit anywhere. We take a window seat and, after a few minutes, she joins us bearing a tray of coffee. 'Ruby will be down with the food in a minute, so she will,' she announces loudly, more to Ruby, I think, than us.

'This your place?' Dan asks.

'It is called Sarah's Place,' Sarah says, sliding into a seat.

Ouch, I think. Dan is unperturbed. 'Nice,' he says.

'It is.' Sarah agrees. 'Ruby,' she calls, 'where are them sand-wiches?' Her tone, outwardly pleasant but inwardly seething. She lowers her voice. 'She's a TY student, about as useful to me as music.'

We all turn as Ruby walks carefully down the café, like a giraffe in high shoes, a plate in each hand and one balanced between her outstretched arms. We watch her approach with trepidation. Dan and I don't dare move as she places the plates on the table and lets the third slide from her arms. 'There now,' she says, with satisfac-tion, as it lands. 'Enjoy.' She dances back up the room.

'I can't wait until she goes, so I can't,' Sarah whispers. Raising her voice, she calls, 'Clean out the coffee machine while we're quiet, will you?'

'I just have to finish cutting up that gross-looking vegetable,' Ruby calls back.

'Celeriac,' Sarah shouts. To us, 'Who doesn't know what a celeriac is?'

Neither Dan nor I answer that one.

'She says she wants to work as a chef but she hasn't a clue.' Sarah takes a bite out of her sandwich and chews with abandon. 'What is it ye want to know?' Chew. Chew. Chew. 'Like, I can't help ye at all really. All I can say is that we were to meet Lisa for a run last Friday and she didn't show. It was Paul made us call her mother. You should talk to him.'

'We'll do that this afternoon,' Dan says. 'Can you tell us the last time you saw Lisa?'

'We didn't hang around together or anything like that. She's not my sort of person. She's like,' she flaps her hands, bits of coleslaw falling from her sandwich, 'while I'm like . . .' Sandwich down, she assumes a zen pose. 'The only things we had in common were running and the fact that we were both free on Friday at seven. Not the basis for a great friendship. I mean,' she rolls her eyes, 'she was non-stop talk, usually about herself. I preferred to run with Liam, if I'm honest. She hung back with Paul because he was slower.' She makes quote signs on 'slower'.

'You don't think he was?'

'I think she just wanted to annoy Liam by running with Paul, and Paul liked her so he played along.' She pokes her sandwich. 'She's put cheese in and I asked her not to. I'm lactose intolerant. I think she's trying to kill me, I do really.'

We watch her pull all the bits of cheese out of her sandwich, before she says, 'I know Lisa's dead and all and no one deserves that, but she was weird. All Goody Two Shoes with people and then she'd turn mean.' She takes a tentative bite and chews, decides it's okay and takes a bigger bite. 'What was I saying? Oh, yeah, you should talk to Liam. Now, there is one pathetic bastard. The amount of times I told him to tell her to fuck off but he wouldn't, so he wouldn't. Like, she totally used him. Totally. And she knew he didn't like her always running with Paul but, like, she made out Liam was being inconsiderate for wanting to run fast and leave Paul behind. Liam isn't inconsiderate, he just didn't like Paul that much. She was the inconsiderate one.' Then she flushes, realising, I think, that she's said too much. 'Sorry, I know she's dead and that but . . .' Her voice trails off and she looks away from us.

Dan catches my eye.

'No need to be sorry, we need honesty, and if you didn't like her, you didn't like her,' I say.

'I never said I didn't like her,' Sarah backtracks. 'She was, she just . . . Anyhow,' she pulls back, 'there's nothing I can tell you . . . I have no idea how she ended up on that bog. None. Sorry.' As if to close off the conversation, she takes another bite from her sandwich.

'Tell us the exact sequence of events that Friday,' Dan says. 'Who arrived first?'

'Me. As usual.' She speaks through a mouthful. 'Then Paul arrived and he was hyper – I mean, he's hyper anyway but he was afraid he'd be late. He got held up with the old woman who lives near him or something – I don't know exactly. He was going on a bit about it. Then he takes out a sandwich he's bought and asks me if I want some. Like, who eats before a run?' She waits for us to answer, and when we don't, she says, 'No wonder he's so bloody slow. Then Liam trots up all fired up because he got a promotion or something. I wasn't paying attention to them, really. We waited about twenty minutes for Lisa – we always had to wait for her because she didn't drive. But you'd think she'd start out earlier rather than hold us up. Sometimes Paul or Liam would give her a lift but she hadn't answered their calls so they'd left it. Anyhow, we waited and then Paul and Liam said it was odd, so Paul tried her phone again and nothing. Then Liam rang her mother and her mother just freaked out, so she did, so Liam went over there and Paul tried Lisa again, and when he got no answer, I just went on the run. Honestly, I thought it was a big drama over nothing.' She stops. 'But, sure, I was wrong.' There is a tinge of something in her voice that I can't read. Regret, maybe. 'And that's it,' she finishes.

'You said Liam didn't like Paul?'

'That's just my opinion. I mean, Liam never said, he wouldn't, he's too nice, but like, Lisa used to be Liam's friend and now she was ignoring him for Paul. So why would Liam like him?'

'Any idea why Lisa was ignoring Liam?'

'Because, and I'm sorry now to talk bad of her, but she got off on it. She liked making him suffer.'

A beat, but she doesn't say any more.

'All right.' Dan hands her our card. 'If you think of anything else, let us know.'

'I will.'

'Can we get these to go?' He indicates the sandwiches. Sarah carries our plates back to the counter and we hear her loudly ordering Ruby to pack them up.

'There's a view of Lisa we haven't had before,' I observe.

'Except from Liam's mother.'

'Sarah really doesn't like her.'

'Maybe she fancies Paul and Lisa was in the way,' Dan says.

'Or maybe it was Liam she liked.'

'Or maybe Lisa was a bit of a bitch.'

We stop talking abruptly as Sarah makes her way to us with the wrapped sandwiches. 'There you go,' she says.

'Where were you between three and five last Friday?' Dan asks.

'Where I always am.' Sarah waves a hand about. 'Here.'

'And was anyone else here?'

'Just customers. I was on my own, the rush had eased.'

That'll be easy to check.

Dan nods, 'That's all for now and,' he holds up the sandwich, 'thanks.'

'Fine. Enjoy. Ruby,' she calls, as she stomps back up the shop, 'that coffee machine isn't going to clean itself, so it's not.'

Paul is working near my home place on the site of an old monastery. It's about a half-hour drive from Achill Sound, some of it along steep cliff roads. I'm amused to see Dan avert his eyes from the stunning scenery.

'Not a man for heights,' he says.

'But we drove some of it last night when we went to my place.'

'It was dark then so I didn't notice,' he says.

I chortle and he glowers at me. I know every bend and twist of this road. In my probably biased opinion, it's one of the most beautiful places in the world. I love the way it changes from day to day, moment to moment. The light over the cliffs, the way the sun catches on the waves far below, the sweep of the bay, the ever-shifting clouds. Today, though, the sky is a uniform grey and the landscape is blurred by the fine drizzle of misty rain. Still, the smell of the spray is heady as we step out of the car in front of the monastery, which is undergoing refurbishment and will in time be a visitor and heritage centre.

It stands with its back to us, and as we walk around, a gaping door, not yet replaced, faces the sea. The air is fresh and wild, and the sound of the Atlantic is thunderous.

While it's desolate outside, inside the building it's a hive of activity, with high-vis, hard-hatted builders everywhere.

We ask for Paul at the entrance and are given hard hats and are pointed to the rear of the building. 'He's back there doing a bit of repointing,' the builder says. 'Don't keep him too long or I'll dock his pay.'

His laugh follows us as Dan and I pick our way carefully through cables, blocks and large beams of wood. The noise of hammering, sawing and pounding tears at the air. The outline of what will be a stunning place is already evident. In the back, a team of brickies is working together, laughing over something, and Dan and I stand and watch for a moment, noting the interaction between the men.

'Paul McCarthy?' Dan calls.

Two or three look up, but a guy we hadn't noticed, hidden from view by the shadow of a lamp, stands up, pushing his hat back on his head and hitching up his work trousers. 'That's me,' he says, in an accent I can't place. It's a blend of the island and the rest of the country. 'Are yous the guards?'

'That's right. Is there somewhere we can talk?' Dan asks.

'Boss,' Paul says, 'can I use your office? They're here to talk to me about . . . you know . . . Lisa.' He thumbs in our direction.

The laughter dies and his boss, the man who'd been telling the joke, nods. 'No problem at all. Take your time.'

'Through here.' Paul leads the way, skilfully navigating cables and blocks in heavy work boots.

We enter a makeshift office with a table and two chairs. Paperwork piled high is spilling out of wire baskets. Safety notices hang crookedly on the wall. Paul indicates the chairs and sits on the edge of the desk, arms folded.

He's small, almost like a kid, but lean, his face pocked by old acne scars. Dark hair falls across his forehead, almost covering one eye, which is a pity because all that scarring makes his eyes look quite beautiful, large and a deep dark brown.

'This place is looking good,' Dan remarks, staring about.

'It's coming on slowly,' Paul agrees, with a quick shy smile. 'Backbreaking, though, so it is, repointing all those bricks.'

'Be worth it in the end,' Dan says.

'As you know, we're here about Lisa,' I say. 'We hope you don't mind answering our questions.'

'Be glad to, though I didn't know her long, maybe six months or so. I joined her running club. She was lovely, so she was.'

'When was the last time you ran with her?'

'The Friday before last. There was me and Liam and Sarah. The usual. I sort of fell in with the three of them when I joined. They were nice people, welcoming.'

'How did Lisa seem that Friday?'

'No different. Like I've gone over it and over it and she was all right.' He sounds bewildered.

'You said you talked when you ran? What about?'

'About Lisa.' He flashes us a grin. 'Once she got going, you couldn't stop her. I was usually too knackered to reply, mind you.' A wider smile.

'Anything you specifically talked about?'

'Just . . . our jobs, how our training was going. What races we were entering.'

'She ever mention any trouble she was in? Any problems she had?'

A flicker of something I can't catch. 'No.'

'She ever say she was having trouble in work?'

He takes a moment, then says, 'She could have, yes, just briefly.'

'Can you remember what she said?' Dan asks. 'When she said it?'

A long moment. Paul takes his time, clearly trying to remember. 'Not exactly. It was . . . She just said there was a bit of hassle but she was sorting it. That's all.'

'How did she seem when she talked about it?' Dan asks.

Paul winces. 'I don't know. It was so brief. Scared, maybe? I don't know.'

'Why did you think she was scared?'

'I just . . .' a shrug '. . . I don't know. Maybe she wasn't.'

'If you thought she was scared, would you not have asked her more about it?'

'She just mentioned it and moved on. Like I said, she just talked.' He runs a hand through his hair. 'I don't know.'

Dan's not convinced, but he'll let it go for now.

'Let's go back to last Friday,' he says instead. 'Tell us what happened as best you remember.'

'Sure.' Paul sits up straighter, more confident now. 'Right, well, I got to the meeting point at the tourist office. Sarah was there first. She's always first and she always moans at us for not being on time.' A hint of annoyance, which he curbs. 'Anyway, I got there and made some small-talk. It's hard with Sarah, though she was nice in the beginning. Then Liam came and I was glad about that. And when Lisa didn't turn up Sarah got into a right one, moaning and saying she was going out anyway and she wasn't hanging around and that she had to go back to work and she was on a timetable, the usual.' He rolls his eyes, throws us a grin. 'I never want to get so fast that I have to run with her.'

Dan smiles back. 'She sounds hard work,' he agrees. 'Then what happened?'

'I rang Lisa. Liam was going to but then he said for me to do it.'

'Any reason why he wouldn't? I thought they were best friends.'

'I think maybe there was some tension between her and Liam, like they had a row over something, I don't know the details but he seemed wary of her so he didn't want to ring. Then when there was no answer, Liam rang the landline in her house and her mother answered. Next thing, I hear Liam tell her to calm down and that he'd go over to her, and he did, and then Sarah said she was going running anyway and I just went home because I didn't want to run with Sarah.'

'Tell us more about Liam. You say he was wary of Lisa. What makes you say that?'

Paul sighs. 'Liam was into Lisa, it was so obvious. But she, I don't know, wasn't into him or she was cross with him. I just felt caught in the middle, to be honest, like in the last while she'd just ignore him or interrupt him when he said something. And she talked a lot to me in front of him. It made me uncomfortable but, sure, what could I do? And he just stood and took it. Like, he had no respect for himself at all.'

'Did you ever ask Lisa or Liam about it?'

'Nah. I didn't want to get involved. I just wanted a running partner. And most of the time, it was fun.'

'So when Lisa didn't show, was anyone worried?'

'Not until Liam rang her mother and her mother said she hadn't been home from school. That was odd all right.'

'But you went home?'

He takes a second. 'Yeah.'

'But if you thought it was odd . . .?' Dan lets the question hang there.

'I'm not sure I get you?' Paul's voice hitches up a notch. 'What could I have done? She wasn't missing then. Like you'd just imagine she was delayed or something.'

'I suppose,' Dan agrees. 'Where were you between three and five last Friday?'

'Here until almost four – we knock off early on Friday. One of the lads drove me home. I was back in my house by four.'

'What's your co-worker's name?'

He supplies it.

'And after you got home?'

'I visited my neighbour soon after I got back. That was around a quarter past. My neighbour, she's, eh, going a bit . . . senile and forgetful, I suppose, and she likes me to call in and turn her heat

150

on for her and that. Then I left to get ready for running.'

'What time was that?' Dan asks.

'Six thirty-ish.'

'What kind of a car do you drive?'

'A brown Focus.'

Not our car, then.

'And you live?'

He gives us his address on the outskirts of Doogort, in one of the reclaimed cottages on the bog road. And the name and address of his neighbour. Another alibi for Pat O'Neill to check out.

Dan nods. 'Thanks for your time.'

I wait until he's showing us out before I say, 'Do you know what I find funny?'

'What?' Dan asks, playing along.

'The fact that Lisa told Paul about her trouble in work and she never mentioned it to her parents. Or anyone else.'

'Yeah.' Dan feigns surprise. 'She did tell you about the work stuff, didn't she?'

Paul flushes. 'Only in passing,' he says. 'It wasn't a big confessional.'

'She must have liked you, Paul.' I tap him with my notebook on the chest, then ask, 'Seeing as she talked to you, did she talk about her work with Family First?'

He's wrong-footed now. He'd thought we were going. Though he seems harmless enough, with the innocent eyes and the soft voice.

'That was the counselling line she did?' he says.

'That's right.'

'All she said was that she did a Thursday all-night shift sometimes.'

'Would she mention any calls she had?'

'Is all that stuff not private?'

'Supposedly.' I smile, like I'm asking, 'Is anything ever private?' 'But you know, if a call really got to her, she might just tell a friend.'

'I don't know.' He seems baffled. 'I would think if it was confidential . . .' His voice trails off and he looks as if he's considering it. 'Anyway, we just talked about our jobs.'

'Because she told Liam about a call, yet she never told him about the trouble in school.'

'Maybe because she was cross with Liam. I already said.'

'Did you ever meet her outside running?'

'Nope.'

'You didn't fancy her or wish for something more?'

'No.' He sounds appalled at the very idea.

'You wouldn't know where she lived or anything like that? You weren't that close?'

A pause. 'I knew where she lived – I gave her lifts to running. She didn't drive. I called into her a while back.'

'For?'

'A book she was lending me.'

'What was the book called?'

'I don't remember. It was about running. Had a picture of a runner on the front.'

'Did you give it back to her?'

'No. I still have it.'

'You work on many projects like this?' Dan asks, throwing Paul off balance yet again.

'Now and then. Usually I'm just a brickie.'

'It's great what you're doing here,' Dan says, 'making a brand-new place out of something old.'

'I prefer new builds,' Paul confesses. 'Doing it from scratch, making a whole great something from a whole lot of nothing. A place like this has a list of regulations and a pile of history and the historic architect is a pain in the arse.'

We commiserate with him over that, thank him and say our goodbyes.

We're out before Dan asks, 'Do you think he changed his tone when he was talking about his work to when he was talking about Lisa?'

'He was definitely more relaxed, but he would be, I suppose.'

'Yeah, but it's worth noting, hey?'

When we get back to the station, there's a Post-it on my desk to ring Peter Casey. I have to sit down before I can dial, my legs have gone from under me.

'Peter, it's Lucy. What have you got for me?'

In the background, someone is shouting, 'Fuck off,' and I hear smashing sounds.

'Not a lot, Luce,' he half shouts down the line. 'Two months ago, the boys in Castlebar were alerted that he was living down there. He seems to be behaving and keeping a low profile. There's a Facebook account in his name and the pictures certainly look like his. I can't authorise any intrusion onto his page, though, you know yourself. Put that down!' His last words are to someone else. 'Sorry, I'd better go. It's getting a little rough here.'

'Thanks.' I can barely get the word out. Castlebar? For fuck's sake. That's only a fifty-minute trip up the road. I know for certain now. Maybe I knew all along. Maybe I've been living in Fantasy Land.

'Holy shit,' I hear Dan exclaim, and his voice seems to be

coming from far away. Then he says it again and there's a certain amount of excitement in it. I look up and see Larry showing Dan some photographs, which can only be stills from CCTV.

'It's a positive ID on Pete Ryan's car coming out of Luck Lane around the time Lisa vanished,' Dan says to me.

'Holy shit.' Now it's my turn. 'Let's see.'

Larry, beaming, holds out the image and there is the car Pete and I saw outside the Ryans' house. The registration is clear as day.

'So, we have conclusive proof that he lied to us,' Dan says.

'We also know that a car passing by twenty minutes before that spotted Lisa,' Larry says. 'We're still running the trace on the car before Ryan's, the blue zero nine Fiesta, but that trace on PULSE will take a day or two.'

'Let's go to the Cig with this.' I stand up. 'I'd say it's enough to bring him in.'

The three of us head towards William's office. From inside, we can hear him roaring down the phone at someone. It's not like him to do that. We stand there like three schoolkids, until I eventually knock on the door and push it open. William beckons us in, puts his finger to his lips and motions us to sit down. Into the phone, he says, 'When I know, you'll know. I'm not going to make up information to keep the vultures happy. Right? Grand.' He slams his phone onto the table and looks at us. 'Pretend you didn't hear that. What's happening?'

'Larry IDed Ryan's car as the one coming out of Luck Lane.' I push the image across the table to him. 'It's the same time as Lisa disappeared. It's also the white car that took a little longer than others to exit.'

'The person in the driver's seat sure looks like Ryan to me,' Dan says.

'There's only one person in the car, though.' William looks at us. 'Where's Lisa?'

'Maybe he hit her, dragged her in – come on, it's the same car. He lied about his whereabouts. That should be good enough.'

'Have you IDed the blue Fiesta that went in before this car yet?'

'It'll take another day or two,' Larry says.

'If we can get the blue Fiesta to say he saw Lisa, maybe we'd have a stronger case against the driver of the white car,' William says.

'It's Pete Ryan's car,' I lean across the desk, push the image further towards the Cig, 'and he lied to us. That has to mean something. His wife lied for him. Come on, Cig.'

William has a reputation for caution and that can be a good thing in a detective. Cover all your bases, leave no room to be surprised. I'm all impulse: I'm up on my feet, hopping from foot to foot, as he ponders the angles. 'All right,' he finally says, sitting back in his chair. 'I'd prefer if we had the blue car IDed, but get a warrant, arrest him and the wife.'

'Let me and Luce question him,' Dan says. 'We've already met him so he knows us.'

William looks at us. 'Are yez not a bit rusty?'

'No!' That's me. 'I know not a lot happens here but we're both level three and Westport is busy enough.' It's not and we all know it. 'What I mean is—'

'All right,' he interrupts, holding up a hand. 'I'll supervise. You and Dan question him and I'll get two boys sent to Westport to question her. I'll ring the station in Westport, let them know she's coming. Organise a search warrant for the house and the car while they're being detained.' A pause. 'Get yourselves prepared. Get the background from Ger.'

I nod.

Dan looks at me.

For all my brave words, I hope we don't fuck it up.

17

A few hours later, the warrants have been secured and we've prepped for the interview. It's time to pick up Ryan. When Stacy, the reporter from *Island News*, spots Dan and me as we cross into the public area of the station she hops up from a chair, where it looks like she's been freezing her arse off. She's slightly over-dressed in a sparkly top and leather trousers.

'Any progress on the investigation?' She hurries alongside us as best she can. She's shivering.

'Were you out last night?' Dan asks in amusement, taking in her clothes.

'Twenty-first,' she says. 'I came straight here. Well?'

'Go home and get some sleep.' Dan laughs. 'Then when you wake up, contact the garda press office.'

'I already have and—'

'Dan, can I have a word?'

The sonorous voice stops Dan in his tracks and I bang into him from behind. Stacy stops talking to gawp at the man at the counter who'd been talking to Matt.

It's Fran. Fran with his rumpled clothes and tousled hair, like he's just climbed out of bed. His nonchalant easy way of moving, his half-crooked smile and speculative blue eyes. Where Dan is all sharp suits and polished shoes, Fran has a haphazard thrown-together air. I love the guy.

I grin at him and then, with a lurch, remember where we are.

No one in the force, bar me, knows that Dan is gay. I found out one night after he'd been beaten up by two men we'd tried to arrest. Initially Dan had resisted all attempts from me urging him to contact his next of kin, but when the doctor told him he'd have to spend one night at least in hospital, he'd asked me to get him his mobile and he'd called Fran. Afterwards, he'd turned to me and said flatly, 'He's coming in.' Then, 'Yes, I'm gay.'

I hadn't said anything then, not a word. Maybe I should have. But I didn't know what he wanted of me.

Since then, I've watched him being evasive or rude whenever anyone asks him about his private life. And maybe he's right, because in a way, I understand. It's a tough job, being a detective. For a woman it's harder than for a man. You just have to put up with the misogynist comments because – and I quote: 'How on earth would you deal with real savagery from real savages if you can't take a bit of a joke?' It's worse for gay men because it's such a macho environment. Though things are improving.

Dan and Fran, though, are made for each other. They're like the best comedy double act. They're so totally opposite, yet get each other. But, right now, Dan looks cornered. 'What do you want?' he asks curtly, as if talking to a stranger, and I wince. 'We're just off to pick up someone.'

'You are?' Stacy says. 'A suspect? The murderer?'

'I want to talk to you,' Fran says, in his lazy way. Laidback. Casual. 'You haven't been around the last few nights. I can't get you on the phone.'

Beside me, Dan sucks in his breath. Fran eyeballs Dan, almost like a challenge.

'Who are you picking up?' Stacy asks.

'Can you give me a moment?' Dan turns to me. 'I'll find out what this fellow wants.' He says the last bit for the benefit of Matt at the desk.

Fran's mouth lifts in what can only be described as a sardonic smile as Dan crosses to him. 'You can talk while we walk to the car,' he says.

'Gee, thanks,' Fran says.

'Are you a witness?' Stacy, oblivious to the undercurrents, plants herself between the two men but directs the question to Fran. 'Have you important information for the detective?'

'I do, yeah,' Fran says.

'Can you get lost?' Dan snaps at her. Then to Fran, 'You. Come.'

'Are you a police informer?' Stacy asks.

'For Jaysus' sake—'

'What the hell are you two still doing here?' William's arrival cuts Dan off. 'I thought yez were on your way.'

'On the way where?' Stacy asks.

The Cig takes in Fran's crumpled appearance. 'Matt at the desk will deal with you. Have you been robbed?'

'I want to talk to Dan,' Fran answers.

'Unless it's police business and to do with this case we're working then it'll have to go through Matt,' William says.

Neither Dan nor Fran says anything. They just stare at each other.

'Who the hell are you anyway?' the Cig says, sensing the mood but unable to fathom it.

And the answer when it comes is quiet. But deadly.

'No one important,' Fran says, and there is a pause. I don't know if he's waiting for Dan to refute those words or not, but Dan stays silent. I can't see the expression on his face.

'We won't be too long.' I fill the awkward silence.

'Doesn't matter.' Fran throws a smile in my direction and my heart goes out to him. What a shitty way to be treated. 'I'll be going.' He pushes past Dan and leaves, the door slamming behind him.

I want to shake Dan, tell him to do something . . .

'That was weird,' Stacy says. 'I thought—'

'Out of my station,' the Cig snaps at Stacy.

'It's a public place. I'm entitled to be here. The public have a right—'

'Out!'

'Come on,' Dan says to me. 'Let's get going.'

We leave to the sound of the Cig ordering Matt to evict Stacy.

'Sorry about that,' Dan says, as I join him at the car pool. 'I know I handled it all badly but—'

'Badly? That was appalling.'

'It's a fucking murder case! I don't have time for domestic shit during a fucking murder case.' He takes the keys for our regular car and hands me another set for the second. I'm about to ask again when he holds up a hand and glances sideways as the two guards accompanying us arrive. 'Leave it, Lucy, right now. I can't do murder and Fran at the same time. Like, if I think about it, I'm just not focused.' He unlocks his car and slides into the driver's seat. 'I'll lead, you follow.'

It's probably best if I say no more so I trail him as he pulls the car out of the station and takes the turn towards St Jude's. It's drizzly, grey and oppressive, one of those days when you think it might never be bright again.

Pete Ryan's car is in the driveway, which is good news because it means he's in. We haven't called ahead in case he rings his wife to get a story straight.

Dan and I give the front doorbell a good long press and it jangles inside.

Pete answers, a tea-towel in hand. When he sees it's us, he starts back a bit. 'What do yous want?' His voice hitches up at the end, a tiny note of fear.

'Hi, Mr Ryan,' Dan says easily. 'We're here to arrest you on suspicion of the murder of Lisa Moran. You are not obliged to say anything unless you wish to do so, but anything that you do say will be taken down in writing and may be given in evidence. Do you understand?'

'This is nonsense,' he says, already backing away.

'Do you understand?' Dan asks again.

'Yeah.'

Dan notes the reply in his notebook. 'We'll also be searching the premises,' he says as two gardaí enter the hallway.

They'll be looking for a weapon, a Lenovo laptop, Lisa's Michael Kors bag, any of her clothes. Anything basically that can tie the Ryans to Lisa.

'What the hell is going on?' Mrs Ryan shrieks, coming to join her husband at the door. She's wearing silk pyjamas, a cigarette dangling from her lip.

'We're arresting you, Mrs Ryan, on suspicion of accessory to the murder of Lisa Moran. You are not obliged to say anything unless you wish to do so, but anything that you do say will be taken down in writing and may be given in evidence. Do you understand?' I ask.

'We did nothing!' Mrs Ryan gawps at us. 'Did we, Pete?'

He has paled. A small shake of the head.

'Do you understand?' I have to ask again.

'Of course I fucking do!' she says, though she sounds like she could cry. I jot her response down. Then, 'I have to pick up the girls from school. I can't be going to the station.'

'That's no problem,' I say. 'We'll give you ten minutes to arrange to have them picked up by someone else.'

'There is no one else,' she says. Then, jabbing her cigarette in our direction, 'You just have it in for him because of before. That's all. And—'

'You lied for your husband, Mrs Ryan,' I say. 'Now, let's not do this on the doorstep.'

Her mouth falls open. 'Only because he's innocent. Only because—'

'I'll go,' Pete says, stopping her mid-flow. 'She knows nothing. I'll come with yous.'

'I'm afraid we need you both.' I'm firm. 'If you won't come voluntarily, I'll have to—'

'All right, give me ten minutes,' Mrs Ryan says. 'Let me just . . . call someone.'

A while later I deposit Mrs Ryan at Westport garda station, which takes ages as I've to talk to the member in charge and explain why Mrs Ryan should be lawfully apprehended for six hours. She is searched and her phone is taken, which causes her to have a fresh meltdown. The woman is living on her nerves.

Then I head on back to Achill, where the same procedure has been undertaken for the detention of Mr Ryan.

Larry calls just as I'm pulling into the car park. There's a note of urgency in his voice. 'It's his car all right,' he says. 'I've just picked it up again about fifty metres from Luck Lane, after he exited the junction back onto the main road. The registration this time is even clearer.'

'That's great. Has Dan organised the custody record for Pete Ryan?'

'He's all trussed up and waiting,' Larry says.

Just before I go in, I text Luc. *Hey, are you around this evening? I want to talk to you.*

Then I switch my phone off.

I always like to imagine that the perfect garda interview is like the perfect dance. When it goes well, it's dip and bow, twist and turn. I'll be taking notes this time because Pete seems like the sort of man who responds better to other men than to a woman. Dan will befriend, reel in, clarify and pounce. It's a ballet of precise articulate beauty.

There are only two interview rooms in the station. Interview One is where we bring those we think are guilty, because its stark bare walls, uncomfortable seats, lack of windows and one-way mirror make the witness long for home. As a rookie, I used to worry that an uncomfortable interview room might make a witness say something that wasn't true just to escape the claustrophobia, but I soon learned that is not the case. Innocence is too important to the innocent.

'Sorry this place is so grim,' Dan apologises, as we bring Pete in. 'Cutbacks, you know.'

'Can we just get on with it?' Pete snaps. 'I don't know what you think I lied about.'

He doesn't seem intimidated. Not yet.

'We'll be as quick as we can,' Dan says. 'Do you need a solicitor?'

'No.'

Just as Pete settles into a chair, Larry arrives in with a file. He flicks a glance at Pete and leaves the file in front of me. The file contains the pictures Larry took from the CCTV but we'll bide our time before we use them. Pete Ryan glances uneasily at it, but he doesn't ask what it is, which is interesting.

The thing to do now is to spin the web. Dan, who will be doing the questioning, gives him the caution again while I flex my hand in preparation for all the writing I'll be doing. It can be hell on the fingers.

Dan informs Pete that the interview is being recorded on DVD, and then I listen as he makes small-talk to which Pete merely grunts. Dan then switches to asking him about his shift today and Pete tells him in terse, blocked sentences how busy he is, how much he needs to get out of here. At least he's talking, I think. At least what he's telling us now is the truth.

'Grand.' Dan smiles once more and settles back in his chair. 'We'll do our best for you. So, can you take us through your day on Friday again?' He asks it like Pete is doing us a massive favour. 'Just take it piece by piece.'

'There isn't much to it. I got up at seven, the usual time.' We listen, not saying a word, as Pete takes us through his day, pretty much the same as before. 'I finished up about three fifteen, collected my car and drove home. I was back by five.'

'And your boss lives where?' Dan asks, though he knows fine well.

'Near Newport.'

'On the mainland. I see. And that's twenty minutes' drive from your house.'

'On average, yeah.'

'If you left your boss at three fifteen, it would mean you were definitely home by five?' Dan says, nodding.

'That's right. Maybe earlier. I wasn't, you know, looking at a clock.' His eyes slide away.

'So, to get home, which way would you go?'

Another tiny pause. Then slowly, like he's treading on ice, he says, 'I come in from the main road, over the bridge, through the town.'

'What road is that now?'

'The R319.'

'Then what?'

'I took a right off that road, up towards my estate.'

'Is that the way by this garda station and McLoughlin's Bar?'

'Yeah. It's the only way to go.'

'And you did this on Friday?'

'I already said. It's the only way.'

'I know that, but did you go by McLoughlin's Bar on Friday in your car before five o'clock?' Dan is sitting back, relaxed.

The silence stretches.

'Mr Ryan?'

'You wouldn't be asking me that if you thought I did,' he says.

Dan says nothing.

'No,' he says softly. 'I didn't go that way.'

'Why not? You said yourself it's the only way, isn't it? You can't go—'

'I got a fare on the way back. I'm not supposed to but people who know me call me up. It's just . . . extra money. I barely make ends meet so sometimes I pick up fares that my boss doesn't know about. I drove the fare to a house just outside Mallaranny so I got delayed and then I drove home.'

He would have had a legitimate excuse to be passing the school at four, then. Clever.

'So, does that mean, Mr Ryan, you would have been around the school between four and four thirty on Friday last?'

More hesitation. 'I can't quite remember the time.'

Now. I push the file towards Dan.

'That's okay,' Dan says. He removes the still of Pete's car from the file and slides it across the table to him. 'Do you recognise this vehicle?'

He studies it. Glances up. 'No. It looks like a BMW, though.'

'It's a still taken from the CCTV at the Bank of Ireland ATM just before four fifteen. That's beside the school. Were you there at that time after you dropped your passenger off?'

'It might make sense if you were delayed with an illegal fare,' I interject helpfully, and see him flinch on 'illegal'.

'I probably was but that's not my car, if that's what you're trying to say.'

'But you travelled up the main street.'

'Yes.'

'Then what?'

'I went home.'

'You didn't take any detours?'

A pause. 'No.'

'What is this?' Dan slides the image of his car heading into Luck Lane in front of him.

He glances at it. 'I dunno.'

'And here you are exiting the Lane some minutes later.' Another picture.

'Me?' Ryan tries to laugh. 'The number-plate . . . it's not—'

'And here you are, just passing the first house off Luck Lane back on the main road.' The final picture complete with clear number-plate. 'And again.' The more damning picture. 'What were you doing up there?'

The colour drains from his face. His jaw goes slack. 'Not what you think,' he says.

'I'm not thinking anything,' Dan says. 'But you've got to admit it looks pretty suspicious, you driving up that lane the same time as Lisa Moran disappears. Maybe you can take us through your story again. How about that?'

'I didn't kill her.'

'What happened, then?'

Silence. He's eyeing us. He's scared, though, his eyes darting between me and Dan. My hand is aching from the writing. I flex my fingers. I hope I won't have to write much more.

'All right.' A sigh, maybe relief, as he looks down at his hands. 'I did drive up that lane, I did.' His shoulders slump. 'I'm not proud of it. I let my customer off, was driving home and when I came by the school and I saw her coming out – just walking, like nothing was wrong – I was raging.' He looks at Dan.

Dan nods in encouragement. 'I can understand that,' he says.

'I'd planned on going home,' Pete says. 'I had but I pulled in and kept watching, like I don't know, and she seemed so happy and it was that smile . . . I don't know, I just . . . I went after her. I just . . . I went after her.'

Dan and I keep silent, keep still, like cats watching a mouse come out to play. One false move and it'll run. I can't believe he hasn't asked for a solicitor.

'Not right away, I just sat awhile, I think, and then, before I knew it, or even thought about it . . .' He looks at Dan. 'Well, I'd started after her, only she'd gone ahead so I couldn't see her at first.' He swallows. 'I didn't have a plan. I didn't know what I was doing. I just . . . wanted to scare her maybe. Warn her off.'

And here it comes, I think.

'I drove up the main street, only, like I said, I couldn't see her. I thought maybe she'd gone into a shop or something, so I pulled into a space opposite one of the shops, Lavelle's, I think it was, and gave it a couple of minutes but still nothing, and I was about to go home but I thought I'd try Luck Lane, you know, seeing as I'd gone to all the bother and it was on the way home anyway.'

'Of course.'

'But she wasn't there either.'

The words clang into the air, shattering what we'd thought he was about to say. Is he playing us? The best ones do. Dan flicks a glance my way before leaning across the table and saying slowly, 'You're telling us you didn't see her?'

'Yeah.'

'There was a red Clio two cars ahead of you and he saw her,' Dan says.

'I didn't see a red Clio, I saw no car, and I didn't see her.' He folds his arms.

'What did you do when you were driving up Luck Lane?' Dan asks.

'Nothing. Just drove up slow and then, when I didn't see her, I reversed back a bit but she wasn't there.'

Clang again. That would explain the delay on his car exiting.

'If a car in front of you saw her and you didn't, then where did she go?'

'Maybe there was more than one car in front of me.'

I glance at Dan. The Cig was right. Without tracing the blue car, which was in front of him, we can't even push him on this. Fucking rookie mistake.

'So, you didn't see her, though you admit going up after her?' Dan says.

'Yeah. I followed her because I was raging and, like you said, it's understandable.'

Dan twitches, a small tell that only I'd notice. He wants to thump this guy. Turning our words back on us. 'You're saying you didn't see her?'

'Yes, which was probably good for her.' There is a silence after he says that. He flushes but doesn't amend it.

The thing is, the car after Pete's says they didn't see her either. There's a tap on the door and I excuse myself as Dan suspends the interview for a moment.

William meets us at the door. 'Yez are doing well, but I'm not sure we'll get any more from him now. According to the boys in Westport, the wife says she lied because she knew he'd picked up an illegal fare and didn't want to get him in trouble. We can't get into his phone – wouldn't you know it's an old BlackBerry. Who the fuck uses BlackBerrys now? It'll take a while and, to top it all, they've found nothing at the house.'

'Fuck,' I say.

'The only light on the horizon is we had the list of blue Fiesta cars and regs in an hour ago. I've got the lads working on it. Lynch says the Fiesta in our CCTV seems to have some kind of a sticker on the front window, which will help with ID. But we've nothing to charge the Ryans with right now.'

Shit, I think.

'Is there no way we can hold him beyond the six hours?' I ask.

'Not now, but we'll get our chance again if there's anything on the phone or in the car. O'Neill reckons he can crack the phone in a day or so.'

We go back in to Ryan. He looks anxiously up at us.

'We're suspending questioning for now. Interview ended at . . .' Dan glances at his watch and rattles off the time. 'We'll see how the search of your car and house pan out.'

'You're going to search my car? My bloody car? I need my car!' Ryan stands up now and lunges towards Dan.

Dan stands his ground. 'When your time of detention is up, you'll be released by the member in charge.'

We leave to the sound of his roaring.

18

Dan and I are having a quick coffee. I'm typing up the Ryan interview and discussing our next move, when one of the guards who'd been tasked with reading all the counselling journals arrives.

'Excuse me?' she says nervously, as she clutches a file close to her chest. 'We've finished reading the journals. Here's the report.' She lays it in front of Dan, like a gift.

'Can you summarise?' Dan asks. I can tell he's in a bad mood but I'm not sure if it's because of Ryan or Fran.

'Okay,' the guard says, flushing and hopping from foot to foot. 'Me and Sandra read the fifty journals, looking specifically for references to a boy called Sam. Only one other person ever had a phone call from him.' I think she wants a reaction.

'We knew that, and?' Dan says.

'This fellow Tony . . .' she leans across Dan, totally invading his space, and opens the file '. . . he wrote this.'

I join Dan around his side of the desk to have a read.

Sam (7) phoned 23:15. He said his mammy was being bold and that he was not allowed to leave his bedroom. He was very distressed; he said his mammy is no good at taking care

of him. He was crying and asking me to help. I gave him the
number for the guards and Tusla but in the end he hung up.

'Was that call before or after Sam started ringing Lisa?'

'About a month before,' the guard says. 'Lisa got her first call from him in June. This is May. Then he kept calling Lisa, just her. Isn't that curious?'

'Lisa might have told him when she was on,' I offer. 'Or he might have called other times but when it wasn't Lisa on the line, he hung up. They get a lot of hang-ups.'

'They do, but if the boy is that desperate why would he wait for just Thursday night?' the young guard says.

Dan and I look at her with new interest.

'I read the journals,' she says, gaining confidence. 'A lot of the same callers ring up but they talk to everyone.' A beat. 'I'm just saying,' she goes on, getting red, 'like if he's that desperate.'

She has a point.

'Maybe he felt he had a bond with her,' Dan muses.

She nods eagerly. 'I think he just wanted to talk to a woman.' Before Dan has a chance to ask how on earth she's jumped to that, she ploughs on: 'I rang this Tony, just to double-check his notes. He sounds,' she screws up her face, 'quite feminine on the phone and his name, see, Tony? It could be mistaken for a girl. Maybe, I'm thinking, Sam found out Tony was a guy, changed to Lisa and stayed with her.'

'It's a bit of a leap,' Dan says, thinking. 'All right, here's what you'll do. Get that report into the book. Also get on to Tony again, ask him if he can remember what Sam sounded like. Accent. Age. Words he used. Just if he can remember. Don't put any ideas in his head.'

'I did. He said he just sounds like a child, though the accent was West of Ireland for definite. No words he can remember the child using.'

'Good,' Dan says. Thinks. 'Also ask him if he ever revealed to Sam that he was a bloke. If not, then maybe you're on the wrong track but might be worth checking if there are any reports of anyone loitering outside the Family First offices in recent weeks.'

The guard nods.

'Good work,' Dan says, and her face pinks. She's almost knocked down by Larry as he comes in.

'Lucy, Jesus,' Larry says.

'It's Dan but I'm open to being upgraded.' Dan smirks.

Larry doesn't even laugh. 'Jordy just saw it. There's a zero nine blue Fiesta registered to a Pascal Smyth. I'll give yez a medal if you guess where he lives?'

'Not Doogort Bog?' I say. In my head, the name rings a bell.

Larry hands us a piece of paper. 'Oh, yes. Do you want some regular lads to go with you?'

'Nah. If this car is a local, then it would make sense for him to be up that lane on the Friday. We'll check it out first. See what he saw. You get Ryan's car TEed as a matter of urgency.'

'That's in hand.'

'Great. Come on, Dan.'

He's got his coat on already and we're out of there.

19

Pascal Smyth, whose name niggles, lives way out on the bog. There are pockets of this island that are totally isolated, though with a car, you're always in touch. We head out on the twisty road towards Doogort, dark now with black rainclouds, our headlights slicing through the grim drizzle. Whop, whip, whop from the wipers.

The turn-off rears up suddenly as it always does and we're driving up through the bog on solid road, the land spread out on either side of us as we crawl towards the coast. We drive past the walking trails, and out in the distance, we can see the flutter of white tape that marks off the spot where Lisa's body was found. It should be coming down tomorrow as all searches are now complete. Lights of houses scattered about the bog puncture the encroaching darkness, and all in front is the flat land and the deepening glow of a dying day.

'This place gives me the creeps,' Dan remarks.

I smile because it's in my bones, and while it's eerie out here, it's also savagely exquisite. I want to inhale it into me.

Rainclouds scud across the sky and the road gets narrower as it begins to dip and rise and dip and rise. What is left of the purple and yellow heather brightens suddenly as the heavens open and rain pounds ferociously onto the car. I flick the wipers to double-speed but they make little impact against the deluge.

'I'm going to have to pull in,' I tell Dan. 'It's impossible to see.'

I indicate, though there is no one behind us, and we pull into a small indent in the road used when two cars are passing in opposite directions. The car shakes with the ferocity of the wind as it howls across the bog. We sit in silence, waiting for it to pass.

'Maybe Ryan was telling the truth,' Dan muses after a bit. 'Maybe he didn't see her.'

'He's still not being totally honest with us,' I say. 'It just doesn't add up.'

'Why?'

'Think about it. It was his wife who was pushing the case about Lisa being too hands-on with Kara. The teachers all con-firmed that. The wife is the one with the axe to grind, not Pete. Why would he suddenly flip and go after Lisa?'

Dan nods. 'Still, he didn't ask for a solicitor.'

'No, but I knew he was lying yesterday and I was right. Today, I dunno, I still think he's holding out on us. This abduction took planning.'

'He was a businessman, pretty successful. I'd say he's a planner.'

'Let's see what his car and phone turn up.'

We lapse back into silence. Maybe I should ask him about Fran, but it's rare in the job to have moments of quiet and I think neither of us wants to break it.

After five minutes or so, the rain loses its ferocity, the clouds part and what is left of the sun peeps out. I pull back onto the road and drive on.

Google Maps leads me on and on, through endless brown and

gold. Eventually, we end up on a road with barely enough space for one car, grass growing down the middle. It's a driveway of sorts, and after about three hundred metres we come to a small cottage, with a sagging roof and a straggly garden. I pull to a stop before a half-and-half front door, painted black but peeling badly.

Something stirs in me. This place looks familiar.

Dan and I get out and the silence embraces us. There are tyre tracks but no car.

'Hello,' Dan calls. 'Anyone about?'

Birds flap and tweet but no one comes.

It doesn't look as if anyone has been here in some time. The grass, what there is, is not trodden down as you would expect. But someone must have been here because of the car tracks.

Dan knocks on the door but no one answers. We try to peer into the house but the off-white lace curtains hanging in the window impede our view. We take a walk around, Dan going in one direction, me the other. A precarious water tower, some fencing, stone walls, a falling-down barn. There is something familiar about it, just out of reach.

'That barn,' I say.

It's distinctive, built of wood, sagging and rotting. The door has come off, leaving a gaping wound in the building, and that's when I remember. 'Dan,' I call, and he, coming from the other direction, strides over. 'This is the house from the Smyth case.'

He looks questioningly at me.

'You're probably too young to remember but it happened, I guess, about twenty-odd years ago. I was in Dublin, but I remember the pictures. This is definitely the place. The uniforms in the station should know it, too, though they're young so maybe not. There was a woman found murdered in a barn.' I remember how

I couldn't believe that such a thing could happen in my home place. 'And there were two children here,' I say. 'They got taken away.'

'You sure?' Dan asks.

'Yes.' It had been the biggest news on the island ever. 'The husband was charged. He got out years ago. I can't remember all the details.'

'Someone comes here,' Dan remarks. 'The lock on the back door is pretty new, as if the old one broke.' He glances at me. 'I don't like this, Golden.'

Neither do I. The place has a feel to it, but I push that thought back. It's fantastical and not how I should be thinking, but sometimes you just sense things. 'I'll call for back-up.'

Then Dan holds a hand up and suddenly I hear it. A scraping, coming from somewhere nearby. A whine, quite faint but audible.

'Hello,' Dan calls, and we wait.

More scraping.

We run to the back window and, through the dirty net curtains, we see an elderly man lying on the floor, an upended walker alongside him. A dog, pawing wildly at the door.

'Hello!' Dan pounds on the window. 'Hello!'

The man doesn't stir.

'I'll call for an ambulance,' I say, 'and get the first-aid kit. You try to gain entry to the kitchen.'

'I hope the dog doesn't go for me,' he says, as he knocks a hole in the glass of the window.

When I arrive back, Dan is outside, and inside, the dog, a miserable-looking thing, is lying flat out beside the old man.

'It's not a first-aid kit you'll be needing,' Dan says. 'It's a dust suit. I've called for back-up.' At my look, he says, 'The auld fella is dead. I checked his pulse. Not long, I wouldn't think. But something happened in that house. It smells of bleach and death.'

'Was he murdered?'

'No, I'd say he fell. I've asked for the Tech Bureau to come down, just to check the place out, and a doctor. The super is sorting it now.'

Half an hour later, a team arrives. Dan explains what we found and we stay as Forensics get to work.

About twenty minutes later, we're handed dust suits and asked to go inside. The body of the old man lies splayed across the kitchen floor.

'Natural death,' we're told. 'The interesting stuff is up here.'

Once we cross the kitchen, past the body, the smell hits us. A mix of bleach but also something underneath it, something sweet and sour and hot and sticky and cloying. Someone has died in this house, I think. That someone could still be here, yet the smell is faint.

Behind us, I can hear the dog howling and growling as the team try to get near his master.

The stench of bleach hugs the air, makes its way onto our tongues.

Dan goes upstairs with some of the men while I enter the open door to the living room, where some others are working. It's dated but surprisingly clean compared to the kitchen. An old armchair in front of an old TV. I press a switch and the screen flickers on. The floor is covered with grey lino and the walls are painted white. No pictures but a lot of newspapers are piled high against the TV.

'I want them bagged,' I say.

'Lucy.' Dan's shout alerts me from upstairs.

I turn and head up.

The smell of bleach is stronger now. Large patches of the boards on the landing are a sizzling white, and the trail leads into the bathroom where Dan is standing with one of the team. It doesn't take long to see what has snagged their attention.

The room looks clean, it has been painted recently, but just over the bath, very faint, the letters BiTch are scrawled. A huge capital B and T, as if the writer was infuriated and finding it hard to control himself. The paint job was obviously meant to get rid of it.

'That's not all,' someone says to me. 'Have a look in here.'

He pushes open the door to the bedroom. Women's clothes lie scattered on the floor, as if they have been discarded. Jeans, white hoodie and a glittery blue T-shirt with the words *Live Life* in silver. More bleach.

Someone is taking photographs of them.

'We'll bag them up and get them removed for a tech exam,' one of the team says.

I give him the details of the exhibits officer on the case and ask the photographer, 'Are there any shoes there? Socks?'

'Doesn't seem like it.'

'I want all results as quickly as possible. Let's see if there are any connections between this place and our case. I need a complete search done of the house and the barns and the grounds. I want to know where Pascal Smyth's blue Fiesta is.'

Then, unable to look any more, I turn away. With as much composure as I can muster, I head downstairs and out into the air.

My phone rings. It's the sergeant-in-charge. 'Lucy, I'm looking

179

at Pete Ryan's custody report here. He's being released now. Is that right?'

'Yes, make sure it's all done by the book. You know yourself.'

'Will do.'

I look back towards the house.

Dan approaches. 'I've told Jordy to stay with Forensics. He'll have a report by morning. Want to get a coffee?'

'Yeah. What'll happen to the dog?' It strikes me suddenly that he'll be left behind. That all his loyalty will come to nothing.

'Probably bring it to the pound. It looks half starved.'

I hope he finds a new home.

The Captain

He stops eating his supper, toast held aloft as the newscaster announces that the body of an elderly man has been found in a cottage in Doogort but that foul play was not suspected. The cottage has been cordoned off.

So, the old man is dead, he thinks. Rotted away, just like his life. He feels a bit sorry. Then he doesn't.

He wonders will they search the water tower. He remembers it being built, going up, piece by piece, day by day. That big rust-coloured water tower, looking in through the window at them as they ate their tea. Shining in the bright light of early morning, winking at them in the evenings as the sun passed over the land.

He slept in his room, looking out onto it. He talked to it and sometimes it talked back.

He loved the big boggy landscape of his home.

He loved how he could find his way about the bog, knew where to put his feet without sinking into some stream or other, without getting sucked into the marsh.

He loved the will-o'-the-wisp on dark nights.

He loved everything until he didn't.

20

I arrive home late enough that evening, battered and exhausted. It's been a hell of a day, a total curve ball in the investigation. My mother appears in the kitchen doorway and I feel a flash of irritation. What now? I think. Can she not see I'm bloody wrecked?

'How was your day?' she asks, her voice pitched about an octave too high.

'Not good.' I walk into the kitchen, determined to knock back some wine.

Luc is at the table, looking a bit chastened, a bit morose, and I remember that I'd texted him earlier to talk to him.

Shit!

He's all long, easy limbs, yet still managing to dress as if his clothes are ten sizes too big. Enormous runners, baggy jeans and a black hoodie with a picture of a skull on the front. There's a piece of toast dangling from his mouth. He whips it out as I enter, and stares at me, like a feral cat, wondering what the deal is.

I want to yell at him, to shake him hard so that he tells me what's up. But I can't. Instead, I rein in my shit day, take my time placing my bag on the counter, dreading the next few minutes. 'I need you to tell me what's wrong, Luc.' Good, I sound reasonable yet concerned.

From the corner of my eye, I see my mother nod at him.

So she knows.

I can't decide if I'm hurt, angry or relieved that he's confided in someone.

Luc, his head still down, brings his eyes up to study me. His resemblance to Rob in that moment makes me catch my breath.

'I think it might be good if you sat down,' my mother says.

'Is it that bad?'

Luc shrugs.

'Is it Rob?' I can't contain the crawling anxiety, 'Has he contacted you?' Before he can answer, I go on, 'Because I'll have you know now, it would not be a good idea to meet him.'

His expression tells me I've got it wildly wrong. 'Me dad?' he says. 'Is he out of prison, then?'

'Yes,' I try to brush it off. 'A couple of months now.'

'You never said.'

'I didn't think you'd be interested. I didn't think it would matter.'

His look withers me. 'You just didn't want to tell me,' he says, and I flush. 'Do you honestly think,' he goes on, 'I'd be stupid enough to get involved with him?'

'This is not what you were going to discuss with your mother, is it, Luc?' my mother says, in this conciliatory tone.

And I wonder how long she's known. She brought him up when I was struggling to make ends meet. When I was so focused on getting my respect back from my colleagues that I lost sight of him. He trusts her. She was his fun person. The stab of hurt that he doesn't see me like that is a physical pain. 'Well, Luc?' I say.

'It's embarrassing.' He winces. 'Like, I don't know how to put it quite.'

'I won't mind, whatever it is,' I say, trying to be supportive.

'Off you go.' My mother sits beside Luc, like an ally.

He shifts about in the chair, pulls the sleeves of his oversized sweatshirt down over his wrists. Dips his head, brown hair tumbling across his face. 'I know this is gonna be a shock to you, right—'

It hits me all of a sudden and I want to cry for the sheer relief of it. And hug him and tell him it's fine. It will all be fine. 'Are you coming out?'

'Coming out? What?'

'You're gay, isn't that it?'

'Will you let the boy speak?' my mother snaps. 'Would you ever bloody get on with it, Luc!'

'I'm not gay. In fact, Mam, I'm going to be a father.'

The words land like a bucket of cold water. I gawp at him.

'Now, that's not too bad, ey?' my mother says, and I realise I've been standing with my mouth open.

'He's just eighteen,' I start to babble. 'He can't cook, he listens to dreadful music, he's only in Leaving Cert year and he doesn't even like babies.'

'I don't know any babies,' he says sort of defensively.

'Who's the girl?' My mind is spinning.

'She's just this girl I know.' A shrug.

'Do you know her well?' Crap. Crap. Crap.

'I should hope so,' my mother pipes up. 'He got her pregnant.'

'Nan,' Luc says. 'Jesus.'

'How well do you know this girl? Is she your girlfriend? Are you in a relationship? Did I ever meet her?' I slide into the seat beside him, pressing closer with every question. I know I sound hysterical but it had never entered my head that this was his news. Part of me is relieved that it's nothing to do with Rob, but the other part is saying that this fatherhood thing is for life. And he's too young. He's still my baby.

'I don't know her like I'd know you or me nan,' Luc says, sounding just a bit wary. 'I just know her from around, for like saying hello to.'

Holy mother of fucking crap. I have no words.

'Anyway,' Luc continues, 'her mother is being supportive and she's letting her have the baby and I just thought I'd tell you.'

'But your music and your plans and—'

'He has everything all thought out,' my mother says. 'He's being very mature about it.'

Has he never bloody heard of contraception? What are they teaching him in school? What should I have taught him? Eighteen and shackled with a child.

'Tell her, Luc,' my mother says.

'Yes, yes, go on.'

Luc eyeballs me, then stands up. 'I will when you don't sound so – so hysterical.'

Is he lecturing me?

Him?

'I'm not being hysterical.' That's a lie, right there.

'You said you wouldn't mind whatever it was.'

'I didn't think it was this. Do you realise what you've done? All your plans and—'

'It's not as if he's meeting Rob,' my mother chimes in.

'Mam, will you just take your beak out?' I snap. 'How do you think I feel when my own mother knows something like this and I didn't?'

'We knew you were under stress with work,' my mother placates.

'And I told Nan because she doesn't go off the deep end,' Luc says unplacatingly.

'I'm not going off the deep end,' I say, going off the deep end. 'You only told her because—'

'I've offered to take the baby on the weekends and for holidays and she says that's great,' Luc interrupts. 'And I'm going to get a part-time job and give her money for it, and when it gets bigger, I'm going to bring it to GAA matches and rock concerts.'

The innocence of it all blindsides me into wanting to hold him and hug him and not let him go. And yet out of my mouth tumbles, 'Every baby's dream, being looked after by a dad with a crummy job. Well done, you.'

I'm not prepared for the hurt on his face. I want to say sorry but then he takes a step towards me and says, with biting bitterness, 'At least it'll have a dad. A dad that won't let it down by bankrupting a bloody bank and turning half the country into a wasteland, while his ma, who is called Tanita by the way, thanks for asking, she'll be around for it too. She won't be rushing off to look after strangers who've had shitty things done to them. She'll be there for her own kid. So there.' And knowing he's got me where it hurts most, he stomps out of the kitchen. After a few seconds, the door to his bedroom slams and that sound is soon followed by the muffled thud of pumping music.

My body sags suddenly and I lean against the countertop. It's been a day of too much.

'He didn't mean that,' my mother says, after a second. 'Well, maybe the bit about Rob, but not the rest of it.'

'How long have you known?' I ask.

'Not long,' her red face gives her away, 'maybe a few weeks. The girl wasn't sure if she was keeping it so he sort of hid it for a while.'

'A while? When is this baby due?'

My mother flaps her hand about. 'A couple of weeks or so.'

'A couple of weeks or so? Aw, no.'

'I know it's a—'

'Don't say "shock", just don't. He's kept this from me for months. That girl must have decided way back to keep the baby. And he—'

'He was worried he'd let you down.'

'He's let himself down. He's let that poor girl down. I'll have to ring her parents.' I pull a bottle of wine from the fridge and twist it open. 'Just leave me alone,' I tell her, taking the wine and a glass out with me.

She follows me into the room in time to see me pour my second glassful. Sitting in beside me, she hands me a plate. 'Banana and peanut-butter sandwich,' she says. 'Peace offering.'

She knows me well. 'Ta.'

After a moment, she says, 'You've done a great job with Luc, you know.'

'*You've* done a great job, you mean,' I mutter, opening the sandwich and rearranging the banana.

'Just eat it,' she says wearily. Then, 'Do you not think that I didn't doubt myself when I was bringing you up?'

'That's not—'

'It's the same,' she pre-empts me. 'When you brought that Flash Harry Robert home, I blamed myself, I still do.'

'You liked Rob,' I say.

'I did in my arse.' At my surprise, she says, 'Oh, there's no doubt he was charming and funny, but underneath, he wasn't anything. There was nothing there but you were mad about him and I couldn't stand in your way. And I could see why you married him, Lucy, even if you couldn't.'

'I married him because I loved him,' I say.

'You married him because he had money,' she says back.

'That's not true.' Of all the things my mother has said to me, this is the most offensive.

'He made you feel secure,' she goes on. 'And that was my fault because I never did. How could I? Without your dad we were always on the breadline.'

The insight startles me. 'No, you did great. That's—'

'And Luc knows you worked hard so that he'd never feel insecure,' she says, interrupting me. 'He knows that. I've told him. He's so proud of you.'

I'd like to believe it, but I hardly even feel proud of myself.

'And I know he's only eighteen,' my mother goes on, her voice softening, 'but it takes a man to stick around for his child.' And with that she stands back up, her knees creaking. She waves at the plate. 'Eat up your sandwich, there's a good girl.' A moment. 'Grandmothers need their strength.'

And I realise that Luc is about to make me into one. And I don't know how to react other than to catch my mother's hand.

She gives mine a squeeze.

And she leaves.

21

Day Four

The Cig seems uneasy as the team files into the incident room the next morning. He's flicking through a sheaf of papers. 'That was some find yesterday,' he says to me, as I slide in beside him. 'Forensics did a luminol test in the bathroom. The bleach didn't get rid of everything.'

He passes me a picture of the darkened bathroom lit by ultra-violet light. Swathes of blue spatter adorn the walls. The word BiTch stands out starkly over the bath. Blood.

'Christ.'

'From their preliminary findings, it seems a girl, judging by the clothes, was in the back bedroom, voluntarily or not, we don't know. Then something happened and she was dragged to the bathroom. That's where we think she was murdered.'

'The clothes don't match what Lisa was wearing, though,' I say. 'Could we have another victim here?'

He nods. 'We're working on the assumption that the cases are linked somehow. The car we can't locate links them. If it's the same car. But obviously we need more.'

'Obviously,' I say, and I sound sarcastic.

He looks at me sharply but wisely says nothing. Maybe he thinks it's residue from the house of horror yesterday. And some of it is, no doubt. But it's also the house of bloody horror that Luc has landed himself in. I can't imagine a baby in our lives right now. And I don't even have time to adjust because in a few weeks' time I'll be a grandmother.

Dan joins us.

'O'Neill thinks he's cracked the stuff on Ryan's phone,' William says to him.

'About bloody time,' Dan snaps, and I wonder who rattled his cage today.

'You two better perk up a bit,' William warns.

Dan's phone pings and he glances at it, flicks it off and shoves it back into his pocket.

'Fran?' I guess.

'They don't call you Detective Sergeant Lucy Golden for nothing,' he says, a bit sourly.

'Did you get to talk to him yesterday in the end?'

'Through the letterbox,' he says, without humour. 'We broke up. Last night I slept in my car.'

'Aw, Dan!'

'Lucy? Dan?' William makes us jump. 'Anything you'd like to say?'

'No, Cig,' we mumble, turning away from each other.

'Because you were doing a lot of whispering there. I hope it was about this case!' Without waiting for an answer, he eyeballs the room. 'None of you will have a life until this case is solved. We will work around the clock if we have to. Yesterday, thanks to the good work of Larry, Jordy, Lucy and Dan, we got a break so let's see where it takes us.' He nods to Jordy.

190

Jordy, looking more dishevelled than usual, hauls himself to his feet, tucking in his shirt as he does so. A cough. He's always uneasy talking to the room. 'I was tic-tacking with the guys on the scene yesterday,' he says, his voice wavering, then finding its level. 'The initial impression is that the old man, who we believe to be Pascal Smyth, fell at the scene. He was suffering from cancer and was at an advanced stage. They don't suspect foul play. However, it is suspected, based on findings, that something suspicious occurred in other areas of the house.'

He goes on to outline what we found at the scene yesterday. He tells the room that the newspapers, some of which dated back twenty-five years, chronicled the case of Pascal Smyth's murder of his wife. 'Papers he couldn't possibly have kept as he was in jail when they were printed,' Jordy says. 'The clothes we found are being tested for forensics and an ongoing search of the farmyard is taking place. Despite the bleaching, fingerprints were found at the scene,' he goes on, 'Pascal Smyth's and three others. We have no idea how long those prints have been there. But they prove the old man did have visitors. Three different ones were found inside while the fourth was on the glass at the back door. That, we think, was the local health nurse who, according to herself, had never been inside the house. Pascal Smyth's health was so bad there is no way he could have murdered Lisa Moran. It's very unlikely that he would have carried out the other assault we believe took place in the bathroom.'

'Does it look like anyone visited the house recently?' someone asks.

'Aside from the nurse, who only stayed a short while, not that we can see, though a new lock was fitted on the back door and the front room is in a surprisingly clean condition. There has

191

been no trace of the blue Fiesta we were initially looking for on the site.'

'Let's find out if that car was sold or stolen,' William says. Then, 'Have we background on the original Pascal Smyth murder? It might be good to know that.'

I'd hinted to Mick that it might be an idea to have the details for today's meeting and I'm pleased when his hand shoots up. 'I took it upon myself yesterday to familiarise myself with the case, Cig. I'll go through the highlights for everyone.' A clearing of his throat before he begins. 'I talked to the investigation officer who was here at the time – he's long gone now. Seems there were tabs on Pascal for about ten years after he was out but what with one thing and another—'

'What other?' William snaps. 'The island is hardly coming down with murderers that he had lost sight of.'

Mick wisely doesn't try to defend his statement. I think he's used to being picked on by the Cig now. 'Twenty years ago, the body of June Smyth, Pascal Smyth's second wife, to whom he'd been married for eleven years, was found in a barn on a farm on the bog. She had been beaten but the cause of death was suffocation. It appears her husband stood on her throat and blocked her windpipe.'

There is a murmur around the room.

'What happened to the first wife?' William asks.

'According to the reports at the time, she died in childbirth four years before he remarried. We're having another look back but it doesn't appear to be suspicious in any way. However, June Smyth, the second wife, was wearing a grey tracksuit when found.' After that bit of news has been digested, he goes on, 'The position of her body at the time of death tallies with the position of Lisa Moran's.' He holds up an enlarged photograph of the murder scene in the barn and he's right: there is a similarity in the positioning of both bodies and she has a look of Lisa Moran too, small, blonde. 'And finally,' Mick says, 'there were two children sitting in a car in the farmyard when Pascal Smyth was picked up. A two-year-old and a six-year-old. They were deeply traumatised as you can imagine. Neither of them spoke initially. The elder of the two boys later confessed that they had seen their father covered with blood emerge from the barn. As there were no relatives on either side, both children were taken into care.' He pauses. 'Their names were Ken Smyth and Samuel Smyth.'

Sam.

What are the odds?

'Thanks, Mick. What did the neighbours say at the time?'

'Nothing,' Mick says. 'Nobody knew anything. It's isolated and miles from any other house. Apparently the couple kept to themselves and the eldest boy had just started attending the local school. Other than that, the children didn't mix.'

'Any history of violence in the home prior to the murder?'

'Not that we were aware. But around here . . .' Mick gives a shrug.

'Around here?' the Cig says, and I want to kick him for his sarcasm. Mick has done a good job digging out the case.

'That's the way it is in this place,' I say. 'Everyone knows but no one knows.'

William stares at me. I seem to specialise in contradicting him. Then he mutters, 'Christ. Right, anything else for—'

Just then, Susan arrives, plaits bouncing up and down, her glasses hopping. 'Sorry, everyone. I've just got some news now.'

'Aren't you and Mick on fire today?' William remarks drily.

'I put a bit of pressure on the boys at the house yesterday to get detail on any fingerprints at the scene as soon as they could. They got back just now with one of them. It's in the system. It's a woman and her name is Pearl Grey.'

I see Mick give Susan a surreptitious thumbs-up.

'The interesting thing is,' Susan overrides the chatter that has greeted her news, 'the woman, identified as Pearl Grey, was twenty-five years old when she went missing eight months ago from Castlebar. She failed to return home after putting in a shift in a local call centre.'

'Call centre?' I interrupt. 'What kind of call centre?'

'I'm getting to that,' Susan says. 'It was a helpline for children.'

The room erupts but William gives the tiniest cough and it dies down. 'Anything else?' he asks.

'No evidence turned up at the time when Pearl disappeared. It was like she vanished into thin air.'

The Cig nods. 'All right. Lucy, Dan, go tic-tac with the guards in Castlebar who handled that case, will you? Find out more. That's connection number two. I want Pascal Smyth's two sons traced. Susan and Mick, get on it.' They nod, like eager kids being invited to a party. 'Now,' William goes on, 'let's not assume! Yesterday we had Pete Ryan in. He's proved himself a liar, let's not rule him out. Any word on his car, Larry?'

'I'll have something today, Cig.'

'Good. Alibis all checking out?'

'We checked out the three running friends yesterday evening,' Pat O'Neill pipes up. 'Sarah was picked up on CCTV leaving work, as was Liam. It's impossible, we estimated, for Sarah to have had sufficient time. Liam we traced in his car as far as Achill Sound but after that the car goes off grid because we've no CCTV. His mother says he was at home from four to six thirty, though. We've no proof that he was anywhere else. Paul McCarthy left work with a co-worker at three forty-five. That car hasn't been picked up though the co-worker says he dropped Paul at his house around four. We picked up the co-worker's car in Achill Sound fifteen minutes later as he left the island, so that fits. Paul says he went to his neighbour and I interviewed the neighbour and she confirms that he called in just after four and they had a lovely evening together, chatting and drinking tea. He turned on her heat and made her a sandwich and, basically, he's the son she never had.' There's a ripple of laughter. Pat adds, 'You'd want to see the state of the place she lives in, the poor auld dear. She says Paul is a great neighbour, that he fixes anything that needs fixing. Anyway, that's those three done. I'm checking out the teachers today.'

'Good. All right, remember, everyone, wherever this man Sam and his brother are, be aware that they have witnessed terrible things. They will need careful handling.'

William goes around the room, asking about door-to-door and phones but these have drawn blanks. 'Anything on this boyfriend that she was meant to have?' he asks. 'Are we any closer to finding out who he is or if he is?'

'No,' Dan says. 'There was one but he hasn't come forward. It was back in March, so it might have no bearing on the case anyway.'

'But it might so we need to find him. If he's nothing to hide, he should come forward.' William turns to Jim. 'Give out the job sheets and remember, everyone, I do not want any leaks. If I see one column inch in a newspaper, I will come down so hard on whoever talked. Is that understood?'

A bobbing of heads.

'I don't care if she offers to show you her knickers, the answer is to refer them to me or the press office. Have yez got that?'

I notice Matt go very red.

'Yes, Matt, it's you I'm talking to.'

Then, amid the jeering, William strides out of the room.

22

We drive to Castlebar in silence, both of us a bit pissed off with our lives. I'm glad I'm driving: it gives me something to focus on. Dan is doing a search for hotels and Airbnbs on his phone. Good luck with that, I think.

The drive takes almost an hour but it's worth it to talk to the investigating officer and maybe re-interview a few of the people who knew Pearl to see if we can connect her and Lisa.

When we get there, the DS, who has been expecting us, leads us into one of their interview rooms. He's carrying a large file and lays it on a table.

'Summary,' he says. 'Pearl went missing last year after a shift in a call centre. Disappeared off camera and wasn't seen again. She was a hairdresser, worked most evenings until six, then went home to the flat she shared with her boyfriend. On a couple of days during the month, she would do voluntary work for a children's helpline. It was on one of these nights she never came back.'

'Did she keep a journal at all about the type of calls she may have got on the line?'

'No, but there is a report from her supervisor at the time.' He pulls it out and hands it to us. 'She said that Pearl was issued with

197

a gentle warning during one debriefing session. She was getting too close to a number of the callers. She was afraid at the time that her words might have upset Pearl.'

My heart picks up a beat as I take the report and skim the details. 'Does this woman still work for the helpline?' I ask.

'The helpline is gone,' he says, 'but the woman is still about as far as I know.'

'Anything else of significance?' I ask. 'CCTV of cars or anything?'

'It was the perfect disappearance,' he says. 'In the beginning we thought she'd just left her partner but he was convinced she'd been taken. We focused a lot of our attention on him – he had a rep for bad behaviour – but there was nothing. He insisted she wasn't suicidal, that their relationship was good. But her credit cards were never used, her passport was left behind. If it was an abduction, the guy had it all planned out. The case went cold.'

'Where is the boyfriend now?'

'I checked this morning. He's gone to Canada.'

That's a relief: we don't need another suspect.

'Any cars spotted in the area?' I pull out a picture of Pascal Smyth's blue Fiesta. 'We're interested in finding this.'

'Like I said, it was perfect. No CCTV. We did pick up CCTV of some cars in the vicinity and interviewed the drivers but it was needle-in-a-haystack stuff.' He hands the file to Dan. 'You're welcome to read it. I can send you over the highlights. Anything else, just shout.'

'We'll take any CCTV you have,' Dan says, and I think, Good call.

He promises to send it over.

★★★

We grab lunch in a cheap café that smells of grease and chips. I try to eat the cheese sandwich I've bought as Dan skims the file. He has the ability to speed-read and extract important information. At first, I didn't trust it so I'd give him little quizzes but he'd always be spot on with his answers.

My sandwich is hard and dry and tastes like chips. I can't eat much anyway. It's not the case, it's just that my thoughts keep diverting to Luc. I know I'll have to find the time to ring the girl's parents and introduce myself but, really, is there a guidebook for that? I put the sandwich down and heave a sigh.

'Problem?' Dan asks, looking at me over the rim of his coffee mug.

'I don't want to talk about it.'

'Fair enough.' A wry grin. 'I guess I deserve that. Sorry for being grumpy this morning.'

'I wasn't too chirpy myself.'

He smiles. Nods towards the file. 'They did a solid investigation.'

'Good.'

More silence as he goes back to scrolling his phone for somewhere to sleep that night. I pull a corner of crust off the bread and crumble it between my fingers. Up at the counter, the dipsy-looking waitress changes the music playing to some kind of rap, the crushing sounds causing a baby at the table opposite to howl. She apologises and turns the music back to generic pop.

Dan huffs out a sigh and stabs his phone screen in frustration.

'You can stay on my sofa for the length of the investigation,' I say. 'We both know you haven't a hope of finding anywhere while it's going on.'

He looks up at me. Hesitates. 'Aw, no . . . Better off not.'

'You won't be fit for anything sleeping in your car. Now, I reckon my offer is the best you'll get. Take it or leave it.'

He sets his phone down and looks directly at me. 'Then I'll take it and thanks.'

'You're welcome.'

'And we'll agree, no discussing of the case off duty.'

I'd been about to say the same, though I'm not sure how realistic it is. 'Agreed.'

'Thanks, Luce.' It's heartfelt.

'No bother.'

Another bit of silence before he says tentatively, 'Is it Rob?' He sets his mug down and leans towards me across the table. In a low voice, he says, 'I heard you on the phone yesterday asking about him.' Before I can respond, he goes on, 'You've been distracted. Is he being a problem? Tell me to mind my own business, if you want, but if it's Rob, that's serious.'

His concern is so raw that I'm moved. He has never asked me about Rob before and I appreciated it. One time it was all anyone knew or cared to know about me.

'No.' I shake my head. 'He's not being a problem.'

'Good.'

It might be nice to confide in an impartial someone, I think. And I really need to focus on this case. The Morans are trusting me and Dan to do our best. We can't let our personal lives mess up our focus. 'It's Luc.'

'You don't have to. It's—'

I go straight for it. 'He's going to be a dad.'

'Feck off!' And he has the nerve to chortle.

'Not the reaction I was hoping for,' I say. So much for concern.

His smile dies. 'You're serious?'

'I'm serious.'

'Right.' He seems a bit lost at that.

The woman with the baby leaves the café, and the waitress switches back on the rap, then takes a manky cloth and wipes the table.

'You'll be a grandmother.' Dan says it, like it's just occurred to him.

'Not helping, Dan.'

'Sorry.'

He sips his coffee while I stare at my arid sandwich. 'It's due in a few weeks.'

Dan coughs as some coffee goes down the wrong way. I hand him a paper napkin. He dabs his mouth and coughs some more. 'The baby is due that soon and you're only finding out now?'

'Yes, and it would help if you didn't find it so bloody funny.'

'I don't. Sorry.'

'I wish I hadn't told you.'

'It's not the worst thing,' he says, trying to redeem himself. 'Babies are supposed to be, you know, bundles of joy and all that.'

'I don't ever remember putting in a request for a bundle of joy,' I mutter, and his mouth twitches. I flop back in the chair. 'Look, I know it's not as bad as him seeing Rob, but I could have dealt with that. This,' I shake my head, 'there's nothing I can do. Him and that poor young girl are in it for life now.'

'The baby will grow.'

'That's it? That's your contribution? The baby will grow?'

'It will,' Dan says. He pulls my sandwich towards him. 'You having that?'

'No.'

He bites into it, chews for a second. 'The baby will grow and in a few years it'll be in school and, anyway, it's worse for his girlfriend.'

'It is but she's not his girlfriend, just someone he likes saying hello to apparently.'

Now his grin broadens out – he can't help it.

'It's not bloody funny.'

'I know. But, Jesus . . .' He has to put the sandwich down because his shoulders are shaking. 'Gives a whole new meaning to "You had me at hello."'

'You had me pregnant at hello.'

And, somehow, it makes me laugh.

23

The ex-supervisor, May, is a small woman, hunched over with arthritis. Her head is bowed in permanent prayer, and when she looks up at us, it's at an angle. She invites us into her kitchen and shuffles before us. She folds herself into a chair, like a bird. 'You're asking about Pearl,' is all she says.

'Yes,' Dan says. He sits opposite her while I stay standing.

The kitchen is old and dated but tidy. I don't see how she can possibly keep it clean in her condition.

'We have reason to believe that her disappearance might be linked to her work on the helpline.'

May gives a tiny gasp, like a hiccup.

'We'd like,' Dan continues, 'if you could go back over the information you gave the guards at the time.'

'Of course,' she says. 'But I must say everyone on the helpline last year was lovely. I can't believe—'

'We're not saying that anyone on the helpline was involved, though we'd like a list,' Dan says. 'We're working on the assumption that her death may be linked to a call she had. Did any calls in particular upset her?'

May swallows. 'Yes. Yes, in fact a couple of calls did. That was my fear, that something I'd said to her – I must admit I was a little sharp with her the second time it happened . . . Well, I thought she'd gone and killed herself because she was a very sensitive girl.' She pulls a tissue from her sleeve and dabs her eyes with it.

That was exactly what Amanda had said about Lisa in Family First.

Dan and I give her a moment, then Dan asks, 'What happened for the second time?'

'She wanted to get involved. She was quite insistent. I told her in no uncertain terms that we'd have no use for her if she did that. She got upset. That was the last time I had contact with her.'

'What did she want to get involved in? Can you remember the case?'

May frowns. 'Not really. She'd been with us a few months, getting on fine, then one day, at a debriefing, she said she found it hard to leave the children and hang up. A couple of the others agreed with her. There was nearly a mutiny.'

'Did she keep a journal?'

'They just filled out sheets, statistics for funding, no identification anywhere.'

'Think hard. Is there anything you can remember about the case she wanted to get involved in?'

'No. Some of the other people on the phones might – they were at the meeting – but it was over a year ago. I'm sorry.'

'That's all right,' Dan says, with a smile. 'Tell me, did she have regular hours on the line? For instance, was she working every Wednesday or was it mixed from week to week?'

May shrugs as much as her bent body will allow. 'Most of our volunteers worked the same hours. They tended to fit it in around their lives, you see. As far as I recall Pearl worked every Tuesday until nine.'

'Was there anyone she was particularly friendly with on the volunteer team?'

'I don't know.' May is apologetic. 'Most of them were friendly with each other.'

There's not a lot to be gained here. 'All right, thanks.' I wave her to stay sitting. 'We'll show ourselves out.'

In the car, Dan contacts the station to ask them if they can pull a list of volunteers on the helpline Pearl worked for with a view to setting up interviews with them all. 'Let's see if anyone else can remember who Pearl wanted to help.' He heaves a sigh. 'At least we have a definite link between the two women. It has to be enough. But this guy, whoever he is, must have come across them in some other way. He had to know them, know what they were like.'

I think over what the young guard had said yesterday. 'Maybe he did see them.' I pull out the image of Pearl from the file. 'Hasn't she a look of Lisa? Blonde, twenties?'

'Yeah,' Dan agrees.

Just then my phone rings and it's the Cig.

'They've found a body on the farm,' he says, without any pre-amble. 'In the water tower, no ID as yet, fairly decomposed but we have reason to believe that she was wearing a grey tracksuit at the time of death.'

'Thanks.'

After he hangs up, Dan looks at me. 'I have an idea,' he says. 'It's a bit of a long shot and we need the super on board.'

I smile, because I like the way he's thinking. And because we now have the car, the tracksuit and the helpline as links. 'I'll call William back and ask him to talk to the super.'

When we get back to the station, Mick and Susan are tapping away on the computer, trying to trace the sons of Pascal Smyth and some details on Pascal's first wife. 'I've shaken the foster agencies up a bit,' Mick says, 'so I should have news by tomorrow. What I did find out was that the boy, Sam, was two when he was fostered, his brother was six and, by all accounts, a little wild. The tragedy was they were separated because it was thought that the older boy would run and take the younger boy with him. I'll keep plugging away.'

There are four notes on my desk, one from Joe to call him, another from Kev Deasy, the third from Pat O'Neill saying he'd got into Ryan's phone records AT LAST and will get back to me, and the fourth from the Cig, asking us into his office when we get back. There's also a note to say that the fabric found inside Lisa Moran's bra was a polyester scrim with a bonding agent and an exterior PVC coating. Then a note, saying it's the sort of fabric that would be found on the exterior of durable products – punch bags and so on. I think about that.

'I'm going to call Joe now before we go in to the Cig,' I say, and Dan makes a scared face as I stick my tongue out. I hope Joe is still there, though I think he lives in the mortuary.

'Joe!' he snaps.

'It's Lucy Golden.'

'I have the prelim on Pearl Grey.' Without waiting for an answer, he fires the information down the line at me. 'The body was badly decomposed but, due to the water temperature, not as badly as might have been expected. It's obvious that death was most likely caused by a violent beating or strangulation. Her jaw-bone was shattered as was her cheekbone. You don't get that from being flung into a water tower. The grey fabric found appears to be identical to Lisa Moran's. That's it.'

'Can I ask one thing?' I interrupt, before he hangs up. 'Could Lisa Moran's injuries have been caused by boxing gloves? The fabric found in her bra was the sort found on punch bags.'

He gives this due thought, for which I'm grateful. 'Yes.' I sense him nodding. 'Yes, her injuries could be consistent with that.' And he hangs up.

Then I call Kev. 'Story?' I say.

'The taxi driver who brought Lisa home that night called. He said he remembered, and he wasn't sure if it was significant, that earlier in the year, when he was waiting for Lisa to come out, there was a guy hanging around. He couldn't give much of a description only to say the guy was wearing black, about five eight he reckons, and that he was hidden in a doorway and stood out when Lisa came out of the building. He says it might be noth-ing, but it jarred with him at the time. I pressed him on the date, but he's not sure.'

'Thanks.' I put the phone down.

'Let's head into the Cig,' I say to Dan.

William is watering his bonsai tree when we enter. He straight-ens up, gives a bit of a cough, as if he's slightly embarrassed to be caught in such a domestic act. He plants the watering-can on the windowsill and motions for us to sit.

He takes his own seat behind his desk. 'I talked to the super—'

'Great. Did you—'

He holds up his hand. 'Patience, Lucy.' He waits a couple of seconds to make sure I won't speak, before he goes on: 'He thinks it's a good idea, and if it's his modus operandi, it might actually shake him free. So, the super will go live on the steps here at six tonight for the news and they'll run it again for the nine o'clock. I want the two of you there. Give it a bit of gravitas.'

'Great.' I say. 'I—'

He holds up his index finger, which also means 'shut up'. 'I'll see you both at the steps at six. Lucy, would you get a hat for yourself. You look like a skunk.'

'What—'

'Just do it,' he snaps.

'Fine.' I jump up and stomp out.

'Be worse if you smelt like one,' Dan whispers, coming up behind me.

I belt him. 'He has no right to comment on my appearance. I could have him for that.'

'Be easier to get the hat,' Dan says.

The Captain

He likes the dingy days and the drizzle. He peers out onto the streets as he drives by and sees the minions, walking, umbrellas held high against the wet. He sees the driver in the car behind him looking anxious, as if her life actually mattered. Putting on lipstick while peering into her rear-view, smiling at herself. Does she not realise that, if he chooses, he could extinguish her? Like the way he used to do with the ants when they invaded the house one hot summer.

That woman didn't like the ants: she put all sorts down to kill them.

He sat outside, cross-legged on the ground, staring down on them, like a god. He'd fix his eye on one and follow its progress across the yard, watch the way it stumbled over bits of grass and carried crumbs on its back. Working away. Being important. It had no clue that, in a second or two, it was going to die. He liked the choosing and the following and the making plans as to how he would do it. A foot? A rock? A piece of glass to burn them?

He didn't like the fact that he couldn't hear what they went through.

And then there was the blonde girl, from way back, five maybe she was, on the beach that summer's day. Oh, the terror in her eyes had been magnificent. And then—

'Sam.'

The word snags on his attention, like a briar pulling him back to the present. The item had moved on. He knows it had something to do with Lisa Moran. Calmly, methodically, he flicks the switches on his radio until he comes to another station where the news has only just begun.

'Gardaí on Achill Island, where Lisa Moran's body was found four days ago, have issued the following appeal.' A man's voice, deep, serious. 'As part of our investigation into the brutal murder of Lisa Moran, we would like to talk to anyone who works on a children's helpline or, indeed, any other type of helpline, and has recently or in the past been contacted by a young boy calling himself Sam. It is believed that this child might be in some distress.'

Black swamp clouds.

Fuck. Fuck. Fuck.

He wonders if she will.

Of course she will.

But forewarned is forearmed.

Maybe, he thinks, this can be her test.

24

'Are you sure about this?' Dan asks, as he hefts his case and sleeping bag from the boot of his car. 'You can change your mind if you like.'

'Unless you're going to make up with Fran in the next ten minutes I guess I have no choice.'

'Not going to happen in the next ten years.' He has the stubborn look on his face I've seen so many times in our partnership. It usually occurs when we're interviewing a witness we both know is guilty.

He seems pretty certain but he's mad about Fran. It's inconceivable to me that they'll break up. They're like my poster couple for happiness.

'Come on so, you total idiot.'

He flashes me a grateful look and dumps his belongings on the back seat of my car.

As I pull out of the station, I say a silent prayer that I'm not making a huge mistake. I go home to forget, to take my mind off whatever shit I've seen that day. I sit in a bath or listen to music and I push the images of the battered women and drugged-up young junkies and sobbing kids out of my head. And then I go in and do it all the next day. And murder, that's the icing on the cake of cases. It consumes the whole team, trying to find the guilty, trying to unearth the stories behind the killings. You take it with you through the day, the image of the victim, the voices of the witnesses, the stories, the endless reports. It's harder to shake off a murder investigation by closing your eyes. Sometimes you barely make it home, especially near the end of a case, because you want to keep poring over and over the stories until you tease out the strands, the knots, until it all makes a perfect tapestry. You get to know someone so well that you never knew existed while they lived. With Dan in my home, in my face, this murder is all we'll ever talk about. I won't be able to get away from it. But he can't sleep in his car because this case, until it's solved, will take up everything we've got.

My mother is amazed when Dan arrives on the doorstep.

'Fran threw me out,' he tells her wryly. To give her credit, she takes only a moment to absorb that before standing back to allow him in with his black bag. 'I've the kettle on,' she says matter-of-factly, 'so you just have a cup of tea and try not to let it upset you.' A pat on his back as he goes by before she turns to me. 'Lucy, I saw you on the news. That was a very peculiar hat you were wearing.'

'I know.' I say nothing more.

'Is it one of your own?'

'Nope. In there, Dan.' I point to the living room. 'Just leave your stuff behind the sofa.'

He goes on in and I follow my mother into the kitchen.

'What was all that about a boy called Sam? Is he in danger?' She flicks on the kettle.

'We don't know as yet. Mam, can we not talk about the case? Where's Luc?'

'He's the usual, in his room. Came in from school, went on his laptop. He says he's studying so I have to believe him. Ate his dinner, we saw the news. I recorded it just in case you wanted to see yourself.'

'No, I don't, it's fine. Should I go down to him?'

Her hesitation tells me what I already know.

'Do you have the number of Tanita?'

Another hesitation.

'I have to ring her and her family!'

My mother flaps her hand. 'I'll give it to you later, though maybe run it by Luc first.' She places a mug in front of me and sets one ready for Dan as she says, 'There was more than just you on the news. They brought TV cameras into Achill Sound and interviewed half the place. Do you want to see that?'

'No, thanks.'

The kettle clicks off and she makes a pot of tea while I stick four slices of bread into the toaster. I'm sure Dan will eat some.

'Is Dan very upset?' she asks, in an undertone. 'He was with his girlfriend a long time, wasn't he?'

Respecting Dan's wishes, I hadn't told anyone about his sexuality, but I'm not sure I want to lie by omission to my own mother. 'About four years. Don't ask him about it. He'll take your head off.'

'Between you and him, I think I'll move out so.' But she's smiling and I smile back.

'Ah, Dan,' she looks up as he comes in, 'would you like to see yourself on the news?'

He clearly doesn't want to offend my mother because he says, 'Yes,' then winces as I shoot him a murderous look.

My mother fiddles about a bit with the remote control. I hand Dan a plate of toast and he slathers it with butter. Luc drifts in. Looks at me. Then at Dan. 'Hey,' he says.

'Dan's staying for a bit, until after the case.'

'Oh, right.' He nods to Dan, ignores me, shuffles to the press, grabs a handful of biscuits and heads back to his room.

Dan smiles gamely in the tense atmosphere.

My mother presses buttons like a pro and seems to juggle about three remote controls to find what she wants. 'Here we go,' she says finally. 'Now, you do look a bit weird, Lucy,' she warns.

'Which is why I don't want to see this.'

But there I am, standing beside the Cig and the super, and the bright blue hat, which I'd borrowed from Susan, who clearly has a much bigger head than mine, is the most attention-grabbing thing in the whole picture. Everyone else looks very official, standing straight and tall, staring ahead, hands behind backs, like cool security guards. In contrast, I look as if I'm in the picture by mistake.

'Jesus.' Dan chortles and that starts my mother off.

'It's funnier when you see it the second time. Now, wait for this,' she says as the report moves back to the studio.

'We went onto the streets of Achill to talk to the locals,' the newscaster goes on, 'a lot of whom are concerned for their safety.'

'Fuck's sake,' Dan snaps. 'Bloody irresponsible. What—'

I'm about to tell her to turn it off when Mrs Dempsey appears onscreen. They got her with the school behind her. 'That's Lisa's boss,' I tell my mother before she asks, 'the headmistress in the school.'

'I know Delia, sure she taught you,' my mother says. 'Fond of the drink, she used to be. She's aged well. I was admiring her suit.'

214

'Lisa was a dedicated teacher and she will be a loss to us,' Delia says. 'We're devastated and that's all I have to say.' She puts up a hand against any more questions and walks off.

And then, mercifully, the screen goes blank and my mother exclaims in dismay.

Behind her back, I mouth, 'Phew' to Dan, who smiles.

Later, as my mother and Dan are watching TV, I head on down to Luc. I knock and he tells me to come in. As I push the door open, he says, 'I thought it was Nan.'

I let the words hang in the air for a moment, then say, 'I'm going to ring that girl's family and talk to them. I just thought I should let you know.'

'You won't!' He hops up.

'Actually, Luc, I will.' On this I have no problem arguing. 'I am, whether you like it or not, your mother. This girl is having your baby, my . . .' it feels all wrong '. . . grandchild, and the least we can offer them is our support.'

'I already did that. You are not to call.'

'It's not up for discussion.' And as he yells at me, I turn on my heel and walk out.

The Captain

A man who could adapt was a man who could survive, he thinks, as the call clicks through. It was far worthier to beat dangerous foes than placid ones.

Once before he had beaten a dangerous foe. He could still remember the crunch of bone, the terror in the eyes. The crack as skull hit ground.

He'd promised himself at the time that there would be no more. And, sure, he'd meant it too.

And then, quite by chance, he'd seen him with that blonde girl.

Smiling with the blonde girl.

More betrayal.

After everything.

Those blonde women with their soft voices were all fucking bitches going about saying one thing, doing another.

People needed to know that.

Bam fucking bam.

And the rage had poured forth like a volcano.

Pearl. Lisa.

And now . . .

He shouldn't call, but he has to.

At the other end, the phone is picked up. Before she can say anything, he says, 'It's Sam.' He waits a second, gathers himself. 'They broke their promise.'

Emma remains silent. Usually she tells him to take his time, he's safe now. And she adds 'Sam' to the end of her sentence and the way she says the name, all tender and caring, makes him want to slam her face into a wall for the lying she's doing.

And then the feeling comes. The memories. And he gulps hard so he won't cry.

'They broke their promise in a bad way.'

'Would you like to tell me about it?'

'No.' Tears now. 'I'm scared you'll tell.'

'This is a confidential line. We can't talk about our work to anyone.'

His heart might burst out of his chest. You don't tell. You can't tell. That's private. Family business. Telling people is bad.'

'What do you think you want to do?'

'I want to go away from here.'

There is a long silence. He has learned that that is a good sign. He breathes in, deep.

'How do you plan to do that?'

Emma is good at her job. She never tells him what to do. He'd normally hang up now, leave it, but he has to test her before it's too late. 'I don't know.' He dissolves into tears. 'I don't know. I just want to not be here. I need someone to come and take me away. They will kill me.'

'It's okay, Sam,' she says.

'Can you help?' he hiccups. 'Can you help me?'

The answer is a long time coming, but finally she whispers, 'Where are you?'

'Erris,' he answers, for he knows she lives nearby. He also knows a location he can name. He tells her he can run fast from his house to a place nearby. He's a fast runner. They get too sleepy with all the drinking to chase him at night. That's what he says.

She asks when. Not tomorrow, she says, because she's on the line again, until the early morning, filling in a gap.

He asks for the next day and she agrees. After work she'll be there. She won't let him down, she says. She describes her red coat.

Afterwards, he realises he's crying.

He takes a tablet and sleep comes.

25

Day Five

The next morning Dan and I are up before my mother and Luc. It's weird having Dan in the house. As I come out of the bathroom, he's hovering at the door, and we do a sort of dance, a sort of 'Oh, I didn't know you were there' and 'I've just got here', and then I have to search for a decent towel for him to have a shower. It feels a little too intimate but there's nothing I can do about it now.

I make some porridge for us and we eat it standing up at the kitchen counter while gulping down a mug of coffee.

'You and me arriving in the same car will send the rumour mill into overdrive,' Dan says.

I'm tempted to say that if he came clean to the boys in the station, no one would be talking about us, but I resist. 'Only thing worse than being talked about is not being talked about, right?' Then at his impressed look, I say, 'I didn't just make that up. That's Oscar Wilde.'

'I knew that,' he says.

He didn't.

★★★

When we arrive, there's a note on my desk for me to call Pat ASAP.

'You're on speaker, Pat,' I tell him, as he picks up. 'What have you got?'

'It looks like Pete Ryan and Lisa were better acquainted than he let on.'

Dan's eyes meet mine across the table. 'Go on,' I say.

'He knew her well enough to have her phone number. The earliest text is six months ago, though I only went back six months so there could be more. The text reads, *I can't risk it.* And she texts back, *You are pathetic.* Then nothing more until about six weeks ago. They get interesting then. I'm on my way to your office. I'll drop the typescript in.'

He strides in a minute later and plants the pages in front of us.

Dan and I bend over them.

'Here,' Pat says, pointing to some messages he's highlighted, with names as to who is texting. 'They date from the last week in October.'

> 23/10
> 12:34:12
> **Lisa: I need 2 see you Pete**
>
> 12:35:01
> **Pete: No**
>
> 12:35:50
> **Lisa: You'll be sorry**
>
> 12:39:00
> **Pete: I've made my decision.**
>
> 12:39:50
> **Lisa: Please?**

'He ignored that and then two days later,' Pat says, turning over the pages, 'the texts pick up again. Here.'

> 25/10
> 15:01:06
> Pete: What are you doing? FFS
>
> 15:30:01
> Lisa: I said I need to see you. Usual place or else . . .

'And the cherry on top,' Pat says triumphantly, turning to the final page.

> 17/11
> 16:50:29
> Pete: That better be it now
>
> 16:56:46
> Lisa: We'll see
>
> 17:00:09
> Pete: No, we won't. I'll fucking kill you if you come near me again.

'Beautiful,' Dan says, with a smile. 'Have the results on his car come back from Forensics yet?'

'They're expected later today,' Larry says. 'There was a bit of a delay.'

'Get them on it, make it a priority. Dig into his background. The wife said he had it hard. Was he ever fostered? Who are his parents? Check his phone calls, see if he made any to the helpline.'

'I'll look into that but chances are high he could have used another phone if he did.'

'That's a point, but try anyway, and keep on the background.' I nod to Pat. 'Good work.'

'Everyone,' William says, 'we're making progress.' He briefs the room on the latest developments, running through the phone messages between Pete and Lisa. 'We've also identified the boot prints found near the scene of the body. They're used for hiking and walking and generally heavy work.' An image of the identified boot appears. A pause before he goes on, 'We believe that they are the same boot prints that were found on Lisa Moran's neck. We have also established a link between Lisa Moran and Pearl Grey. They were both volunteers on helplines for children, they were both found wearing grey tracksuits and they were both badly beaten and suffered a lack of oxygen before death. Jim?'

Jim hands out the job sheets, explaining to each person why they've been assigned a particular job, keeping us all in the loop.

'Thanks, Jim,' William says. 'Let's get cracking.'

As people start to shuffle out, he beckons me and Dan towards him. 'We'll see what Forensics find in Ryan's car before we go hauling him in about the phone texts. I'm not jumping the gun again.'

'I agree,' I tell him.

Kev, the young lad who was on phones, pushes his way up the room towards us. 'Sorry I missed the meeting but I got a lady on the line who was contacted by a Sam last night. She saw the appeal this morning.'

'Is she local? Can she come in?'

'Bangor Erris, and she's coming in at eleven.'

'Talk to that girl when she comes in,' William says to me.

26

Emma Dowling sits opposite us, twisting the mug of tea she has requested in her hands. She won't drink it, she's too nervous. It's probably just as well: the mugs here never seem to wash properly and are permanently stained.

The first thing that strikes me is that Emma looks a little like Pearl.

And Lisa.

And that she's living in Erris, which is only a short car trip down the road.

The hair on the back of my neck prickles. I just know we're close.

'Emma, thanks for coming in,' I say. 'We'll take a written record of your statement, all right?'

'That's fine.' A quick, nervous smile. 'I hope I can help. Sam rings me at least once a week. Twice this week.' She puts down the mug and leans forward. 'Is he okay?'

I glance at Dan. His face is impassive. He's ready to write.

'Can you take us through what happened or happens when Sam calls you?' I ask.

Emma looks a little confused. Guilty almost. 'But is he—'

'It'd be better if you just talk us through what Sam says to you,' I say. 'But I'm almost certain Sam is fine.'

Emma relaxes. 'Good, because I think I messed up.' Her voice wobbles. 'I think he might be in trouble. He always rings and we have a chat, and he's normally upset because his mother seems to be abusive. He says she hurts him or hits him. Lately, though, the calls have been getting more distressing. She chains him up, leaves him to freeze outside, that sort of thing. And you're not supposed to get involved, see, that's drilled into you, but last night he begged me to help him and I said I would and—'

'He asked you to help him?' I interrupt, which I should never do. I want to kick myself and I know Dan is cursing me.

'Yes, but I should have done it sooner. I told him tomorrow.'

And I do it again. I lean so far across the table, I startle her. 'You're helping him tomorrow?'

Tears stand in her eyes. 'Yes. But he's all right, right? I haven't left it too late?'

'I'll be back in a second.' Dan says, giving me a warning look to stay quiet and to let her talk.

Then it's just me and Emma. In a moment, Larry arrives and takes Dan's place. It's noted in the written record.

'Emma,' I say, 'it's really important you take me through, step by step, what Sam said to you. What you said back – try to remember every word. From the very first call if you can.'

She nods, still upset, still thinking that something has happened to Sam. I wonder how she handles the horror stories she must hear on the helpline – she looks far too sensitive.

Hesitantly, a little jumbled at first, her story comes out, her words occasionally tripping over themselves but eventually, through questioning, I put a shape to it. As she talks, it's like a coldness creeps into the room and I shiver at the conversations she held with this person, the last one almost identical to the ones Lisa documented in her journal six weeks or so before she disappeared. It's as if time stops, as if the air grows thick. And Emma's words fill the space. I know in my gut that, for the past few weeks, this girl was within sniffing distance of a killer.

Larry must feel the same but we give nothing away.

'Does Sam call anyone else on your helpline?' I ask.

'No. See, he asked me when I was on – he trusts me.'

'What sort of a voice did the boy have? Accent? High? Low?' I lean forward, willing her to give us something we might use. 'Think hard.'

Emma cracks a wobbly smile, before she screws up her face and says, high and childish, 'Emma, is that you? My mammy is bold.'

Larry recoils.

'I'm a good mimic,' Emma explains. 'Sorry, I should have said.' A pause. 'That's what he sounds like. Exactly. West of Ireland accent and just . . .' a gulp '. . . innocent. And sad.'

'You're saying he definitely sounds like a child?'

'Of course. Why wouldn't—' I can see the penny drop. Shock in the brown eyes. She rears away slightly, her coffee sloshing. 'Is Sam not a child? He sounds so . . .' Then the question, almost like she's scared to ask: 'Who do you think it is? I—'

'We don't know, Emma,' I cut her off. 'Maybe it is a kid, maybe not. We're trying to find out.' And if he is a child, I think suddenly, where is he getting such frequent access to a phone? Maybe his parents are drunk and he sneaks theirs. But if he's so scared, would he risk it? My skin prickles.

'Is he calling a lot of helplines? Is that why you put the appeal out?' A moment, as more pennies drop. Her voice spirals. 'Is this to do with the Doogort murder? She worked on a helpline too, didn't she? Is it part of that?'

A moment before I nod, I see the fear creep into her eyes.

'Oh, my God.' It's said quietly. 'Was he – was he after me?'

'We don't know yet, Emma, but you did the right thing in coming forward. We can keep an eye on you now.'

'Oh, my God,' she says again. 'What happens now?' She looks from one to the other of us as if we have the answers. 'I said I'd meet him tomorrow.'

I ignore that for now and continue with the questioning. 'Have you met anyone new over the past while, Emma? Think hard.'

My firm tone seems to ground her a little. 'I work in the men's department of a clothes shop in Ballina,' she says. 'I'm always meeting people.'

'Anyone stand out?'

'No.' Pause. 'You *do* think this man is after me!'

'We don't know,' I answer, 'but, like I said, we're going to take care of you.'

'How?'

'That's what we need to figure out and we need you to help us,' I say. 'So, think again, anyone watching you or befriending you?'

'No. No one new.'

'Think.'

She does but still shakes her head.

'What about anyone here?' I place a number of pictures before her, Ryan included.

She stares at them for a moment, then says, 'I don't know . . . but if I only saw him once, you know . . . I'm useless with faces. I'm good with voices.'

I tuck the photographs away.

'Does Sam sound like anyone, then?' I ask. 'I know it's a child's voice but maybe there's a word he uses or a tone?'

A longer pause, but it's finished with a shake of her head. 'I can't believe that it isn't a little boy.'

I nod to Larry and we both stand up. 'Can you wait here for about ten minutes, Emma? We just want to run something by the SIO.'

'Of course. Yes.' Her hands shaking, she finally brings the mug to her mouth and takes a sip.

Dan joins me in the doorway. 'The Cig is contacting the super about putting a team together tomorrow, providing what we have is solid.'

'Solid? Is it not enough that she and Lisa received the exact same phone call? For all we know Pearl got it too.'

'And the fact that they all look the same,' Dan says.

'Which means he's scouting out these girls.'

He nods. 'That's if we're on the right track.'

'But we are,' I lean towards him. 'Can't you feel it?'

He grins.

'I have the press crawling all over me after that appeal last night,' the super says, on video link. 'I also have about thirty assault cases, a spate of petty burglaries by some feckers who drive down from Dublin, some idiot who comes in every day claiming the guards are corrupt, a flood of people complaining that Doogort Bog is still out of bounds, and you want me to set up a young woman with a potential killer? As well as that, you have no proof other than she'd win a lookalike contest with our victim.'

'Super, I—' I try to interject but he's on a roll.

'Do you know how many guards are already on this case?'

'Yes, but all I'm asking—'

'Nineteen. And have you got anything concrete yet?'

'Yes. The fact that—'

'Lucy,' William warns me quietly.

'Nineteen,' the super repeats.

'This is our best chance,' Dan wades in. 'If this man is responsible for the deaths of two women, we need to take our best chance. If we do nothing, Emma could be in danger anyway.'

'We could pull people off some other line of the investigation,' I say. 'At best it's only a couple of days we need them for.'

'And if we get him, we do have fingerprints and DNA at the Smyth farmhouse crime scene.'

'It's all "if".' The super shakes his head, 'You don't know for certain this is our guy?'

'The definite link between Pearl and Lisa is the phone line,' William says, in the cool way he has that makes people listen, 'and now we have proof that Emma is getting the exact same calls too.' He glances at us. 'Lucy and Dan are solid detectives.'

I feel pathetically grateful to him for that. Maybe after all this time, I've redeemed myself and extracted my reputation from Rob's.

Outside, through the window, we can hear someone cursing as they're dragged into the station. On screen, the super taps his pen on his desk, thinking. 'I want this kept quiet,' he says eventually. 'I do not need to read about a cock-up in the paper.'

'Absolutely.' Dan amuses me by crossing his heart.

The super gives him an odd look. 'Has Emma agreed?'

'Yes,' I lie. 'She's well up for it.'

William shoots me a sharp look and I avert my gaze.

'Right,' the super says. 'Give me a list of who you want. I'll make a few phone calls. I'll put the armed support unit on notice.'

'We'll need eyes on Emma as well until it's over,' William says.

'All right.'

'Thanks, we won't let you down,' I say.

'No, you won't,' he says, and disconnects.

'Emma's agreed?' William raises his eyebrows.

'In theory.' I flash a quick smile and leave before he can ask any more.

Emma is not happy. 'I never want to talk to the creep again,' she says. 'No.'

'It's our only chance to get him,' I say. 'We think he's a killer, Emma.'

'I know,' she says. 'And no.'

'If he goes on to kill someone else . . .' I let it hang. I feel bad for guilt-tripping her, but I get the feeling with Emma that it will work. After all, Sam has been doing it for weeks.

'That's – that's unfair. I'm not responsible for what he does.'

'No,' Dan agrees, 'but . . . I suppose you are responsible for what you do.'

'Or don't do,' I add.

This is unorthodox but sometimes you bend the rules, and I can see how much Emma resents our words. This girl owes us nothing. I hate how I'm prepared to use her, but Dan and I are on the scent now and, to be honest, we'll do pretty much anything to get our man. In a way, it makes us similar to our SO and that's a chilling thought sometimes.

'You'll be safe,' I say. 'You just have to live your life as normal for today and the next. We'll be watching. If he feels safe, so are you. Tomorrow night, we'll replace you with an officer. You won't have to meet him.'

The silence drags on. Emma fiddles with a ring on her right hand. The sounds of the station seem very far away.

Finally, she looks up. 'Just the next couple of days,' she says quietly, and Dan and I exhale in relief. 'I am not meeting him. And after this I'm going to take holiday leave.'

'Thank you,' I say. 'We'll be in touch and we'll have a team with you for your next shift in case he calls.'

She picks up her bag and glares at us. 'I just wanted to help,' she says. 'Not be treated like bait.'

Then she's gone.

27

After lunch, I decide to bite the bullet and ring Tanita's parents. Larry is scanning the CCTV from Castlebar so he's oblivious, and Pat has gone off to get a sandwich before re-examining the alibis of everyone we've interviewed. Again. Dan has gone with him.

I have the mobile number of Tanita's mother, which I forced out of my own mother. Facing the worst criminal would not have me as nervous as the prospect of speaking to this woman.

'Hello?'

A middle-class accent, I think in relief. And I'm appalled that I'm relieved. I'm a snob, I think in horror.

'Hello, is that Katherine?'

'Yes. Who is this?'

'My name is Lucy. I'm Luc's mother.'

A pause. 'I know who you are.'

How does she know who I am?

As the silence stretches, I jump right in, just like the guiltiest criminal. 'Sorry I didn't call before now, but, well . . . I only found out two nights ago and it's not that Luc didn't tell me, though he didn't, it was . . . Well, I work and, anyway, I know now and . . .' My voice trails off. 'Anything we can do, we will.'

'You've all done enough.'

It takes a second for the words to land, and when they do, I don't know what to say. Well, I do, only it would destroy any future relationship between her and me. So, I opt for, 'Well, we want to do more.' Which is precisely the wrong thing to say as well.

Another pause, this time longer. 'Thank you for your call but we have it in hand.'

'And, eh,' Christ, I'm babbling but I can't seem to help it, 'maybe we could all meet up, get to know each other.'

'Well, as I said, thank you for the call.'

And dial tone.

'Feck's sake,' I can't help exclaiming. It was easier and odder than I'd expected. A woman of few words.

'All right?' Dan asks, as he comes back in with a couple of coffees and a sandwich.

'I just rang the other grandmother.'

'And?' Dan chucks a sandwich at me and one to Larry, who is still peering hard at the CCTV.

'Honestly, she sounds like a cow.'

'Moo,' Dan says, as he unwraps his food, looks between the two slices of bread, sniffs approvingly and takes a bite. Chewing, he asks, 'Have you met this young wan?'

'No.'

'Is Luc on social media?'

'You can't hack his account!'

'I'm not. We're just going to look at it. That girl will be a friend of his.'

'Isn't it private?'

'He might have a public account, so . . .' Dan begins tapping buttons. 'So . . . let's see. Luc Golden.'

232

I say nothing, not wanting to stop him, but not wanting to tell him to keep going either.

'Most kids his age don't bother with Facebook,' Dan logs into Twitter and types Luc's name in. After some moments scrolling, he shakes his head. 'Let's try Instagram.'

And bingo.

I should have known that Luc would have an Instagram account. He is his father's son, after all. Rob, when he wasn't defrauding millions, was a keen photographer. Dan finds an account for a 'Luc Golden' and logs in. It's his. There are plenty of pictures of Luc with his friends, bright, colourful, amazing shots of happy kids. Drunk kids. A girl features a lot: Luc has his arm thrown over her shoulders, she's smiling up at him. He catches her in the act of eating an ice-cream, of sticking her tongue out. He takes shots of her hair as it flies about her face in the wind. He likes this girl. I wonder if it's Tanita.

'Great pictures,' Dan comments.

'Rob was a photographer,' I say.

'At least Luc inherited the good stuff.' He's scrolling through the comments and the likes on each picture, checking who they are. 'Oh, oh,' he says. 'This looks interesting. Here we go, a comment from a Tani.' Dan enters her name into Instagram and her photographs pop up.

'Me and the bump,' is her last picture. It shows her side-on, hand on her belly, supporting a huge bump.

She's not a bad-looking girl, though she's wearing way too much make-up and has eyelashes the length of my little finger. As Mick enters, I scroll down her page.

'All right?' Dan asks him.

There are pictures of her with a dog, of her barely dressed, of her with Luc. My heart squeezes as I see the big happy face on him. At least she was someone more to him than a—

'I managed to find one of the sons of Pascal Smyth,' Mick says, and my attention is immediately diverted.

'And?'

'I've got a home address for him in Castlebar. Plus a work address.'

'Isn't that where Pearl lived?'

'Yes,' Mick says.

'What do we know about this guy?'

'His name is Sam. He's single, though he's in a relationship. No kids. He manages a clothes shop in Westport. No priors.'

'Where is he now?' asks Dan, already pulling on his jacket.

'The lads in Westport say he's working. The name of the shop is Spaced. It's a hippie sort of place by all accounts.'

I think I've heard of it.

'You up for it?' Dan asks, glancing at me.

'Sure.' I pull on my jacket and scarf. 'Lead on.' I turn to Mick. 'Anything on the other brother?'

'Not yet. Susan's located his last set of foster parents, and they're happy to be interviewed. Do ye want to cover that as well? They're in Castlebar, which is only up the road.'

Dan looks at me. Everything is local. This whole case is from around here. It must mean something.

'Would it be better to wait until tomorrow night and see what pans out?' Dan wonders. 'See if he turns up for Emma?'

'We're just going to talk to this guy, just doing our job,' I say. 'If it's him, he won't spook. If it's not him, we might learn something anyway.'

28

Westport, where Dan and I are usually stationed, is a busy little tourist town with a large number of shops scattered across a few different streets. We drive up and down, along the banks of the Carrowbeg river, and finally find Spaced. It's situated in the middle of a row of brightly painted shop fronts. It looks fun and friendly and young.

I pull in.

It's a clothes shop, selling, from what I can see in the front window, hipster fashion. The window display is chock-a-block with white T-shirts sporting pictures of album covers while others bear slogans about saving the planet.

As we watch, a woman comes out of the place. Blonde. It registers like a punch. She calls, 'Goodbye,' to whoever is inside before blowing a kiss. Then she pits herself against the wind as she pushes her way past us up the street.

'Ready?' Dan asks.

'Sure.'

A bell rings as we enter and a young man with a long brown beard and well-cut hair emerges from a room in the back. He smiles amicably at us and takes up position behind the counter.

He's total hipster, jeans so skinny, his legs look ready to snap. A white T-shirt and a brown corduroy jacket.

'We're looking for Samuel Smyth?' Dan says.

'You're looking at him,' the man says, in a surprisingly soft voice that barely rises above a whisper. 'What can I do you for?'

There is something familiar about him, though I can't quite put my finger on it.

'Are you the son of Pascal Smyth?' Dan asks, and Sam jerks like he's been shot. His face, what I can see of it under the beard, bleaches white.

'Why?' Softer again. He has pressed his palms onto the countertop as if to steady himself. His fingers are long and slender.

'We've a bit of bad news,' Dan says.

Sam's gaze flits from Dan to me and back.

'I'm sorry to have to tell you that your father was found dead two days ago in his house near Doogort Bog.'

Sam nods. 'I heard on the news.'

'I also have to let you know,' Dan continues, 'that a woman was found on the property. Also dead.'

'He didn't—'

'It's unlikely,' Dan says, anticipating the question and Sam swallows hard. 'Now, I'm sorry,' Dan goes on, 'but we need to ask you some questions.'

'What?' Sam says, slightly bewildered. 'I can't tell you anything.'

'I know.' Dan rolls his eyes. 'That's what I said to my DI, but he's sent us out to interview you so I'm afraid it has to be done. I'm Detective Garda Dan Brown and this is Detective Sergeant Lucy Golden. Is there a place we can go, or I could arrange to have you down to the local station later on?'

'I haven't been to that house in a long time.'

We let the silence hang.

He sighs. 'I suppose it'd be better to get it over with.' He comes out from behind the counter, feet clicking in tan cowboy boots. He turns the 'Open' sign on the door to 'Closed'. 'We can talk in the back. There's not much doing now anyway.'

He leads the way to the room at the back of the shop. He's terribly thin, shoulders as narrow as a wrist, tiny waist. I'd imagine his face under the beard is hollowed out. This, I think, is a man who does not want to take up space.

Sam grabs a chair in the tiny storeroom while Dan and I sit opposite on two large boxes of stock. 'Well?' he says. He seems to have recovered.

'You don't seem too upset about your father?' Dan observes.

Sam's expression doesn't change. 'You're the guards. You know who my father was, what he did.'

'Who was he to you?' Dan asks.

Sam blinks. Then blinks again. Head dips as he massages his forehead. 'I don't know, really. I was only two when . . . when she . . . when he . . . I never saw him after that save for once a few years back.'

'How was that?'

'Awful,' he says simply.

'I mean, how was it that you saw him a couple of years ago?'

Sam flinches. 'Look, I have a partner and she doesn't know anything. I never—'

'Did he contact you?' Dan pushes.

'He wrote me,' Sam says, each word a struggle. 'A letter. I didn't think he knew where I lived. Told me he was back on the farm. Asked if I wanted to visit. Said he was sick, said he was fucking sorry for everything.' A long silence but in it I can see

Sam battling with the memory. 'So . . . I went.' He pauses. 'And it was shit. A mindfuck. He denied even writing me. Told me he loved me but to keep away. He made an eejit out of me.'

We watch as the memory plays out in the tiny twitches and tics of his facial muscles.

'I pushed my way in then. I told him he couldn't mess with me. He was just, fuck's sake, he was a small man. All my life, in my head, I'd thought he was huge.' His voice breaks unexpectedly and he wipes his nose with the back of his hand, sniffs a bit, then abruptly stands up. 'Sorry. Just – just a second.' He leaves the room and a few seconds later we hear sounds of vomiting.

Dan raises his eyes at me but we don't speak. The walls are paper thin.

'Sorry about that,' he says, coming back in. 'Stomach bug, I think.'

He's changed his T-shirt but he still smells of vomit.

'No worries,' Dan says. 'Can I ask if you recognise this lady here?' He passes Sam a picture of Pearl.

Sam shudders and drops the photo as if it's burned his hand. 'That's Pearl,' he says.

'That's right. She was found in your dad's house,' Dan says.

Sam's only response is to wipe a hand across his face.

'Any ideas on how she got onto your father's farm?'

Sam puts up his hand. 'Can you stop with the father? Please? His name was Pascal.'

'All right,' Dan says. 'Any ideas?'

'Don't know. Don't know.'

'Did you know Pearl?'

'No, I just . . . She was from Castlebar, where I'm from . . . It was in the paper when she went missing.'

'How about this girl? Do you know her?' Dan hands him a picture of Lisa.

A moment, then puzzled: 'That's the murdered girl, the one found on the . . .' He stops, raises his eyes to us. 'What's going on?'

'Would you know of any link between your father, Pearl and this girl?'

A second before he throws the picture down. 'I think you should go.'

'Fine. When can we catch you at home?'

'You can't come to my place. I don't want Evie to know.' He rises and suddenly he doesn't look as harmless. Jabbing a finger in Dan's direction, he says, 'She has nothing to do with this shit. She's – she's untainted by it, for fuck's sake.' He turns away and leans a hand against the wall, bows his head. When he turns back to us, his eyes blaze. 'My ma, whom I barely remember, was beaten and choked. I was two. I had no clue what was happening. I was dumped on a family that took me in because they were paid to do so. My brother, the only person left, was taken away from me. I have seen my old man once in twenty-odd years. I don't see Ken any more. I don't have anything to say.'

'Do you know where your brother is?'

There's a weird look on his face, haunted almost. 'No.'

'When was the last time you saw him?'

'I can't . . .' He shakes his head, squeezes his eyes shut. 'Can you just stop? Please.'

There is a silence.

'Sorry if this is upsetting,' Dan says quietly. 'You've been great. Have you any idea where your brother is, just so we can inform him about Pascal?'

'He won't care.'

'Even so.'

'Last I heard he was in England. But that was years ago. He came to see me in my foster carer's house. I was, like, fifteen. First, I was delighted to see him and then it just got weird. We couldn't do the normal stuff and we can't talk about what went on. So, it's easier not to talk at all.'

There's a world of grief in the remarks.

Dan feels it, too, because he says, 'That's hard.'

A shrug.

'Did you ever ask for help when you were growing up?'

The silence that follows is oppressive. Sam's expression shifts, his eyes close off, he pulls slightly back from us. 'What has that to do with anything?'

'I'll take that as a yes,' Dan says. 'What sort of help did you look for?'

'We looked for none,' he says. 'How would we trust anyone? So, take it as a no.'

Outside someone bangs on the shop door.

'Are we done?' he asks.

'If your brother contacts you, let us know.' Dan makes to hand him a card but Sam doesn't take it. Dan leaves it on the table. 'It's important we speak to him.' Then he asks, 'Where were you last Friday between three and five?'

'Hello? Hello? Sam! Is this place open?' the person outside roars.

'That's the boss.' Sam moves to the door. Then, over his shoulder, he says, 'I was here, working. Why?'

'We'll need to confirm that with someone,' Dan says. 'Who would know?'

240

'The other shop owners, if they remember.' Sam opens the door to a tall, middle-aged man.

'What's going on here?' He glares at all three of us as he steps inside. 'Sam, you've been told before—'

'They were selling,' Sam says. 'I shut the shop for ten minutes while they showed me their wares. I've no cover today so . . .' He lets the sentence hang. 'I'll be in touch,' he says to us, as we pass him.

'Nice lie,' Dan whispers to me.

'Smoothly told,' I say back.

We call Larry to request CCTV footage from shops in the area.

29

Molly and Alan Brennan are elderly, a little uptight. Their house is tiny but trim with nothing out of place. Things are polished and shiny. A little like them.

They have no idea where Ken is but invite us in for tea anyway.

'Children from chaotic backgrounds like order,' Molly says, as she leads us into a pink and grey dining room with curtains straight out of the 1980s. There is an old-room smell of floor polish and stale air. Alan comes in bearing a tray with tea, little delicate sandwiches and a plate of biscuits. As Dan and I sit down on an over-soft sofa, Molly gets a side table and positions it in front of us. Then Alan sets out the tea. 'Eat up,' they say in unison, before taking their seats.

Dan and I don't need to be asked twice. Dan takes about five sandwiches and settles back on the sofa, his notebook balancing on his knee.

'Egg,' Alan says. 'And cucumber.'

'Tasty,' Dan says.

'It must be rewarding being a foster parent,' I begin, trying to put them at ease.

'Yes.' Molly smiles brightly.

'Very.' Alan nods like his head might fall off.

'Did you foster many children?'

'Loads.' That's Molly.

'Plenty,' Alan says.

'What does it involve?' I ask Alan.

'At first,' he begins, licking his lips and clapping his hands together, 'it's just for one or two nights.'

'That's right,' Molly says.

'For children whose parents are in hospital and that, but then, as time goes on, you get the more challenging cases.'

'That's right,' Molly agrees.

'Was Ken difficult?'

'Oh, yes,' they say together, laughing a little and then looking guilty.

'You can't blame the boy,' Molly rushes to say, as Alan does an eye roll. 'His circumstances were complex so that wouldn't have helped. He must have been about ten when he came here.' Her voice dips. 'He'd been very disruptive in the other houses. But then again, by all accounts no one heard the half of what went on in his home. He and his brother never talked about it. They say the boys saw the blood . . .' The words hang. 'And then to lose his brother . . . He was . . . ruined.'

'It was very sad,' Alan chimes in.

'Very sad,' she agrees. 'And we did our best but,' she looks at Alan, 'I think he was too far gone.'

'We had him for eight years,' Alan says. 'And it was too long.'

'Don't say that.' Molly tsks. 'We were just too late,' she says then. 'Too much had happened to him.'

I glance at Dan, who is helping himself to another sandwich. He'd better be writing this down. He catches my look, shovels the sandwich wholesale into his mouth and picks up his pen.

'They tell you not to ask them about themselves,' Molly goes on, 'the agency and that. The children do tend to open up in their own time, once they trust you. Kenneth didn't have any trust for anyone. He spent a lot of time on his own, didn't mix with other children.'

'He was odd,' Alan says, braving a look from his wife. 'I don't like to say it about our foster children but Kenneth *was* odd. He had a way of looking at you that was . . . downright scary.'

'He did not,' Molly snaps. 'I never saw that.' She appeals to us: 'Honestly, I never did. Sometimes he could be sweet. He was a sad boy.'

'He was. And he was blank.'

'Blank?'

'Blank. He was blank. And that's . . . well, I found it uncomfortable.'

'Blank.' Molly rolls her eyes. 'He was just quiet. That's all. He didn't laugh much or enjoy things but he never did anything bad either.'

'He killed the goldfish.'

'They were old,' she says. 'We all let him down. Everybody.'

I get the feeling Molly would find good in Lucifer. It's a nice trait, which I sadly lack. 'And you don't know where he is now at all?'

'The moment he turned eighteen, he left,' Molly says. 'We did offer him a room.'

'*You* offered it to him,' Alan says, and I wonder how many rows they've had over Ken. 'I was glad he left.'

'I know he went abroad that time,' Molly says, 'and worked. He was a worker, I'll give him that. But it's been years now and we haven't heard a word from him. Our other long-term children always keep in contact but Ken never did. Alan sometimes looks him up on the internet for me, but there's never anything.'

Alan nods, but his eyes slide away from me.

'When he left, he left,' Molly says. She straightens, crosses her legs. 'It hurt but you learn to let go.'

'Would you have a picture of him?' I ask.

'I don't think so,' Alan says.

There were no pictures of the boys in the paper at the time. The only ones we managed to find were taken by the social workers when they went into care. The pictures are blurred.

'Alan, go and look in the box under the stairs,' Molly says, 'the wooden one we used for toys.'

'It'll take hours,' Alan says.

'We don't need it now,' I say. 'If you find anything, it'd be great if you could email it to us or drop it into the station in Achill as soon as you can.'

Alan smiles bleakly, not enamoured by the idea at all.

I hand him my card. 'My email is on that. Contact me. How was he at school?'

'Aw, sure, I forget,' Molly says. 'He was good at art, I do know that. There's a picture he did for a Leaving Certificate project. It's in the attic. Alan will hunt that out too.'

Alan throws her a pained look. 'Are you sure it's there? I don't want to waste—'

'I am not going to throw out a painting by a foster child, am I?' she says. 'It's there all right. I wasn't mad about it. Sort of a weird-looking thing, but I know he got an A for it.'

'The picture and a photo would be good.' I smile, thinking we might get some prints from it. 'Thanks for your time.' I stand up and shake their hands as Dan helps himself to a couple of biscuits. He's polished off the whole tray of sandwiches by himself.

'I got it all down,' he says, under his breath, as we leave. 'You don't need to look at me like that.'

I have to smile.

30

We are in William's office.

'Forensics say she's all over it,' Larry tells me, on the phone.
'There is no doubt that Lisa Moran was in Pete Ryan's car. He's had
it cleaned recently too, but they found one hair that matches Lisa's
DNA and also a fingerprint on the dashboard. Unfortunately, we
can't say when she was in the car, but she was there.'

'And he's rung that helpline.' Pat lays the proof in front of
William. 'From his own phone, if you can believe that.'

'And they exchanged angry texts, one when he threatens to
kill her,' I say. Then, 'Did he ever ring Pearl's number?'

'I didn't go back that far,' Pat says.

'It's enough. I want the dossier on Ryan.' The Cig nods to me.
'I want you to read it cover to fucking cover, Lucy, and then go,
rearrest that fucker and find out what the prick knows.'

William said 'prick'. And 'fucker'. How very unlike him.

It's kind of attractive in a weird William way.

'I'll do it,' I say, and am gone.

The dossier Pat has put together on Ryan is comprehensive. To
my disappointment, he is not the missing Smyth boy, because

247

he came from west Dublin and is basically a poor boy who married a rich girl. A clever poor boy, who got to college on a grant and did accountancy. Then, working in a small firm, he met and married the owner's daughter, and in less than eight years was head of accounts and had managed to turn the place around. The photograph Dan and I saw framed in their house had appeared in a society magazine. There are a few more pictures of Pete and Jane on file at various charity functions. Then came the crash when he and his wife lost their jobs. After a year, they also lost their heavily mortgaged house.

There are reports on file from the council about difficulties in rehousing them as they expressed a desire to stay on in the same area and let their children continue at the same school. Eventually, after two years of living in hotel rooms, they took the house in Achill.

'Another bad choice in a series of bad choices,' I remark, flicking through the file.

'There isn't much on his early years, is there?' Dan asks. 'I was hoping he might have been fostered or had a brother called Sam.'

I glance up. Dan offers me a doughnut from a bag he has somehow procured. I take one. 'You don't think he's our man, do you?'

Dan licks sugar from his fingers, then wipes his hands down his trousers. 'I don't know. He's definitely holding out on us, but my gut is pointing towards that house on the bog. Ryan doesn't fit the rest of the picture but, hey, he's lied to us, he's been in contact with the victim, so he has a part to play in this somehow.'

'Yep.'

By four o'clock Pete Ryan has been rearrested, taken from the holding cell and escorted into the interview room. He looks scared now, as he probably should. He slides into the chair almost with an air of apology. 'I knew her, all right?' he says. 'That's what this is about?'

Dan reads him his rights, explains to him why he's here again. 'This interview is being recorded and filmed,' he says. 'You have a right to a solicitor and—'

Pete waves his hand in the air. 'I've been told all that. Look, I don't want a solicitor. I don't want anyone to know I'm here. Especially not my wife.' A pause. 'She doesn't know, does she?'

Dan ignores him and reads him his rights again, then says, 'Not unless you told her in your allowed phone call.'

'I refused one,' he says. Then, on a sigh, 'I'll tell you every-thing but . . .' he groans '. . . I did nothing to her.'

Dan flashes me a look. 'All right, off you go.'

Pete looks as if he can't believe it.

'We just want to get to the truth,' Dan says. 'That's why you're back again. Go ahead.'

There is silence. After a second, Pete closes his eyes and mas-sages his forehead with his fingertips. More silence and then, 'I wish I'd never met the bitch.' There is no fury in the words, just the tone of deep regret. He doesn't meet our gaze, just stares down at the battered Formica table. 'I am so sick of everyone going on about how lovely she was. The way the papers are making her into a saint. She was no saint – at least, not where I was concerned. Truth? Part of me was bloody relieved when she ended up dead.'

This guy is walking into a whole pile of shit and he doesn't even smell it, I think.

'It was true what I told yez that I met her last year. She was my eldest girl's teacher. And there was this parent-teacher meeting and Jane couldn't make it so she asked me to go instead because

249

she was worried, you know. Jane worries a lot about the girls. Too much, maybe. Us losing everything has changed her. And Nash was shy and her life had turned upside down, and we'd been forced to send her to that school. And I'd been in trouble and, anyway, I went along to the meeting and . . .' He stops, like he's remembering. 'Well, I had all these questions to ask that Jane had written down for me, but Lisa just said that Nash was a lovely child and she was a pleasure to teach and that she was very bright and it was the nicest thing anyone had said to me in the last few years. I was hungry for it, you know?' A shaky sigh. 'To hear your child praised by a stranger is wonderful. To not be judged because I'd been in prison was . . .' He swallows hard, blinks. 'I started to . . .' A groan. 'I got emotional. It had been a tough few years and she was so kind. I broke down, I did. Fuck, I hate that I did.' He stops, swallows some more and glances up at us.

I can see where this is going. And it might answer one question we have, but it's not going to be enough.

'Anyway,' Pete goes on, 'for a joke, she handed me a comfort teddy, saying it helped the kids she taught, and I laughed and so did she, and then I, well, I left.' He shakes his head. 'But, fucking eejit that I was, I couldn't stop thinking about her. She was like this balm on an open sore. Things were not good at home. I'd been in prison, Jane was stressed out, like I'd never seen, the kids were not happy and Lisa was . . . there.'

I bite my tongue. How convenient to blame everyone else for his seedy affair.

'I pestered her. I'm not proud of it. I rang her in work, I made excuses to see her about Nash, and in the end we had a bit of a thing. I actually think she felt sorry for me.' A pause, then bitter, 'Lisa was, I dunno, drawn to people in need.'

'When you say a "thing"?' Dan asks.

Pete looks like he wants to punch Dan. 'An affair, right? A grubby affair.'

'When was this?' Dan asks.

'Back in January.' He waits for our response, and when we stay silent, he goes on, 'I hated myself. I knew it was wrong but I couldn't help it. Being with her was like being in confession or something. I'd even ring her when she was on the helpline she did and ask her for help, and she'd laugh and tell me to stop.'

Neat, I think. He knows we know he'd been phoning the line.

'And then one morning I just woke up and Jane was lying there beside me in the bed, asleep, and I thought, What the fuck am I doing? I just . . . I love my wife, I do. We have history, she saw in me what I could be and we worked bloody hard. I never wanted to go back to the way I was before I met her but somehow I did and . . . Anyway, me being with Lisa was like me abandoning Jane. Leaving her to cope. So, sometime around March maybe, I told Lisa it was over. She was grand about it, a bit pissed off that she hadn't done it, I think, but overall . . . she took it well, which was why I don't understand what happened after.'

We wait.

'I didn't hear from her for months. I think we were both relieved it was over. And then, about eight weeks ago, less maybe, out of the blue, she rings me up to meet her. I said I would because, well, I liked her and I figured I owed her, and she sounded a bit . . . off, and anyway, she asked me for money. Me? I don't have a bloody bean! Oh, she said she'd pay it back and it was just a loan, but I told her no way. So she told me she'd tell Jane about the affair if I didn't pay her off. I still said no because I didn't believe her. It just didn't seem like her and I ignored her calls and that, but about a week later, she started all the Kara stuff. Like, she knew my wife would go crazy because all the teachers in that school know what Jane's like. She watches them like a hawk. So, I told Jane I'd have a word with Miss Moran and I went into the school and she told me it was my last chance so I paid up.'

'Just for the record, are you saying Lisa Moran was blackmailing you?'

'Yes. I had to take on the illegal jobs to keep Jane from seeing how little I was actually bringing home. And that's it. That's the story.'

It seems bizarre that Lisa would do that. It goes against everything we know about her. But the timeline fits with everything else.

'Tell me about that Friday again. From the beginning,' Dan says.

'Again?' Pete heaves a sigh. 'Right.' And once more he tells us the same story and it squares with his earlier account. He finishes with, 'I went up Luck Lane and it was deserted. Then I thought I'd missed her, so I reversed for a bit and went back, but I hadn't. She was not there.'

'This part of the road,' Dan lays out the pictures of where we think she disappeared, 'you drove by here and saw nothing.'

'Yes.'

'Did you actually see her go up Luck Lane?'

'No. I just guessed it because she wasn't on the street or in the shops, and I thought it would be the only other way for her to get home, even though it was longer. Or I thought maybe she was visiting someone up there.'

Dan leans back in his chair. 'I find this hard to understand,' he says. 'You admit an affair, you admit she blackmailed you, yet you say you did nothing.'

'Yes, I admit to all that. I did not kill her.'

'She was in your car?'

'Yes. But not that day.'

'You're saying Lisa blackmailed you?'

'I said already, yes.'

'She indulged in behaviour that might have lost her her job just so she could get your attention and extract money from you?'

'She seemed desperate,' Pete says. 'It was weird. And, yeah, I told her she'd lose her job but she was confident she wouldn't. That head teacher backed her to the hilt. Maybe Lisa had something on her . . .'

'Oh, come on, we're talking about a twenty-five-year-old girl who volunteered on a children's helpline. She went running, she loved glitter.'

'And she blackmailed me,' Pete snaps. 'And she used my kids to do it and my wife.'

'You must have been furious with her,' Dan says.

'I was.'

'Did you ever threaten her?'

Pete pales. 'That text? I didn't mean it. I was annoyed. It was just a thing to say.'

'But you followed her after school that last Friday when she went missing?'

He flushes. 'I know I did . . . I was still so angry at her . . . I don't know what I would have done to her if I had caught up with her that day, that's the truth. I wouldn't have killed her, I'm not . . . Anyway, I didn't see her. She had gone by the time I drove that road. I told you that.'

'How much money did she want from you?' Dan goes

backwards now, seeing if Pete can keep up. If it's a lie, he'll flounder.

'Two hundred a week, only I couldn't manage that sometimes.'

'What did she want it for?'

'She called it a loan. Said it was for a "good cause".' He laughs suddenly. 'As if that made what she was doing all right. She was a bitch.'

I'm betting this is how she found the money to pay Clive. She'd gone from her father to her ex. Or maybe she'd asked Pete first. Either way, it doesn't matter. I think now of what her best friend had said about her, that she liked getting her own way, hadn't talked to her father for weeks when he refused to comply. Maybe there is a bit of steel in this girl.

And I also think that Sam must have been a very convincing caller. I can feel the hairs on my neck prickle. 'Do you know a man called Samuel Smyth?'

The change of subject startles him. 'No. Why?'

'Ken Smyth?'

'No.'

'Ever see this girl?' Dan pushes the picture of Pearl across the table.

Pete picks it up, then looks at us. 'What the hell are you trying to do to me? That's the girl that was murdered.' He folds his arms. 'I'm not saying any more. I want a solicitor.'

'DG Dan Brown and DS Lucy Golden leaving the room. Interview terminated at three forty.' Dan switches off the recorder and I gather our things and stand up.

'We'll organise that for you,' I say.

'I did nothing,' Pete shouts. 'Do you hear?'

'Can we agree that this is your statement?' I ask, and read back to him what I've written down.

'Yes,' he says. 'I did nothing.'

'Then sign it here, please.'

He does so, then Pete and I sign it too.

'Interview concluded at sixteen forty-five,' Dan says, flicking off the DVD.

We close the door on him.

Dan looks at me. 'D'you fancy a break?'

31

We're in the pub across from the station. The barman serves Dan a strong coffee and me a cappuccino.

Dirty grey light slants in the window, gaudy decorations hang from the ceiling, and a Christmas tree, looking as if it's been attacked by dogs, stands drooping in a corner.

'This is cosy,' Dan says, and I think he means it.

We click coffee cups. In the background Bruce Springsteen is telling us to 'better watch out'.

'Thoughts?'

'He's lied to us twice now,' I say, 'but this time I think he's on the level. And the more I'm finding out about Lisa, the more I'm convinced she was a force to be reckoned with.'

'Yeah?'

'Think how she treated her dad when she didn't get her own way. She didn't speak to him for weeks. Then Sarah described her as saying that she punished Liam for not doing what she wanted, how Liam's mother was annoyed with her. Yes, she was a nice kid, she loved teaching, she was childish in her way, but she was also spoiled and used to getting what she wanted. I'd bet she made her dad's life hell when he left her and her mother. And maybe she viewed Pete in the same light as her father and was punishing him.'

'It's all a bit speculative,' Dan says, 'but, yeah, I can buy some of it, though I think, from what we know of her, she probably would have paid Pete back.'

I nod. 'She was desperate to find Sam. Think how traumatic it must have been for her to hear a child she'd been talking to week after week being beaten and to be powerless to intervene.' I would probably have tried to find him too.

'Why didn't she lose her job, though?'

'I was thinking about that. Delia is a snob. She'd have hated the Ryans trying to push one of her teachers out.'

'Still doesn't explain it.'

'She was near retirement, she had nothing to lose.'

Dan nods. 'I'll see if Jim can get one of the lads to interview her again and focus on the charges against Lisa, but Ryan's story fits with everything we know.' He pulls out a packet of crisps and offers me some.

'You're supposed to buy them here,' I say.

'I did, yesterday, and never got around to eating them.' He shoves a handful into his mouth. 'We might as well keep Ryan on the rack for another while, just in case. Any news from Luc?'

'No. Fran?'

He makes a face, gives me the two fingers and we turn back to contemplating our coffees and our lives to the backdrop of Dan munching. Some other cheesy song comes on and I think suddenly that I used to actually like Christmas. Now I find the cheer and the drinking and the chirpiness depressing. I hate the winking lights and the designer Christmas trees. I hate the frantic nature of it all.

'Isn't this a truly crappy pub?' Dan says fondly.

'Yeah, but at least it's real.'

He doesn't ask what I mean.

Just then, Stacy arrives, a little dishevelled. We haven't seen her in a couple of days.

'Marvellous,' Dan says.

Stacy spots us and, though she knows she shouldn't, she can't help herself. 'Hi.' She waves.

We ignore her but she crosses towards us, whipping out a voice recorder. 'Any more news on the murders?'

'What murder?' Dan says, draining his cup. 'The murder of the nosy journalist?'

'It's my job to be nosy,' Stacy says, pulling off a great woollen scarf, 'and a detective joking about a murder is not a nice head-line. Lugs Larkin posted on his page the other day that he thinks the Smyth murder and Lisa Moran's are related. Have you any comment on that?'

'Yes.' Dan bends down and speaks into the microphone. 'Lugs Larkin is a vlogger. He has, in his own words, a "boring as shit life" and his attempts to spice it up are a little sad, frankly.'

'Can I quote you on that?'

Dan rolls his eyes and we make for the door.

'Have you any suspects in this murder?' Stacy calls. 'I heard you're working on a few lines of enquiry.' We're halfway out before she says, a little desperately, 'Aw, come on, Fran said you were really nice.'

That stops us in our tracks.

'You don't know Fran.' Dan turns to glare at her.

'I met him in the station the day he came in and you both left and he came in here and I followed him because I thought he was a witness but it turns out he's, like, your boyfriend.'

Dan stiffens, like a rabbit in headlights. His eyes dart about to make sure no one from the station is around.

'And he was, like, upset with you because your family don't know anything about him and I bought him a coffee and said you sounded like a bastard, and he said, no, you were generally grand and that he didn't understand it, and then in the end he agreed that, yes, maybe you were a—'

'Shut up,' Dan says to her.

She stops, shocked.

We watch as he stomps out of the pub, slamming the door behind him.

After a moment, Stacy says, 'That Fran is well out of it.' Then to me, 'Can you give me a quote?'

'Yeah. You'd be better off out of it too.' I tip her a salute and leave.

It's about thirty minutes before Dan joins me back at the office. I'm typing up the Ryan statement while wondering if we'll manage to get an extension to his detention and thinking we probably won't. I sense rather than see Dan sit opposite. I'm almost afraid to look at him.

'You probably think I'm a bastard,' he says, after a few minutes.

'You mean Stacy didn't just make it up.'

'That rag she works for? I wouldn't be surprised.'

I manage a smile.

Dan sighs. He massages the bridge of his nose with his thumb and forefinger. Looks about to make sure Larry and Ben aren't around. 'Fran wanted to go to my folks for Christmas,' he says. 'So I had to tell him I hadn't told my family about him.'

My face must say it all.

'It's no one's business.'

'You keep saying that, but there's a difference between being private and living a lie.'

I think I must have hurt him. He stands up, says softly, 'You don't know the first thing about me, Golden, not the first thing.'

I watch him leave.

The Captain

His hand trembles as he dials. She said she'd be working again tonight. He pictures her, blonde hair falling across one eye as she sits at her desk. He isn't sure if there even is a desk, but in his imagination there is. A brown one with a flower on it.

He sees her, in his head, pale arm reaching out to lift the phone.

'Kids in Crisis, this is Emma, how can I help you?'

He's psychic, that's what he is.

She sounds different, though. Or maybe that's just in his head too.

'Emma,' he says. 'It's me.'

A moment. A click. 'Sam?' Like she birthed the word.

He has to hurry.

'Yes.' He gulps. 'Will you really come tomorrow?'

'Yes.'

He starts to sniff. 'Thank you.'

She says nothing. The silence stretches. Then, 'It's all right. I'll be there.'

'And you won't get into trouble?' Sad, pathetic little Sam. The love of the woman's life.

'No one will know,' she says.

She's right. No one will. 'Okay.'

A moment. A gulp. 'I'll see you there, Sam. I'll have a red coat. Be careful.'

And she hangs up.

He smiles, relief filling him from his toes, making them curl and flex.

He makes his way to the all-night café on the corner of Parliament Street.

All the better to see her.

32

It's begun to snow a little as I hop out of the car that evening. Two weeks from Christmas and already the odds on a white Christmas are narrowing because the weather has been unseasonably cold. There's a fine dusting on the path already and I slip a little as I hurry to the front door. It's after eleven and I've just had a text to say that Sam had rung Emma at the Kids in Crisis centre, that the offices were being watched just in case he showed up and that arrangements have been made for tomorrow.

I dial William because I just know he'll still be mooching about on the case.

'The place he's picked in Erris has no CCTV cameras,' William says, without even a hello, knowing what I want before I even ask. 'No surprises there. We're pulling CCTV from around Erris for the last few weeks, just to see if we can spot any car that matches the ones in Luck Lane. But, best of all, Larry contacted me to say he went through CCTV from Pearl's case and he spotted the blue Fiesta there.'

'How does he know it's the same car? We've no reg for the one in Luck Lane.'

'Same sticker on the front windscreen. It's a clearer reg too, not complete but it's our man.'

'That's bloody brilliant.'

I think William is smiling down the line at me. 'And we have a team in place for tomorrow?' I ask then.

'Yes. And we let Ryan go. He wasn't around to make any calls to Emma. In the interview with Delia, she broke down apparently and said she'd been caught drinking on the job by a few teachers about six months ago and she was afraid it would come out if she disciplined Lisa.'

'Lisa blackmailed her?'

'Apparently Lisa never said anything but Delia wasn't going to take the chance. She knew Lisa was popular with the rest of the staff and maybe one of them would think it was rich her disciplining Lisa and it would all come out. Lisa took a chance that I reckon she knew would pay off.'

Delia always had a reputation as a drinker when I was in school. That whole buttoned-up look she has is a sham.

'Are you going to keep tabs on Ryan for now, though?' I ask.

'Yep.'

'Okay. Thanks, Cig.'

He hangs up and I let myself in.

The Captain

The café is a dirty kip, like all-night places always are. And the people in them tend to be junked up or tanked up or half falling asleep. He sits, nursing a coffee, right at the window, across the road from the call centre. Behind him, some young lad is trying to chat up a girl. He can see their reflections in the dirty window. The young lad is leaning in and nuzzling her when all he should do is take her.

Friday night and the shit is stirring.

The fluorescent light is flickering on and off, on and off. Every fucking ten seconds. It's enough to give him a migraine but then Emma pops into his head and he stills and imagines tomorrow, what he will do to her, what she might say and how it all might go.

But he must be certain. He sips the coffee and it tastes shite. Still, he hunches over his cup trying to ignore the hypnotic on and off of the Christmas lights outside. And the off and on of the fluorescent light inside.

The night before the take, he likes to watch his girls. To see the one he has picked. To enjoy the fact she has no clue that tomorrow she will be at his mercy.

He likes that.

There is another reason he's here tonight, which he does not like.

Those guards and that fucking appeal.

Did she go to them?

Is she setting him up?

If she is, he will show no mercy.

His grip on the coffee cup tightens and he has to take deep breaths to relax.

33

'My old man beat the shit out of me,' Dan says, apropos nothing.

I'm in the front room, on my second glass of wine, eating a large packet of salt and vinegar crisps that I found in the drawer under the TV. The house is quiet, everyone in bed, except us two. Before I can think of an appropriate response to Dan's words, he sits beside me.

I wait. Steal a sideways glance at him.

He's leaning forward on the sofa, hands clasped between his knees.

After a bit, he says, into the quiet, 'When I was ten, I came home from school and told my ma that my best friend had kissed a girl. I thought it was,' a rueful shrug, 'hilarious, the way kids do. And my ma was laughing right back and she says to me . . .' He swallows hard, and with a bit of difficulty, he goes on: 'She says, "What girl do you like, Danny boy?" And I said I liked boys, not girls.' He stills, remembering, 'And before I could blink, I was halfway across the kitchen with my mouth busted and my da yelling at me to never say that again.'

I take the spare glass, fill it to the brim with wine and hand it to him.

'Ta.' He stares into it, heaves a sigh. 'I had no clue what I had done wrong, but over the next few years, it was like he was obsessed. I got beaten for anything I did. If I looked at a painting, if I commented on fashion, if I said some fella was good at sport, everything, I was fucking black and blue heading to school.'

'Bastard,' I say.

He takes a gulp of wine. 'Dublin's inner city, where I come from, you can't be gay, Luce. All this gay marriage and equal rights, it's a red rag to a bull where I'm from. Still is. My da was toughing me up in the only way he could. He beat me so the others didn't.'

'He was assaulting you,' I say. 'That wasn't love.'

He throws me a sideways glance. 'If I thought like that, I'd go under altogether,' he says.

'Sorry.'

'So, he's not exactly a man I can introduce Fran to.'

'He can't beat you up now.'

'It's not that I'm scared of him. It's just he doesn't deserve to know, Luce. Fran doesn't deserve my old man's poisoned opinions.'

'And your mother?'

A hitch of breath, a long exhale. 'She stood by while he spat at me, kicked me, punched me. That was worse.'

'I'm sorry, Dan.'

'You can't outrun a childhood like that, Luce. Like you move on and distance yourself but it gets in your head. He hated that part of me and I hate it too.'

I find that unbearably sad. I say, 'Fran is that part of you.'

He turns away.

'Have you told Fran any of this?'

'What do you think?'

268

'I think you should.'

He half laughs as if the idea is preposterous.

'You told me, why can't—'

'Yeah, but . . . you've seen stuff, Luce, you know what it's like out there. You know there's an underbelly to everyone, to society even. Fran, Jaysus,' he laughs slightly, 'he's never had a bad thing happen to him and I love that. He's just . . . himself. He sees me the way he sees me. If I tell him this,' he winces, 'he'll look at me different and I – I'd bloody hate it.'

'You're on the verge of losing him. I don't think you have a choice.'

'I'd rather lose him this way than have him pity me.'

'You're not giving him any credit.'

'Can we just leave it?' He swallows the rest of the wine, then holds out his glass. 'Please?'

I pour him some more and we drink in steady silence. Outside the snow has turned to hail and it hits the windows. A high whistle of wind catches in the eaves. The fire my mother lit blazes in the hearth.

And the silence fills the room, and we stay there, knowing that tomorrow will make or break this case.

I put some coal on the fire while Dan watches me.

He's building up to something. Then, as I sit back down, he asks, soft, 'Will you answer me something, Luce?'

He's angled towards me on the sofa, glass in hand.

'What?'

'Rob. What was he like?'

The drink has made him brave because he wouldn't normally ask me a thing like that. I hesitate, hurt and a bit disappointed in him.

'Sorry.' Dan holds up his glass. 'I just . . . well . . . I think our SO could be a lot like Rob.'

The thought had niggled away at me too. Rob wasn't a killer, but he had the cold detachment that killers need, the ruthless streak to pursue whatever gave him gratification. And on bad days, I think maybe if he hadn't been caught, he might have resorted to murder to hide his crimes.

'You don't have to answer, if you don't want,' Dan says.

I top up my wine. I need a lot of wine to talk about Rob. 'You know what you read in the papers,' I say, trying to stop my voice catching, 'about Rob being a high-flyer, a super-intelligent man and yet Mr Ordinary?'

At Dan's nod, I say, 'That's all true. He played football with Luc and the neighbours' kids, he was on the residents' committee, fundraising committees. The man was,' I raise my glass, 'perfect. I was crazy for him. And through it all, through all the good deeds, he ripped off his employers, our neighbours and friends. And then he ran, leaving me with my job in tatters and our son, who was eight, being picked on by the other kids in school and even some of the teachers because they'd all lost money to Rob. If ever a man was aptly named . . .' I laugh a little. I'm drinking too fast.

'Was the good he did real?' Dan asks, balling up the empty crisp bag and throwing it on the fire. 'Like, did he love you and Luc?'

I've asked myself that so many times. Was it possible that two separate emotional realities could exist in one person or was the good just put on so he could fit into society and cover up his other life? 'Sometimes I don't think he knew what was real and what wasn't,' I finally answer. 'Like if you spend your whole life pretending to be this nice guy while all the time you're cold-bloodedly planning to defraud your friends, how do you ever know who you are?'

He thinks about this. 'Maybe you're both.'

'Or neither.'

It's as if the words cause a few seconds' chill. I think of Rob often as a nothing person, an empty vessel that donned the cloak of respectability. A man with a hole in the very centre of himself that just grew bigger year on year.

'Did you ever suspect?' Dan asks quietly.

The wine is insulation against the rawness of the memories. 'That he was a con man?' I shake my head. 'No. But after he was arrested, I started to think, and I realised I'd brushed off a lot of weird behaviour.' As I take another gulp of wine, I notice my hand is shaking.

'You don't—' Dan goes to say, but I interrupt him.

'No, look, it's sat between us for the past couple of years. You've been great not to ask.'

'Wasn't my business.'

'You're my friend,' I say, and the words hang there, saying everything. After a moment, I stumble out, 'I think maybe I should have put the pieces together – I'm a guard for God's sake – but I didn't. And, anyway, the pieces were so . . .' I try to find the words, and can't '. . . I don't know, like you're not going to assume someone is psychopathic, are you, because of a few things? You deny it. Tell yourself it's okay. Believe the lies.'

'Yeah,' Dan says, and I know he's not just saying it to make me feel better.

We've both seen it happen, and while others may scoff, I believe those people who say they never suspected. Some people live in such deep denial that even if their partner was dragging a dead body across the house they wouldn't question it.

'Once or twice, I remember being a little scared of him,' I confess. 'Like, he'd do things that weren't, you know, very nice and just not see it. It wasn't that he didn't care, it was that he didn't think he should care.'

Dan remains silent, still, studying me.

'There was this time that really stands out,' I say, feeling half ashamed, 'when we were having a conversation about, you know, things you wish you'd done, things you'd like to do, and I told him about this guy I used to go out with, Johnny Egan. I'd been mad about Johnny, the way you are when you're a kid.' I smile a little at the memory. 'Honestly, Dan, I would have walked on hot coals for that guy. I was bouncing off the walls with happiness when we started going out together, but then this girl, Katie, moved to Achill and she was, like, this city slicker, you know – she had the cool clothes, she smelt great and, sure, she set the boys mad and they all wanted to go out with her. And she chose Johnny.' Even now, years later, the hurt of that time leaks through. 'They got married eventually, so maybe it was meant to be, but anyway, I confronted Katie in the middle of the school corridor over it, and while I screamed and raved and lost my shit, she just stared at me like I was dirt and the other kids started laughing at me and I hated her for that. I really did. Anyway, I remember saying to Rob that I wish I'd done something better about it. Been cooler about it. And do you know what Rob did?'

Dan shakes his head.

'He got this foreign property portfolio, which he knew wasn't going to perform, and somehow he tracked down Johnny and Katie, which wasn't too hard as they were still living in Mayo, and he sweet-talked them into investing in it. He got so annoyed when I wasn't pleased about it. "But," he said, "this will make that woman lose her shit. Isn't that what you wanted?"'

'Fuck's sake.' Dan actually sounds impressed. 'What happened?'

'They lost a lot of money and, yes, Katie did lose her shit.'

I should have known that night. I should have known I was dealing with someone whose moral compass wasn't like other people's. 'If Rob wanted something, he'd just go after it,' I say. 'And people fell in behind him. It was like he could read them. They loved him. Me too.'

'Our guy has a way about him too,' Dan says. 'All the stuff you said, I think this guy is a ringer for it. He's getting these girls to do what he wants by pretending to be someone he's not.'

'And, like Rob, he knows his victims.'

'Yep.'

'Which makes him dangerous because they trust him.'

'We haven't managed to find any friends in common, though,' says Dan. I know we'd made a pact not to talk shop in the house, but it was better than talking about Luc and Fran and all that mess.

'It's probably someone in their sphere.'

'Which makes it like looking for a needle in a haystack.'

I knock back some more wine. I'm edgy and restless. I won't sleep: Luc, the girl, the baby, and Rob will be churning about in my head all night. 'Sam rang Emma tonight,' I say.

'I heard. Let's hope we get the bastard tomorrow.'

The Captain

The owner or waiter, or whatever he is, is making a point of cleaning the tables all around him. The place is closing. He's been given the hint to leave. It's just coming up to two and he sees the taxi to bring Emma home pull up outside the building.

He stands and zips up his jacket.

Black.

Nondescript.

He wraps his scarf about his head.

'Happy Christmas,' the waiter calls, and he nearly laughs.

He raises a hand to acknowledge the good wishes and steps out into the cold.

The air bites, the wind stings, little flurries of snow whirl and dance. He moves into position, not directly opposite the building but just to the left of it. This way, he's in shadow. He is unseen, like always.

Tomorrow night she will be his but for now, the night before the take, he just likes to look.

He pretends he's scrolling his phone, in case anyone is interested in what he's up to, standing alone there. The screen gives a faint light that he shades with his hand. The cold bites his fingers – he's glad he has a scarf.

Up the way, across the road, the door of the centre opens and Emma comes out. He inhales deeply. Exhale.

Loving this.

And then . . .

She turns her head back into the building. Is someone there? Maybe the next shift is early but, no, the shift from two until the morning does not work from the office. He knows that. She told him once.

And then she nods. *She fucking nods.*

She climbs into the car and is whisked away.

Who the fuck was she nodding to? The question roars its way through his head, so loud the entire street shakes. The moon dips and the snow melts and he is back in the street, standing, staring after Emma's taxi, and the door of the centre is closed again. Maybe he imagined it. His brain isn't always to be trusted . . . Maybe he . . .

A garda car is making its way up the street. Slowly. Aiming for him. He thinks, *They know. They know, and she told them.*

Fuck.

Hurt tears inside him and anger and fury, yet he has to move on because that car is going to pull level with him.

He thinks of what he should do. And then it comes to him.

He hails the garda car. They won't expect that.

He smiles as the guard, a hulk of a thing, rolls down the window.

'I'm glad to see you, boys,' he says, before they can ask him anything. He opts for a Cork twang. His words slur. 'I don't know where I am and I seen a taxi pull up there and I just took the number off the side of it to call one for myself and then I seen my phone is dead. Could ye call me a taxi?'

'What's your name?'

'Colm Conroy. I lost my friends and I don't know where I am. What street is this?'

'Parliament Street.'

'Grand. Could ye call me a taxi, like?'

'What were you doing here, Colm Conroy?' The cop eyeballs him; he eyeballs him back. He's thinking that this is not one of them who came to interview him so it should be grand. He doesn't think they have a picture of him down the station with 'Chief Suspect' on it because no one ever suspects him of anything.

Maybe if they had, that one time, long ago, maybe then he might be different. But they didn't. No one suspected him of a thing.

'Just looking to catch a taxi. I was out with my friends and they fucked off so I had a coffee in that café, but it's closing now.' Puzzled look. Feign alarm. 'Is something wrong?'

A long moment.

And then the guard points up the road. 'There's a taxi rank at the top there, turn left.'

'Thanks so much. I appreciate that.'

The guard nods a goodnight.

He moves off at a trot.

Were they watching him or not?

Did Emma nod or not?

But he is not STUPID! Did she think he was stupid? That he would just blindly meet her? That is not the way it works.

He will know, in advance, if she has betrayed him.

He will KNOW.

And if she has, he will get her again. Later.

Because it's always been about, and leading up to, PLAN B.

He goes home and he writes out the order.

34

Day Six

I am not in the best of shape when I get into work the next morning. I'd had nightmares about Rob as if talking of him had resurrected him somehow. I'd dreamed that he'd moved into the house, my mother and Luc had welcomed him, and I was the only one who could see what he was but no one would listen.

It was a relief to wake up in an empty bed, see that it was still dark outside and that I was home. And then thoughts of Luc crashed in on me. And the horrible woman who had not sounded very encouraging about Luc's involvement in her family's life: I'm apprehensive at the thought of him being a dad, but I hate even more the idea of him not being allowed to be one.

I'll ring her again today, or maybe – the thought unfurls like a flag in a gentle breeze – see if I can find out who she is. Find out what sort of a family Luc has got himself involved with.

'The Cig is calling a meeting,' Dan says, coming over and handing me a coffee. 'He wants us there in ten.'

He looks good, his confession of the night before all bundled away in a box in his head.

'Coming.' Just then my phone rings. It's a guard from

downstairs. 'Hi, Lucy. There's a package for you from an Alan Brennan and also Jordy wants you. He says he might have a lead.'

When we get to William's office, package under my arm, Declan Mulvey, a guy I worked with once or twice in Dublin, is there, along with a young guard who bears a passing resemblance to Emma Dowling. We all exchange greetings. Declan asks me how Luc is and I have to tell him that Luc is great. Dan is grinning a little until he asks him how his love life is.

'There's such a thing as a love life in this job?' Dan says, and they laugh.

Then, getting down to business, Declan rubs his hands together and my heart *whumps* with a mix of terror and adrenalin.

'I've details for ye on the operation tonight. We've called it "Operation Take". I'm going to talk ye through it.' Declan flicks on his laptop and we gather in a small semi-circle around it. 'As we speak, the boys are setting up for it, cameras and the like being put in. We've made contact with the owners of the farmhouse and they're happy to cooperate.'

'Really?' Dan asks.

In our experience, people never want to get involved.

'Let's just say there were some mitigating factors that made them very happy to jump on board.'

There's a ripple of laughter at this.

'Now,' he points to the road on a map spread out on the table, 'it's a quiet enough area, a long road, a number of scattered houses, isolated. We can't be too obvious – too much activity will warn this fella off. We figure he might go on a dry run so we're being as inconspicuous as we can. Unmarked cars are parked along the route. There are a few entrances and exits, which pose a slight problem, but we're doing our utmost to take note of any car regs passing up and down, so even if this gouger gets suspicious and drives by, we'll trace everyone in and out. There will also be a number of vehicles parked in the farmyard, here.' He indicates the young guard, who thus far has been sitting quietly in the corner of the room. 'This is Garda Carol Joyce. She's agreed to be our decoy. Her height, hair colour and frame match Emma Dowling's. Tonight she'll be wearing a red coat, as instructed.'

Carol blushes, not liking being the centre of attention.

I feel the familiar flutter in my chest. I can almost smell this guy because we're within touching distance. He just needs to jump the final hurdle and we'll see him.

'Lucy, Dan, are you happy to be there?' William asks.

Is a cat happy in sunlight?

'Yes.'

'We'll be getting into position within the next few hours. You'll need to leave about five. We're going in slowly so as not to ring any alarm bells.'

Back at the office, I unwrap Alan's package. There is a picture with a sticker telling us that it's Ken's Leaving Cert project. It's a weird thing. I'm not too sure what it's meant to be. I make a note to get it examined for prints. As well as that, there is an envelope containing a scribbled note and a folded up A4 page.

Detectives

I know I should have told you this the other day but I did find Ken on the internet. However, I never told my wife because she would have tried to make contact with him and I would rather not have that man in our lives. I enclose the picture.

Alan Brennan.

Unfolding the A4 page, I see that it's a printout of a web article showing three men holding a cheque for half a million pounds and forty-eight pence. Behind them, a huge bottle of champagne is squirting everywhere and people are cheering. Two of the men have grins as wide as America. The fellow in the middle looks faintly puzzled at the celebrations. There's a familiarity about him that I can't place. Maybe it's the passing resemblance to Sam Smyth.

I scan the piece. Joe Doyle, Kendall Smyth and Colin Ryan celebrate a big Cheltenham win. It's dated two years ago.

Having some time before we head out to Erris, I can't resist having a poke about myself to see if I can find Kendall as he must now be calling himself. I log onto the internet and key in 'Kendall Smyth' but I find nothing. I try the 'images' but nothing there either, bar the image I already have.

After a few minutes more, I bring the article to Mick. He's lying back, legs on the desk, swigging a coffee. When he sees me, he jumps to attention so fast, his coffee spills all over the place.

'Sorry, like,' he says, as he looks about for something to mop up the spillage. 'I was just having a break.' He takes up his jacket and, before I can protest, he throws it on top of the coffee. 'I thought I'd have—'

'You've just ruined that jacket,' I remark, holding the page towards him. 'Here, information on Ken Smyth. Can you or Susan trace him?'

He abandons his mopping-up operations to have a quick look at the page. 'Jesus. We've been looking all over for him.'

'He's Kendall now. Try to find out where he is, what he's doing now, the usual. Give me what you have by the end of today.'

'Sure thing.'

Jordy pops his head in. 'Lucy, I might have something for you.'

He's been a guard for years, never sought promotion, just been content to plod along in this backwater. I'd have gone mad by now. 'Go on, then.'

'This.' He lays a report in front of me and Mick. 'I thought, with a lot of attention being focused on the bog and on those two boys, it might be worth looking into any other reports of sexual crime or assault up that way. Anyway, I found this, and when I read it, I remembered. I'd done those calls.'

'What calls?' I don't have time to be reading things.

He's unfazed by my abrupt tone and I feel bad but I don't apologise.

'About twenty years back, this man,' a nod to the file, 'John Henderson, came into the station and made a report that his daughter Chloë, who was five at the time, was assaulted by a young man down at the beach on the north side of the island.'

'The one nearest the Smyth house?'

'Yes. He says his daughter called this young man "dirty" and that he caught her by the neck. When confronted the young man ran off, disappeared, they say, into the bog. I was one of the guards investigated that claim and, sure, you know yourself, no one knew anything. Now, I could have this wrong, but we did call to the Smyth house at the time and there was a lad they had working for them there. He was the right age, he was dirty, but Pascal swore he'd been working with him in the field all along, so we ended up with nothing.'

'What did this worker look like?'

Jordy shakes his head. 'Aw, now, that's going back a bit. But I was thinking I could see if I could trace this girl and, sure, if the assault was as bad as she said, even though she was five she might remember his face, you know.'

'Where did the worker come from?'

'He could have been from anywhere. I think Pascal said he was from out of town, summer work, but, sure, it's so long ago and we ended up thinking it was just a bit of a barney between two children, but there was bruising on the girl's neck.'

'Was there a description of this boy on the file?'

'Yes, but pretty basic.'

'Do run that girl down, ask her if she'd mind being interviewed about it.'

'Will do.'

'Good work, Jordy.'

He shambles off. If I'd told him he'd wasted my time, I reckon his reaction would have been the same.

Mick balls up his jacket and surveys his desk. 'I'll need a proper cloth.'

I leave him to it.

Dan is waiting for me in the corridor. Just as we reach the door that leads to the front desk, we hear raised voices.

Dan holds his finger to his lips and gets there before I do. 'Jane Ryan,' he says. 'Let's go out the back way. She sounds like she's having a meltdown.'

We make a dash for the back door, run around the station and into the car pool. Taking our usual, we're soon on the road to Erris.

35

The cold December afternoon is full of quiet activity, but Dan and I are on the fringes and we'll stay there until we apprehend a suspect. We're both jittery. I hope we've made the right call.

I sit on the stone wall that runs around the back of the farmhouse, and when Dan leaves to walk off his edginess, I take the opportunity to go inside and call my mother. I know my mind should be focused on the op, but unless I sort out the mess at home, I'll be completely torn anyway.

I don't have the ability to box things away.

She answers on the first ring. I wonder if she's been waiting to hear from me. She's not at home because I can hear traffic noise in the background.

'Where are you?'

'Just checking up on my own house. Two tenants coming today. Where are you yourself?'

'Work,' I answer. Then, in a rush, 'Has Luc told you much about this girl or her family?'

'Just that she's pregnant, and sure isn't that enough?' A bit of a snort. 'I don't think she's ever been to the house at all. He must have gone to hers. But I never met her.'

I wince. 'I talked to the mother yesterday. She was a bit . . . up herself. What did Luc say the surname was again?'

She thinks. 'I don't know that he ever did. Will I ask him?'

I feel a surge of ridiculous resentment, partly because Luc will probably tell her but if I asked he'd tell me to butt out. 'If you can,' I say.

'I'll ask him when he gets out from school. That should be anytime now.'

'Thanks,' I say. 'Text me when you find out.'

'Why do you need to know anyway?' she asks, the thought suddenly occurring to her. Then, 'Don't go doing the whole guard checking thing. That's not fair. It's an invasion of privacy.'

'What? What? Sorry. I can't hear you . . .' And I hang up.

Damn, she won't ask him now.

I watch the tech guys rigging up the monitoring equipment. It's quite amazing what they can do. Carol will be wearing a brooch with a built-in camera and microphone. At the moment, she's in Emma's apartment and she will walk, under surveillance, to her car, then drive to the pick-up point. That is purely for the benefit of our suspect if he's lurking around. The cold has worked in our favour as Carol will be bundled up and our suspect will not be able, at a few feet, to tell the difference between Emma and Carol.

The wife of the owner of the property is distributing packets of crisps to the people inside the farmhouse. What is it about guards and food? They fall on it like famine victims.

'Tea?' She comes towards me. 'Crisps?'

'Thanks.'

She hands me a packet of smoky bacon and sits down beside

me. She smells of cabbage and warm milk. 'Only smoky bacon left,' she says. 'The rest are gone.' A big happy sigh. 'You must have a very exciting life.'

'Not really.'

'This all looks very exciting.' She sweeps her arm in an arc, encompassing the kitchen, where we are, and the yard beyond. 'I thought you were catching a criminal or something. I said to the lad who called, we're happy to help if it's not one of those gangland fellas yez are after. Sure, they'd shoot you in your bed for looking crooked at them. It's not one of them, is it?'

'No. This is just . . .' I shrug '. . . just a normal criminal.'

'That's all right, then.' She stands up. 'Good luck with it so.'

'Thanks.'

As she walks off, flakes of snow start to drift down, and the sky is the lead grey that means it could go on for a while. By six o'clock it will be pitch dark out here.

The Captain

Emma's voice wasn't as soft as Lisa's. The soft-voiced ones were the ones you really had to watch.

He remembered the first time he saw Emma. He'd sat, half freezing, in that kip of an all-night café, and when her shift ended, he'd left, crept closer, waiting for a glimpse. Then when she had proved that she was one of THEM, he had found out all he could about her. He had met her. Talked to her. Found out about her. Tracked her down on social media. But he hadn't befriended her. That would have been foolish indeed.

He just bided his time.

Today Emma is not in the clothes shop. He's taken the day off from work because he has to do some errands and also check on her. Covered his face, to be sure, worn a hat. This is suspicious, he thinks. There is an ugly old fat cow where Emma normally is.

'Emma not here?' he says, speaking through his scarf as he puts a tie on the counter.

'Aren't you the observant genius?' she says, with a smile.

'Funny.' He makes it sound as if he's smiling but wishes he could smash her smart face in for her. He leans across the counter. 'Is she sick or something?'

'I don't know. I was just called in. What do you want anyway? This tie?' She picks it up. He can see right inside her mouth when she talks – she wears braces on her bottom teeth.

'Please.'

She charges it and wraps it in some tissue paper, then pops it into a fancy bag for him. Her fat arse moves from the counter to the till and back again.

He holds back a snigger.

'For you,' she says. Something about him makes her unsure. Wrong-foots her. She's looking at him oddly. He can feel her breath sliding across his cheek. He moves away, taking the tie with him.

'Thanks.'

Emma not being here does not portend well.

But maybe she's readying herself for tonight.

Putting things in motion for poor sad Sam.

He's done that too.

36

At five, the contact with Carol is established. She's in Emma's apartment, and when her image appears on the screen, I do a double-take. Carol's hair has been styled the same as Emma's, as has her make-up.

Emma has gone home to her parents on our advice. It's better she's away if the operation goes belly-up. She'll be watched carefully there too. With a suspected offender like this, you can bet he's done his research.

'How you doing there, Carol?' Declan says.

'Good.' She nods. The sound is a little behind the picture. The tech guys start to remedy that.

'You know the drill,' Declan says. 'Leave the apartment at five forty. You'll be shadowed as far as the car. We're pretty positive he won't make any attempt to grab you until you're in position as that's the hardest place to cover by CCTV. Park by the gate of the farm and we'll see if he makes contact. Have you got Emma's phone?'

Carol waves it about.

'Wear the hat and scarf, keep your face covered. You'll be observed at all times.'

'Grand.'
'Good luck.'
The link is disconnected.
And then the waiting begins.

The Captain

The trick is to think like the guards. He's good at that. Ten steps ahead of everyone all his life. He had to be: it was his only hope of surviving.

If she betrayed him, he'll know.

Half an hour before Emma is due to leave her apartment, he finds a seat in a local café and orders a coffee. He hunches over his phone, pretending to fire off texts but, in reality, keeping an eye on the front door of her building.

If she's betrayed him, there might be guards in the café, maybe looking out for him. He doesn't care: they won't be able to do anything anyway. It's not a crime to have a coffee. And if they recognise him, he can always say he was just passing through. 'I've got an appointment in Ballina, Guard,' he'll say, with the right amount of deference, 'with some fellow on Done Deal to buy something and sure I thought I'd have a stop-off coffee in Erris.' He feels pretty sure the two men in the Hyundai just outside the apartment block are guards. He'd walked by them to get here. They'd been drinking from bottles of water and chomping bags of sweets. One even threw the bloody sweet bag out of the window onto the street. Pigs.

He just needs to be sure.

At twenty to six he spies Emma coming out of the apartment. His stomach lurches at the sight of her, just like it had the day he saw any of THEM for the first time. He remains hunched over his phone but watches as Emma bends her head against the falling snow and hurries on up the street. The two men he thinks are cops don't move. They just stay where they are. Emma keeps walking.

The two men act like they don't see her and maybe they don't.

He lets Emma walk off a bit, then slowly leaves his seat and moves to the front of the café. They're not cops, he sees now, they're waiting on a woman who hops into the car and they drive off. Too much imagination.

His gaze flits to Emma. She's down the street now to where he knows she parks her car. Maybe it will be all right, he thinks.

Then someone stops Emma and seems to be asking directions. A woman, who had been walking behind Emma, stops too, then continues to walk.

Maybe it's all right.

And then, just as Emma reaches the car, she takes out her key fob and unlocks the doors. His Emma never does that. She unlocks her car from feet away. Not very safety conscious, he's always thought.

He leaves the café, walking in the opposite direction.

His fury could scorch the streets, but he holds it in.

He inhales, deep. Exhales. He has time to make it to his night class if he hurries.

He doesn't need Emma because Pearl and Lisa were good preparation.

Tomorrow or the next day, he will strike.

He will show no mercy.

37

The evening has grown dark and cold. A dry, needling, bone-deep cold that makes you yearn for the fire and cocoa and a normal job. And yet my heart is beginning a slow, steady thump and my nerves are tingling.

We watch from the edges as Carol comes into view. She drives by the farmyard gate and stops at the old stone pillar. Her red coat is visible as she steps out of the car, against the snow. She digs her hands into her pockets and bends her head against the weather.

All around there is silence.

No one moves. It's easy to believe that there are only Carol and me and the cold, and yet I know that not ten feet away, another person is watching and waiting, hoping to act. All along the road, officers are silently waiting, cameras at the ready to pick up registration plates.

Out in the distance, the crunch of tyres on poor road comes rolling across the landscape. The sound increases and the car passes by. I realise I've been clenching my fists, holding my breath, and I want to let it out in a whoosh, only I can't.

And we wait.

And the cars continue to roll on by, the approach of each one causing my heart to thump like a drum. And fall hard when they pass.

Carol stamps her feet to keep out the cold. I watch her pulling her scarf tighter around her face. She dips her head. The cold air has grown savage.

Ninety minutes pass and nothing.

Almost two hours. In the distance a church spire chimes eight and, because everything is so still, the sound comes clear across the countryside.

And the thought grows slowly, like mould, that he's not coming. He must have suspected something yet what could it have been? It's all been so subtle, so careful. But maybe he's been held up. Maybe he'll appear in five or ten minutes. But no. Nothing would have held this guy up. He's a planner. Methodical and careful. He's not coming. He wouldn't wait two hours to show up if he was coming. He'd be too afraid of losing his prize.

Dan lands in beside me. 'He's not coming.' His voice is flat with disappointment. We've blown it and yet I don't know how.

Ten minutes later, Declan's voice crackles through my headset. 'Stand down. All units stand down.'

And I watch, with a heavy heart, as people emerge from the hedgerows and their cars, and as the whole place is pulled apart as carefully as it was assembled.

'How did he know?' I ask Dan. 'Did he know all along?'

'I doubt it,' Dan says. 'He wouldn't have risked ringing her if he'd known. He was checking it out. But something happened between then and now.'

'This is my fault. I missed something. The super will kill us.'

I feel sick as my confidence shatters, like glass on a tiled floor. What a waste of a night, what a waste of resources.

'It was a good call,' Dan says firmly. 'We did good.' He looks into my eyes. 'We did,' he repeats, and I love his certainty. 'Now, maybe if we come up with something. Like, maybe he did pass on the road, spot something, then at least we have his registration.'

I watch as someone wraps Carol in a silver blanket. She's shivering.

'Hey, Mick sent a couple of messages,' Dan says.

I barely register it. All I can think of is that the super will be impossible for the next few days because the budget will have been blown on this operation. I don't even want to think about the consequences.

I move past the bustle and stand at the edge of a field, staring out into the white-coated land beyond. It should be dark but the snow, lying across everything here, lights the place. He is out there and he is bloody clever. I reckon we've met him, or got close to him. I reckon he's spun us a line. And whatever he's said, it's been a lie and we just need to double-check everyone again and—

'Mick found the other brother.' Dan appears at my shoulder. 'He decided that as we were busy, he'd give him a ring himself.'

A tiny shot of hope. 'And?'

'Apparently Kendall lives between London and Mayo. Mainly London. He's home right now for a meeting. He gave Mick his address. If we go now, we could catch him before it's too late.'

'Will he still be around in the morning?'

'Yeah, but—'

'Did Mick check if this guy was in London the days Lisa and Pearl went missing?'

'He did, yeah, but—'

'And was he?'

'He was in London for Lisa Moran all right.'

'He's not our man then, is he?' I feel the weight of this case crashing down. So far, everything we've had has led up to a great big fat zero. We must be missing something.

'Maybe he's lying. Maybe he has information that could help.'

'We can wait for the morning to do the interview.'

'Look, it's not our fault that—'

'But it is, Dan.' I turn to him. 'We were so sure it would work. And you know what, it should have worked. How did he find out? We have to go through it, see where it fell down. I want to talk to everyone who played a part in this. Step by step, we have to see where it fell down.' From the corner of my eye, I see one of the regular lads crossing to us.

'Can I interrupt?' His face is bright and hopeful and I want to stomp on him.

'Looks like you already have.'

He smiles, not bothered by my sarcasm, and I feel instantly mean. 'I think you'd like to know that one of the regs we ran through the system at around six fifteen this evening was Sam Smyth's.'

I jerk to attention. 'You're sure?'

'Yep. It came back about ten minutes ago. Here's the details.'

'What are the odds?' Dan says.

'Let's go and see what Sam has to say for himself.'

38

Sam's apartment is shabby – even the bright throws on the furniture can't hide the lack of money. His partner, a slim, blonde girl with large green eyes, lets us in. She walks like a cat, all grace and prowl. There's a yoga mat in the centre of the room and the smell of incense fills the air. She motions us to a faded green sofa, sits opposite us in a green chair, feet tucked up under her, and stares. She's got piercings in her nose and tongue but none in either of her ears.

'What's this about?' Her accent is generic, hard to pin down. She cocks her head to one side as she studies us. Her tone is mild, calm, quiet.

'Sam is helping us with a case we're working on,' I say.

That comes as a shock to her. Eyes widen slightly and she takes a second. 'What case?'

'Murder of Lisa Moran,' I say casually and watch her flinch, any zen she had being sucked away. 'On the bog in Achill there a week back. He never said, no?'

'No.' A gathering of herself. 'Sure, what would he know about that?'

'That's what we're trying to find out,' Dan says pleasantly, offering her a smile.

She is unsure whether to smile back or not. After a second, she says, 'I hope he's not, like, a suspect?'

'Do you know where he was last Friday between three and five?' I ask instead.

'I'm guessing work.'

Silence descends again.

'Are you planning on attending the funeral?' Dan asks, picking fluff from his trousers.

'Funeral?'

'Sam's father? Didn't he tell you?'

Her eyes narrow further. She sits up straighter in the chair, tosses her hair. 'I'm not stupid. I know fine well what you're at. Trying to get me to talk about Sam, trying to make me think he doesn't tell me things. Well, actually, he doesn't.' A smile. 'He never says anything about his family and that's all right with me because I don't like families and neither does he.'

'Right.' Dan nods, as if impressed. 'So, you won't be going to the auld fella's funeral. Probably just as well. The press will be all over it.'

To give her credit, she remains silent. I begin to think she's meditating or something.

Sam arrives back a couple of minutes later. He stops dead in the doorway when he sees us. 'What have you said to her?' He sounds genuinely fearful.

'Nothing,' Dan answers. 'We're waiting for you actually. I just want to advise you that you're under caution.' He recites his rights as Sam stares incredulously at him. 'We're wondering where you got to this evening.'

'What?' He glances at his partner, then back at us. 'You want to know where I was just now?'

'Yes.'

'I was working.'

'In Westport?'

'Yeah. That's where the shop is.'

'You didn't take a trip anywhere?'

'Just a couple of deliveries.'

'He always does them after work,' the girl chimes in. 'He gets the travel expenses from his boss. And double time.'

'We'd like to talk to you alone, Sam,' Dan says pleasantly.

In answer, the girl slides off the chair and comes to stand alongside him.

'Evie, it's fine.' Sam closes his eyes. He sounds weary all of a sudden. 'Just make us a cuppa, would you? I've a banging headache.'

'No, I won't. I'm staying beside you until these are gone. You'll say something stupid and—'

'I won't because I've done nothing.' A pause. 'Please, just make me tea.' He looks at us. 'Do yous want tea?'

'I'm not making them tea.' Her outrage is a little endearing. 'They said your dad was dead and that you were helping with a murder inquiry. Trying to make me not trust you, trying to get me onside.'

'Then just make me tea.' He gives her a smile, so full of affection that I'm suddenly sure he's not who we're looking for. But Rob was like that, the best husband and dad any kid could have wished for.

Evie hesitates a bit before moving off, a waft of sweet-smelling something left behind. The clattering of delph comes to us through the thin door.

'Where did you make the deliveries?' Dan asks.

'I had one in Westport, one in Mallaranny and then one out by Bangor Erris.' His tone is slightly wary, his gaze flitting from Dan to me and back. 'Why?'

'Where in Erris?'

'I asked you why.'

'Just answer the question.'

'Don't talk to him like that.' Evie's voice.

'It's fine,' Sam calls. Then, to us, 'I had to swing by to deliver a sweatshirt to some young wan who dropped a note in the door of the shop. Paid me double to get it quick.'

'And what route did you take?'

He tells us and it involves him passing the farm. Clever, I think.

'What's the address of the woman who ordered the sweatshirt from you?'

'That's the weird thing,' he says, 'she hadn't. I guess the address must've been wrong.'

Dan looks at me and I look at him. I wonder if he invented this scenario just so he could pass the farmhouse. It'd be clever. 'When you say she dropped a note in . . .?' Dan asks.

'Just posted it through the shop door last night. I never met her. I thought it was a weird sweat for a girl to choose anyway.'

'Can we see it?'

Sam gives us an odd look. 'Sure. It's in the car.'

'We'll go down with you,' Dan says.

Evie picks that moment to back in through the kitchen door carrying a mug of tea and a huge slice of cake.

'Back in a sec.' Sam winks at her.

'You're not arresting him,' she shouts at us as we leave, her composure disappearing. 'I'll have your jobs if you arrest him. I swear, I—'

300

'They're not arresting me,' Sam calls back, sounding remark-ably cheery, though I suppose it's for her benefit.

Sam's car, a battered Volvo, is parked in a designated space. He pops open the boot and pulls out a white plastic bag, with the shop logo on the outside. It's been taped up. 'Here we go,' he says. 'There was fifty in cash in the envelope for a twenty-five-euro sweat.'

'Can you open that, please?' Dan says. He's not buying this new cooperative Sam.

Sam can't manage the tape, so he just rips open the plastic bag. Twenty-five euro flutters to the ground. Sam bends and hast-ily pockets it. 'That's just the change,' he says. He unfolds the sweatshirt.

It's white with a black graphic of the 'fuck-off' sign.

Dan looks at me. A message or what?

'See?' Sam makes a face. 'Most women wouldn't wear that.'

Dan is smiling grimly.

'Do you have the note that was sent this morning?'

'Yeah, back in the shop. It was an order, so I kept it.'

I'd thought he'd say no. I'd thought he'd say it was burned or dumped and that there was no way we'd be able to see it. I have to admit, I'm wrong-footed.

'You have the note in your order book or whatever you use?' Dan too sounds sceptical.

'Yeah,' Sam says.

'We'll need to see it, maybe take it as evidence.'

'Of what?' All of a sudden, Sam slumps against the bonnet of his car. He looks beat. 'You can have whatever you want. I did nothing.'

'You're telling us that someone asked you to travel up that road tonight to deliver that sweatshirt?'

'Yeah. It was weird. People normally order online, but they paid cash so what's not to like?'

'We need that note now,' Dan says. 'And the fifty if you have it.'

Sam shakes his head. 'The fifty is gone to the bank. I can get the order to you tomorrow.'

'See, Sam,' Dan goes on, his face poking right into Sam's, causing him to pull back, 'this isn't us asking you, this is us telling you.'

'And this is me telling you to go fuck yourself,' Sam says, pushing himself off the car and trying to sidestep Dan.

'Let me put it like this,' Dan says, blocking the way. 'Tonight we were watching that road in Erris very carefully because we had certain information about the killer of Lisa Moran. And what do we see? You, in your car, driving on by.'

'I was doing a delivery.'

'Bit of a coincidence, though, isn't it?' Dan says. He is totally in Sam's space now. I can see the guy growing edgy. 'And there we were interviewing you only the other day.'

'Coincidences happen.' He shoves his hands into his pockets and glares at Dan.

'Maybe, but from here, it sure looks like you're in the frame or else someone is trying to put you in the frame.'

'Or else there is no note and you'll forge one in the morning,' I chime in.

'There is a fucking note.' He glares at me, suddenly vicious.

'Then we really need to see it.'

'Fine. I have to tell Evie or she'll worry.'

'Give her a call.' Dan nods to where Sam's phone is poking out of his jacket. 'Let's not waste any more of our time. Hop into our car. We'll give you a lift.'

Sam sees he doesn't have much of a choice. He dials his girl-friend and follows us to the car.

In Westport, Sam unlocks the shop and flicks off the bleeping alarm. Turning on the light, he strides towards the counter, pulls out a large book and flicks through it.

'A lot of the stuff is computerised obviously,' he says. 'I never got a note for an order before. I put it in here 'cause I didn't know what else to do with it.' He finally finds it and pulls it out, slapping it on the counter.

'Get the kit from the car,' I say, and as Dan leaves, I dial up the station and ask for Larry, telling him to make all CCTV from Westport Main Street a priority. 'And tell Ger that I want Forensics called. I've something for analysis,' I finish.

The Captain

Social media. A killer's best friend. People trusting perfect strangers, the fools. He trusted no one, not since . . . not since the auld man had sold him out.

Mothers were the BEST, the old man said. They CARED about things. They cooked and sang and wiped your knee when you fell.

The same as fathers then, he'd said.

But the old man had laughed. MUCH BETTER, he'd said. MUCH BETTER.

And he had been happy and excited.

FOOL.

He contacts Emma on Messenger, under the fake alias he'd created using a photograph of an old school friend she had. An old school friend who had befriended a lot of Emma's friends before befriending Emma.

In the country tomorrow for a week, he types. *Want to meet up?*

I'm not in Galway right now, she types back. *At the parents'.*

Silly, silly, Emma. He knows where her parents live. Emma has not been the most subtle with her Facebook posts.

I'm there tomorrow, he types. *Name a place.*

And she does.

And they arrange to meet at three, saying how EXCITING it is to see each other after SO LONG!

Fucking bitch.

39

Day Seven

It's the tiniest breakthrough but it's something. After last night's debacle, the fact that we have the note is something.

I'm at the top of the incident room, with a copy projected up behind me. 'As you can see,' I say to them all, 'this note was allegedly delivered to Sam Smyth on the evening before or early morning of our operation. It allowed him the excuse to drive up by the farmhouse from which we were conducting Operation Take. This note will be forensically examined and all CCTV from around Sam's shop in Westport has been requested to see if indeed anyone was around at the time specified. We'll have fingerprints and analysis from the note hopefully by the end of today. We also suspect that our SO must have a connection to or grudge against Sam.'

'Maybe it is Sam,' Pat says.

'Yes, that's a possibility we're working on too. He might have typed the note himself but Forensics should help establish that. He might have used it as an excuse to scout out the way the land lay last night. The only thing is, and this is what makes us wary of accusing Sam, the land lay very well last night. We should have had something happen. Before then, we think, our guy was spooked.'

'Maybe he wasn't sure and scouted it out anyway.'

I nod. 'True. We can't discount him.'

Kev raises a hand. 'Actually,' he begins, words tumbling, 'I, eh, had a look into that last night because I hadn't much to do after the phones got quiet. Seems people don't bother ringing the guards on a Saturday night, all too busy enjoying themselves.'

A few titters.

'Is there a point here?' William says.

'Aye,' Kev says. 'Last night, it was dead quiet on the lines and—'

'Is this the story of your life?' William asks. 'Can you get on with it?'

I feel sorry for Kev. He's had the shit-end of this case and never complained.

'Right, Cig.' Kev is unflappable. 'Well, I thought to myself, you know, where along the way could our guy get spooked and I thought, it wasn't yesterday, so it had to be something to do with when he rang Emma. And, like, the only thing we did different there was we didn't leave Emma alone in the charity offices.' He looks around the room. 'She wasn't on her own that night and, eh, I thought that maybe he saw that, you know. That he'd been there, outside the offices, and seen she wasn't on her own.'

'We had a car posted along that road,' William says.

'Aye,' Kev says. 'Just, bear with me. Melissa,' he nods to Melissa, 'she agreed with me. She said that when she read the journals Sam had rung a guy called Tony but then stopped. Why? Because maybe he saw Tony was a dude. So, I thought, maybe he decided, after our plea, to go spy on Emma, or maybe he always does it anyway. But sure, for whatever reason, maybe, I thought, he was waiting to see Emma that night, you know, because that is the only thing in the chain that we did different.'

'And?' William snaps. 'Is this going anywhere? There's a lot of maybes and mights and anyways.' He's in filthy humour.

'Actually, yeah,' says Kev, straightening. 'I found out that two guards who were meant to keep an eye on things, from Ballina station, actually did talk to a guy just down from the offices at around the same time Emma was coming off her shift.'

The room erupts.

'They didn't think to call it in?' William says incredulously.

'No. They said this man approached them, a Colm Conroy, said he was lost and looking for a taxi and maybe he was.'

'Did they get a description?'

'Just that he was of average height, thin, with possibly dark hair. All in black. They said . . .' here Kev winces '. . . they said they gave him directions on how to get to the taxi rank.'

Someone says, 'Jaysus,' like they can't believe it. Someone else laughs.

'I rang the taxi firm,' Kev goes on.

Go, Kev, I think. He's always been overlooked in cases and this could be a game-changer for him.

'Good work,' William says. 'And?'

'It's a bit needle-in-a-haystack so I asked if any drivers had a man in their taxi that night fitting the description given by the guards. One driver remembers a man asking to be dropped off in Castlebar.'

Sam lives in Castlebar. Would he have been so obvious?

'Does he remember if he talked to the guy? What he sounded like?'

'No. But, eh, I sort of thought, Well, if this guy is our SO then he must have been hanging about the street, must have been seen by someone. Like, he didn't just appear out of thin air. So, like, after I finished on the phones, I drove there and it's not the nicest area. You wouldn't hang about too long. The only place our suspect could have been at all was in a car or in this supposedly all-night café that actually closes at two. This café, it's right opposite the road the building is on, so I just went in and asked the owner and he said there was this fella, all in black, hanging about that night. He remembers because he had to start cleaning up to give him the hint to leave. And he says the guy walked up towards Parliament Street.'

'Is there any CCTV?' Larry asks.

'I requested it, but there'll be nothing from the café. The owner agreed to come in and try to describe the guy, but he said he's not great on faces.'

'Would he recognise him again if he saw him?'

'He says he might.'

'Well done,' William says, impressed, and Kev gestures as if it's no big deal. 'Anyone else get—'

'Another thing,' Kev interrupts. Then, 'Eh . . . sorry . . . like . . . it might be nothing, but like, Emma was supposed to be on her own in the offices, so I asked one of the guards who was with her if Emma did anything off as she was leaving and the guard said it was only a small thing but that she turned back as she headed out of the doorway. The guard thinks she was about to say goodbye, then thought the better of it. It was only a small thing but if he was there and saw that, well, he'd maybe think she wasn't on her own, wouldn't he? And he'd be suspicious, wouldn't he?'

Holy shit. I look at Kev with admiration.

William gives what might pass as a smile, and says, 'That's great work, Kev. Anyone else get up off their arses and get me something?'

'I checked up on Ryan,' Melissa says. 'He spent last night in a hostel. His wife threw him out.'

'Where was he yesterday morning?' William asks. 'He didn't pay a visit to Westport by any chance?'

'I don't know, sir. I'll try and catch up with him.'

'Find out where Sam was too while you're at it.'

Larry is again put on CCTV and Jim divvies out the rest of the job sheets.

'When did you say Ken Smyth is due in?' William asks Mick.

'He says he'll be here by two. He can give us an hour. He's flying back through Knock.'

He looks at his watch. 'Right, Lucy and Dan, seeing as ye fucked up so royally last night, get something out this fella.'

'I don't think we fucked—'

'That's it now.' He strides out.

'— up, sir. So, go fuck yourself,' Dan mutters, in an undertone.

Jordy catches us at the door. 'The girl, Chloë, can be here in about thirty minutes,' he says. 'Would any of ye like to talk to her or do you want me to do it?'

'I'll sit in with you, Jordy,' I say. 'Let me know when she comes.'

'I will.'

'There's a man happy with life,' I observe, as Jordy moves off with a slow calmness.

'Lucky guy,' Dan remarks, and I have to agree.

Chloë Spenser, a girl with dyed black hair, looks up as Jordy and

I enter the interview room. She's heavily made up and is dressed in an unflattering tracksuit and runners. She's tapping her foot up and down and pulling the sleeves of her sweatshirt over her hands.

'Hi, Chloë,' Jordy says, and introduces us both. 'Would you like some tea or coffee?'

'No, thanks.' Her voice is soft.

'Wise choice.' Jordy smiles at her, and she manages a watery one back. 'Now, Chloë, I know it might upset you but can you tell us about the time you say you were assaulted down at the beach in Doogort there?'

I take a chair opposite her. 'In your own time,' I say.

'It was so long ago,' she says haltingly, 'and maybe you'll think I shouldn't remember it like I do but it's still so clear because it was like, shocking, you know.'

Jordy nods encouragement.

'I was five, I was on the beach. I'm not sure which one but we were staying in a little house near it and we crossed the bog and it was just there. We had to walk down a sandy incline and it was fun.'

'I know it,' I say. Her memory is good because I'd imagine she has never been back to it.

'Anyway, like I said, I was only a child at the time, small for my age, and I was with my parents and grandparents too – we were on holiday. Anyway, I saw this boy on the beach. Up the way from us. He was about maybe ten or so and he was looking at all of us. He was standing so still and he was looking and, I don't know, something about him made me feel sorry for him.' A small break in her voice. 'I thought he looked sad so I went over to him and he was filthy. He was wearing clothes too small for him and he wasn't washed, and I was only a child and he smiled at me and

311

I said it.' She clenches her hands into fists and winces. 'I said he was dirty or smelly or something like that. I know it wasn't nice, but I was so young.' She gulps hard, hesitates, goes on: 'Then, his face sort of changed, like maybe his eyes, and before I could think, he put his hand on my throat and pulled me towards him and he was squeezing me hard and there was this,' a pause, 'flatness, just nothing, in his face and I was kicking and . . .' tears track down her face, her voice becomes younger '. . . then my daddy saw him and let out a roar and the boy dropped me and ran off. My dad tried to follow him but it was like he just vanished, he said. So, we went to the guards and made a complaint but we heard nothing more.'

'We couldn't find him at the time,' Jordy says. 'I'm sorry about that, Chloë.'

A tear plops off her chin. 'I don't think I ever got over it. I know I should have, it was a long time ago, but sometimes I even dream of him standing over my bed and looking at me, and when I wake up, I grow cold because I know he's still out there.'

'Would you recognise him?' I ask gently.

'I don't know. Maybe if he hasn't changed.'

'If we bring in an artist, could you describe him as he was then?'

'Yes.'

'Thanks, Chloë.'

I leave Jordy with her while I sign out some exhibits for the interview with Ken.

'I'll let you do the talking,' Dan says, meeting me on my way back from collecting the exhibits. 'Grand. Where is he?'

'Interview Two. The guy was out of the country for Lisa Moran's killing.'

'But he's connected to this somehow. We know that that family is all over this. Right, come on.' With Dan on my heels, I stride into the room.

Kendall is at the table, scrolling through something on his mobile. Totally at ease, long legs splayed out, as if all is right in his world. He looks up at us as we enter and, once again, I feel that jolt of familiarity. Is it because he looks like Sam that I think I've seen him before?

He's more groomed than his brother. His hair is dark, slicked back, curling at the ends. His face isn't as gaunt – it's thin but has that attractive quality of looking lived-in. He's dressed well too, a sparkling box fresh white shirt, open at the collar, sharp tailored navy suit. He looks like a man who has made a few bob. His eyes are dark, not giving much away. I get the impression he's short on smiles.

'Hello, Mr Smyth,' I say, offering my hand. 'I'm Detective Lucy Golden and this is Detective Dan Brown. Thanks for coming in.'

'No problem. Is this about the auld fella?' He pockets his phone and shifts a bit on his chair, hands locked in front of him. 'They told me he was . . . dead?'

'Yes, Mr Smyth.'

'Ken, please.'

'Ken. Yes, he is.'

His head dips, then he brings his gaze to mine. 'I'm not going to pretend I'm sad, because I'm not. He was . . . he wasn't . . . Well, he murdered the ma.'

'Yes.' I notice he says 'the ma' not 'my ma'. 'Can you tell me a bit about your family, back then?'

He grows still, as if he's gathering himself in. 'I was six so . . .' a shrug '. . . young. My memory might be wrong. Short on detail.'

'What can you remember?'

'Just the ma, the auld fella and the brother. Few animals. The bog. Bloody endless bog. Sometimes it was as if you were the only people in the world. I learned pretty early on that I could only rely on myself. The ma and the auld fella weren't what you'd call happy. We saw no one way out there. I thought it was just us in the whole world. The rest . . .' He shakes his head. 'I relied on myself, that's all.'

Too many times people who rely on themselves commit the most atrocious crimes. But he'd been out of the country. 'When you say your parents weren't happy, was there violence?'

'No. Not that I remember. Not until . . .' He stops. 'But there wasn't much fun. Tension all the time.'

'Tell me about your brother.'

He looks oddly at me. 'Sam? Haven't seen him in years, nothing to tell. I'm pretty much on my own family wise.'

There isn't much to be gained here. I don't want to upset him.

'That's fine. Would you or anyone in your family, to your knowledge, have known this lady?'

I pass over a picture of Pearl.

He takes a quick glance at it. 'I can't answer for them, but me, no.'

'Or this girl?' Lisa.

He shakes his head.

'Anyone here?' I show him an array of photos, including Pete Ryan.

Another shake. 'No. Why?'

'When your father was found,' I say, 'there was another body in the house. This woman.' I tap the picture of Pearl. 'You're sure you've never seen her before?'

'No. Was she . . .?' He lets the question hang.

'She was murdered. Left in the water tower, wearing a grey tracksuit, badly beaten.'

A small tremor of shock. 'A grey tracksuit?'

'Yes.'

I watch that sink in.

'Like the ma?' His voice is quiet.

I nod.

'Did the auld fella . . .?'

'No, we don't think so.' I let the moment shimmer, to see if he can add anything. Nothing, just a shrinking away from the pictures. 'Any ideas?' I ask.

'What? No! Jesus.' He's shocked. 'How would I have ideas? I haven't seen the old man in years.'

'We're pretty sure the person who murdered Pearl knows your family or is a member of your family or has a grudge against your family. The connections to your mother's murder are too obvious. The fact that one body was found on your farm and the other on the bog.'

'There's only me and Sam left, like. We never knew our relatives. I don't think we had any.'

They hadn't: that's been investigated.

'We've talked to Sam. He says he knows nothing either.'

'Well, then . . . Maybe it's someone else.'

'Sam says he got a letter from your father a couple of years ago, asking him to visit and he went over.'

Ken snorts. 'He would.'

'Pardon?'

'Sam was a kid back then. He barely remembers what went on.'

'What did go on?'

Ken flashes me a look, then dips his head.

'Sam says he went over but your father denied writing the note and was just messing with him.' Saying the words makes me think of something. Something I should have thought of before. 'Excuse us,' I say to Ken, as I gesture to Dan to follow me out.

'Yeah?' Dan says.

'Get someone to ask Sam if the letter he got from his father a year ago was typed or handwritten.' I wonder if our SO sent it to put Sam at the scene. Or if Sam, once again, has invented a letter to place himself at the scene. I wonder if it's a match for the note we already have. 'See if he still has it.'

'Sure thing. I'll call him myself.'

'Get Ben to join me in the interview room.'

A couple of minutes later, Ben arrives and we head back in to Ken. He is scrolling on his phone. He doesn't look as easy now, though. He's hunched over the mobile. He puts it away as I take my seat. 'Let's say it's no one in your family,' I begin.

'It isn't,' Ken says.

'Is there anyone else who would have a grudge against your family? Or Sam?'

A sigh. 'I don't know,' he says, like I'm asking him the impossible. And maybe I am. Then a bit of a snort. 'Except for maybe the Barn Boy. He was weird. I remember there was a big fight over some pups that he blamed Sam for killing.'

'Sorry? The what?'

'The Barn Boy. This guy who worked for us. The ma used to joke that he lived in the barn, that he creeped her out, so I just called him the Barn Boy.'

316

I think of Jordy's report into Chloë. How there had been a worker on the Smyth farm.

'Sam never mentioned him.'

'Sam was only two when we left there. He might not remember him. He was bloody weird.'

'Tell me about him, all you can remember.'

Beside me Ben huffs a bit and flexes his fingers. I want to kick him. This might be the break we're looking for and he's worried about writer's cramp.

It's a second before Ken speaks; his voice is faint.

'I just remember he was weird. I'd catch him standing real still, staring at me and Sam all the time. And he wore our old clothes. They didn't even fit right. He was a good few years older than us. Ma and the auld fella used to fight over him. I think the auld fella felt sorry for him and the ma was scared of him, I think, because one time he was in our kitchen and she jumped so hard and he laughed and she was shaking, I remember. He was smelly too. He seemed way older than us but we were kids so maybe he wasn't. He was just . . . always there.'

'Always there? Not a summer worker?'

'From the beginning. As far back as I remember. But me and Sam, we had to keep away from him especially after the trouble. Though Sam was only a baby so he wouldn't remember it.' He shifts a bit as if the memory makes him uncomfortable. 'One day these guards came to the house and I remember it because no one ever called to us. I must have been about five. They drove up in a police car and it was kind of exciting. And they were asking the ma and da questions and I was looking in the window of the car, excited about the radios they had and that. And then they drove away and I wanted to tell the ma all about the radios but the ma and the auld fella started screaming at each other. And I remember looking at the Barn Boy and he was smiling, just standing to the side of the auld fella, smiling. It was horrible. Then the ma hit the Barn Boy across the face and the da shouted at the ma and Sam screamed from his cot inside and I just went in to him.'

'And you have no idea what the fight was about?'

'No.'

'And your mother hit this boy?'

'Uh-huh.'

'He was an employee and she hit him?'

This comment makes him start. 'Yeah, I guess.'

I leave it with him for a second, see him thinking.

'It is kind of weird,' he adds. 'You'd think he'd have left after that.'

'You would.'

'Maybe he did. I can't remember the last time I saw him.'

'Was he there when your mother was killed?'

There is a long pause. He looks like he's composing himself. 'All that . . .' he swallows hard '. . . that's a blank for me. I can't remember huge chunks of that time.'

That's pretty normal, but also very bloody convenient.

Dan comes back and hands me a folded page. 'Typed,' he says.

No laptop, printer or typewriter was found in Pascal Smyth's house. So, either that note wasn't from his father at all or Sam never had a note.

I turn back to Ken. 'Would you remember what this Barn Boy looked like?'

'Barely.'

'If you wouldn't mind hanging on for a minute or two, I'll get our artist down to do a photofit with you.'

'Sorry,' he holds up his hands, patience running out, 'I'm a bit confused by this. What is going on? I'm asked about stuff from years ago and shown pictures of girls I don't know. Can you just explain again why I'm here?'

'You're here because of your relationship to Pascal Smyth. Two girls have been killed in the past year. We believe these murders are somehow connected to your father's farm and to the murder of your mother.'

'How can that be connected to—'

Ben pushes the CCTV picture of the blue Fiesta towards him, as I say, 'We believe this is the car that abducted Lisa and . . .' My voice trails off because Ken, at the sight of it, has reared back abruptly from the table. His mouth moves but nothing comes out.

'Ken, are you all right?' Ben asks.

Still he says nothing.

'Ken?' Ben says, with more urgency. 'Do you need some fresh air?'

'Oh, God.' He stands up. 'I'm going to be sick.'

He vomits on the floor.

40

Ken is apologetic, mortified and shaking. We give him strong sweet tea, which he clasps in both hands. His carefully constructed façade has crumbled and I find myself looking at a deeply damaged man.

He can't talk, except to apologise, and it takes at least an hour before the shaking subsides.

Finally, at around four, he says that he's all right.

'It was the sticker,' he stumbles out. 'It . . . oh, God,' he lays his head on the table. 'Seeing it like that, I don't know, brought me back and I, well, I'd sort of forgotten. Like lots of things.' He rubs a hand over his face. 'But seeing it . . .'

Dan and I wait.

'That's the da's car,' he says.

Dan looks at me, eyebrows raised. A positive ID.

'Your father's car?' I say sceptically. 'We think it is, but we can't be sure.'

'I'm sure,' he says.

'It's a zero nine reg. How would you know that? You haven't seen him since—'

'That sticker.' He jabs a finger over the tiny sticker we'd spotted on the CCTV. 'It's a Padre Pio one. He always had one of those in his car. He had it the night . . .' he makes a gesture '. . . the night he killed her. I remember now, that night, he came into the house and he was just . . . He grabbed me and Sam, shoved us into the car and told us not to move. He said police would be coming and we were not to move. We had bits of blood on us from him. And we didn't move for like hours, and I remember knowing that something awful had happened and just sitting there, staring at the sticker. Top left.' He puts his palm in the air as if touching it. 'Christ.'

We give him a moment.

'And the Barn Boy?'

He shakes his head.

'Where was he?'

'I don't know.'

'Had he left maybe?'

'I don't know!' He buries his face in his hands. 'I thought I'd left this behind me.'

'I'm sorry. You've been very helpful. Just a couple more questions. You're telling us that there was a boy who lived on your farm—'

'I don't know if he did. He might have gone home at night.'

'Did he get fed in your house?'

'The auld fella would bring food to him in the barn.'

'Right, so we can say he ate in your barn, was still there in the evening, he was beaten and still hung around. Your mother clothed him.'

'No.' He shakes his head. 'That was the da. He used to take my school books, too, and teach him.'

Slowly, like rain filling a bucket, I think I could be getting it.

'So, your father looked after this boy's welfare, on his farm. And this boy was there from for ever.'

'Yeah.'

'Your father had been married before, hadn't he?'

'I . . . think so. Yes. When, you know, the ma was killed, they said "his second wife".' He blinks. Thinking. Then shakes his head. 'Nah, no way.'

'Why not?'

'Because I . . .' He looks like a man whose mirror on the world has shattered to reveal that all he has been seeing is the reflection of everything he's been told. Finally, a nod. 'I suppose it could be right, though I never—'

'Get an artist in here, Ben.'

He hops up and leaves.

'Thanks, Ken,' I say. 'Would you mind staying a bit longer? I know it's inconvenient. We'll take a statement, if that's okay.'

Two hours later, both Ken and Chloë have described the same man. The drawings are remarkably similar. And, again, that niggling feeling in the back of my head.

'If that's our boy, I think he was Sam and Ken's half-brother,' I say to Dan, who is nodding along. 'Pascal's first wife died, but because the children picked up after the murder were six and two years old, it was just assumed that they were Pascal's only children. No one thought another boy was living there, probably his first wife's child. And, as a result, we lost sight of him too.'

'But the neighbours,' Dan plays devil's advocate, 'would they not have known there was another boy there? Would they not have seen him with Pascal?'

'This isn't Dublin,' I say. 'That farm is miles from anywhere.

322

People might have seen the boy in the early days, might even have helped out, but Pascal remarried, and if the family were as isolated as Sam and Ken say they were, I reckon that boy was written out of the family narrative. Pascal could have told people he'd left. No one would be sure of his exact age.'

'Which was at least fifteen at the time of June's murder.' Dan does the maths. 'Pascal was married to June for eleven years, and four years before that he was married to his first wife, who, we think, had the baby and died.'

I nod in agreement. 'I know Mick is looking into Pascal's first wife. Just check in with him and tell him to investigate if the woman had a child at all. And if she did, what the hell happened to it.'

'On it,' Dan says.

'And if we've seen him before and interviewed him, then his alibi is a lie. Has Pat finished his checking?'

'For the main ones, yes.'

'Then we've missed something. I want those files.' I can't think of anything else to do.

I push open the door of the office, nod a hello to Larry, who is at his desk, ploughing through the endless stream of CCTV. I flick on my computer.

Dan nods to Larry too.

'Yez might like to see this.' Larry points to CCTV he has been examining. 'I might just have found our suspect on here.'

We're over to him in less time than it takes to clamp cuffs on someone.

'That Kev Deasy has his uses.' Larry taps the screen. 'He gave us a good lead. Fair play to him. I called a few of the businesses along that street – the street where we reckon he had a coffee or whatever that night – and two of them had CCTV for the front of their shops. Luckily, one at each end of the street. See this guy,' he taps his pen at the image in the top corner of his screen, 'he's in black. He's got the scarf over his face, head ducked down. He's very aware of cameras. Now see where he goes.' We watch as the man in the video disappears from sight. 'That's about where the coffee shop is. Now watch.' He rolls the video on until the time reads 1:50 a.m. The guy reappears, this time zipping up his jacket, head still ducked but there is a moment when he crosses the road, looks left and right, and Larry captures a profile, not very clear but clear enough. 'This is him heading up towards Parliament Street,' he says. 'And here he is, waiting.' He flicks to another video, bottom left. 'He disappears into this doorway, see, but he's forced out of it when, I guess, he spots the garda car – and watch.'

An empty street, save for this man in black, hidden in a doorway. A taxi passes up and out of frame but we can see a reflection of the tail lights as it stops outside the helpline centre. The guy pops his head out, looks upwards, then glances down the street to the way he's just come. He spots the garda car and, the brass neck of him, goes right over. 'I'm going to scour more footage now, see if he pops up anywhere else. I'll also see if we can get an estimate of his height and build too.'

'Blow up that profile, Larry.'

Larry does and prints me a copy. It's grainy and not great quality, but it's more than we had. In my gut, I know this is our man.

I email it to everyone.

An hour later, Dan and I are re-checking alibis. We're getting tetchy. It's like knocking our heads off brick walls.

'I think I, eh, have something,' Mick says, arriving, his cheerful face bright red with what looks like excitement.

'Go on,' I say. It's bound to be better than this waste of time.

He lays some stuff in front of me. 'I've been looking at Pascal Smyth's wives,' he says. 'Now, as you can see, June Smyth and Pascal Smyth, had two children. Boys. Samuel and Kenneth. We know those ones. I couldn't find a third child at all so I looked under the name Smyth to see if there were any children born in a particular range of years. There were loads but,' Mick holds up a finger, 'I'm working on the assumption that Pascal had always lived on the bog and, bingo, I found a birth cert of a boy, Pascal Junior, father Pascal Smyth, dated four years before Pascal married June.'

'And the mother's name, is that on the birth cert?'

'Francesca McCarthy, the first wife. She died on the same day as this boy was born.'

'Anything else?'

'Loads.' Mick smiles. 'So, I found Pascal and Francesca's marriage cert. And Francesca's death cert. And then the trail went cold. There was nothing on the son. Just a birth cert dated two years after he was born. No death cert I could find, nothing in the local schools, but then,' he places a page in front of me, 'I got his PPS number, ran it through the system and guess what? He's changed his name by deed poll to the name of his maternal grandfather.' He takes a breath. 'Paul McCarthy,' he says.

Dan lets out a low whistle.

The running friend of Lisa's.

That flash of recognition I had when I saw Sam and Ken. I'm kicking myself now. Paul McCarthy looked like them.

'It fits,' Larry says.

Then I pull over the CCTV image.

It could be him.

Then again, it could be anyone.

But I can sniff it now, like a hound on the scent. And yet . . .

'That's great, Mick. Right, so we know that in all probability Paul McCarthy is Pascal Smyth's son. We know he knew Lisa. We also suspect he knew Pearl. We don't know that he killed anyone. What we need to do is pull down a picture of Paul from his social media, if he has any, or use that photofit picture we have from Chloë and Ken, and show it around Westport, around Pearl's workplace, go to Ballina and show it around Emma's work-place, and see if anyone can identify him. Don't prejudice it. Put it alongside others. We need to establish a connection between Paul and Pearl and Paul and Emma at the very least.'

'On it,' Larry says.

I rifle through the witness statements and pull out Paul's. Holding it up, I say, 'This is our problem. His neighbour backs up his alibi. He got home at four and popped into hers soon after. He stayed with her until six thirty. There is no opportunity to take Lisa at all.'

'I'm finished with the boot prints now,' Ben says. 'I'll take a trip over to the neighbour and double-check that alibi. Maybe she mistook the day.' He takes the file from me.

'I'll go with you.' My mind hums. Okay: if Paul is our guy, he has to have the car stored somewhere nearby. 'Mick, talk to companies who lease lock-ups in the area, see if any was taken in Paul's name. No, actually, he's far too clever to have used his own name. Get a list of everyone who's taken a lock-up within a ten-mile radius. Any further and he'd never have had the time to get the car and drive it, abduct Lisa and make it to running

326

by seven o'clock. Then talk to the owners – bring photographs along, including Paul's, and see if anyone recognises him.'

Mick nods.

I turn to Dan. 'Get someone to call Ken, see if he'll submit to a DNA test so we can compare him with Paul when we bring him in.'

'Sure thing,' Dan says. 'Let's do this.'

Paul's neighbour lives right out on the north side of the island. As I navigate the twisty, up-and-down roads, Ben reads aloud Paul's alibi again so we're up to speed.

It's watertight.

'Who's this neighbour?' I ask. 'What's her name?'

'Rita Keel. Eighty-one. Lives alone.'

I know Rita. Her husband and daughter were killed in a car crash many years ago. She's a nice woman. Hardly likely to lie.

But something is off. I know Paul is our guy. When he'd told us that Lisa had confided in him about her trouble at work, it had jarred with me. Why would she tell him and no one else? I'd asked him that at the time and he'd brushed it off. Now I realise she probably hadn't told him anything. He'd just seized on it in the hope we'd go haring off in that direction. Paul must be lying about his alibi. But that means his neighbour is lying too.

But why, for God's sake?

And then I remember something. Something one of the lads said in one of the meetings and it clicks. And I think I know how to get her to change her story.

'Ben.' I turn to him as I pull up in front of the neighbour's house. 'Let me do the talking, will you?'

'No problem, Luce.'

The house is tumbledown, but someone has painted the front door – it's a cheery red – and an attempt has been made to tame the overgrown garden. Our knock is answered before we've even taken breath. An elderly woman with bright, intelligent eyes peers at us from a gloomy hallway. The smell of cabbage wafts towards us.

We introduce ourselves and at first, in slight alarm, she says she's busy, that she can't talk. I tell her we'll only be a moment, it's about Paul, that he might be in trouble and we need her to clear something up for us. As I expected, she immediately invites us in and asks if we'd like tea. We refuse.

She leads us into a tiny front room with a blazing turf fire. It's like stepping back into the 1920s.

'Is Paul all right?' she asks, with concern.

'He's grand,' I say.

'I thought you said he was in trouble.'

'We're here to double-check the alibi you gave him.'

'Oh.' A jerk back. Swallowing, she gestures for us to sit down and takes a seat opposite. Her fingers knot themselves together.

'The day Lisa Moran disappeared, you say that Paul was here with you?'

A beat. Tightly, 'Yes, that's right. He calls in every day checking I haven't fallen or hurt myself.'

'And he was here that evening?'

'He was.' She stands up. 'Is that all? I have—'

'He was here for two and a half hours?'

'Yes.'

'Doing?'

A flap of a hand. 'Just . . . talking.'

I stand up too, move towards her, 'Well, while you were just

328

talking, Rita, a girl was abducted and murdered. A poor girl was killed. Someone's daughter.' I feel awful for using it against her but I go on, 'Can you imagine the grief?'

She flinches.

'Her mother needs answers, Rita.'

I wait.

Nothing.

'She needs justice for her little girl.'

I can see her wavering.

'If you're covering for Paul, we need to know.'

Rita blinks, tears in her eyes. 'Paul would never—'

'That mother is half mad with grief.'

'He's a kind man, he helps me out. He would never—'

'Was Paul here, Rita?'

'He painted my door. He takes me to the graves.'

'Was Paul here that evening?'

'He would never—'

'We need to know.'

She looks at me as if she wants to tell but that to do so would hurt her too much.

I play my last card. 'Paul is not your son, Rita. I know you told the guard that he was like the son you never had, but he's not your son. You are not his mother.'

The words land like blows. 'Don't,' she says, like a plea. Then, on a sob that comes from somewhere bone deep inside, she whispers again, 'Don't.'

The world is such a sad place, I think, as I fish a tissue out of my pocket and pass it to her. This poor lonely woman was just ripe for the plucking. I cast a look back at Ben, who's still sitting on the sofa. He shakes his head at me.

Finally, after what seems the longest time, she wipes the last of her tears. 'I'm sorry.' She sniffs. 'It's so . . . hard, knowing that the best part of you is gone. My girl . . .' She stops, not wanting to go there. Instead, she says, with more composure, 'And you're wrong about Paul, he's a good man. He did nothing, he wouldn't, but . . . he wasn't here that night. He told me he'd come home and fallen asleep. He said it'd look bad for him with no alibi and he was terrified, so, you know, I offered to give him one. He didn't want me to but I offered. That's all. He did nothing.'

'He manipulated you. That's what he did,' Ben snaps, cross on her behalf.

'Detective!' I warn. I turn back to Rita. 'When did you offer to cover for him?'

'Monday. After the body – the girl was found.'

Oh, yes.

I take a statement after reading out the declaration to her: 'I hereby declare that this statement is true to the best of my knowledge and belief and that I make it knowing that if it is tendered in evidence I will be liable to prosecution if I state in it anything which I know to be false or do not believe to be true.'

When we get back to the station, we dig a little deeper and we find more.

But it might still not be enough to hand to the Cig.

41

We have laid it all out before William.

'Just because this man is the son of Pascal Smyth, it doesn't prove he killed anyone,' William argues.

'He knew Lisa,' I say.

'Did he know Pearl?'

'We think so. We're just confirming now.'

'Any proof he knew Emma? And don't say you think so.'

'We don't know.'

'Pearl was found on his dad's farm,' Dan says.

'Like I said, that proves nothing. Have we the car?'

'Not yet,' I say.

'His alibi was false,' Dan says. 'Luce said the woman told—'

'And Paul said that woman was senile,' William snaps. 'Maybe she's imagining things. Show me a medical report on her and I'll believe you then.' William looks at us, palms flat on the desk. He sighs. 'Look, we had Ryan in and there was nothing. We had a big operation in Erris and there was nothing. I'm not saying he's not our guy, but he's clever. Where is the motive?'

'He's obviously a fruit cake.' Dan is losing patience. 'Guys like that don't need a motive, Cig, you should know that. He's a serial killer, for God's sake.'

William sucks in his breath. 'We have no proof of that.'

'The women look like his stepmother who we think treated him very badly. Or at least he believes she did.'

'Again speculation.'

'He was forced to live in a barn, he was uneducated and unwashed. That's fact. Pearl was found in Pascal Smyth's water tower—'

'How many times—'

'Chloë Spenser says he attacked her when he was a teenager,' I chime in.

'Lucy, stop it!' William says. 'She didn't name him.'

He's right, of course. 'We need to question him,' I say. 'We need to find out where he was the night Pearl disappeared. Only he can tell us that.'

'But will he?' William says. 'It'd fly if he said he couldn't possibly remember. It was eight months ago.'

Jesus, Jesus, I'm thinking, we need to act now. Just as I'm about to say so, my phone rings. It's Mick. 'Yes?'

'Are you with the Cig?'

'Yep.'

'Put me on speaker.' I do and Mick says, 'Just got a positive ID from a staff member in Emma's shop. Seems Paul was a regular customer over the last while. In fact, he came in asking after her last Tuesday, the night of the sting.'

Dan and I look up at William.

'Two out of three,' Dan says.

And still he hesitates. 'What about getting eyes on him?'

'We could,' I say, 'but I think we're wasting time. Can we interview him about his false alibi?'

'He'll say the woman is senile.' After a second, 'All right, Lucy. Let's meet halfway. Give it a few more hours before you bring him in. I want every effort made to locate that car. To find the connection between him and Pearl. Put Ben on surveillance – he loves that. Where would Paul be now?'

I glance at my watch. 'On his way back from work.'

'Tell Ben to stay out of sight at all costs.'

'Right.'

My phone rings.

Luc's number pops up and my heart hops. 'Mam,' he says. He sounds odd or maybe it's just that he doesn't sound as grumpy as usual.

'Has something happened?'

'It's Tani, she's having the baby.'

Even though I knew it was going to happen soon, it's still a shock to hear it. I don't quite know what he wants from me. 'Is she all right?'

'I think so. She's in the hospital, like.'

'That's the best place for her.'

'Yeah.'

'Are you there too?'

'Yeah. We were on the bus together when she said she had these pains. It's terrible sore, Ma.'

'I know.' I allow myself a smile.

The two men are looking at me. William waves us out.

'I'll just go down and help Jordy with trying to locate the car,' Dan says.

I nod, turn back to the phone.

'Her ma is here,' Luc says then. A whisper: 'She's sort of taken over. She told me to stay outside, that I'd caused enough trouble.'

The bloody cheek. 'It wasn't just your fault,' I huff. 'What did you say?'

'Nothing. I don't think she likes me much.'

How dare she not like Luc? And how dare she be rude to me on the phone? 'Do you want to see your baby born?' I ask him.

He hesitates. 'I don't know. I might not like it.'

I bite back a retort. 'Do you think you should be with this girl during labour?' I can't flipping remember her name now.

'Yeah, yeah, I do.'

'Then go and tell the mother that.'

There's a silence. 'I'm not like you,' he says, and I don't know if it's a criticism or a compliment. 'And they're not like us.'

'What do you mean?' Then, before he can answer, it dawns on me that that girl, whom I have never set eyes on, is giving birth to my grandchild, and while I would wish for things to be different, it's my son's baby and I should be there.

I have a few hours. Nothing will happen until we find the car.

'I'll be with you in an hour,' I say.

I hang up and run to find Dan. 'You're going to have to tic-tac without me for the next couple of hours, Dan. Once we find that car, we'll need a search warrant. Get preparing one. And see if there's any possibility of locating a photo from Paul's teenage years to show Chloë. If she makes a one hundred per cent positive ID, we're cooking. He's got form.'

He holds up his hands. 'I know,' he says, with a smirk, 'I've done this before. Just go. I'll keep you informed.'

I gabble out a thanks, grab my coat from the office and head down to my car.

42

Eddie is up at the desk, showing Matt his feet when I get down.

'There's nothing wrong with them feet that a bath wouldn't cure,' Matt says, rolling his eyes at me as I pass.

Ah, the joys of the front desk.

On the other side of the station, Stacy is sitting beside Malachy, the gloomiest man in Mayo, and he's totally invading her space as he talks at her. '. . . waste of time, the gangsters in the force.' He's almost on top of her as he bends towards her to make his point. 'They're all speeding and running people over and wiping it under the carpet, and then they sell all the drugs they confiscate back to the dealers and build mansions for themselves. You should print that now.'

'I'd need more evidence.' Stacy tries to move away but Malachy is like a limpet. Then she spots me and it's the perfect excuse to hop away from her informant, who overbalances. 'Detective Lucy Golden,' she says, and I wonder how she got my name. 'Any news? My editor says the case has stalled. Is that true?'

'That's one of them there.' Malachy wags a finger in my direction. 'I see her out in all sorts of cars. Never the same one. Day in, day out.'

'They're from the car pool,' I say to him. Then, to Stacy, 'You'll be informed when we've something to report.'

'Is it true that you blew a lot of money on a surveillance operation that went wrong?'

'Where did you hear that?'

'I can't divulge my sources,' she says. 'Is it true?'

'Of course it's true,' Malachy calls over. 'They waste money left, right and centre. She'll be off partying now with illegal drink or something.'

Stacy follows me out. The wind almost knocks the two of us off our feet. 'Where are you going? Are you off to arrest a suspect?'

I push against the breeze to my car, ignoring her.

'Where are you going?' she says, as she runs alongside me.

'That's not your business,' I say. And then I think I'll make it her business – at least it'll take the heat off the boys in the station. 'Do not obstruct my work.'

She'll be very confused when she sees me entering a hospital.

It makes me smile.

I pull up outside Mayo University Hospital, parking illegally. I know I shouldn't but it'll intrigue Stacy.

I race across the road, pretending I don't see her, run through the automatic front doors and into the corridor.

Luc texts me that he's on the first floor and I take the stairs two at a time, panting more than I really should. I used to be a good runner. I have to bend double when I reach the top, gasping for air. It's a bit embarrassing. Behind me, I hear the clip-clip of stilettos and think that Stacy is in hot pursuit. I don't want to make it too easy for her so I plough on through the double doors before she can see where I've gone.

I stop abruptly at the sight of Luc, his back to me, hands in his pockets, his head dipped. There is something so alone in his stance that it hurts me. I call to him and he turns. 'All right?' I say, hurrying towards him.

'She's in that room.' He points to a door at the end of the corridor. 'I tried to do like you said but her ma just yelled at me and only one person is allowed in at a time. I don't want to go upsetting Tani.'

'And does she want her mother there, or you?' He shrugs and I want to shake him. 'You need to find out. You have to be stronger than her mother for her sake.'

He rubs a hand over his face and turns away. We stand there, two islands in a sea of humming, buzzing, crying humanity.

I wait and he waits, and neither of us says anything. Nurses pass between us, looking busy and important. Finally, in the lull, I blurt out, 'Are you scared?'

He turns slowly, looks at me. 'Yes,' he says, so quiet I think I've imagined it. Then, a little louder, 'I don't know what to do, Ma.'

And I don't have to think any more. I pull him into me and hug him hard. He needs me. And he called me. I feel full, I feel joy. And relief. And sadness. And grief. All these emotions go zinging about inside me, ricocheting off my nerves, like pinballs. He leans his chin on my head and we stay like that for a few moments. Then I pull away. 'It's just a baby,' I say. 'And you will figure it out and so will . . .' Damn, I've forgotten her name again.

'Tani,' he supplies.

'Yes, Tani. You'll both be great. And I'll be there and your nan . . . But you need to go back in there and say your piece and see what the girl wants.'

He squares his shoulders. 'Right. Right, I will.'

I watch him make his way up the corridor, trousers halfway down his arse, his baseball cap backwards, huge runners. Flipping hell, I think.

And then I realise he's gone back in there to face that mother because he trusts my advice and I feel – I search for the word and it blooms inside me – privileged. Go, Luc.

I watch as he pops his head into the room and I hear raised voices. I want to run up there and thump that stupid woman but I don't. Then Luc steps in and firmly closes the door. About a minute later, a woman stomps out. Tall, effortlessly elegant, with the sort of swishy hair well-groomed dogs have. She's in ballet pumps and skinny jeans and looks about thirty. Though she's older than that because, to my absolute horror, I know her.

And not in a good way. No wonder Luc had been scant on the details. Boyfriend stealer of my adolescence, the woman Rob had swindled in the mistaken belief I'd be thrilled.

I want to disappear through the floor before she sees me.

But I can't do that. I have as much right to be here as she does.

'Hi, Katie,' I say, in a bright, breezy voice that isn't mine.

She arches her perfectly groomed eyebrows and looks at me in the disapproving way that makes me feel about ten years old. 'It's Katherine now and let's not pretend,' she says, as she sits down on a hospital chair, crossing one skinny leg over the other. She pulls a compact mirror from her bag, flips it open and examines herself in it. It's her way of ignoring me.

Feck that, I think. I sit beside her. 'I didn't know Tani was your daughter.'

She flicks a glance at me, 'Well, she is.'

I know I have to be the bigger person. I have to make it all right for Luc. 'Luc and I, we want to help out any way we can.'

'I'd rather you didn't.'

'This will be my grandchild too. You can't cut us out.'

She takes a breath, holds it, expels it, says, with what appears to be an effort at keeping calm, 'Your husband, your son's father, swindled us out of thousands. And now my daughter is having that man's grandchild. It makes me sick. I don't need your help.'

I refuse to apologise for Rob. I've spent the last ten years doing that and I won't any more. 'Luc is not Rob,' I say, hurt on behalf of my son. 'He's about as different from Rob as you are from me.'

She doesn't know how to take that one.

'And I am not Rob,' I say too. 'I had nothing to do with what he did.'

'You were a guard and you never noticed.' She gives a bit of a snort.

'Yes,' I say, 'and I have to live with that. He fooled me too.'

'Some guard,' she scoffs.

Years of policing and interviewing have given me good training. I will not rise to her. I go back to the main point: 'We will have a part to play in this baby's life whether you want it or not.'

'I made it perfectly clear that I don't want it.'

'Yes, but your daughter obviously does.'

She flinches and I think, One-nil to me.

Just then, the double doors at the top of the corridor blast open and Stacy stands there for a second, breathless and heaving. I reckon she's been up to the top floor and worked her way down. I whip my head away but it's too late.

'Detective,' she says smugly, marching over. 'I see you've apprehended a suspect in the murder case.' She's referring to Katherine, who gawps.

'I beg your pardon?' Katherine splutters. 'Suspect? If anyone should be arrested—'

'Can we all wait somewhere else?' A nurse bustles over. 'This corridor is a throughway. Why don't you all go down to the canteen?'

'My little girl is in that room up there, giving birth. I'm going nowhere.' Katherine folds her arms and eyeballs the nurse.

'I'm afraid—'

'I think you will be,' Katherine says.

God, she hasn't changed. I cannot imagine having her in my life.

'I've dealt with way worse than you,' the nurse says. 'Now, shift or I'll get security and you won't even be within the hospital grounds when your daughter gives birth.'

'I'll have—'

'For feck's sake, come on,' I say to Katherine, as I haul myself up. 'There's nothing you can do.'

Katherine glares at me, glares at the nurse, then sweeps to her feet in one graceful motion, tossing back her hair. She follows me down the corridor, and behind us, I hear Stacy quizzing the nurse on just who exactly is in that room at the top of the corridor. The nurse is telling her to 'do one'.

Stacy catches up with me just as we're about to get into the lift to bring us to the canteen. 'The public have a right to know, Detective,' she says to me. 'Has this monster impregnated a woman now?'

'Her son may be bad but he's not like his father.' Katherine surprises me by sticking up for Luc. 'Or I most certainly hope not,' she tacks on.

'Excuse me?' Stacy says, screwing her face up and wrinkling her nose. 'Sorry? What?'

'This has nothing to do with the case, Stacy,' I say. 'My son and his . . .' I can't think how to describe the girl in relation to Luc '. . . his friend are having their first baby and I'll thank you to butt out of a private family matter.'

She looks devastated, then rallies. 'You weren't on actual official garda business when you parked illegally outside, were you?' She says it like it's a huge scoop.

'No, she wasn't,' Katherine supplies helpfully.

The lift pings and the doors slide open. A woman is wheeled out by an orderly, anxious husband trotting alongside. 'That baby in there will be a boxer,' the orderly tells her, with a grin.

And ping.

Something lodges in my head at the words. Stacy is jabbering on about unprofessional conduct but it barely registers.

Ping.

I grab her arm and say, 'I need you to do something for me.'

She's taken by surprise.

'Talk later,' I say to Katherine, as I step back out of the lift, hauling Stacy with me. She has no time to react before the doors close on her.

'Can you get into your newsroom archives and check something out for me?' I ask Stacy.

She snorts in derision. 'I wasn't born yesterday. I'm not going to be put off again.'

'I need you to do this, Stacy, or I'll have to get on to your editor and he will not be happy if he thinks you've missed a scoop.' Beat. 'If you do this, I promise you'll have first dibs on any information we get.'

'Yeah, right.'

I plunge in: 'I need you to find if there was anything published either in your paper or elsewhere in the past few years on boxing, referencing either a Pascal Smyth Junior or Paul McCarthy.'

'Paul? That weirdo?'

'You know him?'

'Not personally, but my old boyfriend interviewed him after a boxing match once. I remember because he was covered in blood and barely standing and still had his hands in the air like he'd won. Made a great front page. I can get Charlie to call you.'

'That'd be great. Thanks.'

'I'm not doing it to help you. I want whatever comes of this.'

'Yes. First dibs.'

'Right, I'll get on to him.'

She moves away from me and I hear her muttering into the phone. My head is clear on this case for the first time since it began. I bloody love these moments. It's like climbing a hill and seeing it all laid out in front, a tapestry of whys and hows and wheres and motives and opportunity and intent.

Things are slotting together. But we still don't have that car. Or a weapon. We need to prove he was in it, that the girls were in it. We don't have a kill site.

And suddenly the wail of a baby pierces the corridor and I remember where I am. I get that awful sinking feeling in my belly that I frequently had when Luc was a boy. I have to go.

Luc appears in the doorway. 'Hey,' he says, walking towards me, 'are you all right?'

'Are you?' I ask, evading the question.

'The midwife said it'll be a few hours yet.' He looks me up and down, a half-smile. 'Go, if you need to.'

I want to apologise but to Luc, who's heard it so many times before, it'd sound empty. 'I do. We're closing in on this guy and . . .'

I don't finish. In my peripheral vision, I see Stacy looking at me, ready to hand me over to her ex-boyfriend.

'Go on,' Luc says. He doesn't sound angry or resentful.

'I'll be back before . . .' and I think, No, I can't promise anything. 'I'll see you later tonight.'

He nods.

I want to hug him, wish him luck, but we don't have that sort of relationship. Instead, I say, 'You'll be brilliant, Luc. You were there for Tani and that's really important. I'm proud of you.'

'Thanks, Ma.' A wobbly smile. He thumbs to the room. 'I'll go back in. If you see Tani's ma will you tell her it'll be another few hours?'

'Sure.' I'll pop into the canteen on my way out.

As he turns away, I think that the next time I see him, he'll be a dad.

It's too much. My eyes fill.

'Charlie.' Stacy stomps all over the moment by holding out the phone.

I take it from her. 'Charlie, hi.'

'Stace said you wanted information on a Paul McCarthy?' Charlie gets straight down to business.

'That's right. What have you got?' I'm thinking that if Paul boxed, there must be some coverage of him in the papers, especially local ones.

'She said you're the gardaí and that I was to confirm with you that you'll oblige Stace if what I have to say is helpful. I'm recording this now.'

'I confirm it.'

'Thank you, Guard,' Charlie says. 'Now, McCarthy. I only ran into him once or twice. Haven't seen him in a couple of years. He was a strange character but a nice guy to talk to. Quiet and that. But he lived in Fantasy Land. He'd get beat up good in matches, but he always acted like he won. He called himself the Captain.'

'What did he look like?'

'Bad skin, dark hair, dark eyes. Average height.'

'Did he train with a gym?'

'No idea. He'd have to, though, to get into the competitions. I'll have a look back through the archives if you like.'

'That'd be great, thanks.'

'I'm doing it for Stace. What's your number?'

I give it to him and a few seconds later my phone pings. *An easy find*, he says. He's sent me a photo of Paul that made the front page of the *Island News* five years ago. He's destroyed but unbowed. The picture captures a manic glint in those great brown eyes.

The piece is small. Paul McCarthy, a.k.a. the Captain of Central Gym in Westport, lost his bout in fine style on Friday, 22 November.

'Helpful?' Stacy asks.

'Yep. I'll be in touch.'

And I'm out of there.

I call the station on the way to let them know. Paul boxes. Another tick. 'And get someone out to a Central Gym in Westport, ask them a few questions on Paul McCarthy.'

'Sure.'

The phone goes dead.

I calculate my next move. My heart thumps and I can almost feel the blood pumping around my body.

The Captain

He stands opposite the café where he knows she will come. It's a crappy little tea and bun place full of smelly old women and harassed mothers. Screaming kids that deserve a belt.

If you don't belt kids, they don't know what life will be like, he thinks.

His dad had never hit him. He used to say to him, at night, before that other woman had come, with her blonde hair and her laugh and her poison, 'You'll be a great man, one day, and you'll make your mother proud.'

He hoped he had.

Pearl was meant to die in the barn: him and the old man were supposed to do it. Only the old man hadn't wanted to. He was sick, he said, he hadn't the strength. And he didn't want to watch, he said. Or talk about that long-ago day when the other one had died.

He wanted him to let Pearl go.

More betrayal. It cut into his heart that, once again, the old man would choose a woman over him.

And Pearl had worked on the old man, like that other bitch had, and she'd almost got her way, but he'd been smarter. He'd been those few steps ahead of them.

And the rage had come, filling him, making his hands flail and his heart pump and his head roar and he had barely known what he was doing.

And it was the splash of her hitting the water in the tower that had called him back from the fury. Called him back to the earth and grounded him once again among the bog.

The old man had helped him clean up. He'd been crying and blabbing and telling him that maybe he needed help.

And that was the last he ever saw of the old man. He was dying anyway and wasn't the best company.

'You need to go away and try to forget it all,' the old man had said.

How could you forget something that was burned on your soul?

And the pull of the place. He couldn't ever go too far. He'd tried but always the call of the bog, the smell of turf burning at nights, the songs of the birds. The bog was in his blood. Its secrets were his secrets.

And during those years, when the old man had been locked up and those interloper boys had been taken away, once or twice he'd returned to Doogort, and in the darkness of a night, he'd gone back. Stood in the barn, breathed in the stale air and remembered. Gone into the falling-down house and cleaned out the living room where he and the old man used to sit by the fire before she had come. Put a new lock on the place, ready for the old man's release.

He had been a good son.

But that was over now.

43

The station is hopping.

Paul had not turned up for work that morning citing a stomach bug. According to Ben, he does not appear to be in his house in Doogort.

'Where is he, for God's sake?' I snap.

'We think he's in Corr-na-Mona as Emma rang to say an old schoolfriend contacted her out of the blue to meet up,' Dan says. 'We've informed the station down there and they said they'll have a few lads watching the coffee shop tomorrow. Ben is heading down too.'

'If he turns up there, we should arrest him on the spot.'

Dan nods. 'We're getting the warrant. We've no lead on the lock-ups – no one recognised the face or the name.'

'And Central Gym?'

'I did that myself. It's closed but the old manager remembers Paul all right. He said he really liked him, that he was sound. Not the best boxer but he had heart, that's what he said.'

Something niggles, like it's trying to squeeze out.

'He must have stored that car somewhere,' Dan says. 'I'd say he uses it for all his pick-ups.'

'Captain,' I say, remembering what Charlie said. 'See if there are any lock-ups leased under a Captain or a—'

'Captain McCarthy,' Dan says. 'Yes. Yes, there was.'

'Then what are we waiting for?'

The Captain

There she is, blonde head bent over her coffee, long legs crossed, serene. Nothing wrong with her in the whole world that you would notice. And yet does he detect a certain anxious frown between her perfectly sculpted eyebrows?

He hates her. The feeling is just there, not like a gripping rage or searing powerlessness but a calming knowledge of what lies deep inside.

He has seen her laughing, throwing back her slender break-able neck, tossing her hair and laughing in a throaty gurgle. He has seen her blow kisses and choose cards saying, 'Love you.' He has listened when she has prattled on about being good to yourself.

And treating yourself.

Airy-fairy shit.

And he has made smart witty comments to her and she had laughed. They all had.

She had liked his bashfulness. His humour. She touched his arm or leg and he flinched each time she did so. A rolling of stomach and a subtle jerking away.

She always pretended not to notice. Maybe she hadn't.

And here she is, oblivious to his mounting excitement, as he peers across at her.

He walks in and pretends not to see her.

It's a departure from the norm but sometimes change is good. And they'd be foxed, the gardaí, because he'd read that most criminals followed the same MO time after time.

NOT HIM!

Sweets from a baby, he thinks.

44

The lock-up is located about two miles outside Doogort, on a piece of land owned by a farmer called Jason.

'Easier money than farming,' he says, when Dan and I talk to him. 'I just rent them out by the three months, and once they pay me up front, they can do what they like.'

'Do any of these men look familiar to you?' Dan shows him the requisite twelve pictures, one of which is of Paul. 'We have reason to believe our suspect is renting number thirteen.'

Jason shrugs. 'I always forget a face,' he jokes. 'I told that to the guard already. Totally shit at recognising people but I do have the name here.' He pulls out some dockets from a drawer and flips through them. 'Yes, a Captain McCarthy rented it about two years back. I thought the name a bit show-offish, to be honest. He pays me every three months, cash in hand, which I thought was weird. I have the signed agreement here,' he says, as he pulls out more papers from yet another drawer. They seem to be arranged in a very disorderly manner. 'I hate paperwork,' he says, as a pile slides to the floor. 'Leave them,' he says to Dan, who has bent down to retrieve them. 'It's not them – they're the pink ones. I need the yellow ones.'

Ten minutes later, he hands us a signed docket. 'There you go now,' he says.

'Ding dong,' Dan says, passing it to me.

I look at him, not sure what he's getting at.

'The capital T in the middle of the words?' Dan says. 'Just like that "BiTch" over the bath?'

'Nicely spotted,' I tell him, and Dan gives me a half-salute.

I pop the docket into an evidence bag.

'Can we get access to the lock-up?' I ask. 'I have a warrant here.'

Jason waves us away. 'Off ye go, I can't stop ye. I have no keys to any of the sheds, so you'll have to break in or something. If this is a wild-goose chase, I'm taking no responsibility for yer man's door. You can deal with him yourselves.'

'Grand.'

Outside, the squad cars are gearing up to move in on the sheds, which are visible in the distance. About twenty of them sit on the crest of a hill, their doors bright red, the colour pinging in the winter sunlight. They stand out starkly against the brown bog. A backdrop of blue sky gives the place the look of a child's colouring book. I give the nod and the vehicles begin to traverse the rough-hewn, grass-down-the-middle roadway towards the buildings.

'Stay on the road,' Jason shouts. 'The bog can be a bit treacherous if you don't know it.'

We wave our acknowledgement.

'I've a good feeling about this,' Dan says.

I say nothing.

'As the crow flies,' Dan goes on, 'this is not too far from where we found Lisa's body.'

'Some job to carry a body across the bog at night,' I say.

'Not if you know the place,' he says. 'Know where to put your feet. And Paul was born here.'

And wandered about here. I remember Chloë's words – disappeared into the bog. Yes, I think, Paul would have the know-how to navigate this place.

I can't take my eyes off the buildings as they rear up in front of us, large, imposing and silent.

Nothing stirs.

The Captain

'Hey,' he says, feigning surprise, 'you from around here?'

She smiles, crooked teeth in a perfect face, and offers him the seat opposite. Just like the others, the smile is soft.

'I live up the road,' she answers. 'I like to have a coffee here.'

'It's a bit of a dive,' he says, and she laughs that laugh.

'I like dives.' She could almost be flirting with him. 'Nothing pretentious about dives. What are you doing here?'

'I'm meeting someone in about ten minutes, thought I'd grab a coffee. Can I get you another?'

She normally drinks two coffees here. He knows that about her.

'Thank you,' she says.

'Coming up.' He offers her a salute and she smiles again. He covers the lower part of his face with his scarf and approaches the counter. 'Two Americanos,' he says, in a Cork accent.

Then when the dour bitch slaps them in front of him, he adds, 'I'll have a bar of chocolate and a few packets of crisps to try and sober us up.'

The woman doesn't even blink. 'How many crisps?' she barks out.

'Three packs,' he says. 'Salt and vinegar.'

She turns to get the crisps and, quick as a flash, he pours two of his sleeping pills into one of the cups.

Oh, the high of it all. He thinks he might laugh.

45

The bolt on the door finally gives and one of the team catches it in a bag, labels it and places it aside.

The large metal doors are prised open, swinging soundlessly on well-oiled hinges. Someone has been here and has taken care of the place. With the glare of the winter sun, it's hard to make out the inside of the shed immediately, but gradually my eyes get used to the gloomy interior. The space is vast, tarpaulin covering most of the floor. A beige car, a Ford Focus, is parked on the left and some sort of a wall has been built down the middle.

The initial whack of disappointment is immense.

'That's no Fiesta,' Dan says. 'But I bet if we run the reg through the system, it'll say McCarthy has a car like that.'

Someone flicks a switch and light illuminates the space.

And that's when we see it.

Hanging from the ceiling.

The Captain

She is falling now, craning forward to look at him. He stares back at her and grows cold all over with the deathly calm he loves. The one where they become nothing to him, except something he can study, like a scientist.

'I feel sick,' she says. 'Not well.'

His hood is up, his scarf is on. 'I've my car outside,' he says. 'Tell me where you live and I'll drive you back.'

She looks confused. Scared, maybe. He hopes she's scared, that makes it better. 'Call S—'

'Up we go.' He walks around the table and hoists her to her feet. A couple of middle-aged biddies with dyed hair and judgemental stares follow his progress as he drags her out into the night. Her arm is draped about his shoulders. Her head lolls close to his. The smell of her sends his senses spinning, makes him want to yank her hair back and break her neck, but he holds himself in check.

Time enough.

It's better when they're aware of what's happening: the pure terror makes his blood jump in the way nothing else ever has since he was small.

When he was small everything was a wonder, but he had to leave that behind to survive, to push on in this fucking life.

He opens his car and throws her inside. She falls across the back seat and he covers her with a blanket. Just another fellow minding his passed-out girlfriend.

46

Hanging from the ceiling is a punch bag. It's behind the stone wall. As is a small bed, a slop bucket underneath, a cup and plate. Women's shoes. Tracksuits. Lots of them.

The floor is packed dirt. Stains that could be blood spatter it. The smell of disinfectant is powerful.

'Can you turn that punch bag around for me?' I ask one of the Forensics boys and he does, slowly rotating it until I tell him to stop. There, up at the top, a piece of fabric is missing.

This might just be the most solid piece of evidence we have so far. I'm swamped by a feeling I can't quite catch, sadness, gratitude, a sense of how powerless we are in the face of things.

Thank you, Lisa, I think.

In my mind's eye, I see her rolling on the floor, covering herself in the dirt of the place. Getting the grime between her fingernails.

'I want everything here photographed,' I say, 'then I want a—'

My phone rings. It's Larry. 'Just here with Sam,' he says. 'He was at home last week, was nowhere near Parliament Street and his girlfriend could confirm. The only thing is, she hasn't come home yet.'

'Wait there until she does.'

'No. We think she's missing. He says she normally goes to a coffee shop after her yoga class but that she's usually home by seven. She's not answering her phone and it's after nine now. I've called the coffee shop, it was closed, but the owner got on to the woman who was working there earlier and she confirms that Evie came in and was joined by a man she seemed to know. She said Evie was drunk, that a couple of the customers remarked on it.'

And that's when the niggling feeling I had earlier blooms. Only it's too late.

'Fuck!' I say. 'We've been played. He's not gone back after Emma. He wants to hurt Sam.'

It's been so obvious and I didn't see it.

'We need to get out of here now,' I say. 'We need to make like we've never been.' And then I explain to them what's happened. 'He'll bring her back here. I know he will. We need to catch him in the act. Dan, send out a description and registration on the Fiesta over Control. I want this fecker caught before he can do anything.'

'I think it's too late,' Dan says, pointing.

From a small distance away, headlights are approaching. The drone of a car engine can be heard as a car trundles its way along the makeshift gravel path, bouncing.

Dan and I run out to our car and as Dan makes the radio calls, I fire up the engine.

The Captain

In the back seat, she moans, but it'll be a while before she's totally herself. He'll enjoy looking at her as realisation dawns. That's one of his favourite expressions, so it is, realisation dawning. Because it does, like the sun over landscape or, in this case, a cloud over the sun.

When will Sam realise that his girlfriend is not coming home? When will his realisation dawn? Will he worry she's been murdered, like his disgusting mother was murdered? Will he look for her? Will he forever wonder . . .

His headlights snag on something up ahead, something metallic. There is nothing at all metallic between the off-road entrance and the lock on the shed. He rolls down his window and he hears it, another car. Coming closer, its headlights off.

Up here.

Without hesitation, he turns the wheel, hard, the car bounces onto the muck of the field, the tyres slip and slide before gaining purchase and he's firing off in the other direction. Behind him, headlights flood his vision, the wail of a siren howls through the night and he thinks, Shit, shit, shit.

His plan will fail, he thinks.

STUPID!

NO!

He feels he is falling.

Crashing down through the bog to where everything stays for ever. Where bodies and utensils are preserved and remembered and pulled out hundreds of years on, intact. Where hurts and grievances never fade. Where the land remembers and won't let go.

That day, the first day he saw her, he was mesmerised that such a beautiful creature could come to live on the barren, flat land. Mesmerised that such a beautiful creature would come and care for him and his daddy.

And in time, under her rule, she moulded him to the landscape so that he became like the bog, holding and remembering and powerless to let go of the past.

He hops out of his car. If he can run across the bog, he can make it safely away, just like that time many years ago, after the first one on the beach. He could hop from mounds of sedge grass to sedge grass, lead them on a merry dance, see them sink in the marshes. He's managed to take a few steps – the wind is biting, the air the freshest he's ever inhaled. His senses are alive and buzzing.

'Hands up,' the voice commands. A man steps out of the car in front. The man who interviewed him all those months ago. Or was it only a few days ago? His mind is fuzzy on that. The man is tall, wears a shirt and tie and a bulletproof vest.

'Fuck off,' he says, and starts to run. Hop. Hop. Hop.

But the guard is faster: he slams him down into the boggy marsh, catching a fistful of his jacket. He doesn't know the bog, though. He loses his footing and sinks. Down into the bog hole that hides there.

He tries to shake the guard loose but the fucker has hold of his shirt and won't let go. As the guard sinks, he drags him to the ground and now they are eyeball to eyeball, the guard in the hole and him on solid ground. Bam! Right hook, left hook. If he can get out of this, he can hide. Right hook, left hook. And the blood is pumping from the guard's nose and face, and boggy water is streaming into his mouth and still . . .

He reaches out, two hands, and pushes hard on the guard's head. Down.

He hears the man choke and he smiles.

And then, just as the guard's fingers loosen their grip, they come for him, like a herd of swarming dogs and it's too late . . .

47

I watch in a frozen horror as Dan is pulled from the bog hole, Paul shrieking, like a trapped animal, that they have no right to arrest him. As Paul is led to the garda car, cursing and spitting, Dan is laid on the marshy ground of the bog, as still and cold as the night air.

'Let me in there.' I push through the crowd, fall to my knees and start to give mouth-to-mouth. Someone dials an ambulance. One of the other guards takes a turn with me. I fight the panic rising in me. One-two-three.

Nothing.

From across the flat landscape the sound of a siren. As we pump, the lights of the ambulance grow closer and then, just as it reaches us, Dan coughs and splutters and I think I might cry, only I can't. Not in this place, not in front of these men.

I stand aside – we all stand aside – as Dan is brought into the ambulance.

And then I follow it to the hospital.

William is already there. He takes one look at me, at my filthy trousers and matted hair, and orders me home.

'I can't,' I say, folding my arms. 'This is . . . I can't.'

'But you will,' William says. 'You can't do anything here. And you look a state.' A bit more gently, he adds, 'I'll keep you posted. Who's his next of kin? I'll send one of the boys out to let them know what's happened.'

Dan would die, I think. 'Let me do that at least and then I'll go home.'

'You'll frighten the family,' he says firmly.

'Dan lives with just one other person,' I say. Then, because I know that William will meet him anyway, I add, 'Fran. A man.'

William takes a second, absorbs it, and nods in understanding. 'Right. Well, let me do it. What's the address?'

I'm about to protest, but I know it'll be useless. I rattle it off.

'Go home,' he says then, turning on his heel and striding off down the corridor.

Just then my phone rings.

Blindly I answer it.

'It's a girl, Ma.' Luc's happy voice is a shock. Like vibrant yellow on a black background. 'Ma? Did you hear me? Are you okay?'

And I can't ruin it for him, this big moment. His absolute joy. 'I did,' I say. 'That's wonderful.' I inject all the happiness I can into my voice. 'Wonderful. I'll be there as soon as I can.'

48

My granddaughter is red-faced, tiny-fisted, with a cap of dark hair. She lies snug in her mother's arms, wrapped papoose-like in a white blanket. Peaceful and innocent and utterly beautiful. Katherine and I are speechless with the wonder of it.

I have washed and changed and fielded my mother's anxious questions, and am now just trying to enjoy this moment, trying not to let Luc see how shaken I am by the evening's events. Just gazing upon this as yet unspoiled life has me wanting to break down. I have to keep blinking back tears.

Luc looks proud and unsure and awkward and young. Tani, without all her make-up, is a pretty girl, petite, with delicate features. She is besotted with her new daughter and it gives me hope. If a mother loves her child enough and her child feels it, it can protect that kid from an awful lot of damage. It can't make life go away but it builds resilience and confidence, and that's all that's needed sometimes.

'She's gorgeous,' Katherine says, and her eyes are soft and she doesn't look like the superior bitch I know.

'Isn't she?' Tani holds her baby out to her mother. 'D'you want a go?'

Katherine looks unsure. 'I don't know. I—'

'Willya just take her, Ma? She's only small so she can't actually object, can she?'

'All right, bossy boots.' She says it affectionately and Tani places the baby in her open arms. The baby must sense that she's been moved because she squirms and it almost makes me smile as Katherine visibly stiffens. Then the baby opens her eyes and we're struck again with the wonder of her.

'Look at that,' Katherine says. 'Clever little thing.' She starts to coo at her.

'Any names?' I ask Luc and Tani.

Luc nods. 'Sirocco.'

I have no words.

'Sirocco,' Katherine says. 'Do people name their children after warm Mediterranean winds now?'

I'm glad she said it and not me. 'What if they call her "Sir" for short?' she goes on.

'I never thought of that.' Tani's face creases in dismay. 'That would be crap, wouldn't it, Luc?'

'A bit weird all right.' I try to mirror her disappointment, but I'm really thinking, Christ, do not lumber your child with that name.

'We could just tell people we don't want it shortened,' Luc says staunchly, and Tani smiles at him.

'That's clever,' she says.

Luc beams and I think, Oh, my God, he likes this girl. He actually likes her. And I get a lump in my throat and I can't figure out why.

Katherine looks to me for back-up but I shrug. 'Sirocco, it is,' I say, almost choking on the words. It's only a name.

Katherine's face tightens slightly but she says nothing. In her arms the baby starts to wriggle and then, scrunching up her perfect little face, she starts to howl. Quick as a flash, Katherine hands her back to her daughter. Over the wails, she says, 'Your dad will be in later, once he finishes work.'

I do not want to meet him. For one thing, I still haven't tackled my hair. I go hot and cold simultaneously.

'Why is she crying?' Tani asks her mother. 'I only fed her a few minutes ago.'

'Babies cry.' Katherine flaps a hand about. 'You did when you were that age.'

'Maybe she's too hot,' I suggest. 'It's warm in here and she is all wrapped up.'

'Yeah.' Tani lays the baby on the bed and removes the blanket. Luc tries to help but he just succeeds in getting in the way. Tani lets him, though, and I find myself liking her. The baby is wearing the weirdest-looking Babygro. White with a print of a sheriff's outfit. It's truly horrible.

'Good God,' Katherine says, recoiling.

'Isn't it great?' Luc says to me. 'I bought it with the money me nan gave me for my birthday.'

'It was a dead clever present,' Tani says, 'because—'

'– it would have suited a boy or a girl,' Luc joins in, and they laugh.

'She looks great,' I say, and Katherine gives me daggers across the bed.

My phone pings and I pull it out of my jacket.

It's a text from William: *Dan good. Get some sleep. Good work today. William.*

And the tears come, just a couple.

Happy tears.

And gathering myself, I hold out my arms for my new grand-child and kiss her tiny baby-scented head. 'Hi, Sirocco, welcome to the world. It's not a bad place to be.'

20 December

Man Caught for Bog Land Murder

Stacy McCann

Gardaí on Achill Island have confirmed that they have apprehended a man in connection with the brutal murder of Lisa Moran on 5 December last. The body of Lisa Moran was found on Doogort East Bog on Achill Island by a dog-walker. After an exhaustive seven days' search, the police finally arrested a suspect yesterday evening. The man, believed to be known to the victim, is now in custody.

Reports say a detective was injured but is expected to make a full recovery.

49

Paul seems to have gained some equilibrium since his arrest. He's had a wash, a shave and some food. He glances up at Larry and me as we enter the interview room. His solicitor alongside him. We tell him his rights. Tell him we're recording.

I want to punch his smug face in.

'Can we just get this over with?' he says, sounding bewildered. 'Like you made a massive mistake. I'm sorry about your colleague, so I am, but he scared the life out of me, tackling me like that.'

I take a moment. 'Then you'll be able to help us correct it,' I say, sounding more composed than I feel. 'For the record, I'm Detective Sergeant Lucy Golden and this is Detective Garda Larry Lynch. Please state your name and address.'

He does so, and I advise him that he's under caution.

'Now, Paul,' I say, 'we're hoping you can clear a few things up for us, if you don't mind. First, we'd like you once again to take us through the day of Lisa Moran's disappearance. Tell us exactly what you did.'

'Sure,' he replies, big brown eyes eager to cooperate. And then he tells us the same story as before.

'Would you have any idea where you were on the night of April the sixth last year? It was a Tuesday night.'

'April the sixth.' He screws up his eyes. 'I don't know.' Pause. 'It might be in my phone,' he says helpfully. 'You took that so maybe you could check.'

'We'll be doing that,' I say.

'Because April was eight months ago and like, I'm no Memory Man.'

'It was the night Pearl Grey went missing from Westport. Did you know her?'

'No. I might have heard her name on the news is all.'

'I see. And now can you tell us again how Evie Long ended up in your car?'

'Sure.' He is easy, relaxed. 'I know her from yoga class. Have you ever done yoga?'

I shake my head.

'It's great. Relaxes the mind and the body. Your shoulders look a bit tense there, if you don't mind me saying. Anyway, I started it last year because I was having terrible trouble sleeping and Evie was giving it and she's a great yoga teacher. And so flexible. Good for the core too – a good core is very important.' He looks pointedly at my midriff. 'So, anyway, I had to go into Westport, just to pick up this book I wanted, but before I got to the shop, I see Evie and she doesn't look good. She's sort of spaced out, like she's taken something, so I go in and I buy us both a coffee and some crisps and then when she's a bit better, I take her to my car, but sure I don't know where she lives and I figure that I'll bring her to my lock-up because there's a bed there and she can sleep it off.'

'That was nice of you.'

'Stupid of me. Look what happened.' A roll of his eyes.

'It just looked a bit suspicious,' I say. 'Would you not maybe have brought her to your house instead of a lock-up?'

'No.' He almost laughs. 'I wouldn't want her seeing my house.'

'Why?'

'I'm a private person.'

'Ah, I see. Right.' I smile. 'You said your name was Paul McCarthy when you came in, yeah?'

'That's right.'

'Not Pascal Smyth Junior?'

The smile fades to be replaced by such a look of hurt that it startles both me and Larry. Then it's gone, flatness. 'Paul McCarthy,' he says.

'That's right. You changed your name, sorry. I forgot. Why did you do it?'

'It was too much,' he says. The sparkle has gone.

'What was too much?'

'The name.'

'All right, Paul, fine.' I take a deep breath and fling a silent prayer heavenwards. Here we go. 'I'm just going to take you through your statements, bit by bit, if that's all right?'

'Fine by me.'

'You knew Lisa Moran, didn't you?'

'Yes, I ran with her. She was lovely.'

'And at the time she disappeared, which we estimate to be around four thirty, you were visiting your elderly neighbour. Is that right?'

'Yes.'

'You had a cup of tea with your neighbour then watched the news. Is that right?'

'Uh-huh.'

'How long did you stay?'

'Maybe two, two and a half hours.'

'Her recollection is different. She said that you didn't come at all.'

For a moment his mouth drops open. He genuinely looks shocked. Then he rallies: 'She's old. Senile.'

'Not according to her doctor.'

'I fell asleep. She said she'd cover for me. I just went along with it. I'd no idea she was planning to trap me. It was her idea.'

'I see. She was trapping you?'

'Well, obviously.' He says it like I'm stupid.

'You were fully prepared to run with Lisa that Friday, were you, Paul?'

'Yes.'

'You're saying that you got home, fell asleep for two hours and then went to meet the others. Is that what you're telling us now?'

'Yes.'

'So when did you ask Rita for an alibi?'

'Rita offered on the Monday, after the body was found.' He stresses the offered.

'That's funny. Sarah's testimony says you told her you were held up at your neighbour's.'

He narrows his eyes.

'You knew she'd offer, didn't you? You knew you'd be able to manipulate her into offering to give you an alibi.'

'Sarah is mistaken.'

'Tell me, did you really think you'd go running that Friday?'

'Yes, yes, I did.'

'Would it be normal to eat before a run?'

He looks at us.

'Would it be normal to eat a sandwich before a run?'

'I had no sandwich.'

'That's funny, because this is you,' Larry pushes across more pictures taken from CCTV, 'in SuperValu buying a sandwich just before seven.'

He grows completely still.

'Maybe,' I say, 'you knew you wouldn't have to run.'

'I don't care what it looks like,' he says.

'We'll move on to Pearl Grey. Did you know her? Here's a picture of her, just in case you need reminding.'

'I never saw her before.'

'You're positive? Think now.'

'I don't know her.'

'She was a hairdresser in Westport.'

'So?'

'Where do you get your hair cut, Paul?'

'Nowhere in particular.'

I nod. 'Would you, by any chance, have got your hair cut, at any stage, in Westport?'

He hesitates, just very briefly. 'Maybe, once or twice.'

'Try five times. And guess who cut your hair five times?'

'I don't know. I'm not one for talking to those people.'

Larry places the first piece of evidence in front of Paul.

'That's some pages from the appointment book of the hair salon where Pearl worked. There's a Sam Smyth booked in five times for Pearl, but guess what?'

Paul looks at me with disinterest.

'When we showed the staff an array of pictures, including those of you and Sam, they identified you. And see this here,' I jab at a little star beside the name, 'that means you requested Pearl because, you see, when you request a hairdresser, they get paid more. Did you know that?'

'I am not Sam Smyth,' Paul says.

'How about Emma? Did you know Emma?'

'Emma who?'

'Larry?'

Larry lays the picture of Emma down.

'No idea,' Paul says.

'Where do you buy your clothes?'

'From loads of places. Why?'

'We did a search of your house when we arrested you,' I say. 'Would these be yours?'

We show Paul an array of clothes.

'Yes.'

'All bought in Casey's,' I say. 'Some of them never worn, the receipt still in the bag, and guess who served you? Emma.'

'I don't remember her.'

'We found these too,' I say, and Larry shows Paul a pair of boots, recovered in a search of his house.

'My boots, yeah.'

'They match footprints found near Lisa on the bog.'

'So? Loads of people have those boots.'

'They match the footprints found on her neck.'

He looks at us as if from a long distance. The emptiness in his eyes is truly shocking.

'We've sent the boots for testing, I wouldn't say loads of people have Lisa's DNA on their boots.'

He shifts slightly. Smiles.

'You have nothing,' he sneers.

'This your T-shirt?'

A bag containing the T-shirt that says 'Pain is the body's way of growing stronger'. When Paul doesn't answer, I go on, 'You were seen on the bog the morning before the body was discovered. Running. Wearing this T-shirt. You never came forward.'

Paul leans back and folds his arms.

'We also found these in your house.'

Larry takes a picture of a purple laptop and a Michael Kors bag and shows it to him. 'Recognise these?'

He says nothing.

'In the lock-up you rented, we found a little boxing ring. Is it yours?'

Nothing.

'Is this your punch bag?'

An image of his punch bag with the torn leather strip.

Nothing, though his brown eyes seem to deepen.

'See that torn bit there.' I point to the ripped piece on the bag in the picture and Larry places the strip of leather found on Lisa Moran in front of Paul.

'This was found on Lisa Moran when her body was recovered. It matches exactly the fabric missing off your punch bag. Can you explain that?'

A flash in his eyes, like the silvered back of a fish underwater. Then nothing.

Next Larry pushes an image of Paul's signature when he signed for the lock-up.

'Is this your writing?' I ask.

A look so hostile, it'd start a war. 'Yes, so?'

Another image. 'This is a form you filled out to change your name from Pascal Smyth to Paul McCarthy.'

'Yes.'

'You would have had to write that yourself, wouldn't you?'

'Yes.'

'See here,' I point to the capital T in the middle of words. 'And see here.' I lay the picture of the bathroom with the word 'BiTch' in front of him.

'So?'

'That's unusual,' Larry says.

'What?'

'That capital T in the middle of everything.'

'Flimsy,' Paul says.

'Not according to our handwriting expert, who says that in all probability all these were written by the same hand.'

And, once more, that chilling change, the person under the surface emerging for the briefest time. The person Lisa and Pearl met.

Silence.

We look at Paul. He looks back at us. The moment stretches on and on. It's like he's searching right inside us, gauging us. The only sound is our breathing. His gaze moves slowly from me to Larry and back again.

'I liked it,' he says softly.

Beside him, his solicitor shifts.

'Don't!' Paul snaps at him. He turns to me and Larry. 'I liked killing her,' he says.

'Killing who?' I ask.

A smile that grows slowly, that stops just before his eyes. 'The first one.'

'Pearl.'

A long silence and I know then exactly what he's going to say.

'June,' he answers.

The Captain

He digs down into the dirt of memory to find the details. He has not looked at them for a long time, save for his visits to the barn to remember, but telling it might help his case. Even as he finds the story, he wonders if it's worth telling, but for too long, he has wanted to claim her, for too long he has wanted the world to know that he killed her, that he did a favour to everyone. That she deserved it. And that women who go around promising what they cannot possibly deliver, who pretend to care, deserve to die.

June had pretended to love him just to get her feet under his father's table. And he had been dazzled by her. She was like tinsel on his sad Christmas-tree life. He was only a child, four, five, six maybe, and stupid.

He remembered the day she came: the bog dripped gold. He was burying the cat with his spade.

She said she'd love him.

But then those two boys were born and she loved them better and she made him move into the barn because he was bigger and braver, and he moved because she asked. Because he thought, as his heart squeezed, he loved her.

And he was bigger.

He was the big brother.

And the old man said nothing.

He froze in that barn.

And he used to cry, useless weak him. But then, he didn't remember when, one day he wasn't crying any more. One day he was fine about it all.

Until the day by the beach and he'd felt the rage surge up in him at that blonde girl.

The rage that spilled in through his veins and jumped out of his eyeballs. Fist-clenching, head-pumping rage. And he had liked it.

It was as if all his feelings had somehow melted and re-formed and were just waiting to get out.

And when that woman had come into the barn with the old man, that last day, and looked at him, at his fifteen-year-old body, and said, 'You give me the creeps, you weirdo,' that rage had come again.

Bam! Bam! With a wooden plank, he had done what he had dreamed about, what the King of the Land did to those who displeased him. He had just hit her, hard, in the head. He was taller than her by now. Strong from the farm work. Splat went her brains.

Oh, the bitch had gone sprawling. Like a fucking snow angel without the snow and he had kicked her and she had tried to turn around but he was angry and maybe the old man helped or hindered, he couldn't ever be sure. All he knew was that as he stood on her neck, they had watched as the life left her and he had rejoiced in it.

And been calmed by it.

But then she was gone.

His daddy said not a word, just fumbled about in his pocket for a few pounds. 'Take your shoes off. Take the money. Run.'

And he had. His daddy burned the plank, wore the shoes, covered himself in her blood.

It was easy for a teenage boy to disappear, to find bits of work.

And until he'd seen Sam again, with that woman who looked so like June, the fake mother, the rage had stayed buried.

But somehow, after that sighting, he'd seen them everywhere, those blonde, soft-voiced bitches. He heard one on the radio once, talking about how she worked on a children's helpline and he knew, he KNEW, that was where they hid themselves.

So, he'd done what had to be done.

He thinks all this, but when the policewoman with the scarred face asks him, 'Why? Why did you do it?' he can't get it out.

'I killed because it brings me alive,' he says, and it's the truest thing he's said in years.

50

Interviewing Paul is hard going, even though he's cooperating, because it's difficult to be in the same space as him. He makes my skin crawl and the hair rise on the back of my neck.

The room, when he talks of himself, seems to grow oppressive. His character looms over everything. I can't decide if he's pure evil or if, somewhere along the line, life made him into this monster that killed three women. He does not attempt to hide himself any more.

Today should be the last meeting with him. There is one last thing we want to clear up. Maybe it might answer questions.

'Why Sam?' I ask, and watch as he grows rigid. 'Why did you target Sam?'

His eyes widen a little and he swallows hard. Then he inhales and lets it out real slow.

A blink and, with studied composure, he answers, 'I hate Sam.'

'Why?'

A long time coming, then, 'He killed the pups. He liked it too.'

'What pups?'

And now that skin-crawling, prickling sensation fills the room.

It's like a storm gathering force. 'The ones he fucking killed,' Paul says, in this flat, dead voice.

'Sam killed pups?'

Something dark comes down over his face. It's as if he's turning inward and peering at us from a long way off, from down a tunnel.

'Yeah. He did. And he liked it.'

The Captain

He can talk about Sam, he decides. He feels a kin-ness with this guard who has the scarred face. She might hate Sam too: that would be good.

'Sam was the youngest one,' he says, looking at the woman and ignoring the man. 'I liked him at first but she would never let me near him. "Go away," she used to say, when she'd catch me looking, "you filthy thing." That wasn't nice, so it wasn't.'

Neither of them comments. That woman is looking at him as if he fascinates her somehow. He is fascinating. The man is splayed back in his chair. He's tired taking the notes, Paul thinks.

'And?' the woman says, and he realises he's stopped talking, that he's been studying her. 'You were saying that it wasn't nice what your stepmother said.'

'It wasn't and so, one day, when she was busy, I took Sam to see the new pups. He wanted to come and I liked Sam, back then. I gave him a pup. And he held it by the neck and it died. Then I gave him another one and then another and he was laughing and he killed them, not me, but they blamed me.'

'How long before your mother was murdered did this happen?'

'A while.'

'Sam would have been less than two years old, then,' the woman says.

He thinks he hasn't heard right. 'He was big.'

They don't answer that. But Sam was big. Sam killed those pups and never owned up. Left him to get beaten and take the blame. Sam had . . . He stops. A sudden flash of Sam taking his hand and . . . his hand was like a tiny starfish and he had to stoop down and . . . He pulls back from the memory. Stares at the woman. 'Sam never owned up about the pups. I got beaten. I figured now it was my turn to kill and not get the blame.'

He watches as the woman nods.

After that day, he wanted to say to them, he never tried to make anyone happy again.

23 December

Breaking News

A 34-year-old man, believed to be from Achill Island, is due back before the Central Criminal Court later this month charged with the murder of three women on the island and the abduction of one.

Inside:

The History of Achill Island and Its Bogs, page 5

Lisa Moran and Pearl Grey – why were they targeted?

Stacy McCann

51

Dan is sitting on the side of the bed when I visit him a few nights later in hospital. He still looks like shit but he manages a smile as I enter the room.

'Hey, partner,' I say. I'm weirdly emotional every time I see him now. Leaving the grapes and the card from my mother and Luc on his locker, I enfold him in a hug.

He squeezes me tight, then, releasing me, asks, 'How's Granny?'

I thump him gently on the arm, laughing. 'Great. Aw, Dan, you should see her. Tani brought her over last night and she's got more stuff all over the house than I have. Cots and mats and toys.'

'Sounds fun,' he says wryly, rolling his eyes. 'Have you met the other granddad yet?'

'No. Now, piss off or I won't tell you how the interview went today.' I take the chair beside his bed to give him the run-down.

He listens intently, nodding and asking questions before pronouncing, 'Aw, the unhappy childhood. We'd all be killers if that were true.' He pulls open a bag of sweets and offers me one.

I think of him and his relationship with his father. How bad he must have had it. 'It must play a part though,' I muse, as I unwrap a toffee and pop it into my mouth. I study him, ask, 'What do you think went right for you and so wrong for Paul?'

He thinks about that. 'Maybe I just wasn't born an evil bastard.' But he's joking. 'I don't know,' he says, after a bit. 'Maybe he got angry and maybe it had nowhere to go. I got angry and joined the guards. My old man hated that.' He laughs and unwraps another sweet.

He seems much better so I take the plunge, about to broach the subject of William possibly knowing about Fran and him. 'I— I have something to tell you,' I stammer, 'and I didn't say anything before now because I didn't want you to stress over it and so—'

'And here he is,' Fran announces from the door, interrupting me as he ushers William in. 'Told you I'd find him, Will. New ward and all.'

'That you did.' William smiles at Fran. 'Met this fellow in the foyer, Dan.' He crosses to the bed. 'How are you, son?'

Dan is wide-eyed as his gaze darts between Fran and William and back again. He opens his mouth to speak but nothing comes out.

'He's looking a lot better than he did yesterday,' I fill in the too-long silence.

'He is looking better,' Fran says, but his smile has dipped. He knows what's going through Dan's mind. The hurt is written all over his face.

'Good to hear it.' William is oblivious to the undercurrents. 'You did well, Dan. That was brave, hanging on to that gouger under that freezing water.'

'Anyone would have done it,' Dan says.

'Believe me they wouldn't.' William sounds pretty certain of that. 'You should be very proud of yourself, son.' He turns to Fran. 'You should be very proud of your . . .' he hesitates '. . . mate,' he finishes.

I will Dan to say something. To give Fran his rightful place. To say that he's not just a friend. And maybe Fran wills the same because he stands there for a few seconds, leaning towards Dan, but finally he pulls back. 'I, eh,' he thumbs to the door, 'I . . . eh . . . Well, I'll leave you be. I . . . eh, I'm getting a coffee.'

'What? No!' I say. Then I turn to Dan. 'Dan?'

The moment stretches. The silence builds.

Fran and Dan eyeball each other. I hold my breath and look from one to the other.

'Fuck,' Dan says, as he closes his eyes. He sounds like he might cry. 'William, Fran isn't—'

'Don't.' Now Fran has a change of heart. 'Dan, it doesn't matter.'

'It does,' Dan says. 'William—'

'I'm a detective inspector, Dan,' William says. 'Give me some credit.' A quick smile. 'And it's not my business. The only thing that is my business is how you do your job.'

'Still . . .' Dan slowly stands up, holds onto the bed for support, stares at William '. . . that man there,' he indicates Fran, 'he is the love of my life, Detective Inspector.' Softer, to Fran, 'You are, you know.'

Fran smiles his lopsided smile and they hold the look, and it's all quite squirmy, and I feel the ridiculous urge to laugh. Of all the people to witness this moment, William would be the least preferable. He's a relative unknown, a man's man: it's all about the job for William. He plays his cards close to his chest and keeps his own counsel. He doesn't do emotions, I don't think.

'Right,' William says. He doesn't seem to know what's expected of him. He rocks on his heels. Shoves his hands into the pockets of his trousers. 'That's grand so. Well done again.' He nods to all of us. 'I'll be off now.'

'I'll go with you,' I say and, without looking at either Fran or Dan, I join my boss in the corridor.

We walk through the hospital, side by side, in silence and out into the winter bright day. Wind whips my hair and I think that finally, now, I'll have the time to colour it. William zips up his jacket and turns to face me. 'Do the rest of the lads know about Dan?' he asks.

'No.'

'Ah, right . . .'

He starts to walk again. I match my strides to his.

'So, we keep this between ourselves?'

I realise he wants guidance. He's at sea with this information. 'I don't know. I hope that Dan might be ready to let people know now.'

William gives a rare smile and it changes his face: his eyes crinkle up and I see how blue they are. He's not a bad-looking man. I like him, I realise suddenly. He's steady as a rock and he always sticks up for his team. 'Well done,' he says then. 'You did a great job, Lucy.'

'Thanks. It was good working with you.'

'And you were right,' he says.

'About?'

'Mick and Susan aren't totally useless.'

I laugh and so does he, and then we stop, and he keeps smiling, and I feel suddenly embarrassed.

'I've been asked to recommend people for a new department,' he says then, wrong-footing me. 'Would you be interested in a move, Lucy?'

'Where would it be?' I try to sound blasé, as if I get asked to be in a new department every day. Inside I'm fizzing.

'Limerick.'

Bang. Down to earth.

'I'd have to leave Achill?'

'Yes.' A pause. 'You'd be an asset, Lucy.'

And I think that this is what I wanted: this is what I've worked for. I've spent ten years trying to come out of the shadow that Rob left me under. And Luc is talking about going to college in Limerick if he gets his points in his exams, so he'll be close by. But he's a dad now, so that could change. And I'd be leaving my house and my mother and my new grandchild. I'd be leaving Mayo and its beaches and sunsets and mountains and wildness and secrets and clannishness.

And I find I've been chasing something I already have.

'I . . . I like it here, Cig.'

His smile dips. 'Sure.'

I've disappointed him, I think.

He rallies: 'The lads are meeting up for a drink in that dreadful pub Cobbler's to celebrate closing the case. Coming?'

'Lead the way, Cig.'

And he smiles at me and offers to drive, and I take him up on it. I deserve a drink.

As he drives me towards Achill and I look out on the barren landscape, details of the case flip by, images in my brain. Moments that stand out now that hadn't before. I think about Pete Ryan and his wife, how his life had gone so wrong, how our questioning had led to its unravelling, and I feel guilty, but there are always moments of collateral damage in every investigation. Long-buried secrets that rise to the surface, like bog bodies.

'Any word on the Ryans?' I ask.

William glances briefly at me. 'Pete was innocent,' he says. 'That's all we know.'

'But that woman, his wife, her life fell apart.'

William takes so long to answer, that I think he won't. When he does, he says, 'She's not the only person in the world whose life fell apart.'

A brief smile.

I'm not sure if he's talking about me or himself.

And I think that, yes, he's right.

It is possible to recover.

And I turn my face to the road and watch the snow start to fall.

Acknowledgements

I am so lucky in the people I know — all the friends I've made down through the years. Y'all know who you are. I count my blessings every day.

But a special mention to Colm, Conor and Caoimhe, Irene and Imelda, Kate and Sean.

For keeping me company on the writing days: Taylor.

For my agent Caroline Hardman at Hardman Swainson for all her hard work in getting this book up to scratch.

For the crew at Little, Brown for taking a punt on the book and sending me such welcoming emails — Krystyna Greene, Hannah Wann, Hazel Orme and Rebecca Sheppard.

Thanks especially to all the guards and detectives that helped me along the way — my brother-in-law Julian Shanaher, David Donnelly, Conor Gately.

Also to the detective who went through my book with a forensic eye and improved it beyond measure. I will be for ever grateful.

All mistakes are mine.

Thanks to Sean and Claire for reading the book as readers and giving me feedback.

For Achill. PS St Jude's Park and Luck Lane do not exist on the lovely island of Achill!

And thanks to you, the reader, for picking it up and taking a chance on it. I hope you'll love it as much as I loved writing it.